PRAISE F(
TRUST ME WH

"An outstanding debut from an exceptional new talent, this is an absorbing thriller told with heart and wit. Morality and ambition clash on a journey full of twists as *Trust Me When I Lie* takes readers from the cutthroat media landscape to a sleepy town full of secrets. Confident, compelling, and with a surprise around every corner, I loved it."

—Jane Harper, international bestselling author
of *The Dry* and *Force of Nature*

"A killer premise, genuinely surprising twists and turns, and an original, deeply memorable protagonist."

—Dervla McTiernan, author of *The Ruin*

"A hugely original premise, a guilt-ridden protagonist, a plot that won't lie down. A great debut."

—Chris Hammer, author of *Scrublands*

"A gruesome murder, a podcast, now a blockbuster TV series. With the identity of the killer still a mystery, the man behind the broadcasts is desperate for a conclusion. Clever as hell and as timely as it gets, this is definitely one of the must-read thrillers of the season."

—J.P. Smith, author of *The Drowning* and *If She Were Dead*

TRUST
ME
A NOVEL
WHEN
I LIE

BENJAMIN
STEVENSON

sourcebooks
landmark

Published by Sourcebooks Landmark, an imprint of Sourcebooks
P.O. Box 4410, Naperville, Illinois 60567-4410
(630) 961-3900
sourcebooks.com

Originally published as *Greenlight* in 2018 in Australia by Michael Joseph, an imprint of Penguin Random House Australia Pt Ltd.

Library of Congress Cataloging-in-Publication Data

Names: Stevenson, Benjamin, author.
Title: Trust me when I lie / Benjamin Stevenson.
Other titles: Greenlight
Description: Naperville, Illinois : Sourcebooks Landmark, [2019] |
  "Originally published as Greenlight in 2018 in Australia by Michael
  Joseph, an imprint of Penguin Random House Australia"--Title page verso.
Identifiers: LCCN 2019000962 | (trade pbk. : alk. paper)
Subjects: | GSAFD: Suspense fiction.
Classification: LCC PR9619.4.S746 G74 2019 | DDC 823/.92--dc23 LC record
available at https://lccn.loc.gov/2019000962

Printed and bound in the United States of America.
VP 10 9 8 7 6 5 4 3 2 1

For Mum and Dad

"Life and death: they are one, at core entwined.
Who understands himself from his own strain
presses himself into a drop of wine
and throws himself into the purest flame."
                                    —Rainer Maria Rilke

"The truth does not change according to our ability to stomach it."
                                    —Flannery O'Connor

"Reasonable doubts are for innocent people."
                    —Kenneth R. Kratz, Special Prosecutor,
                    State of Wisconsin v. Steven A. Avery

S01E01
COLD OPEN

Exhibit A:

Piece of polyester rope. Length: 70 cm. Diameter: 1 cm. Color: Blue and yellow. Fiber profiles match Exhibit F (fibers recovered from victim's neck). DNA: Not present.

PROLOGUE

It was the dripping that woke her. And the smell.

In the dark—it might have even been night, though it was always dark—she couldn't isolate the sound. She decided it was important to know this, if only because it barricaded her from her usual first thought on waking: he's back.

Steady and rhythmic on the concrete floor: *plink, plink*. Not rain. Rain was the sound of fingers thrumming on a car roof, an almost underwater echo down here.

Plink. Plink. Plink. Not rain.

Her left arm was draped out of the bed; she wondered if she'd finally managed to...if the drip was coming from her wrist. She'd thought about it once but failed for courage. He'd found her cradled in a corner, shard in hand, skin unpierced. Too scared to do it, he'd said, and taken the bottles away.

The bottles were gone now. *Plink. Plink.* Not that either, then.

The dripping sped up. Individual drips blurring together in a spatter. He'd pissed in the corner once, on the floor. Her pulse quickened. Had he come—

No. That had been *loud*. And hot. Steam rising from the puddle as if he'd pissed acid. She rubbed her forehead, a near-physical memory: the condensation, the way it had settled, sticky, on her brow. Not that. It was cold now. It was always cold down here.

She thought it was coming from her right. Elevated, from the roof. A pipe in the ceiling maybe. But she'd scoured the bare walls, and she remembered no pipes. Besides, pipe water didn't smell so cloying.

She sat up. Now the dripping seemed to be coming from in front and behind her. More than one leak, then. She put a foot on the floor and gasped. It was freezing. Wet. Tendrils of liquid snaked in between her toes. She stood up, shrugging her blanket off. Shivered. The dripping was getting louder, all around now. Was she imagining it?

It was hard to keep track of things. The time, the day, the most obvious markers. How long she'd been there. Sometimes she began to lose even the most certain things. Who she was. Who she used to be. In the dark, it was easy to lose yourself.

What was her name again? Sometimes she wrote it down. Traced it in the condensation on the walls. Just to remind herself. Others used to write her name, too. Journalists. Detectives. That sort of thing.

She took a step, felt beads of liquid pool at her heel, tumble down the arch of her foot and suicide off her toe. Near the center of the room it was drier. The residue on her feet peeled off with each step. Shedding skin.

Her name would be gone from the papers now.

In the center of the room hung a long piece of thick cord with a knot at the end. It turned on a single dull light. She swung her arm, missed, rotated her torso, and tried again.

Maybe her name would pop up again. Perhaps an obituary (though the memory of the shard of glass, useless against her pale skin, suggested that particular mercy was out of reach). Maybe one of those retrospective crime shows. Yes. In a couple more years, maybe someone would write her name again. Until then, she had to remember it. In case no one else did.

She felt the cord bounce off her forearm. She wished she had her shoes on. Her soles were gently stuck to the floor, the fluid tacky and deepening around the sides of her feet.

Her name. She tried to focus on that. What did it start with? She knew her parents' names—Malcolm and Helen. But she'd lost their faces now. Her mother's had been the first to go. Her father's soon after. She still had images of them in her head, sure, but those images were distorted.

They were the cinematic versions of her parents, missing the moments that made them real—a slight bruise on an elbow, the black tooth at the back of her mother's jaw you could only see when she laughed: those human flaws. In her mind, her dad wore a suit—he hadn't worn a suit since he'd retired—and a tie he didn't own. His face was a kaleidoscope, composited from a fragmented collection of memories. There was only one face she remembered now.

She shook her head, went again for the cord. The liquid sounded as if it was gushing down the walls all around her now. The sickly sweet smell had crept into the back of her throat. She tried to remind herself of these simple facts often. Malcolm and Helen. *Plink*. Malcolm and Helen. Simple concepts, her mind wrestling them into reality. No one could take those from her. Not even him.

Eliza! Her cheeks flushed with the discovery. Malcolm, Helen, and Eliza. She couldn't believe she'd forgotten so much. Her own name fished, thrashing from the swamp of her confusion. But now she had the name in her head, she couldn't fit into it. It was as if it were someone else's name. Someone else's confidence hitching around Australia. Someone else's charm talking her into work at pubs and farms and vineyards. Someone else's brashness cashing in on some good old-fashioned blackmail. Maybe she couldn't remember her name because that Eliza was dead, nothing but a wisp of lingering smoke from a snuffed-out candle. *You're being dramatic*, she told herself. *You're confused from being down here for...* How long *had* she been down here?

That was a more slippery truth. She'd begun by counting sleeps, but that proved futile when she started sleeping when she was hungry. And she was always hungry. A few months, though—that sounded fair. Longer? A year? Long enough to not be in the papers. Long enough to lose herself. She felt the cord against the back of her wrist and twirled her hand to catch it.

She thought back to the shard of glass, harmless in her hand. He said she'd been too scared. He was wrong. She hadn't been scared enough.

Eliza Dacey turned on the light.

She saw her bloodred footprints leading from the bed. Droplets sputtered from the roof, feeding the dark liquid monster that was consuming the floor. And long, almost-black rivulets ran down all four walls. All a violent, cascading red.

The walls were bleeding.

She was scared enough now.

S01E02
GREENLIGHT

Officer Ian McCarthy of the New South Wales Police Force, after having been first duly sworn, did testify:

Direct Examination
BY Ms. ALEXIS WHITE:

Q: For the benefit of the court, could you state your name and occupation?

A: Officer Ian McCarthy. I am a police officer stationed in Cessnock, and I patrol the surrounding area.

Q: And this area includes Birravale and the Wade Wines vineyard?

A: Affirmative.

Q: You can just say yes.

A: Sure.

Q: And you were one of the first responders to the scene of the murder of Ms. Eliza Dacey?

A: Yes. I was driving, and Andrew Freeman was in the passenger seat.

Q: Tell us what you did when you got there.

A: Well, we arrived around 2:00 a.m. We drove up to the victim. Got out, picked her up, and put her in the back of the car to take her to the hospital.

Q: And why would you do that?

A: I don't— Your Honor, I don't understand the question.

The Court: Rephrase, Ms. White.

Q: Why wouldn't you cordon off the crime scene for a murder investigation? Why did you put her in the back of the car?

A: She might have been alive.

Q: You didn't notice she was dead?

A: I'm not a doctor. She was a bit blue, I guess.

(laughter) The Court: Settle down.

Q: Did you look at the body?

A: Yes.

Q: You saw a naked girl with two amputated fingers crammed in her mouth and you didn't think she was dead enough to establish a crime scene?

A: Uh—affirmative.

CHAPTER 1

MAY

If Eliza Dacey had only had the common decency to wear shoes when she was murdered, Jack Quick's life would have been a lot easier.

At the very least, he wouldn't have been picking through shrubbery at two in the morning. And, probably, he wouldn't be famous.

He pulled foliage aside left and right, bent over at the hip like he was looking for the coldest beer in a cooler. He wished he'd brought a better flashlight—the dull, rusty glow only served to blend the browns of sticks and leaves together.

He straightened up, closed his eyes, and inhaled. The corners of his eyes were hot, tired. He was beginning to doubt he'd seen it at all. It was a two-and-a-half-hour drive out here. Picture lock was at dawn. Not much time left.

It was a smallish area to search. Most of the vineyard was neat, short grass, though this section was a small natural garden that backed onto wilder bush past the fence line. He'd strayed too far in, he thought, and took a step back to center himself against a large gum tree. He winced. He'd rolled his ankle jumping over the fence.

Behind him, trellises raked down a slight incline toward a homestead. It was a red-painted, old-fashioned structure with a tin, peaked roof and strong wooden door. He knew; he'd knocked on it before. Not tonight, though.

There was a small gravel walk between the house and a much newer building, a circular one from which the vines seemed to splay out like spokes in a wheel. This building sparkled in the sun, 360 degrees of curved glass windows. Inside, he knew, were crisp, white tablecloths and palm-sized wine goblets, row after row. Tables, glasses, wines, windows, grapes—vineyards are all about symmetry. It was only five years old too; Curtis had built it when he moved in. Only bought the winery off the old owner, Whittaker, on the condition they knocked the old restaurant down first. Didn't want to be attached to anything old. The new restaurant was a beautiful structure, a bona fide tourist attraction, but Jack hadn't been able to gawk on the drive in—his headlights had been off since Pokolbin.

He bent back over and resumed scratching through the vegetation. Four years was a lot of regrowth. The flashlight was too dim, useless. He pulled out his phone, flicked the light on. It scorched the earth white. Too bright. A beacon. He shoved it back in his pocket.

He chanced a look back at the house. The lights were off. Good.

It was freezing. Mist cut the sky in half horizontally, as if the world had a ceiling. Most of the vines were laden with fruit, but nearby, some of the lattices were empty. He could see their wooden stakes and bald wires, stark in the moonlight. Homemade prison fences. As if there was something in this serene, symmetrical estate that needed to be kept here.

Jack didn't know a lot about wine making, but he knew that soil quality was bantered more than sports out here. Acidity. That was a word they loved using. He looked at the empty vines. The soil here, perhaps it was spoiled.

He got his phone back out, cupped his hand, and angled the light at the ground. The object had been on the right, on-screen. He started at the base of the tree, swept to the right, slowly brought it back in. When he hit the tree, he tilted the phone up and swept to the right again. He hoped he might not have seen it on the screen at all. That he might have imagined it. He leveraged the angle again, swept back out.

There. It was real. He cursed again the dead girl's lack of foresight. He had a decision to make now. The difference between success, fame, a legacy, and fading away like he always had. This would ruin everything he'd worked for. He knew what he wanted to do. He also knew what he should do. Those feelings were not the same.

The homestead lights switched on.

Crunching gravel bore through the silence. A whistle. A faster patter now, many quick, small steps. A dog.

He didn't have time to think; he grabbed the object and ran. *Get there. Come on. Get there.* It was a lopsided run, favoring his left, and he lumbered over the fence hard and landed on his side. Dropped the object. *Fuck.* The grass was wet against his cheek. The mist had settled, descending ghosts.

A strong beam shot up in the air, cutting through the fog. Unexpectedly, he felt a pang of not fear but jealousy: Lauren had a better flashlight than he did.

He pushed himself up to his knees, patted the ground until he found it. He ran to the car, immediately felt dizzy—too much running on an empty stomach—and leaned against the hood for a second. He had a second. Breathed in, tried not to focus on the pain. The dog sounded close now, no more time. He jumped in, tossing his find on the passenger seat, and shot off, no headlights, into the darkness.

The moon was high and bright. Vast quadruple-lane bridges spanned canyons hundreds of meters deep. In the daylight, red-rock cliff faces plunged into deep-blue, glittering water below. But in the dark, the bridges soared over nothingness, long black holes. In between gorges, rock walls loomed, the road a deep wound blasted through each mountain. Not a tunnel, a gash—open to the sky but encased in rock, dark with trickling water on either side. The bridges and cliff walls alternated every couple of hundred meters, giving Jack the feeling he was both in the middle of the air and deep underground. Safe enough now, he flicked the headlights on.

He gripped the steering wheel so hard his fingers were white and the curve of his bones showed through. He'd always had thin, cold hands. Bad circulation. Vampiric fingers designed to protrude from, curl around the lids of, coffins. Not a man's hands, really.

He crunched the transmission into fifth. The mist had settled low on the road, illuminated in the headlights. His car broke it apart, sending the rolling vapors back to the gutters, where it stayed until he'd passed, when it crept back onto the road, reforming like it had never been broken.

After a few kilometers, he had to pull over. His head was swimming; his vision, fuzzy. He took a sip of water. Sometimes that helped, something in the mouth. His hands hurt, peppered with tiny scratches. He'd been looking behind him, but he hadn't seen any following lights. He didn't really expect any, having stolen something that wasn't even supposed to be there.

Stolen. The word tasted bitter. It wasn't meant to be like that.

What felt worse was that, in his mad dash to the car, he'd run right through her spot. The patch of overgrown grass at the end of the final row of grapes, closest to the road.

That was where Eliza had been found. Four years ago. Strangled. Two fingers cut off and shoved in her mouth. Naked. Barefoot.

That definitely would have fucked with the acidity.

The network was housed in a large old-fashioned building about twenty-five minutes' walk and—depending on Sydney traffic—twenty-five minutes' drive from Jack's terrace home. It could be seen from a couple of streets away. Only eight stories tall, yet it loomed, as older buildings tend to do. There wasn't much adorning the outside, just the red-and-blue logo on a spire and a few vacant parapets. Jack had suggested to friends and colleagues that it could do with some gargoyles, just to spice things up. But they'd disagreed, suggesting that objects of snarling menace would clash with the overall aesthetic of the place. Jack couldn't see their point; after all, it was network television.

"Late night or early morning?" Jessica asked as Jack swiped his pass. The plexiglass saloon-door partition folded inward, admitting him into the ultra-modern foyer. Curvy and uncomfortable furniture was scattered across the harshly lit waiting room. Someone had told him early in his career that you had to have a strong back to work in television. Based on the furniture here, this had mostly proved true. The message was clear to TV dreamers: Don't cold call.

Jessica was the day guard, the night-shift guards having just knocked off. Jack had made it back before sunrise, but only just. The breakfast producers, who he always liked to dodge, would be in. He handed her his ID.

"Season finale," he offered.

In this building, if you looked scruffy, it was either a finale, a premiere, or you'd just been axed. Jack knew his hair was too long—it hung down past his ears—and his beard was coming in patches. He tried to remember the last time he'd shaved. Episode 3? He measured time in production schedules now. Monday, Friday, Sunday—meaningless. Instead, greenlight, picture lock, final cut, air date. Jack put his scratched hands in his pockets and shifted his weight to his good foot. Limping and bloodied hands were a sure sign of an axing.

"You're all good." Jess held out the ID just far enough away that Jack had to lean in to get it. Bait. She leaned in too, lowered her voice conspiratorially. "I can't wait for tonight."

Jack nodded. He'd had this conversation with a lot of women. And a lot of men.

"You know, my husband, he thinks he did it."

"Does he?"

"Me, I'm not sure. You're right, you know, about how they ganged up on him. I think…" Jess had become distracted and put Jack's swipe card down on her side of the counter. If he were directing their conversation, Jack thought, he'd film this scene for comic effect. Though he'd need to recast Jessica, whose sensible brown bun and buttoned-up navy security shirt wouldn't cut it. No, she'd need to be younger. Not security, either. Pencil skirt, do something with a blouse. Pretty too. Not for eye candy, but because mockery was easier comedy if the women watching were jealous.

Gum too. Rabbiting on like this, she'd have to chew gum. Jack blinked and fictional Jessica disappeared. He felt a pang of guilt for thinking about Jess that way, which ebbed quickly with the rationalization that he was in a hurry, and, besides, she was still talking. "...feel sorry for him, you know. Hard done by. So, do you think he's guilty, then?"

"I'm really sorry. I'd love to chat, but I'm on a deadline." Jack nodded at his ID. "Do you mind?"

"Oh, sorry."

"It's nothing. Just in a rush."

"Of course." She pressed a button and the next set of saloon doors gave way. The main office floor was huge, crisscrossed with felt-walled cubicles. The carpet smelled of instant coffee—ground in. During peak news hours, this floor heaved with scurrying journalists weaving from desk to desk, printer-ink coffee sloshing in stained mugs. The advantage of having a dedicated edit suite on the third floor: no powwows. Also, not having to use words like "powwow." "See you tomorrow?"

"Maybe. Might not need to come in here anymore." Jack hurried over to the elevators and stepped inside.

"Season 2?" Jess called from the desk.

"Not unless someone else gets murdered, I suppose."

The elevator doors slid closed. Sanctuary.

Upstairs, the door to his editing room was still shut. Taped across the inset window was a piece of paper, hastily scrawled on in black marker:

IF YOU DON'T WANT CURTIS WADE TO CUT OFF YOUR FINGERS, FUCK OFF.

Jack held his card up to the reader and waited for the whir and click. One of the breakfast producers whipped past—tailored shirt, tapered in, the type Jack couldn't wear—until he recognized Jack and reeled to a stop.

"Mate, let's talk about getting you on tomorrow."

Jack had never met this man before. He didn't even know what program "on" referred to. Did this man chat up women this way? *Babe, I'll get you on.*

For Jack, the attention had felt good up until around episode 4, but he knew now no one just gave spots away. If he went *on* this bloke's show, Jack would be doing *him* a favor. Not the other way around. Maybe it was ingrained from producing his podcast on his own, but he still preferred to work alone. A pat on the back, in this building, was because you had shit on your fingertips and needed to wipe it off.

"I don't think—"

"We'll talk. Rough trot. I hope he gets a retrial."

And the man was gone. *Cocaine must speed them up*, thought Jack, pulling himself into the room and leaning against the inside of the door. He closed his eyes and breathed. Almost finished now.

The room was as he'd left it. The lights were off, and he'd made sure to kill the monitors, so the glare when he started them up again made him wince. There was the image he'd left on the monitor, paused. Six hours, five hundred kilometers, and one obstruction of justice ago.

Five more minutes and he'd have greenlit the damn thing. He already wished he hadn't seen it.

That Eliza Dacey had been naked had been one of the cornerstones of the series. The evidence around Curtis Wade had been circumstantial at best—there was no blood; there was no murder weapon. Of course, his footprints had been everywhere, but it was his property. And he'd tried to help, got his DNA everywhere. Idiot. As for Eliza, she'd picked fruit for the neighboring winery for six months, but then left to travel more. No one had heard from her since. That wasn't particularly suspicious—obviously the parents had panicked, tried to get police to launch a missing person search, but no one ever took it seriously. She didn't have friends in town—they're transient, the pickers, and they tend to stick together. By the time it became a murder investigation, they were either back home or on plantations elsewhere. Because a backpacker can't really *disappear*. Everyone assumed she'd taken off—a new group of friends, a rusted van with a slur for a license plate, and off they go. She could have been anywhere from Melbourne to Townsville. Not worth the police resources to chase. Not in this town. Until her body was found on Curtis's property eight months later—and when you'd pissed off a town the way he had, a young dead woman at your feet was an awfully hard thing to come back from.

So it was open-and-shut. Curtis in a cell before the pretty backpacker was even in the ground. The police, headed up by local sergeant Andrew Freeman, hadn't given great thought to the mystery of the dead girl in the vineyard. Curtis was their man, they were sure. *I always knew he'd do something like this*, echoed the townsfolk. That was all the evidence they needed. So in those crucial first few days, they were sloppy. A country police force not used to dealing with homicides. The body was moved, put in the back of a police car that they drove right up to the crime scene. Forensic photos were sketchy, half-assed. A few footprints at the fence line were used to place Eliza at the scene. They said they had a witness too, but no one ever came forward. No one asked why there was no blood where the body was found. No one asked anything, really.

Until, four years later, Jack did.

Before he'd even contemplated making a TV series, Jack had been sitting in a coffee shop with Theodore "Ted" Piper, the prosecutor of the original case. Ted's skin cells might as well have been phosphorus, charged as they were by being in the spotlight. Jack had convinced him that the new wave of true-crime documentaries would be a profile builder. Ted had taken the bait, even styled his short black hair in a wave, despite being fully aware that this was audio only. Jack's khaki unidirectional recorder lay on the table between them, its orange screen a dull glow.

"So," Jack began, after a short introduction, "you're confident that Eliza was killed on the Wade property? And not taken there after her death?"

"Yes," said Ted.

"There was no blood at the scene."

"She may have been moved. From somewhere else. Inside the house."

"There was no blood in the house."

"Find me her blood somewhere else, and then we'll talk," Ted said sharply, noticing he was in the middle of an interrogation.

"Sure. Sure," muttered Jack. The crinkle of his notes as he ruffled through them, which was picked up by the mic, made him cringe when he listened back—such an amateur back then. "So you place her there. Tell me how."

"There's a cluster of footprints by the fence line. They belong to her. It shows that she was there recently. Eight months after she was reported missing."

"They're her footprints?"

"Size 9. We matched the prints to a brand of shoe: ASICS. And the style of the running shoe, color, and design. We've had people verify that she wore them."

More note ruffling. "Pink with silver trim?"

"Yes."

"So how did she get"—*rustle*—"two hundred meters to where she died without leaving a single trace?"

"They're her prints."

"They're her prints?"

"Are you going to keep asking me the same question?"

"You matched them to her shoes?"

"Yes."

"Tell me how you did that again"—Jack leaned forward; even as an amateur, he had an instinct for tone and drama, knew how to drop the bombs—"when she wasn't wearing any."

On the podcast, there was such a gigantic pause that listeners had initially thought the download was broken. Then, faintly, the screech of a chair pulling back, sliding across concrete. Footsteps. Fainter still, the jingle of a café door opening and closing. Jack let the pause go on a few more seconds before fading out, ending the episode.

In an industry of words, that silence had made him famous.

And that led him to here. Ted Piper's prosecution weakened by the fact that a size 9 ASICS could belong to literally *anyone*. A groundswell of support, more media interest. Then the TV offers came in. And Jack's thesis was suddenly in every home: Curtis had been set up; Eliza's body had been dumped.

And that had all been convincing until they'd decided to go back out and shoot an on-location pickup for a recap in the final episode. Which was what he'd been putting the final touches on last night.

Jack scrolled forward two seconds and watched the wobble of the camera change the angle, and it disappeared. He scrolled it back, and there it was again. Scrolled forward. Gone. Barely a flicker, far in the background. But he knew some keen-eyed internet crime solvers would spot it.

If there was one key to true crime—and he took the word *true* with a grain of salt; it was television, after all—it was to solve the fucking case in the finale.

And everything they put on-screen had been, mostly, true. The prosecutor, Piper, was a greaseball. No way had Curtis been justly tried. And wasn't that the real question? It didn't matter whether he was innocent or guilty; the point of the show was whether he got a fair trial.

And such an insignificant *thing* wouldn't change that.

Jack wasn't an idiot. He knew going out there in the middle of the night was the wrong thing to do. But there was a difference between a wrong thing and a bad thing. There was a difference between telling a lie and simply not mentioning the truth.

He thought about Jessica downstairs. Her comments had summed up seven weeks of newspaper, radio, opinion-poll, and bar-counter courtrooms. If she was right, if Curtis was innocent, then introducing such visually damning evidence would do him a disservice. Especially without proper background research. It would be irresponsible—perhaps not as irresponsible as stealing from a crime scene, but irresponsible all the same. If Jessica's husband was right, and Curtis had killed Eliza—because *someone* certainly had—then the killer was already in jail. No new evidence needed. Justice served.

Every way he looked at it, Jack came to the same conclusion. That what he had in the front seat of his car was not enough to *prove* anything either way. No matter which way he spun it, his trumped-up puff piece wouldn't be enough to get anyone in or out of jail. It didn't matter if it was right or wrong; it didn't matter at all. He wasn't a detective. He wasn't even a journalist. He had no responsibilities here. His job was just to tell a story. And that was what truth was anyway, wasn't it? Stories told.

And their story was *supposed* to be that Curtis Wade was an underdog, four years deep into a life sentence for a crime he might not have committed. Jack's team had spent seven weeks and hundreds of thousands of dollars on an innocence narrative. It didn't really matter if it was the truth or not. It was just a TV show.

No. It wasn't just *a* TV show. It was *his* TV show. He'd slaved for years on the pitch, and only after his grassroots podcast had taken off did any network look at him seriously. This wasn't Eliza's story. It was his.

Sure, her image was plastered through the opening credits: milky stare, open mouth. Black tongue. The camera panning across photos of her, to the sound of soft strings, light drums peppered like heartbeats. A cheap trick, a true-crime cliché—that lingering, haunting score—but an effective one. But it was his name on the billing. His whole career depended on this. He had emptied so much of himself into creating this show it was seeping out his pores, thinning him out. He'd had a bath last week and noticed his elbows and knees had gone from islands in the water to jagged shipwreck rocks. All that exertion, it had taken a toll on him. He had so much more to lose than she did.

Hell, she'd want his show to be a success. She'd understand.

He scrolled the cursor back and forth across the footage. The glow flicked across his face. What difference could it make? Two seconds of footage. Two seconds. Back, forth. Guilty, innocent. Alive, dead.

Curtis Wade had been in jail for four years; what difference could two seconds make?

He pressed Delete.

CHAPTER 2

He'd left it on the passenger seat, in full view of the parking garage—an oversight he put down to tiredness. But maybe he wanted someone to notice it. Someone to tap him on the shoulder and tell him to stop. But out of context, his find was completely innocuous. Low risk.

The drive home was a quiet one. The jagged, rectangular peaks of Sydney's skyscrapers were silhouetted into one serrated clump—gunmetal against the lightening blue sky, like the horizon was missing a final jigsaw piece. Every radio station was talking about Eliza, so he had to turn it off. He called his dad hands free, but his brother was still asleep.

"Put me on speaker."

"Once I wake him, are you going to come and look after him?"

Jack sighed. He had wanted to talk to Liam, even if Liam never talked back. "How's the new bed?"

"Makes things easier, lifting him, cleaning him. My back, you know."

"Lay it on thick, Dad. I'll come by this week."

"Be good to see you," his father said. "In person, not on the telly."

"Yeah, I know."

"You're working too much. I saw you on the news—losing weight?"

"Some."

"Take yourself out to breakfast."

He looked out the window. A drive-through McDonald's. Too greasy. He just wanted to get home, turn off all the lights, and sleep through the show airing. Besides, you can't be hungry when you're asleep. An elegant solution. A single stone.

"It's TV, Dad. Must be the angles."

"I thought cameras were supposed to add ten kilos?"

"I wish. This week sometime. I promise." It was always tough, but he'd visit. "Look, ah, can you just let him know I called? I know you hate doing it, but...just tell him. For me?"

"I don't know why you even bother with these phone calls," his father said, "but I'll tell him." He hung up.

It was nice to go against the traffic for once; everyone else was returning to the hive. Upstream. Back in the city, people would be filling those buildings. Thousands of them. Answering phones. Taking meetings. Packed into rising elevators, filling the hole in the sky.

There was one more phone call he had to make. He dialed. The phone rang twice and clicked.

"Mate, it's Quick," Jack said.

"It better be. He's sleeping." The voice on the other end was young, male, midtwenties. A tough age for that job. The phone line had an echo to it, as if the speaker were in a bathroom. "Everyone's fucking sleeping. *I* was sleeping."

"Wake him up."

"Doesn't work like that."

"He's going to want to speak to me. Trust me. Wake him up."

"Hmm." There was a loud clang on the other end, a distant but muffled yell.

"Okay. How about this?" Jack realized he'd subconsciously raised one hand off the steering wheel and was waving it back and forth, as if trying to placate someone in real life. He felt like an outsider in the TV station, coming from his podcast to the big league in such a short amount of time. He didn't fit in with those cocaine-buzzed producers. Yet it didn't take long to catch the tics of confidence and aggression that came with presence on a television screen. His voice dropped a semitone. Platitudes peppered his words. The camera might not add ten pounds, but it made you feel taller. "You know there'll be a book after this. Lots of press. And listen, buddy, you know there'll probably be a chapter or two about your establishment…"

"Are you trying to blackmail me?"

"Nothing of the sort!" Jack had his producer voice in full swing now; if they'd been together in person, there would have been arm-around-the-shoulder backslapping. Such false comradery. "I'm saying that if I write good things about you—how well you do your job, the way you treated him—you might be in line for a promotion, a pay raise. Right, pal? That's what I'm saying."

"You said the same thing about getting me on TV."

"I know, and I tried. But the edit's the edit. We could only fit so much."

"Well, I can only fit so much time on the phone, so—"

"A hundred bucks?"

There was silence, and Jack thought he'd blown it. Then he heard footsteps echoing—not a bathroom, a concrete hall. The man was moving.

Jack was stopped at traffic lights now and ground the gear stick as he waited. He put it into first and rolled forward, preempting the light, but then he heard the distinctive muffle of a phone being handed over and missed the green light anyway.

"Quick." The voice on the other end was deep, rumbling. "You ain't got me out of here yet."

"I never said I'd get you out, Curtis."

"Yeah." Curtis was a slow speaker; every word seemed to haul itself over his lips and slump on his chin. Undereducated but overread. A consequence of spending four years sifting through trial notes, listening to lawyers. Curtis spoke with a vocabulary that belied his lack of high school but a diction that occasionally showed he thought eloquence was a replacement for intelligence. Any prisoner in their first court is the same:

a too-thick neck, in an open-collared, too-tight shirt. *I didn't stab the bitch, Your Honor.* Fast forward a couple of years and it becomes: *I did not implicate those lacerations as identified by the prosecution on this bitch, Your Honor.*

Curtis sighed. "Wouldn't mind if you did, but."

"Keeping well, though?"

"It's gotten better. I'm quite the hero in here now."

"They made you a murderer. I made you a movie star."

"Nah, mate. You made me a martyr. Everyone in here, even the guilty ones, feel they were wronged by someone—a dodgy lawyer, a racist judge, the media. The fucking media."

"Hey now."

"You're okay. For one of them." Curtis laughed. "Thanks to you, I've got the hopes and dreams of everyone in here on my shoulders. If I get out, anyone could."

"*If,*" Jack reminded him. "I never said I'd get you—"

"Be a downer, I don't care," Curtis cut in. "It's a big day today. I am the victim of a gross mismarriage of justice fueled by the incompetence of the justice system."

This was one of his rehearsed lines, inevitably learned from the court papers and chanted in his cell every night, poised for a sound bite. Jack didn't have the heart to tell him it was mis*carriage*. "We'll all watch the finale. They're throwing me a party, setting up the projector."

Jack didn't even know prisons had projectors. Sounded less like a punishment and more like his university dorm. Depends how you define *punishment*, he supposed, changing lanes. "Curtis," he said, "do you remember when I first spoke to you?"

"Yeah."

"Remember what I said? Exactly?"

"You said words were powerful. You said I was a victim. You said words, your words, would make me famous."

"And after that. We agreed on something."

"I woke in a good mood, Mr. Quick. It's a big day for me. I hope you're not about to change that."

Was that a threat? Jack blinked and concentrated on the road; he was overthinking it. Curtis was charismatic, likeable even (if casting a film, Jack had often thought he'd be perfect for a comedian "taking a serious turn"), but there was a hard edge to his words. They crawled down the phone line like a fist emerging from a grave. Slow. Steady.

"We agreed that—"

"I know what we agreed on. You'd tell my story. You'd tell it fair—my side. And I'd tell it to you. But there was one question you promised never to ask me."

"Yes. That question."

"Said it might cloud your judgment."

"I remember what I said. The show's finished. It doesn't matter anymore."

"Are you asking that question?"

Jack didn't know if he was. He didn't know if he wanted the answer. "Let's say," Jack said, "for the sake of argument."

"Okay. We're arguing."

"I found something."

"You mean that literally or fig— You know, whatever?"

"Literally."

Curtis laughed. It was long and satisfied, not mocking—gleeful. "Mr. Quick. You *know* they planted that. You know it!" He was talking faster now, energy pulsing through him.

"What?"

"First of all, whatever you found, let me guess that it doesn't prove shit. But I'll bet, sure as hell, it *looks* bad?"

Jack thought about that. The object was dirty, clumped with mold, and discolored. But was it four-years-in-the-wilderness dirty? Perhaps not.

"You're not saying anything because you know I'm right. You don't care what I did or didn't do. You just care that your goddamn story is screwed."

"Well, that's not—"

"I'm not finished. You said your words would make me famous. But, man, it's the other way around. My words made *you* famous. One little hiccup and you throw me to the dogs."

"Okay. Let's say I'm with you up to here. You say someone planted it?"

"Fuck. Anyone could have. The real killer? Andrew fucking Freeman. Any one of the locals worried about your show. You *know* that. After what I did to that town. After how you made some of them look. Backwards. Hicksville. Besides, your show's made it pretty fucking obvious what pieces of evidence to plant. Blood. An ax. Shoe prints. A piece of rope."

Jack looked at the object on the passenger seat. A good guess by Curtis. Close. "You're already in prison. What's the point in framing you twice?"

"Since you reignited this, the police have swept through my property a dozen times, Mr. Quick."

"Jack."

"Whatever. They didn't look properly the first time, but now everyone's been through the vineyard. Cops. Your investigators. Journalists. Dad told me they brought sniffer dogs. The lot. And you found something with your bare hands *four fucking years* later?"

Jack realized he'd pulled onto an off ramp; he was going so slowly now he'd forgotten he was even driving. While it had been light for a while, warmth had just started to bleed through the windows. Curtis was right: professional investigators had searched that small garden more times than he could count. And he'd found it at two in the morning, on an empty stomach, with a broken flashlight, and an iPhone. They'd gone back after the bulk of the season had aired to film the pickup. It must've been planted. Which meant it was probably fake.

That sounded plausible. He could live with that. There might even be a new episode in it.

"Now, Mr. Quick…Jack," Curtis said. "Did you still want to ask me that question?"

Ignorance isn't bliss, but innocence sure is. Even by default.

"No. Not anymore."

"I get it, man. You need to feel like you're doing the right thing, or right enough. But it's perspective. I think you're doing the right thing, by me anyway. You know that? Lots of people asked questions. You're the only one that wrote down the answers."

"Even Alexis?"

"Especially Alexis. Do you know how much it fucking sucks when your own lawyer doesn't seem to believe you? I know you're just making a TV show; I'm not stupid. But it did feel like you were on my side. On my team, for a while, you know… He's winding me up now." Jack heard Curtis, muffled, say something to the guard. Then he was back. "But the reason you called me now, the reason you woke me up, is because, somewhere deep inside, you don't believe me either."

"Hey, Curtis, don't make this—"

"It's okay." His voice was quiet now, beaten. "Can I go?"

"Yeah." Jack smacked a hand on the wheel. *Idiot.* "Sorry for waking you. Enjoy your party."

There was a clunk as the phone was passed through the bars. Jack tried to think. Curtis had been convincing. Something didn't add up. It didn't make sense for Jack to find this now. And hiding it solved more problems than it created; it was the simple option. TV was all bullshit anyway. But what twisted in his gut, along with his now-painful hunger, was how heartbroken Curtis had sounded. How used. Jack had never heard him like that.

But he was right. Jack didn't know what he believed anymore. And he couldn't decide what was worse: that he'd disappointed an innocent man or that he might have fired up a murderous one.

"I've changed my mind about the book. You can keep your hundred bucks, but you gotta make me badass." The guard's voice snapped Jack back to the car; he'd forgotten Curtis had borrowed the phone. "Jack? Jack? Books get pussy, right?"

Jack hung up.

Now the sun had risen, the traffic into the city was picking up. It was eerie to have so much traffic heading against him, with his side of the highway so quiet. Jack felt like this sometimes, like he was the only one desperate to leave a party that everyone else wanted to get to.

Eliza's face jumped out at him. A massive billboard, hanging from the side of an upcoming overpass. Bone white, sideways. Just enough of cheekbone, nose, lip, and neck to pass the censors. The magic of Photoshop had removed her severed fingers from her mouth. She looked peaceful. Unblemished. Computer trickery had almost brought her back to life.

Six feet under, yet Eliza floated over this city. Over Birravale. Over the nation. She flittered through arguments in bars, whispered conversations in lecture theaters, catch-ups around watercoolers, quiet pillow talk. Everyone watched her, their laptops open, the battery warming their folded legs through the blankets, committing to *just one more episode*. She was in every home. On every overpass. And the last part of her, on the seat beside Jack.

Who really killed Eliza Dacey? Sundays 8 p.m.

And everywhere she went, she took Jack with her. A man she'd never met, their lives inexorably entwined. She followed him into every room. Every locked door. Every bathroom. Saw his every shame.

Who really killed Eliza Dacey? Jack wished he knew. He drove home in silence.

His only passenger, a single pink woman's running shoe.

CHAPTER 3

JUNE

"I'm sure I owe you dinner," Alexis said, sliding into the red plastic booth opposite Jack. She stopped at a long gash in the seat. "But I can spring for something a little less…" She air-pedaled two fingers, hunting for an insult that captured the room.

They were in a grimy pub in the inner west. Jack's pick. He had forgotten the name, though it was put together from the standard formula for naming pubs that sold $10 steaks: randomly match one royal term with one animal. Voila. The Royal Stag. The Queen's Duck. The Imperial Meerkat. Close enough.

Alexis pulled her scarf from her neck as her eyes darted from the unwashed windows to the empty barstools. She folded it, placed it on the table, changed her mind, and moved it to the seat beside her. Glancing at the seat's disemboweled foam, she gave up and put the scarf in her handbag. She'd left the insult hanging, so she settled on silence as the best summation. Her eyes flickered to the manila envelope Jack had on the table.

"No debts here." Jack hovered his hands over the table, palms up.

"It's not a debt." She laughed. "Take the hint when a girl suggests you take her out to dinner next time. What do you want to eat? My treat."

"The best treat, Alexis, would be to not subject me to the food here."

"Fine." She stood. "I'll subject you to the beer."

Jack watched her go to the bar, clear her throat to summon a previously nonexistent bartender, and rap a manicured fingernail on a tap. It reminded him of her approaching the bench. Confident, her long black hair bouncing as she enunciated her points. Except here she wore a leather jacket instead of her courtroom getup—typically a white blouse and blazer. She didn't wear flashy suits like the prosecution, Ted and his team. Alexis chose browns and whites, warm and open and honest to a jury. It was an odd feeling, knowing her so well and not at all, as if he'd gone through her drawers. In fact, Jack had watched so much courtroom footage of her that his knowledge was far more intimate: her tics, her expressions, the way she scratched the back of her calf when she was bored. This was actually only the fourth or fifth time they'd met and spoken. Yet he knew her.

It was curious. Once the show had started to be filmed, at each appeal hearing, everyone had dressed better. One judge had even been late, getting a haircut. Justice wasn't so blind after all.

Alexis finished her cross-examination of the bartender and brought a pitcher of beer back to the table. She poured out two glasses, slid one to him.

"I know you don't think I owe you, but TV and courtrooms aren't so different. You're always paying for something," Alexis said.

"Thanks."

They clinked glasses. Jack struggled with a sip of his beer. He'd had the words in his head for a week, but now that it came time to assemble them, he couldn't fit them together. He'd start with the easy stuff, he decided.

"I believe congratulations are due," he said. "I hear there might be a full retrial."

"A long way to go yet. But everything's gaining steam. The appeals did well. The response to the show, it's been—"

"I know. Crazy."

"That's one word for it."

"So, the retrial…?"

"I don't know the ins and outs of it, if that's what you're asking. If you're looking for dirt." She looked around, her face changing from flirtatious to contemplative, slowly figuring out the meaning of the empty bar. The yellow envelope. She still graced him with a smile. "And here I thought you called me for the company."

"Just the company. I'm not making anything right now."

That was a half-truth: a second unit was filming press conferences and prepping for retrial footage; a team of researchers was scrawling away in a writers' room. A bigger team this time, the network promised, not a one-man show. *To ease your workload,* they said. *To keep you accountable,* they implied. While rumors of the retrial circulated, Jack didn't have to get involved.

"I wouldn't know anyway. I'm kind of out of the picture for a little while. Even if there is a retrial." Alexis shrugged, an exaggerated theatrical gesture. "I might not get it."

"Fuck. I didn't get you fired, did I?"

"You're kidding?" She smiled. "You definitely got someone fired somewhere, but not me. The opposite, actually. My phone never stops. I didn't know electronics could develop anxiety, but it literally can't handle the attention. This"—she hunted in her bag, threw a case of mints on the table, then plucked out a cheap, prepaid phone—"is a new phone. Every criminal from here to fuck knows thinks I can get them out of jail. Get me fired, *pfft.*" She dropped the phone back in the bag and offered him a mint, which he waved away. "You made me look so great out there. Choice angles. I've even been offered modeling jobs."

"Really?"

"Well, just pens and reading glasses and stuff. Lawyer things. But I'll take the compliment. Point is, the partners thought it best I take the heat off the business. For a few weeks."

Jack knew what she meant. Since the finale, he'd been inundated with letters. Most had been the same: penned by a nervous hand, childish— alternating caps and lowercase, squeezing the letters and lines together as the page ran out. Mostly pencil. Often green, a favorite of inmates. When murmurs of a retrial had surfaced in the press, the letters had tripled. The majority to the station, some to his home. Most the same: *Mr. Quick. I'm innocent. I need your help.* Some different. He tried not to think about those.

He scratched his patchy stubble, unsurprised that he hadn't been offered any photo shoots.

"I've had letters too," Jack said. "The retrial will be a media frenzy anyway."

"That's the thinking. Probably better if I head it up in the end, but I'm off until things settle. It's not just me—everyone took at least a week. The office phone rings endlessly; we've had to switch it off. We'd unplug it for a day, plug it back in, and it would still be ringing. Another day, still ringing." She swilled her glass, lowered her eyes. "You get the threats too?"

i will fucking gut you

Large, looping letters. Green pencil.

you got kids tv boy?

Child's handwriting.

He nodded. Took another tiny sip of his beer. Hated it. Alexis had drunk half of hers.

"At least we get it from the ones that are locked up. Ted gets it from the public. His office is closed too."

"Threats?"

"Someone spray-painted the doors. Pentagram. Don't you read the papers?"

Not if he could avoid it.

"Don't feel sorry for him—he just bought a mansion in Point Piper. He must be doing okay," Alexis said.

A phone rang. Alexis rummaged in her bag, pulled one out, looked blankly at the screen, put it back, and pulled out a second one. She declined the call and put it faceup on the table.

"Still getting used to it. Two phones." She smiled. "I feel like a spy."

"I want to ask you something."

"It might not be the best timing. Kind of a *thing*." She tapped the phone. Jack saw her reassessing the empty bar, the reason they were there. It wasn't entirely empty now; the afternoon drinkers were just starting to show up. "Sorry."

"Bad phrasing. I'm not trying to ask you out, no."

"I have standards anyway." She flicked her hair. "I *am* a model now."

"Just pens though," Jack reminded her. "I have standards too."

She chuckled into her beer. He'd brought her here to talk about a murder, and they'd wound up flirting? She saw crime every day, he supposed. This must be so normal.

"So are you going to ask me something, or are we cutting to an ad break?" She nodded at the bar, wiggled her glass in optimism.

"Do you think he did it?" Jack blurted out.

There was the clacking of a billiards break from behind them. Nothing sunk. Someone swore.

"Is that it? That's why we're here?"

"Yeah." Jack ran a finger around the rim of his glass. "I don't know. I've been thinking about this lately. More than usual."

"So Jack Quick has brought me here with an ethical quandary. How juicy *Woman's Day* will find this one."

"Forget it."

"I'm kidding." She reached over and grabbed his wrist, shook it gently. "I'm a criminal defense lawyer, remember. I do my job right and sometimes killers walk right off the stand and out of that courtroom. They look you in the eyes as they go past. And you know."

"And Curtis?"

"Honestly?"

"Honestly."

"I haven't figured him out yet."

"You defended him in court. You might take him to a retrial. You might get him out. And you don't know?"

"You made an entire TV show about him and it sounds like you're not so sure either."

Good point, Jack thought.

"I want to show you something," he said, reaching for the yellow envelope and knocking over his beer in the process. Luckily, it missed everything on the table and flowed harmlessly onto the floor.

"Shit, sorry." Jack righted the glass and dabbed at the table with napkins.

"Top up?" She lifted the pitcher, tilted it.

"Still a third in this," Jack said, waving a hand. "I'm fine."

"Not much of a day drinker?"

"Not much of a drinker." Jack tipped the envelope open. "I wanted to ask you about these again."

Crime scene photographs covered the table. Shoe prints, in grass and mud, of various sizes. Some were zoomed in, black-and-white rulers lined up beside them. Only some. Sloppy. Things missing. Tire tracks through others. Other prints were on a larger scale—press photos, taken from a drone, yellow vector graphics plotting points of significance. There, by the fence, the cluster of footprints. From the bird's-eye view, he could see the parallel rows of vines. At the end of one of the rows, a higher density cluster of yellow. Lots of evidence there, where the body had been found.

Alexis leafed through them without interest; she'd seen them before.

"Uh-huh. Ted's magical"—she curled her fingers in quotes—"'victim placement.' What do you want to know about them?"

"How important are they? To any potential retrial."

"Well." Alexis pointed to the larger picture. "This is probably the most important. It shows that a woman wearing size 9 ASICS was at the perimeter of the property *some time*—and that's important too—within a week or so of the murder. The driveway is gravel, so it's hard to know if she came in from the parking lot or the road or the house itself—which is what Ted proposes. That's a leap though."

Jack marveled at her ability to switch off her cheery tone and dip straight into hard facts. She was, he reminded himself, a brilliant lawyer. No wonder the show had made her a semicelebrity.

"Will Ted use this again? To place her at the scene?"

"Probably not. Yeah, the victim wears a size 9, but we don't know what shoes she was actually wearing. There's no way to match the prints. It's a public winery, so all he'd be proving is that *a* woman wearing size 9 was on the property. Big deal." She slid the photos back to him. "Plus, as you said on TV at least a dozen times, it *might* be her brand of shoe. But there's no way he can prove they're actually hers."

"Why are they clustered?" He pointed to a smaller photo. There, the footsteps seemed to be jumbled around almost randomly.

"The direction changes. If it were Eliza—which it's not, by the way—she's pacing back and forth. Deeper too. Stamping her feet to keep warm." She slid a finger across the photo, back and forth, mimicking the footsteps, making them wander. Jack noticed she had long, slender fingers. Like honey hanging from a spoon. "My guess? She's having a cigarette. No biggie."

"Okay, but because we made it look like the body was dumped, if he shows it wasn't—"

"*We* made it look like nothing, Jack. My defense was rock solid. Your show is your show. But that was the challenge for both Ted and me—placing the victim at the scene."

"And you think she was dumped?"

"I think it's hard to find contradictory evidence to that theory, yes. Come on, you back that up yourself."

"And if, for some reason, Ted were able to match the shoes. Would it change the case?"

"Has he got something?" Her eyes lit up. That lawyerly passion for the chase, the pursuit. A battle begun.

"Just asking."

"Okay." Alexis eyed him cautiously. "Well, it would prove that Eliza had been to the property. It wouldn't prove where she died, because these prints are so far away from the body and look like a casual stroll. For example"—she pulled the photo back and traced a finger in between one of the rows—"if the trajectory showed she ran down this aisle and then stopped"—she planted a finger on the second red mark on the aerial photo, where the body was found—"that would be fairly damning. But it doesn't. Or, at least, not with the patrol car driving through the middle of it."

"So all it would do is prove she'd been on the property. Not that she died there?"

"Which is a fairly safe assumption anyway. Like I said, it's a public winery. Eliza worked for the Freemans. It wouldn't be unexpected that she was in Birravale anyway." She shrugged. "It wouldn't put a huge hole in the case."

"And if she weren't dumped? And he knew it?"

"Well, I mean, if he had physical evidence—there's DNA, fingerprints, the works to consider. But there's no bare footprints of hers either, so someone definitely carried her, at least partly, but her resting place itself is a mishmash of prints and tire tracks. Everyone but hers. You did a good job disproving this yourself. Why are you asking me this?"

Jack sighed. Looked into the dregs of his beer. A rat gnawed at his gut. Alexis was right; the prints themselves didn't matter. The shoe didn't solve anything. Yet there it stood, lodged in his mind. A symbol of the fact that his whole show *might* be based on mistruths. And now that Curtis was getting closer to a retrial and there was a very real chance that he could get out, it had played on Jack's mind more each day. Public opinion was working for Curtis, and Jack had done that too. Eliza had followed him everywhere in the weeks since the finale. Her cold skin jumping out from TV sets and billboards, or the fuzzy family Christmas photo that the newspapers liked. Her smile, her silent pleading eyes. He might have butchered her chance at justice. He didn't know how to explain this to Alexis.

"I can't sleep," he said simply.

Alexis, still holding his wrist, rubbed a thumb against the inside of his palm.

"She's just…everywhere."

"She'll stay. That's what they do."

"It doesn't seem to bother you?"

"Every case"—she pointed to her temple—"is lodged in there some-where. Grisly stuff. Wouldn't even tell you. They just become a part of you. Don't worry. They get nudged down, it fades—you forget about it."

"With time?"

"Or when something worse comes along." She must have noticed Jack flinch. "Sorry."

"You can't tell *Woman's Day* this," Jack said, and Alexis gave him a gentle laugh, more out of camaraderie than humor, "but the show…I made some choices. Editorially. What to show, what not to show. In search of the neatest storyline, the best entertainment."

Alexis said nothing. Took her hand off his wrist.

"In the heat of the moment. You know? It's a bubble, television, and this was a real career maker. And then I stepped out of that studio and back into reality, and Eliza is *everywhere*."

"What are you trying to say?"

"I guess I underestimated the real-world impact."

"You're saying that you made a TV series petitioning Curtis's inno-cence, and now you think he's guilty?"

"No, I don't think he's guilty." He didn't know what he thought.

"But you're afraid he might be?"

Jack nodded. "What if he gets out?"

Alexis paused, as if considering whether to chastise or console him. When she spoke, her tone had softened. "I had a colleague once. We went to university together. She was a ruthless lawyer, coldly focused on winning cases for her clients. Family histories, sexual escapades, everything was on the table in her courtroom. She broke families but won cases. Single-minded. She's in jail now."

Jack raised an eyebrow. Did she know what he had done? Alexis took a sip of her beer, quite relaxed. No. She couldn't.

"Prison witnesses are notoriously unreliable; they'll give evidence against anyone if you offer them extra privileges: cigarettes, money, cable. She had an unwinnable case—knew the guy did it but couldn't pin it to him. She won it. Later they discovered she'd bribed an inmate to say he'd heard something in the yard. Forty packets of cigarettes. She ruined her life for that."

"Why are you telling me this?"

"You like winning. You'd make a good lawyer. No other reason." Her eyes said otherwise. Not quite an accusation, but she was sizing up how close he'd flown to the sun. "On the other hand, sometimes it's enough to do a good thing in a bad way. A small lie for a bigger cause. That's really up to you."

Jack swirled his beer, took a sip, hoped that when he put it down, she would have stopped assessing him. She hadn't.

She broke into a smile. "But you're not a lawyer. Of course you made concessions. Seven hours of TV. *Pfft.*" She flicked a hand. "That's nothing. You built a case for entertainment. Real cases aren't linear, neat, easily solvable. They'd never fit a TV narrative. I think you put a good deconstruction of the prosecution's flimsy evidence out there and, in doing so, made me look like a bit of a superstar. Got me a foot into the lucrative stationery-catwalk industry too."

"I still can't sleep."

She passed the photo back, serious again. "And there's always one mistake that sticks with you. Let me guess. You simplified the shoe print evidence, right?"

He'd told her too much. A timid nod.

"If it wasn't this, it would be something else. You know what your biggest mistake was? Thinking you could do this at arm's length. That you're just an observer. A man on the sidelines. You're not. Not anymore. She's with you now." Alexis paused. "You regret it? The way you presented things in the show? You feel guilty?"

"If Curtis is, I am."

"Bullshit." She surprised him with her sharp tone. "Regret. Guilt. They don't exist. What you're really feeling is grief."

"Eliza's been dead four years. I never even met her."

"You're not grieving *her*, Jack. Whatever decision you made, whatever you think you regret, you thought you were better than that. And then, when it came to the crunch, you weren't. And you know that now."

Jack understood: it *was* grief. But he was grieving himself. The person he thought he'd been. That better version of himself that he kept in his head, the one he thought would always rise to the occasion. His better self was gone now. Crumbled under pressure. Grief: for the dead parts of one's own identity. How selfish.

"A lesson like that only gets learned from experience," he said, tracing his finger through the remnants of spilled beer on the table, not looking at her.

"I've been around. Sorry, probably too dramatic for what you meant."

"If I've influenced the retrial, though—"

"The retrial will be conducted by professionals. Don't get me wrong— every piece of evidence is important. But we'll assess everything on its own merits, not what some television series tells us is true. And we'll double-check the shoe prints, but they'll have little to no play. No one got enough evidence four years ago. Not enough to put him away. That's the strategy: not really whether he did it or not but whether they were able to prove it. We've carefully examined all the evidence."

Not all of it, thought Jack. *I can still place her at the vineyard.*

"Maybe I'm being too harsh on you. You told your story your way. That's fine. I disagreed with some of it. Liked other parts. It was a good show, you made some money—probably a lot—but it's just entertainment. Celebrity has gone to your head if you think people will take it that seriously."

"People seem to be taking it seriously enough to grant a retrial," he said.

"That's exactly it. They aren't, but they're taken in enough by the story of it. It's doubt that makes them uncomfortable." Her phone rang. Again, she ignored it. "Look, I think it's like this: the world is in a state of unrest at the moment. Look at the United States. The politicians in power, they make people unsure. Black kids getting shot by cops. Same here, but there's less blood on the streets. But there's still a sense of working against 'the man.' There's an imbalance, a lack of a sense of justice. And do you know how the middle class responds to this?"

"How?"

"The only way they know how—by clamoring for the freedom of a white guy."

"Huh?"

"This will sound coldhearted, but there are worse things going on in this country than a murdered woman. But that's what makes the news. It's about what we're comfortable rebelling against. Imbalance, Jack."

What had Curtis said on the phone? That he was a martyr. But he'd got the scope of it wrong. Curtis, the success of the show, was only the vicariousness of the middle class—too uncomfortable to fight for any real change, but just comfortable enough to speak out from a couch or keyboard.

But he still felt guilt—grief, whatever—creeping through a hot lump in his gut every time he saw a newspaper and those smiling, alive eyes. He wasn't an observer anymore; he was a part of it. And if Curtis got out, he was a part of that too.

Alexis picked up her phone, read a message, and started gathering her things. "Sorry. I have to go."

"Of course."

"Two things worth remembering, Jack. The first is that the world is bigger than your show, bigger than any single court case. Any lawyer will tell you: you win some you shouldn't, and you lose some you should. It's okay to feel uncertain. Our job is uncertainty. I can turn a case on it just the same as you can spin a yarn. What Curtis did or didn't do"—she stood up, hunched as the table trapped her legs—"that's almost irrelevant. Now, I still owe you dinner. Don't forget that either."

"A nicer place though."

"A much nicer place." She sidled out of the booth. "I will tell you this. Eliza's gonna stick with you. Some of them do. The guy my friend put away, he murdered a sixteen-year-old boy. Opened him up with a hunting knife. Cut him from neck to groin. Shit like that never goes away. You just do what you can to be okay with it. That's why I told you about my friend. It's about choosing between the lies you can live with and the lies you can't."

She laid her hand on Jack's as she said this. Her honeyed fingers circled the small rough spots on the back of his knuckles, those tiny healing scars. Sometimes, women knew those scars. Those lies you can live with. Her hands were soft, and she was smiling. They had ceded the debate, friends again.

"And the second thing?"

"My friend. I lied. She's not in jail."

Alexis wrapped her scarf around her neck, leaned down, and gave him a kiss on the cheek. Whispered in his ear. She had a late-night phone voice, husky with a slight rasp from the beer. A voice that told secrets.

"Best case of cigarettes I ever bought."

CHAPTER 4

Piled up on one end of Jack's kitchen table was the contents of his pantry, a meager haul. A bag of flour. That would be useful. Five tins of tomatoes. Sugar. Ramen noodle packets. Salt and pepper shakers. Pasta taken out of the packet and sealed in a jar. A squeeze bottle of honey. A bottle of tomato sauce, which had barbecue sauce in it. A bottle of barbecue sauce, which had God knows what in it. To say Jack's food supplies were scant would be understating it. The contents of Jack's pantry had all the makings of a cookbook: Jamie Oliver's *Depression in Fifteen Minutes or Less*.

The crockery and cutlery were piled on one of his kitchen chairs. It was past midnight, but he couldn't stop running through Eliza's murder. The shoe, hidden in the back of his closet, played on his mind. He'd paced the house, room to room, but that hadn't helped distract him. The house yawned, open and empty. No doors.

That wasn't true. There were seven of them, all white, wooden single doors, stacked against the wall in his garage. His dad had taken them off the hinges years ago. Jack kind of liked the space, so even when he was allowed to put them back up, he didn't. But that meant that in the middle of the sleepless nights, he felt like he was walking through some abandoned place. Nowhere to hide away. He'd turned on the television, and in the very first commercial break, there'd been an ad for his show, which was playing repeats on the digital channel.

Who really killed Eliza Dacey?

The shoe grew heavier in his mind every day. Jack knew what it was like to make a decision that you couldn't take back, even if you wanted to. Some small, inconsequential choice that grew and grew into something monstrous when everyone was watching. Why had he been fine with hiding the shoe before? Because it was before there was hope for a formal retrial? Because it was before Jack began to doubt Curtis's innocence? He didn't need to know who killed Eliza, but he did need to convince himself that Curtis hadn't.

Jack picked up the flour as a realization thumped him in the chest. If the shoe was planted, then it was by someone who wanted to keep Curtis in jail by stacking up the evidence against him. Someone with access to the victim's clothes. Only one person fit that criteria. Could Eliza's killer, free and unsuspected, have put it there? It must have been planted to be found so late in the piece. Four years on. And, in that case, by helping free Curtis, Jack was doing the *right* thing. Because then the police might have a chance to catch the actual killer.

And turning in the shoe might be what the killer wanted anyway.

Jack dumped the flour on the table and spread it out to the edges with his hands. He needed to look at things from a new perspective. Then he poured half a bag of sugar in a straight, horizontal line, bisecting the bottom third of the table. That represented the main road running through Birravale. He evened out the flour in the top two-thirds and traced crude boundaries. One large paddock for the Wades, taking up most of the center of the table. He took a bowl and placed it in the center of the paddock and a slightly larger plate next to it. The bowl was the domed, glass restaurant; the plate was the homestead. In the top right, west geographically, of the flour, he drew new boundaries: Andrew and Sarah Freeman's property. Another bowl was their house, and two tins of tomatoes their wine silos. In real life, the silos had been repaired. He used more sugar to fill in the Wades' driveway. Dotted along the main sugar-road, he dispersed cups and saucers. The old cinema. The bakery. The few houses clumped together.

He stepped back to examine his miniaturized bird's-eye view of

Birravale. Checked the helicopter photos. He had it about right. Forgot the grapevines. Laid down some parallel lines of spaghetti.

He walked his fingers back and forth near his artificial fence line in the northwest corner. Small divots in the flour. Eliza's footsteps. Maybe her last ones. Maybe completely irrelevant, just a random cluster of her cigarette break. Maybe not even hers. He took the saltshaker and placed it on the plate-homestead. That would be Curtis. He allowed himself a chuckle. Salt, the embodiment of evil. He opened a pack of ramen and lifted the noodle cake out. That would be Eliza. Too big—bad for scale. He snapped her in half. Better. He placed Eliza-Ramen at the end of one of his strands of spaghetti-vines. Near where the old restaurant—since knocked down—would have been, Jack observed from his new vantage point. Eliza's final resting place.

He felt he must be missing something. But, sloppy as the police had been, they *had* searched the property. Hadn't found blood. Hadn't found much of anything. Neither had he. It was as odd as it seemed. And nowhere else to look. Why was she there? Where was she going? Unless she could fly or dig through the ten tons of concrete where the old restaurant supports had been filled in, it looked as if she'd just appeared.

Next, two tea bags on the plate-homestead. Peppermint for Lauren, Curtis's sister. Earl Grey for Vincent, their father. Lauren and Curtis's mother had died during Lauren's birth, so it was just the three of them. He traced out the small patch of bush, unowned land, between the Wades' and the Freemans'.

Finished, he admired his handiwork. He had a dead body, a cluster of footprints, and the place where he'd found the shoe—all so far away from each other as to be completely useless.

It was immediately evident that Eliza couldn't have been at the fence, walked into the middle of the vineyard, severed two fingers, undressed, lain down, and died, without anything happening in between. The prints tapered off from the cigarette stamping, Jack remembered, fading as the ground firmed and turned to gravel. The walk uncompleted. Ominously, fading out in the direction of the homestead.

So, Option One: She'd walked in off the road, up the driveway, walked along the northern fence, had a puff, and then gone inside the homestead. Once inside, someone had killed her and carried her back out to dump her. The trick here was that the exact walk through the vineyard was what Andrew Freeman and Ian McCarthy had driven over on their way to the body. With that interference, it was impossible to prove someone carried the body down there. It was also impossible to prove they hadn't. Ted Piper's favorite, Option One. It had, in part, sent Curtis to jail.

But why would Curtis leave the body out in the open, pointing straight back to him? Why would he call the police first? Why was Eliza even there in the first place? And even with the tire prints, not a single useful footprint, boot or bare. The killer had got lucky with the sloppy police work, but, still, it looked as if she'd been placed there without a trace. It had the actuality of a murder but the feel of a frame-up. Everything just felt out of place, like a bookshelf with a single book backward. And behind every question, the fact that the initial evidence was gathered shoddily. Four years on, it was hard to pull the truth from that. This had been his line in the show, and it would maybe, in part, get Curtis back out again.

Option Two, then. She'd come in off the road, walked through the property, had a cigarette at the only place muddy enough to leave prints, and walked back down the driveway safe and sound. Afterward, someone had killed her and brought her back.

Maybe she had been there and she'd tried to hitch from the road. He moved the noodle cake to the roadside, playing it out in his mind. If someone had slowed to pick her up and killed her right there, it seemed inefficient to haul her over the fence and carry her into the property. Not to mention difficult. Jack had rolled his ankle jumping the fence, and he wasn't lugging a dead body at the time. Plus, in perhaps the only piece of real evidence the prosecution had, Eliza had left a voicemail message on a journalist's phone—Sam Culver of *Discover!* magazine—the afternoon before she disappeared, saying she'd found something *weird* in Birravale. This seemed to point to motive, but Eliza hadn't been sure whether what she'd discovered was technically illegal and had been looking to sell her story rather than go to the police. When Sam had called her back the next day, she hadn't answered, and he'd forgotten about it. Eliza had known something she shouldn't—that much was clear—but no one could figure out what or who it involved. What's more, *Discover!* was a trashy tabloid. Who kills over a puff piece next to "My Ex-Wife's Hamster Gambled Away My Inheritance"? Still, predictably, the prosecution clung to this as proof of premeditation, that someone *may* have had motive. To their credit, they had to cling to something. If it was a random hitchhike killing, there was really no prosecutable case. She could have been killed anywhere, by anyone. Jack thought about this young girl hitching a ride. Bright halogen eyes approaching from the dark, slowing. A white girl in a car's headlights looks just like she does on an autopsy table. Scorched. Colorless.

They had never found what cut off her fingers. What strangled her. Maybe they were in the trunk of a car, thousands of miles away.

Hang on. Something wasn't right. He took a mixing bowl and flipped it, placed the Freemans' tomato-tin wine silos on top of it. Better—it hadn't been right being flat. It was uphill. He got down on his knees, eye level with the table. He imagined the bush blocking out most of the silos from the position of the body.

Shuffling on his knees, he moved—used to kneeling, his knees clicked with familiarity—counterclockwise around the table, and now he could picture seeing the wine silos in full.

He stood up. He was directly in line with the clump of Eliza's footsteps. At that point, she would have been able to see the Freeman house. She'd been having a cigarette, stamping her feet from the cold, in full view of Andrew and Sarah Freeman's homestead up the hill.

Had they seen her? Minutes before, supposedly, she died? Disappeared from the earth and reappeared, barefoot, two hundred meters away?

Jack shook his head. Of course, this all assumed the footprints were made on the same night as the murder. And that they were even hers (he still clung to this doubt). And it still didn't explain the dumping, the lack of physical evidence. Curtis's house had been checked, and there hadn't been a scrap of evidence there.

Andrew and Sarah hadn't mentioned seeing Eliza in their testimonies. But maybe they'd been asleep. Out. Maybe no one actually asked them. Besides, did a single glowing ember stick in the mind?

He looked at his playground of Birravale. There wasn't enough there to prove a man innocent. But there wasn't enough to prove him guilty either. Nothing he knew *proved* anything, and it wasn't worth potentially burning his career by raising more questions. In criminal law, the onus of proof was always on the prosecution, not the defense.

Jack took the Eliza-Ramen noodle and put it on the plate-homestead next to Saltshaker-Curtis. He covered them with a bowl, masking them from view. As if Curtis and Eliza were in the bowl-house together.

"Did you go inside that house, Eliza?" he muttered. "What happened to you?"

He whacked the table in frustration. Everything clinked. A small puff of flour rose up and tickled his nose. He was tired now. At least the mental exercise had done that. He'd clean up in the morning. The food would go to waste. He didn't care.

He would keep the shoe quiet. It proved nothing. Nothing added up the way Ted Piper and his team said it did. And Jack couldn't keep focusing on this. He had a new show to start working on, money to make, and his health to consider. He could feel the stress building. He didn't want to get sick again. The only way to move through this was to accept his mistake—grieve for it, Alexis would say—and leave it behind.

Sure, Jack's version didn't stack up either. He still didn't know *who* had killed Eliza. But looking at the table in front of him—at the upturned bowl that hid Eliza and Curtis inside that house—there was doubt. Just a flicker. An ember in the dark. Just enough.

He took the bowl off Salt-Curtis and Eliza-Ramen, left to their hidden mysteries. He must have hit the table harder than he thought, because it was all disordered now. The saltshaker had fallen over and shattered the noodle cake.

Coincidence, thought Jack.

He walked back through his doorless house and finally into bed. Even still, he couldn't sleep. Couldn't get the image out of his head of the mess on the plate. Of Eliza, broken into pieces.

Did you go inside that house, Eliza? What happened to you?

Eventually, sleep took him. Decision made.

The lies you can live with.

CHAPTER 5

SEPTEMBER

Jack scratched his chest. They always put the tape right on the hair, and then the lighting made the sweat pool around it. The sound guy came over and whacked Jack's hand, pointed at the lapel mic poking through Jack's top button and then at his own ear. Jack nodded. He knew what that meant. *Stop fucking up my sound, amateur.*

Ted Piper sat across from Jack. They hadn't sat in an official interview together since Jack had blindsided Ted on the original podcast. Ted had refused to take part in the TV show, so Jack had had to build his character through preexisting interviews, courtroom footage, and press conferences. The prosecutor wore a sharply cut blue suit. It fit him perfectly. Jack tugged at his own shirt. It was collared, but he'd forgone the tie, which he was regretting now, if only so he could neck himself if it didn't go well. He smoothed his shirt over his stomach, which seemed to have inflated since he'd chosen the shirt this morning. He felt ill. Live national television. He was never good at live stuff. Why had he had breakfast? Never eat before a show.

Ted's smooth, professional beard was shaved in at right angles down his cheekbones. Jack toyed with where he'd cast Ted. Didn't quite fit a drama, too smug to sustain a full hour's attention. A deodorant commercial, Jack decided. Ted's hair was slick, short cropped, and black with a scatter of gray. Good lawyer hair. Black meant youthful enough to be energetic, but gray meant old enough to be experienced. Looking at it, Jack became convinced his was too messy. He ran a hand through it. Before he'd finished, a woman with a can of hairspray appeared. She swatted his hand away and started spraying and pecking with her fingertips. She shot him a look. *Stop fucking up your hair, amateur.*

Ted smiled at his discomfort. *Damn it*, thought Jack. His teeth were superwhite too. But his pants were too tight. No bulge. Small victories.

They were sitting on a circular stage, in two padded, semispherical chairs. The type that had no armrests, so your hands slid awkwardly into your lap or your arms hung over the sides. Jack fidgeted, couldn't get it right. Both his and Ted's chairs were angled at forty-five degrees to an opposing seat—which was currently empty. That one was leather. Host's privilege.

Jack preferred interviews behind a desk. In the middle of a soundstage, he felt marooned. But this was less an interview, more an interrogation.

Cameras and lights were placed around the stage in quarters, glass eyes pointing inward: tall hulking sentries. The stage floor itself was concentric circles: an inner brown rug; the outer circumference the exposed stage itself, a reflective black. It looked slick on-screen, but it was just shiny black plastic.

All this for three people talking. Words will make you famous, Jack supposed.

He wasn't the only minor celebrity. Birravale too had quickly become infamous. Googling *winery deaths* even a year ago would only turn up a few hits: workplace safety accidents and an old Italian winery that tried to blend methanol with their sauvignon blanc and wound up killing twenty-three people and blinding dozens of others. Now, though, pages and pages of fingerless Eliza Dacey. Her death usurped the twenty-three haphazard Italians. Because Eliza was young. Eliza was pretty. Eliza was on TV. She mattered more. Her ghost was a soft cathode glow, now.

"Gentlemen." Vanessa Raynor stepped onto the stage. Casting notes: prestige actress. That one was easy. She gave both Jack and Ted a double-clasped handshake. Her smile was warm, but the firm grip announced that she was in control. This was her show. Her stage. She strode back to her chair and Jack half expected her to let out a battle cry. Instead, she crossed her legs and put her hands on her knees. Perfect hand placement. Someone rushed up and henpecked her straight blond hair, ran a lint roller down her black blazer. "Thanks for being here."

"Thank you for having us," Ted said.

Jack just nodded. He was getting used to these shows, more comfortable in them, erring on the side of confident. His doubts were now buried in a shoebox at the back of his closet, and since the end of the series, he'd been on enough panel shows, speaking for Curtis, that he'd managed to talk his way into believing in his innocence again. Besides, he wasn't here to vouch for anyone; he was here to show his face, get a good sound bite or two, and use the increased profile to renegotiate his deal with the network. Vanessa would ask him the same old questions about the same old murder. As far as he was concerned, that whole case, and everything with it, had run its course.

"This is perhaps a bit different from what you're used to." She nodded at Ted. "Shall we put your hand on a Bible? Make you feel more at home?"

Ted crossed his heart, leaned over, and smiled. "He's the one you need to worry about. I always tell the truth."

"Mate, it's fucking television," Jack said, scratching at his microphone and avoiding the glares of the audio crew. "The only thing telling the truth on you is how tight those pants are."

One of the crew laughed. The hairstylist scurried off, and an assistant holding a clipboard stepped in. Blond, slight, midtwenties. All production assistants looked the same because they never made it into the middle-aged diversity of face and figure—once the glamour of television wore off, they realized how shit a job it was and quit. This one bent and whispered something in Vanessa's ear.

"Okay," Clipboard Lemming said, straightening. "Everyone, this is live TV. Once we go up, that means you can't say 'fuck.' But that was really good. We want to lead with that exchange, okay? Sets up the tension between the two of you. Can you do it again?" She stepped off the stage and stood next to one of the cameras.

Vanessa smiled at them both. "Make it look natural. Just the start, then we'll be live. Play nice."

"Live in five," called the lemming, hand up, fingers splayed. "Phones off."

Ted rummaged in his pocket, pulled his phone out, switched it to silent. "Sorry. Always forget," he mumbled, pocketing it.

The lemming's fingers surrendered one by one until she had a fist.

Before Jack could say anything, the music had started and Vanessa was talking. He knew that was key: to plunge them into it, catch them off guard. On his left, a monitor showed the current framing. To his right, over Ted's shoulder, Vanessa's intro scrolled up the teleprompter in black and white. Jack found himself reading it, rather than listening to her.

> VR: I'm here today with the lead prosecutor in the Wade case, Mr. Theodore Piper. And the filmmaker who blew this case wide open, Jack Quick. Gentlemen. This is, perhaps, a bit different from what you're used to. Shall we put your hand on a Bible, make you feel more at home? *elegant laugh*

All Jack could think about was how fast they'd been able to put their spontaneous banter into the teleprompter. That, and how terrifying an *elegant laugh* from Vanessa Raynor would be. *World leaders have been eviscerated on this stage*, he reminded himself. *Better men than you. Worse men too.*

Then he heard Ted say, like the suck-up he was, "I always tell the truth," and realized everyone was looking at him. Clipboard Lemming Number Two, by camera 3, spun her fingers in a wheel. *Hurry up.*

"Mate, it's fucking television," Jack said. Forgot the rest.

Clipboard Lemming shook her head, mouthed at him: *Don't say "fuck."* He felt a scurry of activity behind him as people dived for radios to tell someone to hit the censor button.

Vanessa shot Jack the look he'd seen before from the techie and the makeup girl but took it in her stride. "Excuse you, Mr. Quick."

"Sorry. I'm a bit nervous." He laughed. Elegantly.

"We do have a delay. Only seven seconds though. We'll have our fingers on the button, just in case." She smiled at the camera, not at Jack, reassuring the families at home. "But please do keep in mind that we are a family-friendly show."

"Right." Jack nodded. "Noted. Let's crack on with discussing the torture and strangling of Eliza Dacey then, shall we?"

Before Vanessa had even thrown to the footage, he knew where they'd start it: on a thunderous Sydney day, in the parking lot of the Long Bay Correctional Complex.

On the monitor behind Vanessa, the footage started to play. It showed a beautiful, slowly setting sun, casting the gathered crowd in a gentle ochre. It looked serene, but it had been freezing, Jack remembered; he had worn a scarf and an overcoat. The wind had whipped off the sea and climbed the cliffs. You couldn't tell on the screen, but a rolling mass of gray lumbered over the bay. It would have been colder still inside the prison.

It had been noisy too. A large crowd, everyone chattering. Cameramen spat on lenses, reporters primped hair, shifted so the light wouldn't ruin the shot, but the frame captured a smidgen of the high concrete walls, the guard tower over their shoulders. Hopefully, a man with a rifle would wander into shot. Add some gravitas.

Vanessa had probably been there, Jack thought, though he couldn't remember seeing her. He remembered Ted, who had only gone because a rival network had paid him enough to film his reaction. The man who could *get you on* was there. So were the Wades: the sister, Lauren, and father, Vincent, leaning heavy on a cane. In retrospect, Jack could see the illness waning him. At the time, Jack had thought it was the stress, the grief of a parent struggling with his son's guilt, but he could see it more clearly now. Cancer. Took him fast. Grabbed ahold and shook the bones from him. Five weeks later, he was dead. They'd only buried him a week ago. Jack hadn't been there, but he'd okayed the network's call to send a second unit. The family had gone with a clichéd headstone: *Rest in Peace.* A bit rich, Jack thought, seeing as he planned on interrupting the funeral footage with commercials. Thirteen minutes of ads per hour was both the legal maximum and the network minimum. *Rest in 78 Percent Peace* would have been more apt.

That day at the prison, Lauren had seemed more grown-up too. She'd been a teenager during the case (high school must have been a *joy*) but was now around twenty. Jack remembered her as a quiet sixteen-year-old, seated in the back of the courtroom with her father. The first day, she'd been puffy eyed and petulant; the second, less so. Every day from then, there was a bit more of the world in her face. By the end of the case, she sat stoically, as if the horrors of her brother's crime had leaded her very skin. Though they kept away from everyone else, the Wades had two police officers with them.

He'd seen Alexis there too. She'd shaken his hand before heading into the throng to be interviewed. She didn't command as high a fee as Ted or himself, but she'd gotten plenty of bookings. They'd made her partner at the firm too. Jack thought he'd even seen her on the side of a bus, wearing spectacles.

Vanessa Raynor shifted in her chair, and Jack slipped out of the memory and back into the room. After this interview, he was going to give Alexis a call. See what she was up to. She owed him dinner, after all.

On-screen, milling in the prison parking lot, was the same crew as at the trial, the appeals, the retrial. This ragtag group of journalists and producers, interns and camera operators had managed to become a strange little family themselves over the last few months. A traveling circus following the ghost of Eliza Dacey through the courts and jails of Sydney.

There had been a roar from inside. As if a football game had just been won. The prisoners must have been allowed out in the yard. Today was a special day. Then it was quiet, the wind picking up the cheer and whisking it away, as if the hope inside the walls was forbidden from escaping.

But the people outside the prison were quiet now too. Because there were two figures behind the glass door entryway, talking. It was hard to see what they were wearing, but it appeared neither were in the green tracksuits of the inmates. Cameras were turned on. People craned their necks. Reporters started talking, variations of the same phrase—"first exclusive"—crossing over each other. A "this-just-in" lasagna.

We are live and seconds away from what we believe to be…

The figures shook hands. And then one of them walked to the side, held his pass against the doorframe, and the doors slid open. A few small raindrops began to fall.

Curtis Wade, in civilian clothes—cheap jeans and a plain hoodie— stepped into the dusk.

A free man.

He'd gotten fat.

People either get fit or chunky in prison, and Curtis had opted for sedentary imprisonment. Maybe he'd been treated better the last few months, on account of the show, and that could've porked him up too, Jack supposed. Four years had aged him a decade. Curtis had gone to jail just north of thirty, but he'd come out with gray hair and a rough, white beard. His eyes seemed set far back, sockets punched in like fingers in dough. He walked slowly, almost with a limp but not quite. It was more a slow method of discovery; he was savoring new steps. Four years was a long time to run laps—or not, as seemed evident—in a yard.

After a few seconds of stunned silence, everything happened in a flurry. The cops, previously with Lauren and Vincent, rushed forward and fell into step on either side of Curtis. Reporters broke ranks like kids at the

starting pistol of an Easter egg hunt, running left and right, yelling instruc-
tions at the camera operators. One bypassed Curtis entirely and knocked
on the door to the prison. Jack had a camera jammed in his face and was
asked for his opinion.

"No comment," he said, turning away.

"Fucking hell, man." The operator lowered his camera, pissed he'd
traded a better shot coming over. "Why are you even here?"

"Make a path!" one of the cops yelled as she guided Curtis through the
pack. "Come on, you know how it works. Back up!"

Eventually, when they realized he wasn't going to give any of them
an interview, the pack thinned out, and Curtis was free to pick his way
through to his family. (At the time, Jack found it odd that Curtis's sister and
father hadn't rushed straight up to him either, but on viewing the footage
again now, he could see that Vincent was well past rushing anywhere.) But
then Curtis changed direction. He pushed into the middle of the throng,
looking left and right, scanning for something. Someone.

He locked eyes with Jack.

Fifteen cameras swiveled in Jack's direction. Reporters scattered out of
the way so as not to impede this reunion. If you could call it that. It was
the first time they'd ever actually met in person.

Curtis walked over. Held out his hand.

Fifteen lenses and millions of eyes watched as Jack reached out and
shook it. But Curtis wasn't having that and pulled him tightly into a hug.
His beard was stiff and scratched at Jack's neck, his nose wet against his ear.
Curtis was crying. Jack put his spare arm around him and patted him on
the back. Watching it again while Vanessa shuffled her notes and readied
for questions, Jack remembered that image well. His slight frame dwarfed
by Curtis's red-eyed bear hug: it had been blown up on the front page of
every newspaper in the country.

But it was what Curtis said next that really stuck with him. Watching
it again in Vanessa Raynor's studio, Jack saw it play out again in almost

sickening slow motion. Curtis pulled away slightly, then bent down and spoke, low and quiet, his breath hot on Jack's ear: "Eliza Dacey thanks you for justice."

Six perfectly chosen words. Essentially meaningless. But just odd enough to feel provocative. Chilling. And not whispered, but said with a quiet sincerity, just loud enough that the mics would pick it up. Clever. No, not clever: shrewd.

That was the first time Jack realized he had underestimated Curtis Wade.

CHAPTER 6

"So…" Vanessa snapped Jack from his reverie, brought him back to the present. "Tell us how you got Curtis Wade out of jail?"

An easy start. That was one of the preapproved questions.

"To be honest, I didn't think anything would happen, legally speaking. I wasn't trying to get anyone anywhere. I was just interested in telling the other side of a story, the side that gets skipped, slips through the cracks. I wasn't prepared for the public response; I don't think anyone was. Australia set him free—I just opened up the conversation."

He thought that was most of what his publicist had written down.

"And what drew you to this story?"

"I just found the circumstances around his sentencing so unclear. I felt someone needed to step in and sift through the evidence again. Try and have a clear view. Start again, from the beginning."

"That's the detectives' job though, isn't it?" Ted cut in. "You know, professionals."

Vanessa made a small pat downward with her hand. *Settle, you'll get your chance.*

"Normally, I'd agree," said Jack, "but Curtis was up against it, in a town that disliked him—"

"Because of what he did to the Freemans' winery?"

"Yes, we can come back to that. But he was a victim of a biased police force, a biased jury, and not to mention a vitriolic prosecution campaign." Jack looked Ted in the eyes. "Set up by, you know, professionals."

"So you wanted to give the little guy a voice?" Vanessa said.

"I think everyone deserves to be heard."

"And Eliza's voice?"

That was not a preapproved question. He faltered. Almost heard his publicist's head *thunk* on the desk from the green room.

"But, Mr. Piper"—Vanessa switched the momentum—"you felt you had a pretty strong case?"

"Of course we did."

"So where did it all go wrong?"

"These guys—I want to say this now so it's out in the open—are just a gaggle of filmmakers. They are not professional investigators; they're not lawyers. They aren't bound by chain of evidence, they aren't bound by duty to the court."

"We had consultant—"

"You had retired police detectives consult, that's true. Retired. May I finish?"

Jack waved a hand dismissively.

"It's a TV show. I'm not denying you made some convincing arguments—you did. But you edited your arguments into existence; you moved things around. There are hundreds of hours in the trial alone, and your show was only seven. You're not even a documentary crew." Ted directed his accusation at Vanessa, as if Jack wasn't even worth the vitriol. "You know, these guys, what they're making, it's classified in the network's budget as a drama. A drama. Fiction."

"That's just a label for the number crunchers. Everything we showed was true."

"It's what you didn't show that concerns me."

A shoebox, pushed to the back of Jack's closet, flickered in his mind. He shut it out.

"So what you're saying is…?" Vanessa guided the accusation.

"I'm saying you made it up. And you got lucky," Ted said.

"Lucky? Your evidence didn't hold up in the appeals court, I don't need to remind you. On top of that, Curtis Wade was retried by a jury of unbiased peers."

"Unbiased? Everyone in the country has seen your show. Everyone has had your opinions beamed into their homes as facts. There aren't twelve people in this country I could make an unbiased jury out of."

"You're just mad because everyone in the country saw you be an arsehole."

"Family show, Jack," Vanessa cut in.

"Yes, of course." Jack tried to remember what his publicist had told him; he had to time it right. "You're forgetting something. We didn't actually present any evidence. All we did was show that yours was not up to scratch. You hack-jobbed him. Reasonable doubt is for *everybody*."

"You're forgetting something too. You got a killer out of jail. You have to live with that."

"No blood, no matching footprints." Jack counted on his fingertips, becoming more animated. The exaggerated defense of someone who knows they're wrong but hopes to get by on bravado. "No motive—"

"We had motive," Ted cut in. "Eliza left a voicemail with a journalist at *Discover!* magazine. She had something she felt might be illegal, that could be newsworthy."

"She found something"—Vanessa tapped her ear, fed some fact by a producer—"*weird*, I believe was her wording."

"*Discover!* is a tabloid," Jack said. "If it had been a severe enough motive for murder, she might have gone to the police. Or at least the *Sydney Morning Herald*."

"She wanted money," Ted said, comfortable in this area of discussion, "so she made a mistake and called the wrong magazine. That doesn't mean she deserved to die."

"Of course she didn't *deserve* to die," Jack sniped. *Control*, he reminded himself. *Don't be drawn into emotion.*

"But she knew something she shouldn't. This much is clear." Vanessa stepped back in, switching sides again to whichever argument would stir the most drama. "We agree on this, gentlemen, correct?"

Jack nodded. "But that motive is all but useless without context, which you do not have. If I may return to my original point? There wasn't a shred of physical evidence, yet somehow you posited that she'd been killed on the property."

"And that was a contentious point?" Vanessa asked.

"Of the appeals? Yes. It came down to whether her body had been dumped or not."

"We proved that the cord used to strangle her was the same cord Curtis had spools of in his barn—"

"My team tested the same cord at hardware stores across the country and got eleven identical fiber profiles to the one you used to convict him. Eleven serial killers, then, according to you. Better go round them up. All of them work at Bunnings Warehouse stores—should be easy to find. Grab me a sausage while you're down there."

"Explain"—Vanessa pointed at the camera—"for the viewers at home?"

"Simply," Jack said, "there was no DNA evidence on the rope in Curtis Wade's barn. The *brand* of rope—quite a common brand—had matching fibers in Eliza's neck, but that's it."

"It all seems very convenient," Ted said. "That he even owns the same brand of rope. He got rid of her clothes, her shoes, he cleaned up her blood; it makes sense he would have got rid of the murder weapon. We weren't positing that it was the exact murder weapon, just that it came from the same spool."

"Just like you can't ascertain that the shoe prints were actually hers?"

"Again, we proved that it was *likely*," Ted said. "I don't know why it bothers you so much that a murder victim's footprints are at a crime scene. That's what happens, you know."

"I agree. A lot of the evidence was"—Jack pulled his fingers into air quotes—"*convenient*."

"Easy evidence is more a sign of a sloppy killer than a corrupt police force," Ted shot back.

"That might have been good enough the first time. The absence of evidence is not evidence. Your excuse that he cleaned it up is not good enough. There's no blood on my car outside; how many people do you think I ran over on the way here?"

"I hope you have a good libel lawyer." Ted was fuming. "You're making it sound like I'm the one that framed him."

Jack shrugged.

"If I may," Vanessa cut in again, "we have limited time left here, so let's try not to get too personal. So, Jack, it's agreed in the courts—"

"We'll appeal," corrected Ted.

"It's been *temporarily* agreed in the courts that the physical evidence wasn't up to scratch," Vanessa said. "So, let me ask you, Jack—if Curtis didn't kill Eliza, who did?"

"I don't know."

"But the real killer is still out there?"

"I suppose."

"Your documentary—"

"Drama," said Ted.

"Yes, Ted." Vanessa's glare challenged Ted to interrupt her on this point again. She turned back to Jack. "Your docudrama seems to imply that three million dollars of corporate espionage might be good enough motive for a frame-up?"

"'Corporate espionage' are strong words for some spilled wine," Jack replied.

"Six hundred thousand liters."

"Point taken. Look, the Freemans and the Wades have beef. No doubt. And I'm sure it influenced the local opinion toward Mr. Wade in the end. But I wouldn't read any more into it than that."

"Andrew Freeman is the local sergeant too, is that correct?"

"I'm not going to sit here on national television and accuse Andrew and Sarah Freeman of murdering someone, if that's what you want."

Vanessa looked at her notes. There was just a glimmer but enough to know—he'd stumped her.

"See, that's how I know you don't care." Ted had found the guts to pipe up again. "Because if you are right, then Eliza's real killer is still out there. And you're not doing anything to find them. And I think that's either because you *want* them to kill again, for the press. Or"—Ted paused and let it sink in—"you already know who it is."

The shoebox flickered in his mind.

"Nothing to say to that?"

"No, Ted. I just…"

"You look tired. Thin too. Every time I see you, you look like you've halved. Stress? Trouble eating? Something keeping you up?"

"Fuck off, Ted."

"Family show, Mr. Quick," Vanessa cut in, but half-heartedly—she was loving it.

"Yeah," Ted said. "Watch your language."

"I'll watch my language," Jack said, "when you stop being such a cunt."

Vanessa sliced a hand across her throat, and the red lights on all four cameras flickered out. "I think it's time we all took a bit of a break."

Jack felt his phone buzz in his pocket. Then again. Again. He checked it: fifteen calls in the last ten seconds. All missed, bouncing off each other. One text got through, from his producer. **What have you done?!** It made him smile. He turned his phone off. Ted might have thought he'd gotten the better of him, and maybe he had struck a nerve somewhere there, but Jack felt like he'd regained some control. His publicist's words rang in his head: *Ninety percent of all interviews are disposable. Just get a few good sound bites. Go viral. Call him a cunt if you have to.*

In retrospect, she had probably meant it figuratively.

Before they came back from the commercial break, Jack knew something was wrong. The minions had mobilized; there was movement everywhere. People were talking into their radios and phones loud and fast. He heard Vanessa tap her earpiece and say, "Are you sure?"

Then someone stood in front of camera 2 and whirled her finger above her head. He heard someone yell they were coming back early, and his life changed forever.

"We welcome you back with some breaking news."

Vanessa was talking, but she sounded distant. This definitely wasn't in the preapproved questions list. He risked a glance at Ted, who looked equally anxious. Breaking news? This wasn't a bulletin type of show.

"I'm here with Jack Quick and Ted Piper, two men intricately involved in the case for and against Curtis Wade." Jack noticed a somber mood about the lemmings; Number One was looking at her shoes. Vanessa was building up to something. "Alexis White, who you'll remember as Curtis Wade's defense counsel, has been murdered."

Ted put his head in his hands. Jack's mouth dropped open.

"I'm hearing that"—Vanessa touched her earpiece again, nodded— "I'm hearing that she had two fingers cut off and placed in her mouth. A replica of the Dacey killing."

Two fingers. In her mouth.

What have you done?!

The next thing Jack felt was the stage driving into his shoulder. His chair had toppled sideways. On the replay, much later, he saw Ted Piper launch out of his chair and crash-tackle him, knocking them both to the ground. There, in the studio, he looked up and saw Ted, his face the palest white, grappling with his neck. Ted landed two solid punches, broke Jack's nose on the second, before the audio guy pulled him off.

Jack lay there, blood dripping onto the back of his tongue. Sour metal. It was only a shoe. It had probably been planted. It wasn't supposed to matter. He could see the TV monitor, sideways now, from where he lay.

The interview stage set had been replaced by vision of an external reporter, which then cut to a static image.

He knew what they were going to show before they showed it. Because it was exactly what he would have done. Sensationalist maybe. But great TV nonetheless.

A vertically split image, two pictures side by side. On the left: a white sheet, pixilation over the worst of it, evidence markers, a cop standing frozen, on his phone. Alexis's crime scene. On the right: Curtis Wade, in front of Long Bay, leaning in and embracing Jack Quick, the man who got him out.

And running through both images, the words:

Eliza Dacey thanks you for justice.

S01E03
NAIL-BITER

Exhibit B:

Photographs. Size 9 women's shoe prints. Photographs 1–7: Footprints catalogued at the northwest fence line on the Wade vineyard. Photographs 8–10: Clusters of unidentifiable prints, various sizes, intersected with tire tracks. Victim's shoe size: women's 9.

Handwritten Note: Defense notes that without victim's shoes, unrecovered, we can't confirm these footprints belong to the victim and therefore represent her final movements and place her at the vineyard before death. Expect objection; we'll see if we can scrape it through. TP

CHAPTER 7

PREVIOUSLY

Put your hand around the neck, Curtis.

Curtis braced himself. *Most people think it's the middle, but you've got to grab it around the neck first,* his father had said. *Now, feet apart. Farther. Shoulder width. Good. Let the power come from weight and not from your arms. Slide your hand up the handle as it descends. Power from the arc. Gravity, you cover that in school yet? Newton? No, Lauren, you can't have a swing. You're too young. Careful now, Curtis.*

A child is always impressed by his father. Splitting wood like butter, clean through the middle in a single stroke, Vincent's hand effortlessly gliding up the wooden handle as if greased. Two perfect pieces falling to either side. Over time, Curtis learned that if you aimed along the grain, you needed very little strength. The wood would split itself, provided you found the right fault. But a father looks strong regardless, ax in hand.

Curtis remembered letting the ax rotate slightly in his hand on his first swing. It hit the wood flat and ricocheted. Shock jarred his wrist and rippled up his arm. Silly. His father had muttered, hand on his back, "You okay?" Compassion. Maybe. Or looking for weakness, for his son's fault in the grain. Curtis nodded, but he'd actually sprained it. Had to cut his sausages with one hand that night; Vincent wouldn't cut them for him. Instead, he insisted the whole family eat one handed. Even Lauren, who was barely walking. Succeed together, fail together. Curtis's flaws spread out across the family. *All for one and one for all. You cover that in school yet?*

But up here, as an adult, it was different. It was the middle of the night, firstly. And he was panting from the battle up the hill: pushing through scrub, climbing the fence. Plus, although Curtis was older and a much better swing, he was swinging the ax sideways not downward.

And, of course, he wasn't cutting wood.

High up, he could see a few dim lights in the town. This view better than his. The sky above was free from city light, so clear he could almost make out the curve of the atmosphere.

Feet apart. Shoulder width. Hands at the neck.

They'd come for him after this. Fuck 'em. Let this town bathe in its own pride. Let this town run red.

He swung the ax.

CHAPTER 8

SEPTEMBER

There was blood in Jack's vomit.

The doctor had predicted this. Jack had felt it, pooling in the back of his throat, cold liquid rolling through his sinuses. Drowning from the inside. He'd swallow the majority while he slept, his doctor said, and in the morning the body would naturally expel it.

"Expel?" Jack had asked.

"Vomit," elaborated the doctor. "Vampire's hangover."

Oh, Jack remembered thinking, *the good old days.*

Jack finished retching, flushed the toilet, and moved to the sink. He swished water around in his mouth and spat. The acidity of bile fizzed on his gums. He took his toothbrush from his pocket—it was always in his pocket, some habits stayed—and brushed. He felt light-headed, braced himself against the sink.

His face was a swathe of colors. One of his eye sockets was black, purpling downward onto his cheek. His nose was a moldy yellow with scabs of red beneath each nostril, a white strip of gauze across the bridge. He prodded his cheek, examining the bruised skin in the mirror. Alexis's neck, he thought, would have been equally discolored. Her throat mottled. Decaying. He felt her finger on his wrist, a soft kiss on the cheek—muscle memory from their meeting in the pub—gagged again, hung his head over the sink.

There was a knock. There were doors in his father's house. His father, Peter, had put them back up when Jack moved out. Another soft rap. His father's voice through the door: "You okay?"

This was hard to run from. Loved ones watched bathroom doors like prison guards.

"Fine," he called back.

"Careful."

"It's just blood, Dad."

"Blood?" Panic. Slight, controlled.

"From my nose."

A pause. His father processed it. Probably trying to figure out if it was a lie.

Jack hadn't had a problem with food—or at least not a severe one, he told himself—for several years. He was better now, at least medically speaking. Percentages, that sort of thing. Those numbers on a piece of paper that men with glasses would nod over, say he was fixed. Fixed enough to put the doors back on anyway. Originally taken off the hinges on doctor's orders, so Jack couldn't lock himself away in a bathroom. But the bedrooms, the closets—anywhere you can tuck yourself away with a plastic bin or a garbage bag—had provided a compromised refuge. So those doors had to go, too, during the worst of it.

Fixed enough now, they'd said. Door approved. You're much better, they'd said. *But you're never really better. Not from this.*

Some habits take hold: vagrant customs striking up camp inside, under a bridge in your rib cage, lighting a fire. A toothbrush in a pocket. Saying he'd already eaten or was just about to head out somewhere else. Choosing low-carb drinks that didn't trigger—vodka, gin, soda water. Accidentally knocking the glass over when someone bought him a beer.

Top up? Still a third in this. I'm fine.

Well before he'd stolen Eliza's shoe, Jack had been very good at lying to people.

People thought it was about weight. But that wasn't all of it. People asked for reasons, and they didn't always exist either. His presence on panels, at news desks, his interviews in chairs without armrests conducted by slick career presenters—sure, they were what his most recent specialist had labeled High-Risk Activities. But at its worst, in his twenties, Jack hadn't even started in TV. He knew he'd struggled with his weight after his brother's accident. And when things had started to spiral, watching the numbers tick down on the scales felt like something, perhaps the only thing, he could control.

Because control is a core part of this disorder. Maybe that was why Jack took the shoe in the first place. He was addicted to controlling his own story just as he was addicted to controlling his body. What came into it and what came out. Control. There were other buzzwords specialists had used along the way: *Low Self-Esteem, Self-Worth, A Need to Prove Yourself.* As if naming that fear could paper over it. This is what you need. This is why you're broken. Take shelter in these labels.

His father, in particular, always wanted to look for a reason, something tangible above that core, terrifying truth that maybe there was no reason at all behind: *there is something wrong with your son.*

A problem with food, they'd say at home. They didn't use the other words to describe it anymore, the ones the doctors used. Because those words were imbued with something worse when spoken aloud. Not a grown man's problem, those words.

Jack still remembered sitting inside the GP's office fifteen years ago. Peter next to him, voices and words nothing more than muffled tones barely penetrating through the fog that encased him as it so often did back then. He'd fainted in a media lecture. It was a soft fall, onto carpet. An octogenarian would have sprung back up. Jack had broken his wrist.

Back then, Ted's punches would probably have imploded his brittle skull. But one thing had stayed the same: his father was still picking him up and taking him to the hospital.

His father had nodded a lot in the GP's office, while Jack held his wrist and felt acutely the individual bones inside him. Every muscle and bone within thrummed with awareness—the body's natural response to threat.

That feeling in itself was addictive. A heightened clarity, crafted and honed from adrenaline. Fear. A body stuck in a perpetual fight-or-flight response, so afraid of itself.

The doctor explained some of these things; others Jack figured out much later. His father didn't understand but nodded along with the doctor's melodious cautions. At the end of the consultation, the doctor handed him a pamphlet. It was pink with an apple on the front: *15 Signs Your Daughter Isn't Eating Properly*. I'm sorry, the doctor said, it's all we have.

Not a man's problem, then.

It would take several more years until Jack was officially diagnosed. Because in order to *officially* have the disease, Jack had to tick off *all* the required medical symptoms. Including, up until only recently, an irregular menstrual cycle. He couldn't tick that box because he didn't have that symptom (*If he had a cycle*, his dad snapped at a GP once, *I'd consider that irregular*), and so, technically, he wasn't sick. The bureaucracy of bulimia.

Jack's father cleared his throat, piercing the memory.

"I've made breakfast when you're ready. Take your time." There was something akin to relief in his father's voice. A broken nose was a more physical pain. Easier to talk about, father and son.

Jack looked in the mirror. His cheeks hung slack, past white and into gray. His hands gripped the side of the basin, cuticles gnawed into scabs. Still had that tic too, chewing his fingernails, a straggler's fire glowing dimly within him. You get cold hands when you don't eat. Bad circulation. That stuck around, ill or not. He thought about Alexis's touch again, how cold her hands would be now.

Alexis was dead. He tried to wrap his mind around that fact. No, not just dead. Murdered. And probably by the man he'd helped get out of jail. Jack's father was scared he was vomiting again, that he had his old broken son back. His son was broken, all right.

Jack may as well have strangled Alexis himself. His cold, chewed fingers wrapped around her neck.

The urge came again. His jaw ached, and his eyes pulsed as he bent over the sink. The tendons in his neck pulled taut as guylines. Nothing but air came out. The fire glowed familiar.

Who could have wanted Alexis dead? Curtis was the obvious suspect. Four years was plenty of time to stew on the past. To plan revenge. Was it revenge against the woman who'd failed to keep him from a lonely four years behind bars? But then, why her? Why not kill Ted, who was surely more responsible? Did that mean Ted was next? And what if Jack's show was right all along and Curtis was innocent? That meant someone had duplicated the original murder and was trying to pin it on Curtis. Worse still, that whoever killed Eliza was still out there. Not two separate murders, but simply the original killer striking again.

But those were just theories. Noise. Fanciful thoughts to mask the truth: that it was his fault. He'd turned a blind eye, and now Alexis was dead. The shoe might not mean shit in the larger scheme of the crime, but it was a symbol of Jack's involvement. Shoe or not, if his show hadn't aired, Alexis would still be alive. He was sure of it.

He could hear his dad calling up the stairs. He took a painkiller and swallowed it without water. Felt it land. Kept it down. The mirror was blood flecked. He looked exhausted, gaunt, and beat-up—but he'd looked like that before and people hadn't noticed. Because when men look drawn, people assume they're working too much. That was why this remains an invisible disorder, especially in a grown man.

Not a man's problem, then.

He had been working too much; that much was true. Enough for no one to notice that he'd started avoiding certain foods. Nothing major, just the stress of the TV show. And that was how it started, small choice by small choice, gnawing away at you. Meanwhile, parts of him faded. The only problem—it was hard to disappear when you were in front of the nation: Sundays, 8:00 p.m.

He steadied himself against the sink, hands gripping the white porcelain.

There were scars on the back of his knuckles, roughly healed calluses that Alexis had run her fingertips over. Russell's sign, they're called. One symptom he could tick off. Soft skin continually broken from crashing against the back of teeth. Not a man's hands either.

Maybe it was the aspirin slowly dissolving and fizzing through his system, but Jack felt resolve surge through him. He still had his police contact: Ian McCarthy. He could build a new case. But no cameras this time. He could do better.

The ghost of Alexis's fingers feathered his wrist.

But first, a more immediate challenge awaited him downstairs.

Breakfast.

"The Nail-Biter Killer," Peter said, dropping the *Sydney Morning Herald* on the kitchen table. "It's got a ring to it."

Peter had wispy, gray hair, sparsely placed, barely fending off balding. He had hazel eyes and sunspots on his neck from a life lived. There's a moment in every son's life when a parent suddenly strikes them as *old*, and Jack had reached his with his father. He moved slower now. Cracks in his face like a gingersnap.

Jack took a seat. It was cushioned, with a wooden frame. It wasn't a kitchen chair. Peter had brought it in from the living room especially for Jack, his own chair merely plastic. Jack supposed that one chair was normally all he needed. His brother was always upstairs. Peter turned back to the bench.

Jack scanned the paper. The front page had a close-up picture of Curtis, red letters splashed diagonally across him. Of course, the copy editor had added a question mark—*The Nail-Biter Killer?*—to protect from defamation. In the body of the article was a smaller photo of Ted flying out of his seat into Jack, his blue jacket flailing behind him in blurred motion. A quick profile on Alexis. A hotshot young lawyer. A little infographic of her biggest scalps—the murdered son of a property developer, her first big trial, won in blazing fashion. Made her name. The killer, only twenty-two years old: James Harrison. Jack remembered it from the papers. Bullet-point list of more killers. It seemed Alexis excelled at murders. More reports, pages three and four. Jack didn't feel the need to open it.

"They think it's a serial killer, then," Jack said to his father's back. He took a sip of his tea. Too hot. Too sweet.

"You're not a serial killer until you get a catchy name."

"It's not that catchy," Jack lied. He wished he'd thought of it.

"Digital dismemberer? Finger feeder?"

"Stick to retirement, Dad." Though he was glad for the levity. Besides, "digital dismemberer" wasn't too bad. He filed it away.

"You probably don't want to talk about it."

"No."

"But the police called."

"Of course."

"Anytime today, they said."

Jack nodded.

"I think it's pointless, you know," Peter went on, seemingly unsure what to say but keen to fill the silence with something. "You make TV. What use could they have for you?" He meant it compassionately, but it came out cutting. He backpedaled. "I meant they shouldn't need you to come in and do their job for them."

"I know what you meant. It's okay. I want to help."

"I'll come. If you want." Peter put a plate of toast down in front of him.

"No. I need to stop somewhere first."

Jack picked up a slice of toast. Thick Vegemite. The salt shocked his tongue; he hadn't eaten since the hospital. His jaw hurt from retching, but he did his best.

"My jaw hurts." He made the excuse without prompting, aware that he was eating too slowly. They used to have a stopwatch. Not anymore, but something ticked between them still. Jack changed the topic. "What do you think, then?"

"About what?"

"The victims. Eliza. Alexis. Either." Jack shook his head, her name a boulder in his mouth. "Alexis, mainly."

"Did you know her?"

"Yeah."

"We don't have to talk about it." Peter flipped the paper sports-side up. Curtis banished to the laminate.

"It's okay," Jack said. "I want your opinion."

"Did he kill her?"

"No." Jack felt it explode out of him, and suddenly he was sobbing. Black eyes and bruises. Crying on the kitchen table. All the slickness and manipulation of television slipping away. No edits, no cuts. Just a child again, in his father's house. "I think I did. Making that fucking show."

His father stood up, wrapped his arms around him. It was a tight hug, tight enough to feel the warmth of tea on his breath. The smell of an old man too: bathroom water, public changing rooms, that almost-clean aroma that follows the elderly—simultaneously wet and dry. His father didn't say anything, not that Alexis's death wasn't Jack's fault; he just held Jack and let him get it out in heaving, ragged breaths.

After a time, Jack pulled away. He wiped snot on his sleeve. Red in it. "Sorry. Should I feed Liam?"

"He'd like that."

Peter bustled around the kitchen while Jack finished his tea, grainy down at the bottom now. Peter handed him a bowl of porridge, bananas squished on top. Mushy stuff, kid's food. Sludge. Two children in this house. Jack headed upstairs in silence, wishing his father had just said it wasn't his fault. They bristled inside him, those missing words. Maybe— unlike his son, that professional liar—Peter Quick could only bring himself to tell the truth.

He opened the door to his brother's room. Liam was propped up on pillows in the new bed Jack had bought. Jack had made sure it was state of the art, moved all angles. To make Liam's home care easier for his father. Liam's head drooped to one side, too heavy for his neck. Something beeped softly—oxygen maybe. Jack wasn't sure. Liam needed most things. Jack sat down beside him, unnoticed, and thought about his brother. Back when they were kids. Cheeks caked in orange dust. Blood leaking out both ears. Chest crumpled, jumbled under desperate, pushing hands, like a bag of assorted tools.

A lie becomes the truth when you're the only one who knows it's a lie, and you're the only one telling it. The thought jumped into his mind.

A lie. That was the first time he'd thought of Eliza's shoe like that. Not just an untruth. Alexis had seen it straightaway for what it was. And now he would go to the police station that afternoon and lie to them as well. Because if he told them the truth, he was ruined. He looked at his brother, silent, unknowing, but alive at least. Brain damage does that to a person: humanity reduced to its basic functions. Only truths in that body.

Jack ladled the sludge of nutrients into Liam's tube. Thought about the way his father had put the sugar in the tea and watched him drink it. That mistrust. That all he needed was a little *more*. Now, force-feeding his brother in his father's house, Jack knew his dad still didn't understand. He would never be better, not from this, even when the physical act was gone. Despite his doorless house, the door was always open to this disease. It was never a matter of an extra spoonful of sugar. It was never a matter of running upstairs, slamming the bathroom door, and shoving your fingers in your throat.

Your fingers are always in your throat.

Nail-Biter.

CHAPTER 9

Alexis had lived in a town house in Sydney's east. Had. She'd died in the alley behind it.

A patrol car blocked the lane off at one end, blue-and-white tape strung between a streetlight and the nearest tree. Likewise, Jack assumed, on the other end. He recognized the cobblestones from the media pictures. The garage door, backing onto the lane, was fully open. It had only been a third off the ground in most of the press photos, a toothless yawn of dark. As if Alexis had been in the middle of lifting it. The laneway sloped downward, dropping away to reveal, over the triangular roofs of the wealthy, a hint of the sparkling harbor. The tip of the famous bridge. You mostly saw the tips of things in Sydney.

Jack dawdled across the road. There were no reporters. They would have been packed in behind the tape last night, squabbling for position under stark generator lights. They'd gotten their shots, Alexis sprawled on the uneven bluestone. The body would be in the morgue now. No white sheet, no front page. Nothing urgent here.

Instead, the reporters were camped outside Jack's place. That was partly the reason he'd stayed at his father's. He'd taken a cab here. He didn't want to be anyone's story.

There were no detectives either, from what Jack could tell. Just a lone officer, a shadow inside tinted windows, parked in the lane. Forensics would have worked the scene overnight, got the laneway cleared first in case Sydney's tempestuous weather turned and big, fat, plum-like drops of rain washed evidence away. Then they'd follow up with the house. They might have overhauled it last night. Or perhaps they were taking their time, figuring out what they were looking for. A house is not an easily interrupted crime scene, which meant they had more time. No sprawling vineyard, no dogs and flashlights needed here.

Jack kept his distance. He didn't want the officer to recognize him. Then he saw the door to the patrol car open and, not wanting to see anymore, turned and started walking away. He heard a clunk, a car door slamming, and resisted the urge to turn around. *Keep walking.* He waited for someone to grab him by the shoulder, spin him around, the ice of steel on his wrists—even though he hadn't done anything wrong. Yet.

Nothing happened. Jack risked a glance. The officer was walking away from him. *He must have to patrol in increments, walk around the block,* thought Jack. *Either that or he was just a lazy cop.*

Jack chewed his lip. *Do it now or leave,* he chided himself. He'd go to the station afterward and help the investigation. Immediately after. But first, a quick look. That tenacity that made him a good documentarian, that scavenger inside him, had awoken, sniffing, stiff whiskers and bared teeth. And underneath it all, his need to control his own story. He knew the case against Curtis intimately; he might see something they hadn't. Something they couldn't, hidden behind red tape and bureaucracy. The rodent knocked at his skull, elation and anxious energy rising within him, an adrenaline not so dissimilar to his hunger at its worst. The rush. The hunt. Just a look.

He ducked under the police tape. His number of crime-scenes-interfered-with rose to two. Who's counting?

Jack hurried to the garage door, sticking to the taped perimeter. Some of the blue cobblestones were chipped with white scars. A scuffle? He remembered the garage door, only a third raised. He pictured Alexis, bending over to fling her rolling garage door up, someone looping something around her neck, yanking her backward, heels bruising as they ricocheted against the uneven stones...

In the middle of the lane, the grout between the stones was dyed a dark black, as if permanently wet. Blood soaked in. Blood that hadn't yet been cleaned by pressure hoses and burly city workers in orange jackets. The last of Alexis White. A stain to be scrubbed away.

The sun disappeared as he entered the garage. Alexis's car, a Mazda sedan, was parked nose in. Jack took a quick inventory. No dark patches here. A bicycle hung on a hook. A few plastic boxes were piled in a corner. Nothing seemed out of place. He wondered what was in the boxes—surely a person's standard junk. They didn't look like case files. Case files would be useful.

Eliza had found out something she wanted to sell—what if it got her killed? And what if Alexis had found it out as well? It didn't matter; he couldn't open the boxes even if they were case files. He couldn't leave a trace.

The garage connected directly to the house. He pulled his sleeve over his hand and gave the door a push. It swung open. Not because it was busted; someone had simply left it ajar. Sloppy police work. The rodent scratched in his skull; his heart thundered in his chest. He stepped into the house.

The first thing that hit him was how neat it was. Snowy carpet underfoot, a tasteful hall runner. The hallway led straight through the house and to the front door. The kitchen was directly to his left, a sitting room at the front, also on the left. On his right, leading backward, a flight of stairs. An old, stale smell tickled at him. A physical smell, one that sat high in his throat. It was at odds with the cleanliness. Still, no one had died here—that much was clear.

A quick look, nothing more, he told himself. Just enough to be helpful to the police. Treading lightly on the carpet, Jack poked his head into each room. Nothing seemed abnormal. There were no broken windows. He rattled the handle of the front door with sleeve-covered fingertips. Locked. Nothing impacted in the doorframe either. No signs of a struggle. Certainly, it seemed that no one had broken in. Until today.

He tried to picture Curtis, dully lit under the porch light, rapping on Alexis's door. From the inside, a blurry silhouette through rose-colored stained glass. Do you let an ex-con into your home, even if they are your client?

Maybe you don't. So they wait for you outside.

He walked up the stairs. The stale smell lingered. It was time to go, but his curiosity would starve him if he didn't check everything. In the bathroom, there was a single toothbrush in a glass. So much for her *thing*. No men's clothing in her bedroom either. Ceiling-high mirrors slid back to reveal her courtroom clothes. As expected, a swathe of neatly hung browns and whites.

Something caught his eye on her dresser. A small cardboard box. Suddenly the smell of the place made sense. An old smell, one that soaks into the walls and the carpets and never really goes. He picked up the pack of cigarettes. She was a smoker.

Interesting. Jack hadn't thought she was the type. He thought he knew her. But then again, his idea of her came mainly from trawling through endless hours of footage. Alexis had never been a real person to him; she'd been a highlight reel. He'd created her. But he'd used only the best bits, exaggerated through regret and memory. Everyone builds their own versions of themselves—happy, healthy, full—to present to the world. Just as they build versions of others. Director's cut. The incongruity of life viewed behind a camera lens with real life playing out beyond the viewfinder.

The mints in her handbag. That she'd pegged Eliza's movements as that of a smoker. It made sense that Alexis smoked. But it was still a shock to Jack; it went against his mental casting list. What else had he got wrong? *Who* else had he got wrong?

Time to go. He turned to the bedroom door, but it was blocked by two policemen. On the left was the patrol officer he'd seen outside. He was a young bloke, Caucasian, but with a tribal tattoo around one bicep. One hand was on his hip, fingers drumming his belt, ready to unsnap. The other cop was unarmed, out of uniform in a tan suit. Tall and thin, wispy brown hair parted to one side. Calm gray eyes. In charge.

"Jack," Brown Suit said, "would you like to come with us?"

CHAPTER 10

Detective McCarthy wasn't at the station.

Jack didn't know who he should have expected, but he'd kind of hoped for Ian McCarthy. McCarthy was a Central Coast detective and the first responder to Eliza's death. He had a bull's shoulders and a hefty frame. In a movie, he'd definitely be a henchman (not the main villain—didn't have the jawline for that) who barges the hero through a plaster wall or two. But his size was contrary to his disposition. McCarthy was a relaxed, jeans-and-R.M.-Williams-boots kind of cop who left the gun at home most days. Talkative too, and a bit thick; things slipped through his teeth as if oiled. And, most importantly, not a fan of Andrew Freeman. He'd been a perfect source for the documentary.

Instead of McCarthy, the new detective sat across from Jack in an airless, glass-boxed interview room. Middle-aged and lanky. Ladled into a brown suit that looked like it had been ironed onto him. A long, thin nose that could cut bread. He'd told Jack his name; Jack had forgotten it.

It had been hard to focus when they guided him past reception and the general clutter and noise of the busy police station had come to a screeching halt. Officers turned and watched. Coffee mugs clunked on desks. Whispers. *He's here.*

"Where's Detective McCarthy?" Jack asked.

"McCarthy works in Newcastle. This isn't his case."

That made sense. This was a Sydney murder now. And much more high profile. No need for a country cop. Get someone who's better at taking photos of footprints, someone who doesn't thunder a 4WD through the middle of a murder scene.

"Do you want a lawyer?" asked the detective.

"Do I need one?"

"Depends. Where were you yesterday, from dawn until around midday?"

Jack took his phone out, placed it on the table, pressed record.

"You can't have that," said Brown Suit, nodding at it.

"I'll need your name again, Detective—"

"Winter. And I'm the one doing the interviewing. Put that away." He nudged the phone an inch back in Jack's direction.

"I want to be assured this is being recorded."

"Contrary to what you might think, Mr. Quick, we as a police force are not in the business of grand conspiracies. I guarantee you this interview is being recorded, and that it will not be manipulated, deleted, or misconstrued in any way. I have no interest in winding up the villain of your next feature. Besides, I'm not the one who broke into a crime scene."

Jack nodded. Pressed Stop on his phone, pocketed it. This one was definitely not a country cop. Jack got the feeling Winter was used to high-profile cases and that he'd steamroll Jack, TV camera or not, to get a result.

"I don't need a lawyer," Jack said, "unless I'm under arrest."

Winter shook his head, a quiet refusal to give Jack any extra ammo.

"For the benefit of the recording," said Winter, then raised his voice almost comically, "no, you are not under arrest. You've come here voluntarily. Correct?"

"Under request from police, yes."

"Under *polite* request from police." Not a question.

"In that case, I am politely here voluntarily."

"You don't want a lawyer, then?" Winter opened a notebook, raised an eyebrow.

"No."

They were talking for the recording with simple words that had simple meanings. But even the calm, poker-faced Winter poured subtext through his words. Understated meaning that could be used later. In court, if it came to that. Both of them aware of how important minor details could become—how with television documentaries and podcasts wielding microscopic focus on the tiniest discrepancy, anything could become a linchpin of a case. So that was how they talked: each on their guard, having two conversations at once, only one verbal.

"Do you want a coffee?" Winter asked.

Subtext: *I am treating the interviewee with respect.*

"Do I need one?"

Subtext: *How long will I be here?*

"Depends." Winter returned to the beginning. "Where were you yesterday, from dawn until around midday?"

Subtext: *Did you kill Alexis White?*

"I had a preparation meeting with my publicist ahead of my interview with Vanessa Raynor that evening. The meeting with the publicist started at ten, finished around lunchtime. Before that I was alone, at home."

"That's not much of an alibi."

"I'm not much of a suspect."

"You made one of the most watched shows of the year." Winter hadn't written anything yet, but his pen was poised, waiting for something. "But now Curtis is out, and your story has come to an end. Maybe you need a new one. Maybe you made one yourself."

"That's thin."

"As ice. I have to ask. Rule you out." He was playing it by the book, ticking all the boxes.

"I don't need to kill someone to manufacture a story. I have the profile to make anything I want to make. You've got nothing if you're trying to verify an alibi from dawn. Every single person will say they were at home in bed and that'll hold up. What was the time of death?"

"I'm interviewing you, remember, Mr. Quick."

"Would you like me to politely leave?"

"It's in the papers, I suppose." Winter put the lid back on his pen.

"Yes. We are actively interested in the period just before dawn. Let's say 5:00, 5:30-ish. And I'm telling you that so you can tell me if you heard from her around that time." Winter rolled the joints in his neck. "I know what you're doing. I know why you were in her house. We don't need some renegade civilian chasing after this one, Jack. You're here to tell us anything useful and then leave it to us."

This is pointless, thought Jack. Winter clearly didn't subscribe to the give-a-little, get-a-little ethos of television (or, more accurately, give-a-little, get-a-lot). He could find more out from McCarthy later. "Finish your questions then," Jack said.

"You knew the victim?" The cap came off Winter's pen again.

"Which one?"

"There's only one victim."

"I knew Alexis, yes. But there's two victims here. Is Curtis Wade not a suspect?"

Jack felt very hot in the neck, his mouth dry. He wasn't nervous at the questions. He was angry. The police were only doing a half job. They were treating the murders separately.

"I'm not commenting further on the investigation."

"Listen, I want Alexis's killer found too. I am actually trying to help you here." He was getting carried away, but he didn't care, letting emotion get in his answers.

"I can't say you've been very helpful so far, Mr. Quick."

"I'm trying now, for fuck's sake," Jack snapped.

Winter blinked, unflustered by Jack's sudden rise in volume, steady gray eyes fixed on him.

"Who cuts off fingers? If Curtis killed Eliza Dacey, then you need to look into him. You can't treat these cases in isolation."

"Curtis Wade was proven innocent in a court of law for the murder of Eliza Dacey. That case is *unsolved*. And you endorsed that, championed it even. We have *no* motive to accuse him of a new murder, based on the similarities to a murder that, legally, he *did not* commit. It's called double jeopardy, Mr. Quick."

Winter was calm, even, but Jack had a sudden creeping feeling he'd walked straight into something.

Winter let the bomb drop. "Are you now saying you have evidence to think otherwise?"

Fuck, thought Jack. Winter must have already interviewed Ted, who would have tried to implicate Jack or suggest he knew more than he was letting on. He could see it in Winter's eyes, a twitch of his cheek, a hint of ecstasy. Jack should have realized. Winter drip-feeding him ammunition, coddling him with titbits of information, which suggested he might be as leaky a tap as Ian. But it wasn't ammunition at all; it was false security. Jack's show had gone to great effort to make the cops look corrupt. *Every* cop was compromised.

Winter was looking for a reason to sweat Jack. Humiliate him. Better still—though he didn't yet know he had the means to do it—send him for a stay in Long Bay himself. That wasn't his play though. His intention was to try to force Jack away from the case, rather than draw him into it, even as a suspect.

"I put my evidence on-screen," said Jack. "That's all there was. Evidence that was independently assessed ahead of the retrial." The same lies he'd used on Vanessa Raynor's show. But this time not just lies: felonies.

"I want to know what you think though. Personally."

"My opinion was expressed in the final show."

Winter sniffed. Jack's head ached, his nose pulsing. No more to be won today.

Winter asked some more background questions. Jack gave him the details of their meeting in the inner west, the last time he saw her briefly at Long Bay, and what he knew about her personal life. Very little, it seemed. After he'd finished telling Winter that Alexis had left the bar to meet with a new boyfriend—or casual fling, he wasn't sure—Winter tapped the back of his pen. Seemed interested.

"Called her, you say?"

"Twice. I didn't see exactly, but that was the implication. Phone buzzed twice anyway. Could have been two different callers, I suppose."

Winter wrote something down at last.

"Okay," said Winter, "now let's talk about the breaking and entering."

"It was just an enter, actually. The door was open."

"Fine, call it trespassing."

"Trespassing involves private property. The owner is dead, so…" Jack shrugged.

"Trespassing involves you being an interfering little shit and being somewhere you're not supposed to be."

Jack tapped his phone, dormant in his pocket. "Did you record that?"

"I don't care. I'm not charging you." Jack must have looked surprised. "Not because you haven't done anything wrong, but because I don't need any more media around this thing. I walk you out of here in cuffs and my days will disappear to press conferences, petitions, more bottom-feeders like you. I don't need it. But I also don't need you around this investigation. I don't want to see you, at all, unless I ask for you. If I see a single camera, I'll find a way to charge you with obstruction. You are not a police officer. Let us do our job."

"I'm here to help."

"I look at you sitting here, and I'm horrified that you genuinely don't know what you're doing wrong. Look around this place." That whispering rustle as Jack was guided into the interview room. The sprawl of desks—corkboards and photos of Alexis pinned up. Her name on everyone's lips. "You want me to look into Curtis Wade because you regret your part in getting him free? And, yeah, maybe he *did* kill her, but you're the one who butchered any chance we had at lining up the similarities. You're telling me you want to help? You're the one who's handed him everything he needs to deny it. You've helped enough."

Winter leaned over and pressed a button on the table. Recording off. Considered his words, lowered his voice. Those gray eyes were now steel.

"You made Andrew Freeman out to be a villain, and you made the rest of the Hunter cops look like headless chickens. You fuck with one of us, you fuck with all of us. I see you snooping again, I charge you. Got that? Now"—he pointed at the door—"I think you have a busy day of fucking off to take care of."

State of play? Jack tapped out a text message as he walked into the sunshine of Kings Cross. The smell hit first, the bright day encouraging the concrete to sweat out last night's deposits. Wafts of kebabs, cigarettes. Piss. A jackhammer rattléd his teeth. It seemed there was almost constant construction work in this part of town. Every day, new apartments, bars, gyms. Spires of cranes reached into the sky. Sydney gorged itself on construction. Always rebuilding itself, knocking itself down.

His father sat behind the wheel of a VW Golf across the street, jutting out of a loading zone. Jack felt his stomach roll. Not hunger. That was a sense he knew all too well. This was different—unease. Because something Winter had said spooked him. There was a buzz in his pocket, a reply from McCarthy.

> Not supposed to talk to you. Instructions from the top. Curtis not a primary suspect. Sydney guys interviewed him already. Not forgotten, but nothing to move on. Innocent, remember? Copycat killer preferred theory. Or...

A car horn rippled through him. He'd had his head down while crossing the road. He looked up, copped a middle finger at a passing window, and hustled across. Pulling open the door to his father's VW, he looked back down at his phone, but that was the end of the message. An ellipsis showed McCarthy was still typing.

"How'd it go?" Peter asked.

"As expected," he said.

Or? he typed.

He could picture McCarthy at his desk, pecking at the letters with a single finger. McCarthy wasn't great with technology. He'd never even heard of podcasts, and, luckily, he didn't watch TV. Having leaked most of the case details to Jack, that was probably a blessing. On television, Jack had edited McCarthy to look like a classically incompetent small-town cop. The comic relief: letting criminals slip under his nose while he sipped tar-black coffee out of a polystyrene cup, boots crossed on the desk in front of him. Thank God McCarthy didn't own a television, Jack thought. Otherwise he'd be pissed, and Jack would lose his only source.

Peter pulled away from the curb. Jack's phone buzzed.

Original killer.

A brief pause. A second text.

Delete these texts.

Shit. Jack closed his eyes and let his head loll back on his neck. Shit.

Alexis's murder couldn't be tied to Curtis, because the only evidence the police seemed to have was circumstantial. Mainly, the matching MO to Eliza's death. But Curtis couldn't be linked to that—he'd been tried and acquitted. Double jeopardy, like Winter had said. In order to tie Curtis to the MO of the new murder, they needed new evidence to tie him to the first. That would enable them to try the second murder with precedent. *Fresh and compelling new evidence,* Jack believed was the legal speak.

Jack was the only one with any potential physical evidence. Just like Winter had said, Jack might not only have allowed Curtis to kill again, but he might have primed him to get away with it too.

Before, even when Curtis was walking free across the Long Bay parking lot, Jack had always fallen back on the fact that *maybe* Curtis was innocent. He'd hung his hat on reasonable doubt. On his flour-dusted musings in his kitchen. But now Alexis was dead, and he had the only piece of evidence that could place Eliza at the vineyard. That could show precedent *and* MO and bring Curtis back into the picture on Alexis's murder. Not reasonable doubt anymore. Reasonable suspicion.

But bringing that knowledge forward would mean admitting to tampering with the case. Obstruction, Winter had threatened. Accessory even, in the hands of a particularly cavalier prosecution. Even a vague confession would lead to warrants, searching of footage. They might find nothing. They might find everything. He would have to find another way.

But he was locked out of the Alexis investigation. He'd burned every cop from here to Byron, McCarthy was off-limits, and Winter was out for blood too. But there was no way Winter could solve the case if they weren't looking into Curtis Wade.

Jack was the only one who knew everything about the Dacey case, top to bottom. More than every lawyer and every detective on the case. Who better to tie the two together?

"Can you drop me home?" he said, noticing his father about to exit the freeway.

"I thought you could stay until you felt better?" Peter said but flicked the indicator off and prepared to remerge. His words like Winter's. Subtext: *You're on the precipice of a relapse here; you shouldn't be on your own.*

"I have to go away for a few days."

Peter nodded. They both knew where he was going. Back to Birravale. To open up old wounds once more.

There was only one way to clear that black mass in his gut, the one that couldn't be thrown up. That fear. That guilt. That grief for himself, Alexis would have said. Because as long as her murder remained unsolved, she would weigh heavy within him. She would follow him just as Eliza had, and one ghost was enough for Jack.

He'd spent his whole adult life lying to others: to his father, to himself, to his own body. Enough.

If he was going to find out what happened to Alexis, he was going to have to find out what really happened to Eliza Dacey.

The truth, this time.

CHAPTER 11

The suspension rather than the road signs told him he was getting close. It had been lightly raining the whole drive, clouds settled in low over the road. Jack had stayed an extra night at his father's, so was doing the drive in daylight this time. The canyon-spanning bridges soared over rolling tree-tops, the light wind rippling them together, puffs of mist spiraling out of the rolls of green fire. Since the freeway turnoff, potholes had cropped up with more regularity. The seats shook, the road thinned, and the white lines disappeared. This was a road where you pulled over to let another car pass. Where a cyclist rode in the dirt or copped a Get-the-Fuck-Off-the-Road. The cracked blacktop sloped away from the center, eroding into the dust at the edges. A long, fat snake of a road, bulbous at its middle, digesting a meal.

As he passed into Birravale proper, Jack stopped at the single set of traffic lights. There was only one road through this part of town. He'd used footage from here in his show: locals, with jeans rolled up to their knees and red-stained shoes, mops and squeegees and strong bristled brushes in their hands, pushing the miniature flood to the drains. Scrubbing the road. All out together, lining the road with bent backs like a prison chain gang.

Another image surfaced in his memory—a steel table with a yellow L-shaped ruler on it. Next to that, an ax. The ax head was a dull chrome, the handle long and wooden. The handle was stained a deep maroon at the head, the color crawling up the shaft, until tapering off about halfway. It was a powerful image: Curtis's ax, varnished in red. But the stain was wine, not blood. Nevertheless, seeing as they hadn't been able to match her finger wounds to *any* weapon at all, the prosecution clung to this image. With its own nonverbal power. That red-handled ax the very definition of red-handed—and it *was* guilty of something, all right. Of tearing through Andrew Freeman's storage tanks, of soaking the main street in wine. But of playing a part in Eliza's murder? Never proven.

On Jack's left, he passed "Australia's Best Pies" splashed across a two-by-four plank hanging from the awning of the bakery's veranda. That was the fourth such sign he'd seen on the two-and-a-half-hour drive. Inside, there'd probably be a third-place ribbon from over a decade ago: Best Vanilla Slice, Hunter Valley Showgrounds 2004. Country bakeries gave him a run for his money in the honesty stakes.

He drove past a sign for a bed-and-breakfast. He'd prefer the motel on the other side of town. He drove past a pub, the dilapidated cinema, then past another pub—named the Royal Stag, of course. It was curious that there were two pubs in this tiny town, though perhaps the wine drinkers needed a break every now and then, lips and teeth pink, searching for a cold one at the end of a day.

The wineries were where the real money was. There was a small constellation of them, most within a fifteen-minute drive down back roads from the center of town. The Wades', then the Freemans' would pop up on the right at the edge of the town. Jack was now driving slightly uphill. The road climbed until the Freeman place, up at the top of the hill, cut into the side of the hilltop like a millionaire's tree house, before dropping over the crest and winding downward. Over the crest, the corners could only be taken at forty. In the wet, fifteen. A confident driver could get down the other side in thirty minutes. Some drivers, unlucky ones, had found ways to get down it faster. Crosses and flowers periodically dotted sections of mended fence.

Jack drove past single-story, flaking-paint, weatherboarded houses, rusting cars and rusted dogs scattered on front lawns, hoses curled on steps like dead snakes. Wheelie bins with yellow lids lined the curb. The Brokenback Range sat on the horizon, the mountains hulking guardians, the lushness of their canopy looking soft, like fur, from a distance.

The motel owner was standing in his garden, waving a hose back and forth over the garden, disregarding the general moistness in the air. He idly watched Jack's car pull into the lot, ceased waving the hose, the stream of water puddling in the low end of the garden and trickling over the curb. Jack parked in front of a random room. No competition here. There was only one other car in the lot, a corroded white Holden utility vehicle. Salt's victim.

He got out of the car and stretched. The owner put the hose down and retreated into the office. Jack could see him through the window, taking up residence behind the desk, ready for a booking. He reached out to the wall, flicked a switch. The sign above the driveway flickered from *Vacancy* to *No Vacancy*. Jack looked around the empty lot and sighed, got back in his car. Another lap of the single street ahead.

The pub was empty but full too, rooms booked by shadows. Though the owner at least had the decency to tell him to fuck off.

Jack hadn't thought it would be quite so obvious. Then again, a murder ripples through a small town in ways it doesn't in big cities. Alexis was probably already banished from the features section. But Eliza had burned a scar through this town like fire through snow, and that takes a long time to heal. Four years hadn't been enough. And here was Jack, ripping the bandage off again.

His last resort was the bed-and-breakfast. The light was fading now, and the cold was creaking through him. The B and B was a two-story house, roof sagging with age, but freshly painted. A swinging sign on the letter box had a phone number on it. Jack didn't bother calling it; he hopped up the wooden stairs and knocked on the door. He heard a screen door rattle. The woman who opened the door did a double take. She was elderly and wore a lot of makeup. Sagging with age but freshly painted.

"Do you have a room?" he asked without giving his name. Crossed his fingers.

"How many nights?"

Alexis's funeral was in two days.

"Don't know. Just start with two," he said.

"I'll see what I can do." She shuffled inside, disappeared behind a door. Jack took two steps in, stood on the rug but close to the door. She hadn't said no, which was a good sign, but she hadn't said yes yet either. It didn't seem like she'd recognized him, but elderly women did passive aggression better than pub owners.

"I have two nights," she called. She came back into the room with a red-covered book, filled with neat, ruled lines and looping cursive. "Four hundred."

"Two hundred a night's a bit steep," Jack said, though he knew it was pushing his luck.

"Is it? Gosh, sorry. Four hundred *per night*. Eight hundred total." She didn't look up from the book. "I'm guessing everywhere else is full. Special rate for you, Mr. Quick."

Jack felt his shoulders drop. He imagined the motel and pub owner calling her up, agreeing to run him around, jack the price up, split the profits. She'd be treating them all to drinks later.

"I could go to Cessnock," said Jack. "It's not that far."

"I suppose it isn't."

"I suppose the motels are full there too."

"They might well be."

"Okay, then. For four hundred, I hope the breakfast's good." Though he didn't care about the food; he just wanted to needle her. "Credit card okay?"

"Yes, we're not Neanderthals out here. That was without breakfast, by the way. You want the breakfast rate? Another fifty."

"I thought this was a B *and* B. Without breakfast is fine."

"Oh." She scowled at the book. "Have to give priority to the breakfasters. Premium bookings, you know?"

"I'm getting the idea."

"Only breakfast specials left."

"Okay, nine hundred then." That seemed to make her happy. She nodded, hooked a key off the wall, and gestured for Jack to follow her up the stairs. He couldn't help himself. "Why let me stay at all?"

She thought about this for a second, didn't turn her head. "I'm not much of a fan of Brett Dawson, the bloke that runs the motel. You'll do all right, helping me stick it to him."

"I'm leverage?"

"Well-paying leverage." She flashed him a dark look as she opened a bedroom door. She was reading him, he supposed, trying to figure him out. "Besides, the cops were here yesterday, and they let him go. I'm assuming you're here to fix that."

"You mean you think Curtis did it?"

"Doesn't everybody?"

"Do they?"

"Bit late to be asking these sorts of questions is my guess." She raised an eyebrow. Alexis was dead. A bit late, indeed. "We weren't surprised, you know. They never fit in here, with their tacky restaurant and windfall fortune—everyone here works for their success." Jack didn't stop her to point out she'd just ripped him off nine hundred bucks for a room. "And then that dispute with Andrew Freeman. He's a good man. That's just nasty stuff, all of it. Of course, we were heartbroken when that poor woman was found. But"—she held open the door and gestured him inside—"I can't say any of us were surprised."

"Were you here when it happened?"

She paused in the doorway, keen to leave. Her response was sharp. "I didn't see the murder."

"What about when Curtis attacked Andrew's wine?"

"I live here, don't I?"

"What was it like?"

She raised her eyebrows.

"For nine hundred dollars, I should think I could trouble the hostess for five minutes of her time." Jack said, his producer-voice creeping into his tone.

"You ever seen six hundred thousand liters of anything all at once?" She shifted slightly, mild surrender. "What do you want to know? It came down the hill, poured through the whole town. It was all over the road. Stained it, actually; I swear it's darker now. It even got into the wood here; that's why I repainted the house. We swept it into the gutters, but there were pools of it, for weeks, lying around in potholes and gutters. In the heat, the town stank. Like it was rotten."

"And that was the last straw for most of you? With the Wades?"

"You take an ax to Andrew Freeman's wine vats, you take an ax to Birravale."

"Everyone feels like this?" He stepped past her into the room. Saw a double bed. The room was sparsely furnished, but there was a water heater bolted to the far wall and homely knitted blankets. It would be warm.

"Of course. It was worse for some. Everyone with a cellar will tell you—and that's everyone 'round here, mind you…"

"Tell me what?"

She turned to leave. "It was like the walls were bleeding."

The next morning, Jack woke, dressed, and stepped out early. When he opened the door, there was a plate on the carpet. On it, a single banana and a carbon-paper handwritten invoice. *Breakfast. $50.*

Jack stepped over it.

Now that he was here, he didn't really know what he planned to do. Interview the locals? Wait for someone to confess? He knew how to edit a crime so it cut to credits at the perfect time, right when the heart was thrumming, so that, like an addict, you needed another hit. But actually solving one? How did people do that in real life? When there were no shortcuts or expository credits sequences to fill you in on what you missed last week? He needed a place to start. Fortunately, years in television had taught him what all good narratives started with. Conflict. Tension. You don't start a series with everyone in harmony—you drop them in discordance. You disrupt them, kick a beehive, and then see what falls out.

Jack had spent the night rewatching his show. He tried to view it from the prosecution's perspective this time. Instead of dismantling the evidence, where it had been enough to merely show that there *had* been gaps, he now needed to fill those gaps. Wherever he'd called them out for making a leap—on placing Eliza at the Wades', on the voicemail providing a motive, that the story she tried to sell pertained to Curtis Wade—he'd always looked to discredit the evidence, rather than present a counter theory. So that seemed like a good first step. What did Eliza know that she thought she could sell? Why had she been at the Wades'? Jack didn't know where to start, but he figured he might as well go kick some beehives.

Curtis Wade's pebble driveway slipped underfoot. There were tire ruts equidistant from the edges, the gravel loose enough to leave no footprints. It had taken him about fifteen minutes to walk there from the B and B. He'd stopped shivering quickly, though the grass underfoot was yellow and frozen and cracked when he walked. The Hunter Valley was Mars. When the sun was up, it boiled—he pictured pools of stinking wine beside the road—but as soon as it dipped below the horizon, everything snap froze. Heaven and hell, all at once.

There was only one media van at the base of the drive. Blue and silver, with a satellite on top. Jack couldn't see anyone through the windows; he assumed they were sitting in the back. The news crews had come here initially: there had been bustling crowds of jostling microphones, helicopter shots. Some intrepid reporter had hovered a drone with a GoPro attached over the house. Curtis had sauntered onto the patio, rifle at his side, and had a few shots at it. A sharpshooter he was not, and though that was great footage, it was the last time Curtis had left the house. The driveway was so long, all private property, that there was nothing left to do but skulk at the bottom of it. And after two days with no money shot of detectives leading Curtis, shackled, down that long drive, the experienced journalists had headed back, leaving behind a few interns in case something exploded. Alexis's murder wouldn't be solved here, nearly everyone had accepted. But Jack had nowhere else to start. The driveway was slightly uphill. Gum trees folded over the drive like arms reaching out from the dust. Jack was panting by the time he reached the front patio.

The house itself was older than the restaurant, which Jack had observed with awe, about three-quarters down the drive, the frozen windows adding a hint of extra sparkle in the morning light. Fifty meters farther on, the house itself had no such spectacle: a stone chimney stack, timber walls, and dirty windows. A kelpie slept on the porch. Wilted plants hung from the front awning like corks on a bushman's hat. There was a garage with the door folded up. Jack could see a tarnished hatchback inside, jaw open and engine exposed. A pickup truck, much shinier, in the other parking spot. He also caught a glimpse of a messy tool bench. A dirt bike.

Jack took a few long breaths and stepped onto the porch. He stood in front of the door and steeled himself. He wondered if Eliza had done the same thing. *Did you go inside this house, Eliza? What happened to you?*

The kelpie lifted its head momentarily and then rested its jaw back on its paws. There was yellow, crusted mucus around its mouth and eyes. It reminded him of himself. A dog with no bite.

He knocked on the door.

There were thuds from inside and then the jangling of a lock. Curtis opened the door. He was wearing shorts and a tank, graying wiry hairs spindling out from his chest like the head of a worn toothbrush. His mustache was stiff and gray; you could have polished a shoe with it.

"Well," he said, "we got a lot to talk about."

S01E04
CUT

Exhibit C:

Message Received, 03/20/2014, 4:52 p.m.

Hi. Um, Sam? You don't know me. My name's Eliza. I'm from England. Right, you probably don't need to know that. I've been living and working in a town called Birravale for the last six months. Anyway, *inaudible* I've found something here. I thought you might be interested. I figure it's one of those things that might go viral, people would share it, you know? Might even be, I don't know, illegal? Either way, it's pretty weird. Could be a good feature. So, you know, do you buy stories? I can't tell you any more until we talk figures. Call me back?

CHAPTER 12

PREVIOUSLY

Wind tore past Jack's ears as he tried to keep up, but even standing and pumping his legs as hard as he could, his pedals spun, frictionless. They whipped around, rapping his calves, grazing the skin with tiny metal teeth. The ground dipped, his stomach held in the air for a second, and they zipped through a stagnant puddle. Mud shot off Liam's back wheel and sluiced up his spine. Jack felt the same wet shock to his T-shirt as he followed a second later. Then the ground was tilting up again, and they were out of their seats again, piston legs. The sunlight was dappled by the overhanging eucalypts.

Liam outpaced him, not only because he was older, but because he had a newer bike. He'd been raving about these things called *gears* that apparently made riding easier. He had brakes on his handlebars too. Ones that you used *with your fingers*. Jack still had to lock his pedals backward to skid to a stop. Liam had let him ride the new bike once, telling him to squeeze softly. Jack, of course, had ignored his advice and gone straight over the handlebars, with Liam collapsing in laughter. Jack didn't ask to borrow his brother's bike again, but trailing him up the hill, he wished he had some of those magical gears.

Liam was at the crest now, yelling down at him. "Get there, Jackie. Come on. Get there. Get there!"

That was Liam's favorite thing to yell at the football players—either on the TV or when Dad found a game to take them to in the city. *Get there!* Who cares if you got crunched over the top of the ball, provided you *got there*. Liam's assistant-coach career was famous around the house.

Jack focused on the ground, watching his front wheel slide occasionally left and right when hopping over a rock. Liam was right though. In this case, there was only one way to the top, and that was up. Jack counted the number of times the orange patch on his front tire—from two weeks ago when he'd run over the remnants of a Carlton stubby bottle—passed under his handlebars. No way but up. Get there.

He made it, panting, to the ridge. Liam was coasting in circles, with his body on the left side of the bike, both feet perched on the single pedal, occasionally dropping his outside foot to paddle the ground. The playing card lodged in his back spokes thrummed lazily.

"Nice of you to join." Liam swung past him.

"That hill got bigger, I reckon."

"Or you got smaller."

"Can I have some water?"

Liam hopped off the pedal, trundled to a stop. He had a water bottle strapped to the frame, another fancy addition that Jack didn't have. Liam tossed it underhand. Jack pulled the rubber top open with his teeth, the first mouthful tasting like an old car. Jack spat it. The second squirt was much better.

"You refill this?" he asked.

"Monthly." Liam smiled. "Where are we going?"

"You should see your back. Dad'll freak."

Liam and Dad had just had an animated discussion about Liam removing the rear mudguard on his new bike. For aerodynamics, Liam argued. When he'd next got home with a gash of mud from his arse up to his collar, Peter said that he wasn't allowed to sit on the couch until he'd washed. Liam, who'd wanted to watch *Gladiators* without delay, chose to stand in the lounge room. Peter was fine with that, as was his parenting style for the most part—he was happy to let the boys make their own choices and live with the consequences. His favorite saying was *That's not a threat, boys, it's a promise.* An hour later, with Liam still standing by the coffee table, Dad wafted past and sank into the couch with an indulgent sigh: *How are those aerodynamics treating you?*

"It was worth it," Liam told Jack later that night, his pale face peeking out from the top bunk. "The bike goes wicked fast."

"Swim?" Liam looked up; the sun was harsh, though some clouds were brewing. "We'll dry."

"We rode up the hill for nothing, then."

"Not for nothing!" Liam spread his arms out as if showing off a kingdom. "For glory! For fame! Swim?"

"All the way down to the river?" Jack grimaced. "Nah."

"Maybe on the way back. Up?"

"Up."

Jack dragged his bike off the dirt road and leaned it in the shrub. Liam, careful of his paint job, carefully wheeled his Giant over to a small clearing, where he propped the bike upright against a tree. It was a bush bash from there, the two kids in a twig-snapping cyclone along a lightly cleaved path. Liam, ahead, peeled back the larger branches and held them for Jack, who took this as a brotherly courtesy before being whopped in the face with spring-loaded foliage. Spitting gum leaves and spiderwebs, he'd give chase until both of them were doubled over, panting and laughing. The farther they went, the steeper it became, and soon they were scuttling, hands and knees slipping over shale, kicking the big rocks and watching them gather clumps of soil as they caused avalanches down the hill.

Black under fingernails, they reached the top. A rock formation loomed above them. The top had been carved by the wind and rain into lumps that resembled knuckles. The Fist. They called it that because, from a distance, it looked like a giant curled hand, a sentient mountain just awoken, punching the sky. In the middle, there was a large crack that you could squeeze into, as if the whole thing had been struck by an ax. No matter how dry the day, the crevasse was always water slicked, fronds sprouting from the sides. The outside of the Fist was marbled and smooth from thousands of years of rain; there was no way to climb it. But if you put your back against one side of the crevasse and the soles of your feet against the other, you could shuffle your way up to the top. And, once up there, it was so high and so clear. Rolling waves of greenery like coral, shoals of birds wafting on thermals, everything rippling together as if joined in nature's slow, rhythmic current. The boys loved it. On top of the Fist, they punched the sky. *Is this aerodynamics?* Jack asked once, spreading his arms and letting the wind ripple his T-shirt in his armpits. *Kind of,* Liam replied.

The Fist was massive, and with its imposing, black, slicked-rock walls, Peter would have been much firmer with his punishment than a no-sitting-in-the-lounge-room rule had he known they were going up there. He'd probably have taken their bikes away for good.

Liam had already poked his head into the fissure, rubbed his hand on one wall, inspected the grime, and cleaned the moss on his shorts.

"Looks okay," he said.

"Looks slippery," said Jack.

"Huh?"

"Dad says it's pretty dangerous." Jack looked up; the tops of the trees were rustling. "It's getting windier. Maybe we should come back tomorrow."

"You're the one complaining about coming all the way up here for nothing." Liam rolled his eyes.

"I know."

"And now you don't want to come up?"

"Dunno." Jack looked at the ground.

"Well?"

"Let's just go swimming."

"You scared?" Liam played his ace. The Achilles' heel of any ten-year-old: *You scared?*

"I'm not scared. Dad says—"

"Dad says lots of things. That's his *job*."

"I am *not* scared." Jack braced his feet to shoulder width, trying to assert himself.

"People aren't scared of heights, Bro," Liam said. "They're scared of the ground."

"We should come back another day."

"Suit yourself. Stay here. I'll be back."

"Wait—"

But Liam had already levered himself into the gap. He dried his hands on his shirt. Then he shouldered the rock, twisting his weight until he had one foot up. Liam was tall; he'd always been good at this part. Jack squeezed his eyes tight. They felt hot. He wasn't scared, he told himself. He'd just spied the clouds coming in from the right, and at the very least he didn't want to ride home in the rain. And if it rained while they were up there, how would they get down? His eyes stung. He wasn't scared. He opened his eyes.

Liam was halfway up already, folded into the crease, soles flat on the wall, knees on his chin. He reached out a hand.

"Last chance—you coming up or not?"

CHAPTER 13

Jack had been inside the Wade house before, to interview Vincent and Lauren during filming.

But it still struck him with the same sense of déjà vu he'd felt the first time—a place he'd never been but knew intimately from poring over crime scene photographs. He knew the carpet in the bedroom had been torn up and replaced in the left corner years before. He knew that the cornice in the lounge room shielded a slight crack rippling through the drywall. The doorways he knew especially. His team had built a silicon hand and slammed it in every door, trying to match the finger wounds.

Curtis led him into the sitting room, and Jack absentmindedly flicked on the light as he stepped over the threshold. Just like his familiarity with Alexis, knowing her from videotape, he knew where every light switch, every scuff was. He'd seen every inch of this house before. At 100x zoom, in 4K HD.

But this time the walls didn't glow blue with black light and the hallway was clean of plastic yellow numbers.

Curtis shot him a look that implied he would be the one choosing whether the lights stayed on or off in his house, but he didn't say anything. Jack sat on the frayed couch (he felt comfortable sitting on this couch—they'd scoured it for splatter) and Curtis shuffled off.

Jack heard clinking from the kitchen. He took his time alone to look around. Off-white carpet. Dark wood furniture but nondescript. Mass made. Everything here was cheap. The couch he was sitting on had a broken beam, and the cushion threatened to swallow him. Jack shuffled forward, perched on the edge. The bottom of the couch had a thin red stain on the skirting. That had excited the police at first. Until they'd tested it: wine. With the winery placed as it was, between the Freemans' and the town, it bore the brunt of the wine damage. The Wades had refused to replace the couch. They'd only replaced the carpet out of absolute necessity. Defiance, Jack figured. Curtis didn't want to admit the damage he'd caused, even to himself.

The house smelled clean, as if bleached. Scientific. It was almost unnaturally neat, a side effect of being pulled apart and put back together again by so many forensic teams. Residue of fingerprint dust and luminol was soaked into the walls and the carpet. All of this was long gone, of course. But four years hadn't been enough to make it feel like a home again. Eliza might not have stained this house, but suspicion had.

Curtis came back with a plastic tray laminated with watercolor drawings of cats. On the tray was a fancy, white teapot; two maroon, yellow, and blue mugs with football team logos; and a small saucer of milk. A collision of finery and practicality. Curtis was doing his best to put on a show of civility. He set the tray down on the table between them and lifted the teapot. It rattled in his hand. The courtesy was a thin shield for his discomfort, poking through in his shaking hand.

"Tea?" Curtis said.

It felt absurd. An ex-convicted killer who might have killed again, whose hands were supposedly more comfortable wrapped around a wine-stained ax handle, was instead holding a delicate teapot. A seriously messed up tea party. Jack managed a nod.

"I reckon I owe you this conversation, Jack, but I don't want to be pulled into anything here. You and me, we're square," Curtis said while pouring. The growl was familiar.

Jack nodded again.

"No cameras," said Curtis.

"This is for me."

"It always was." Curtis added milk, dropped a teaspoon in the first mug with a clatter, and pushed it over to Jack. Both mugs were the same team, from Brisbane. The Wades used to live up north.

"Do you miss it up there?"

"Byron? Well, the weather, of course. But not the tourists. I'd say I like the peace here better, but"—he waved a hand—"you know."

"I'm surprised you came back."

"I'm not hiding."

"No. It might be easier to get away though."

"Now I'm getting framed for murders in Sydney too." Curtis shrugged, blew on his tea as if discussing sport or weather. "So it doesn't seem to matter where I go, really."

"You still think you're getting framed?"

"Well, I didn't fucking do it. So yeah."

"Statistically, being framed for one murder is low enough odds," Jack said, "but being framed for two?"

"It's the same guy. Just means they really hate my brother." A voice came from the hallway. Lauren Wade had appeared, one leg crossed behind the other, leaning against the doorjamb. She had long, black hair; it fell across her flannel shirt. She wore jeans and no shoes. Despite the age gap, the family resemblance was there—the Wade charisma—but she was slight, long limbed. Her arms were folded. Watching the interview footage from the original investigation, Jack had felt sorry for her: a sixteen-year-old shouldn't have to see such things. But she was different here, on the other side of womanhood, relaxed against the doorway, her voice firm and confident. She didn't invite pity. "What's more likely—that two people in this town are running around murdering people, or that it's just the one killer and they've found themselves a good scapegoat?"

"You don't think it can be two killers?" Jack asked.

Curtis was leaning forward, listening to his sister.

"I think a copycat is pretty unlikely. Remember, too, they never caught the first guy."

They might've, thought Jack. *He just poured me a cup of tea.*

"Statistically ridiculous." Curtis echoed Lauren, mimicking her larger words. The word *statistically*, with its hard consonants, rattled through his teeth like a playing card in a bicycle wheel.

"Like I said," continued Lauren, "strikes me that it's the same killer both times. So you just need to catch him."

"You've met?" said Curtis, apologetic as if introducing friends at a party. Lauren and Jack both nodded. "You should thank her, you know. She said you'd come here, said I should talk to you."

"Thank you," Jack said to the doorway. Lauren just flicked her wrist. She'd said her piece. "Why wouldn't you want to talk to me?" Jack turned back to Curtis. "I got you out."

"And you seem really happy about that. Fuck man, I feel like we've slept together." He made to move quickly, an arm extended. Jack flinched from the incoming hit, but when he looked up Curtis had barely moved at all. He was meters away. "Could you be more uncomfortable?"

"This is hard for me."

"I'll bet. You knew Alexis, so it's different now that you care about the case and not the money."

"It was never about the money. You're right though. It does feel... different."

"Did you fuck her?"

"Curtis," Lauren admonished from the doorway.

"It's okay," Jack said. "No. We were more colleagues than friends, actually."

"I ain't a psychologist," said Curtis, "but you've come all the way out here to try and solve the murder of a woman you barely knew. The only person who'd do that is one that feels responsible for getting her killed. Or one who's fucked her, depending on the pussy."

Jack didn't respond. He gripped his mug tightly, letting it warm his hands. He felt light-headed, hungry, not up to a verbal sparring match. Sometimes his hunger made him sharp, and sometimes, like now, it just made him tired. He regretted not eating that expensive banana. Curtis reclined in his chair. Barely perceptibly, Lauren shook her head. If Curtis was telling the truth, and she'd insisted he let Jack in, she was disappointed in the direction the conversation was going. What did she have to gain from Curtis talking to Jack? That was a better way of looking at the room. What did everyone have to gain here? Curtis was, as always, petitioning his innocence. But Lauren? She didn't buy the copycat theory. If she thought it was a serial killer...was she here because she was afraid?

"You're right, Curtis." Perhaps some slack in Curtis's direction might loosen his tongue. "That's why I'm here. I think that by making my show, I might have gotten her killed."

"Damn fucking right you did!" Curtis clapped his hands, then saw Jack's expression. "Not like that, you idiot. I already told you I didn't kill her. Copycat or serial killer, right? Well, how do you think they chose their newest victim? Your TV show. Credits play like a *menu*."

Jack hadn't thought of that—that the show might have been the cata- lyst. There had been rabid fans. There were even T-shirts: TEAM CURTIS was black with white letters; TEAM ELIZA was the inverse. ("People just like to rally," Peter said once, perusing the paper, which had a photo of the shirts clustered outside the court. "Doesn't matter what the sides are.") What if it was a fan so avidly on Team Eliza that they'd taken it on themselves to right some wrongs? And who better a target than the head of the defense? Apart from Curtis himself, he supposed. He thought about the pentagram sprayed on Ted Piper's office doors, Alexis's office closing, and reminded himself to check with both their offices for threats too. Curtis had a point; Jack had brought a whole raft of people into the public eye for scrutiny. Jack's thoughts immediately went to Eliza's parents, but he knew they were still in England—as sensationalist as it would be to have two seventy-year-olds hop on a plane to Sydney to commit a murder. *People like to rally*, Peter had said. But Jack disagreed: people loved to hate. The pleasure of choosing a side was only so you could hate the other one.

"You think?" was all Jack could say to Curtis.

"Fuckin' buffet."

Jack knew to take Curtis's theory with a grain of salt. As in prison, where Curtis had pointed the finger at Andrew Freeman over and over, his ideas had a familiar theme: anyone but me. It was the same as his default it-must-be-planted response when confronted with any physical evidence. A response that, Jack had read, was on the rise thanks to documentaries like his. Every criminal was now a victim of a huge conspiracy. *You see, someone planted the knife in her, Your Honor.*

Jack had to change tack. "Tell me about Andrew Freeman."

"What about him?"

"He set you up the first time."

"This *town* set me up the first time." Curtis's voice pitched slightly, and Jack knew he'd hit the one thing that always got him talking: Andrew Freeman.

"Help me understand why."

"We never fit in here." Curtis stood up, walked to the window, pulled the curtain back. Across the vineyard, thin ice glittered on the vines. Behind it was the steep hillside and, on top, the Freemans' two imposing cylindrical silos. "Lauren and me. Our father. Apparently, you've got to be born into wine—you know that?" Jack didn't, but he nodded. "We never came from money, let alone grapes. But when our old place sold up, we thought we'd make the change. We had enough to buy outright, so we moved here and built the restaurant."

Jack had heard this before, but he was content to let Curtis talk. *Enough to buy outright.* Curtis was understating it. A conglomerate had bought out his family's Byron Bay land to build a resort. The true sale price was undisclosed, though Jack had propagated in his show that it had been astronomical. That was close to the truth. The Wades had lived on a secluded property and were hardscrabble battlers; they got by on odds and ends— gardening, housework—when they needed a bit of cash. But their land, passed down through the generations, meant they didn't need to set their sights further. And then, literally overnight, because of luck and location, they were millionaires. It was all part of Jack's narrative—creating the rift between Birravale and the Wades, the rich, cashed-up blow-ins who didn't deserve respect. Once you force people to pick sides, you have hate. Once you have hate, you have motive. Jack created that. And it worked, despite being mostly bullshit. The problem was, Curtis clearly still believed it.

Visually, it worked in the show's favor too. The crime scene photos from inside this house of millionaires—with their cheap furniture and discolored carpets—seemed abnormal. Why spend so much money on the outside of your house and none inside? *Something is wrong here*, it seemed to say.

"I was looking forward to it, moving here. We thought it would be fun, or interesting at the very least," said Lauren. "Fifty percent success rate on that, I'd say. Hasn't been much fun, but it's sure been interesting."

"Elitist pricks," muttered Curtis, closing the curtain.

"Honestly, like a bunch of teenage girls," Lauren added. "That animosity was there *before* Curtis chopped open the silos."

"They deserved it. Broke my windows."

Tacky. What the B and B matriarch had said rang in Jack's head. The town hated the new restaurant because it was glossy, expensive, and, worst of all, new. Everything Birravale wasn't. Someone had smashed Curtis's restaurant windows, and so he'd gone and flooded their town with their own wine. Petty acts of escalating revenge. But how does that end in two dead women?

"Okay, so I see the friction there, I do. But, honestly. Two women are dead. This isn't some schoolyard rivalry. I'm just trying to understand why, if they hate you so much, they'd go to such lengths to frame you for not one, but two murders? Innocent women."

Curtis flinched. There was something. Even dead, he hadn't forgiven what he saw as Alexis's incompetent defense. He hated her. Maybe he was glad she was dead, even if he didn't kill her.

A *tsk* from the doorway.

"What?" snapped Curtis. He turned back to Jack: "Four years." As if that was an explanation.

"My point is," Jack said, "why didn't Andrew just lead them here with pitchforks and torches. If murder is on the cards, why not just—"

"Because they're cowards," said Curtis, and Jack was slightly surprised by how much he seemed to believe it. Jack blinked away his confusion. At the moment, both of them knew Jack was accusing Curtis of murder, yet here they were, talking around it, presumably for Lauren's benefit. She was still there, casually leaning against the door. Not quite casual, Jack realized. Coiled. It was her eyes that gave her away—scrutinizing the room. Not casual at all but protecting her brother.

Blocking the doorway too. Jack tried to ignore that. "Curtis, maybe Lauren should leave us in private?" said Jack.

"She'll stay. You think I killed them. She knows that, don't ya, Sis?" Lauren nodded. "We can keep talking. It's okay."

It was then that Jack remembered he'd actually told Curtis he had an extra piece of evidence. Curtis didn't know what it was, or whether it was even incriminating, but was it why he'd let Jack into his home? Jack was now very aware of Lauren blocking the doorway.

"Why are you really here, Jack? The cops have already been through." Curtis held out his wrists. "No cuffs. I'm a free man, and there's no reason to charge me. I am"—he sounded the word out into syllables—"co-op-er-at-ing."

"I just—" he started, but Curtis held up a finger.

"You're here because you *want* me to have killed her. Because then it makes it all about you. First thing you did when you got here, said *you* think *you're* responsible. But if I didn't do it, and I didn't, then it's not about you anymore, is it?"

"You should go," said Lauren.

"You invited him. He stays." Curtis turned back to Jack. "I want you to face up to me, Jack. I think you're still on my side a little bit. The cops saw I'm innocent straightaway. Yeah, I got motive. Help me out here. Why did I, hypothetically, kill Alexis?"

Jack stared at his hands. Answered quietly.

"Can't hear you?"

"Jail," Jack muttered.

"Huh?" Curtis had heard it that time, Jack was sure, but he wanted dominance. Prison tactics. Be the big dog.

"Jail. You blame her for sending you there."

"You're goddamn right I do. Oh…" He tapped a finger to his lips, his voice lilting with a high, mocking tone. "Hang on! I'm so angry about getting sent to jail for four years that I publicly murder my lawyer and arrange her body as a calling card, pointing straight back to me! Leading inevitably to… Come on, Jack, you know this one."

"More jail time," Jack conceded. The motive was circuitous. It didn't stack up. Then again, since when was Curtis strictly logical? The right kind of outburst…

"Even the cops knew that, and that's why I'm not in a cell. Stupidest fucking murderer out there. You think you're all wrapped up in guilt she died, but you're all wrapped up in this." He reached over and flicked Jack on the forehead. His finger was sweaty, left a bead on Jack's brow. Jack didn't rub it away. Prison tactics. Don't give in. "Bashed her head in too—they tell you that?"

Jack shook his head. He hadn't known the cause of death; he'd thought she'd been strangled.

"Someone's put a lot of effort into making it look like I'm a serial killer. But they beat her first. She died quickly; a single blow, I'm told. They were trying to fish details out of me, is how I know," he said, anticipating Jack's question. "The strangling came after. She was already dead. Ergo, staged. Ergo, copycat. Ergo, there's the door."

"It's not a copycat," Lauren repeated. "It's the same killer."

"And Eliza?" Jack found himself saying, louder than he'd intended. He saw Curtis's face darken, the muscles shift in his neck. By the doorway, Lauren unfurled. "If they're copying a murder, who are they copying?"

"Did you just ask me what I think you did?" Curtis grabbed the armrest, cocked his elbows, preparing to rise.

"Careful." Lauren took a half step into the room, and Jack realized she hadn't been supervising the room to protect Curtis. She was there to protect Jack.

Jack stood up to leave.

"Sit the fuck down."

Lauren flinched. Jack sat down.

"When we first met, you told me a few things," Curtis said. "You remember those?"

"I told you my words would make you famous."

"And there was one question you promised you would never ask me."

"I did."

"Are you asking that question?"

Everything around Jack seemed to slow. The steam lingered on the rim of his mug. He gently placed it on the tray so he wouldn't spill it. Was it hot enough to be a weapon? Probably not. He could hear Curtis breathing, a fat man's whistle. Jack shouldn't have come.

"I am," he said.

"Okay. Ask it properly." Curtis ran his tongue over his teeth, bulging his lips, clawed the armrest. Jack swallowed, straightened his back.

"Leave him alone," said Lauren.

"Ask. It. Properly."

Jack was properly scared now. Curtis's hands had shaken when he poured the tea. That rage had simmered underneath the whole time. This meeting was a trap. Jack saw, on the top of the bookcase behind Curtis, the stock of a rifle. The same rifle Curtis had shot at the drone with? If Curtis got up and made a move for the gun, could Jack get out of the room fast enough? He figured he probably could, but he was too far in to back out now. He took a breath and said the words he'd promised not to.

"Did you kill Eliza Dacey?"

Curtis ground his jaw. For a second, Jack thought he might go for the gun and kill him right there. Instead, he stood and went to the door, brushing past his sister. The question, now voiced, had torn through whatever bond the two men had formed during the documentary. Maybe Curtis really had thought Jack still was on his side. Jack was starting to see just how black-and-white Curtis saw the world: Andrew Freeman a villain; himself a hero; Jack his sidekick. In prison, those fictions must have been comforting.

Curtis paused in the doorway. He had sounded heartbroken on their last prison phone call, but now he wasn't disappointed; he was furious. His shoulders shuddered with each breath. In turn, that incensed Jack—what right did Curtis have to be pissed off?

Lauren was stoic, still coiled, but aware that the knife-edge had tilted back to safer ground as Curtis made to leave the room. Curtis turned back.

"You think so little of me." Curtis's voice was thick, holding back hot, livid tears. "And you're the smallest man I know."

Then he was gone. Deep in the guts of the house, a door slammed.

CHAPTER 14

Lauren walked with Jack to the driveway in silence. It was different outside, her face relaxed, hazel eyes not analyzing everything. She accompanied him down the driveway without asking, still no shoes, blackened toes kicking at the largest stones.

The sun was high, the sky completely clear, though the trees that lined the drive filtered the light, dappling the ground with long streaks of shadow. Shade to sun in rapid blinks, it was like walking through an old cartoon optical illusion. A zoetrope, Jack knew they were called. He'd made one when he first studied film—you spin the cylinder and watch the bear dance through the slits. Lauren blinked in and out of Jack's vision. The world reduced to a frame rate.

"He'll calm down," she said at last. "Sorry. I thought that would go better."

"Your career as a fortune-teller would be short-lived."

"I foresee"—she touched a finger to her head and waved her other hand in front of her—"unemployment."

Jack surprised himself by laughing. Throughout their interviews, they'd never traded pleasantries, even during breaks. Lauren and her father were rigid and focused, the two of them set up on that broken couch, Jack's voice offscreen. The spotlight on, heating the room, dust rising from the carpet with the temperature. It was clear that Lauren had been coached to respond only to the simplest of questions and with the simplest of answers. At the time, Jack thought he was getting the yes or no answers of a moody teenager (even at twenty, he still thought of her as the sullen sixteen-year-old in the courtroom), but now he realized how unfair he'd been: to ask about such horrors, about murder and violence and her own brother, of a girl who barely knew the world. He'd seen her as a character to play in his narrative, but here she was, real and young and laughing alongside him. Jack supposed that was it—they were always talking about her brother. Outside, alone, it wasn't about Curtis. And she seemed alive to him, for the first time.

"You didn't have to pitch my case," he said. "Thanks though."

"We both want the same thing, you know? I want the world to see what really happened to Eliza too."

"You knew her well?" Jack asked. Lauren raised an eyebrow. "I know, I've already asked you this. But you might remember some small detail. It would help me, at least, to go over it again."

"We were kind of friends, I guess. Though maybe she thought I was just some kid that pestered her. I thought she was *the* coolest. When she was working at the Freemans', I was only fifteen, remember, and I'd lived in country towns all my life, and here's this confident, amazing, twenty-five-year-old who's traveling the world on her own like a goddamn boss." She placed a hand over her mouth and her shoulders lifted, stifling a chuckle. A good memory bubbling out of her. "She swiped a bottle off Andrew once, and we drank it sitting out here, under the vines. That was a nice night. It's how I like to remember her."

Lauren tilted her head and soaked in the sun as if recharging. She looked back at him and smiled.

"Come back tomorrow night," she said. "We'll have the restaurant to ourselves. I used to fill in with the chefs, so I can make you something."

"Yeah. Okay..." Jack said, but he must have hesitated, because Lauren immediately called him out.

"Did my brother scare you?" she said. "Fuck, he scared me too! You're lucky. You can imagine if I ever brought a boyfriend home..."

Now they were both laughing again. A magpie took flight with the sudden noise, rippled through the air. Their laughter faded, and there was no more to be said. Jack kept expecting Lauren to turn back to the house, but she stayed with him, thumbs poking out the front of her jean pockets, palms flat on her thighs. They crunched down the drive.

"He killed her," she said. Kicked a rock.

They kept walking. The world flickered.

"He's guilty," she said. "He always will be. It doesn't matter if he actually did anything or not. There's been too much press. Too many podcasts. Too many shows. Don't you see? Even the supporters, well, Alexis dying has changed their minds. Yours too, I can see it. In the public eye, he's guilty. It's just a different prison he's living in now. A bigger room." They'd reached the end of the drive. The van was gone. "So sometimes it's easier to just think he killed her. Because even if he didn't, wherever we go, my brother will always be the guy that strangled that young woman. No. My *family* will always be the *family* that strangled that young woman." She sighed. "And now we've gone and killed another one."

Jack didn't have anything to say. Lauren's life sucked away by her brother's actions. The only way to move the spotlight was to get the real truth out there. She needed him. He turned to leave. She reached out and grabbed his arm. Hard. Farmer's fingers clinched around his bony wrist. Her hand was sweaty and slicked his skin. She shot a look back at the farmstead.

"Help us."

Lauren turned back at the main road as if some invisible force field separated the Wade property from the town. It may well have.

Leaving that house had been like stepping back into the world. Curtis kept all the curtains closed. Jack wondered if Curtis had done that prior to his visit to intimidate him, but more likely it was to block out photographers and their drones. The main road of Birravale was clear, and the light so sharp that everything looked colorless. The Brokenback's usually vibrant canopy was bleached a pale green.

The road was narrow, so Jack walked in the dirt. Crumbling blocks of bitumen scooted off his toes, the road shrinking ever inward. A sheep transport blew past him, and he felt the world shake. The smell of piss and wool bathed him. Hot diesel lingered in his sinuses. The truck rattled on.

Jack liked walking. Out the front of the hospital, where they'd been fed, he hadn't been allowed. The nurses had forced everyone to catch the bus home. They'd supervised them to the stop, watched them board, and ticked their names off a list. Packed full of calories, the message was clear: we don't want you wasting them walking home. No one had the guts to get off at the first stop, in case the driver was a snitch. Someone would always cause a fuss though. *I don't have any change*, they'd complain, animatedly patting their pockets. The nurses were ready for that—producing ziplock bags with the exact fare in coins inside. *Was Sydney's public transport funding so bad*, Jack used to joke, *they had to prop it up with fares from bulimics? We're light*, another patient said once. *Saves fuel.*

His phone rang. A blocked number. The man on the other end was talking before he could say hello.

"I hear you've been hassling the Wades."

Winter.

"I wasn't hassling. I was invited."

"No journalists are allowed on the property. Do I need to take you through Trespass 101 again?"

"I'm not a journalist. I told you, they invited me."

"Curtis did?" said Winter.

"Lauren, actually. Why didn't you tell me how Alexis was killed? She wasn't strangled; she was beaten. Curtis told me."

"I don't have to tell you anything. You're not a detective. What else did he say?"

"I don't have to tell you anything either," Jack parroted.

Jack ran his hand over the steel railing, a minor barrier where the road bumped, crossing a small creek. The road had started to level out, and Jack could see the whole town in a straight line, every building lining the main street, with their purposes labeled on their awnings in large block letters, as if they were all attending the same high-school reunion, sticky labels on breast pockets. Hi, my name is: NEWSAGENT. It looked like less of a town and more of a movie set. He supposed that was actually half-right. Birravale wasn't a real town; it was a service depot. Just enough drink and food and beds to recharge the wine guzzlers. A community reduced to its basic functions. Like Liam in his bed. He reached the end of the railing. Rust roughened his fingers, and he rubbed them on his jeans. He was sweating, and it had only been a short walk from the Wades'.

How had Winter known he'd even been there? The van. It wasn't really a media van. The satellite on top must have been fake.

"Why are you keeping tabs on Curtis if he's not a suspect?" he said.

"Bad press. If the Wades are talking to you, you might be useful. Tell me something."

It was clearer now. Winter might be a good detective—Jack had no idea—but he was also a media cop. The sort they bring in on the high-profile cases. His job was as much PR as it was solving the actual crime. That was modern policing, Jack supposed. Curtis was actually on the radar, but Winter didn't want to blow into Birravale with helicopters and hand-cuffs. Not until he had bulletproof evidence, anyway. And Curtis wasn't letting anyone without a warrant on his property. Except for Jack. So they could help each other out.

"Curtis said he didn't do it," Jack said.

"Tell me something *new*," Winter said.

"He's right about his motive. As much as I want to believe it, it's not there. How much of a case do you have?"

"Not enough. Help me clarify some things from your interview. This isn't us working together…" Jack imagined Winter leaning back in his chair, checking the office for prying ears, dignity shaken that he was asking Jack Quick for help. "Just so we're clear."

"That low on suspects, are you?" Jack couldn't help rubbing it in a little.

"The company line is that we are actively pursuing several promising leads."

"So. Fuck all."

"We are actively pursuing several promising leads." There was the sound of Winter flicking through a notebook. "Her boyfriend. Do you have any clue who he was?"

"I don't think it was technically a boyfriend. She was flippant."

"Is it you?"

"Fuck's sake."

"I have to ask," Winter said, one of his standard lines.

"It's not me."

"Is it Curtis?"

Jack paused. Winter, whether he knew it or not, was being obvious. Like with Eliza, a rape kit would have been used. Judging by the way Winter was flinging out darts at any target, Jack guessed that, like with Eliza, the kit had turned up nothing. That meant that she hadn't slept with anyone in the week or so prior to her death, the longest period that DNA collection could be considered viable. Or, at the very least, she hadn't slept with anyone they had a profile on. People who watch crime shows think it's as easy as punching into a database, but most average citizens aren't on it. Curtis was—his DNA collected during the first arrest. Jack had a sudden flash of Alexis pinned under Curtis, the whistle through his teeth, fat and panting.

"I'd be surprised," he said.

"I have"—more rustling of pages—"that the boyfriend called her twice during your meeting. And sent her a text. Right?"

"Like I said, I didn't see her caller ID, but it seemed like the same guy rang her a few times."

"Hmm," Winter muttered. "Time?"

Jack told him. A Land Rover thrummed past.

"Don't see it," Winter said to himself. There was a *clack clack clack* down the line, the tapping of a pen against his teeth. *Of course*, Jack thought. Winter was looking at phone records.

"Which phone?" Jack said.

"Hmm," Winter said again. "Interesting."

He hung up.

Jack held the phone in his hand, recovering. *Which phone?* The police hadn't known about her second phone. And if her boyfriend was a new fling, it was likely that second phone was the one with his messages and phone calls. She'd told him it was cheap, prepaid. Hard to trace. Was it in the house when he was there? He tried to remember. And why hadn't he told the police?

He'd just forgotten. Surely. But maybe, subconsciously, he'd held it back on purpose. Because a part of him wanted to be the one to solve the damn thing. *If I didn't do it, it's not about you anymore*, Curtis had said. Maybe he was right. This whole investigation just an exercise in selfishness.

Jack's thoughts were swirling. He was close to town now, walking on the footpath instead of the dirt. He needed someone to talk to. A good listener, someone who wouldn't judge him. He was still holding his phone. He dialed his father.

"Hey, Dad," he said.

"How's it going?"

"Is Liam there?" *Awake*, he meant. Of course he was there. He couldn't physically be anywhere else. He'd meant to say *awake*.

"He's here." They'd almost become used to that accidental language, imagining him as a real person, just for a glimmer.

"Can you put me on speaker?"

"Jack," Peter said gently, "I don't know if this is—" He stopped himself short of saying *healthy*, as if the word itself might leap out of the phone and make his son sick. He sighed. "Okay. Let me grab the paper."

There were a few moments of quiet, then a crinkling of paper, a series of thuds, and some crackling interference. Peter had walked up the stairs, gone into Liam's room and sat in the armchair, crossword smoothed on his lap. His voice, when it came, was from farther away. "You're on."

"Hey, mate," Jack said. "How are you doing, Liam?"

There was no reply except the soft, intermittent beep of a machine, and the gentle scratch of Peter's pencil.

"Listen, that case we've been working on. Can I run some things past you?"

A quiet beeping.

"I just don't understand. If a boyfriend murdered her, it almost makes sense. It was a single blow to the back of the head, you know? That's a murder of passion. Violence like that comes from fire, anger or impulse, right?" Jack saw it in his mind, a hulking shadow in the cobblestone lane, weapon in hand. Alexis's boyfriend panicking. Staggered by what he'd done. Needing to draw attention away from himself, to run. Realizing, as he slipped Alexis's second phone into his pocket, that the perfect cover was as clear as the impending dawn: imitating the most high-profile crime in a century.

No answer but the dull scratch of a pencil in the background.

"No, I don't know who she was sleeping with, mate. I don't know her type." He paused, waiting for answers that weren't coming. "You're right. I really didn't know her at all."

Beep.

"What about her fingers, then? People don't carry around pliers just in case. They could have rummaged in her garage, I guess."

Beep. Beep. Scratch. Scratch.

"Good point. We *were* never able to match Eliza's wounds to a weapon." Jack's researchers had tested all kinds of weapons on replica silicon hands. None had matched Eliza's fingers: mangled stumps like the chewed end of a cigar, a glint of white in the center. "So what you're saying is if Alexis's wounds match Eliza's"—Jack finished Liam's imagined sentence for him—"it could tie the murders together."

Beep. Scratch.

"I need to see the coroner's report. You're a genius, Bro."

Peter cleared his throat loudly. Jack's time was up. There was some kind of stopwatch always running in this family.

"Dad's wrapping me up. I'll see you soon." Then to Peter: "Thanks, Dad."

"I know he can't hear you, but I don't like you telling him those things." Peter's voice was slightly thick in the air. "He's peaceful."

"You don't have to sit in."

"Part of me hates it. And the other part of me...if I shut my eyes and listen"—he breathed—"it's just like you're brothers again."

They paused on that misuse of tense—Liam was still alive; they were still brothers—but Jack knew what his father meant. They murmured goodbye.

Right, Jack thought immediately, *the coroner's report.* He only had one option there, damn it. He texted McCarthy.

Finger wounds. Coroner's report. Help me out?

Then quickly added a second green bubble below.

Last favor, promise.

He'd reached the Royal now. A blackboard out the front promised counter lunches. He knew he had to. Being here on his own—dark thoughts and dead women swirling through his head—was harmful enough. The longer he went without eating, the harder it would be to keep it down later.

He stepped inside. Framed posters—ALCOHOL: AUSTRALIA'S MOST EXPENSIVE DRUG and GAMBLING: KNOW WHEN TO STOP—ringed the room uselessly. Immediately, the air changed. Dampened. As if the very atmosphere was laden on an atomic level with an extra ion or two of beer, latching itself between hydrogen and oxygen. A new molecule, brewed and bonded here: shit-faced dioxide.

Jack took a seat at the bar. The bartender who'd told him to fuck off yesterday was behind the taps talking to the motel owner, Brett Dawson, who was ignoring a parmigiana. Two younger blokes in their midtwenties were standing on either side of him, leaning on the bar. They were both handsome (*Alexis's type?* Jack wondered), with blond hair darkened from sweat and dirt-browned hands curled around their glasses. A yellow vest was folded on the counter. Trade workers. As well as running the motel, Brett ran some construction around town. They'd helped on Curtis's new restaurant. Knocked down the old one for Whittaker too, the previous owner, who, out of spite, had filled his cellar with concrete to deaden the land for the new owners. Jack had seen the invoice for the concrete fill. TV research was not all glamorous confrontations with potential murderers; sometimes it was just sifting through receipts. Not a bad side gig— thirty-five grand for pouring concrete into a hole. One of Brett's buddies snuck a fry off his plate. The bartender looked across at Jack, and Jack gave a noncommittal wave and plucked a menu from the stack.

The menu had nothing he felt he could order. He snuck another glance in Brett's direction; the chicken looked enormous. He wanted it. Wanted to walk over there and tear it apart with his hands and cram it in his face. But he knew if he got that, he'd eat it all. And then he'd feel it festering inside him for the rest of the day. It would be all he could do to keep it down. Eating was always a tightrope walk inside his stomach; too much and he'd want to purge, too little and he fed the other side of his disease. Every meal was trying to flip a coin and land it on its edge. He frowned. The menu was all burgers and fries and schnitzels. He wanted something benign. He considered leaving, flipped the menu over. On the back there were the kids' meals. Smaller portions. Spaghetti Bolognese. Better.

He placed the menu upside down in front of him in what he hoped was a clear enough sign he'd finished reading it. While waiting, Jack noticed a TV hanging from the cornice across the room. Daytime TV was playing. Nothing interesting. But in a newsbreak, Ted Piper popped up in his familiar blue two-piece, spouting sound bites. So Alexis still qualified as news. It took a few more moments for the bartender to catch on; he held a finger up to Brett, excusing himself, and waddled over.

"Decided?" He was gruff but not impolite. Perhaps he'd accepted that they'd failed to drive Jack away. Or perhaps, like the B and B owner who'd put Jack's financial utility above her dislike of him, the bar owner had realized there were only four people in the bar and only one of them was currently eating. He needed every customer he could get. As long as Jack was spending, he'd earned himself a begrudging courtesy. Brett Dawson was the only one with a horse still high enough.

Or maybe the bartender wanted to make Jack eat something he'd rubbed his balls against.

Jack introduced himself, extending his hand over the bar.

"I know who you are. Alan Sanders." He wiped his hands on the front of his apron as if about to take Jack's hand. He didn't. Was Jack imagining Alan's furtive glance to where Brett and company were? "Decided?" he asked again.

"Spaghetti Bolognese, please."

Alan made a show of leaning over the bar, peering at the floor beneath the stools.

"You got a kid?"

"Huh? No."

"Spaghetti's for kids."

"I know."

"It's for kids. *Only.* You have to order an adult meal."

"I'm not that hungry."

"Does this say 'Under Twelve'?" Alan picked up the menu and jabbed a finger on the spaghetti. "Or 'Not That Hungry'?"

"Mental age," called Brett, and the lads beside him laughed. "Give it to him."

"Are you on one of those city diets?" Alan asked. "Or are you just a cheapskate?"

"Neither," said Jack. "I just want the small spaghetti. I'll pay full price. Charge me for the parma."

"If you're paying." Alan shrugged, then said almost to himself, "Sydney wankers. It's not gluten free, if you're wondering."

Jack ignored him. Next time, he was going to the bakery.

The meal was out suspiciously faster than you could even microwave it. A boy in a white T-shirt and a black apron scanned the room and brought it over. He was young, twelve at the most. Child labor laws didn't apply in small towns, apparently.

"You order the kid's meal?" he asked. Jack nodded. The kid placed it down in front of Jack and then said, completely without irony, "In all my years as a chef, I never seen that before."

If the kid was even a year older, Jack would have insulted him. So much material to work with. Instead, he thanked him and twirled a forkful while examining the bowl. No pubes. Not from that chef, anyway. He took his time eating, feeling each bite slide down his throat. Surprisingly, it tasted quite good—real mince and tomatoes—and by the end, he wanted more. Looking down at the empty bowl, he was glad to have eaten it. Mission accomplished. That never changed, whether he was doing well or not, that small feeling of victory. The coin successfully flipped. His internal acrobat straightened on the tightrope. Bowed.

What next? He needed to talk to Andrew Freeman, but he didn't know how to make that introduction. Until meeting Lauren tomorrow night, he had nothing to do. But something was circling in his head. Lauren in the driveway. She had a pretty laugh, he recalled. But that wasn't what he was thinking of. It was her, glancing back to the house. Chewing her lip.

"Help us," she'd said.

Not "Help me." Not "Help him."

Help *us*.

CHAPTER 15

There was someone sitting on the step when Jack got back to the house.

Jack's next thoughts came in rapid succession. The first, that he'd recognize the straight-backed posture of an off-duty policeman anywhere. The second was to wonder if anyone within two hundred kilometers *wasn't* keeping tabs on him. And the third, that Andrew Freeman looked happy to see him.

Which was odd, seeing as he'd refused every single interview request during filming and because Jack had made him out to be, at worst, a conspiratorial murderous prick and, at best, just a regular one.

"Andrew." Jack nodded in greeting.

"Is Mary-Anne treating you well?" Andrew said, standing, and Jack realized he'd never gotten his hostess's name. She was an uncredited extra. Andrew was in his sixties and country skinny, which meant he was thin but tightly wrapped in sinew, a skeleton wound in rope and dipped in skin. He was wearing bright-blue shorts and had a cyclist's calves, overstuffed like a sock full of doorknobs. "Thought I'd come and welcome you to Birravale."

"You missed the welcome parade," Jack said.

"That bad, huh?" Andrew had crossed the lawn now. He opened the door of his Subaru Forester, tilted his head toward the passenger seat. "Hop in. I wanna show you something."

It was a short drive back up the hill to the Freeman winery. Jack was impressed by how steep the road became beyond the Wades', the gradient pushing him back in his seat. He could see in his mind tendrils of thick wine bleeding down the hill, pouring into town. Andrew's car was impeccably clean, even the floor mats vacuumed and shampooed. There was an earthy smell, though, one not easily vacuumed out: a dusty, almost-spiced tinge that he couldn't place. Outside, a yellow sign announced they were approaching a *CREST*. Behind it, there was another yellow sign—*STEEP DESCENT* and a zigzag squiggle. Jack wondered if that was where Andrew got his calves, pumping up that hill every day.

Andrew hooked into a driveway before they reached the sign. They passed under an arch with *Birravale Creek Wines* nailed up in wooden letters.

"Where's the creek?" asked Jack.

"Nowhere." Andrew smiled. "It just sounds good. Have you ever heard of a winery not named after nature? Those are the rules: landmark, plant, or animal."

"Maybe there was one, back in the day?" Jack suggested. "Family business?"

"My wife's. Yeah, maybe. Hopper's Crossing's as close as we get, I reckon. Doesn't matter. We like the name. Besides, a creek means the wine's flowing. 'Swamp' doesn't quite have the same ring to it." Jack didn't laugh. "Sorry. Winemaker's joke."

"What's the Wade winery called?"

"Vineyard."

"Huh?"

"The Wades own a *vineyard*. They only grow grapes, don't make the wine. Brewed off-site. Blends." Jack could hear the distaste as if Andrew had just taken a sip of it.

"What's their vineyard called then?" Jack realized he didn't actually know. He'd always just thought of it as the crime scene.

"Wade Wines."

"The exception that proves the rule?" Jack said.

Andrew pulled off the drive and onto a small square of clipped grass where there were about a dozen cars parked.

"Nope. Like I said. Landmark, plant"—he switched the engine off—
"or animal."

They parked, and Jack got out, followed Andrew toward two buildings.
A wood-walled homestead, with a tin roof peaking steeply toward the sun.
Aztecs could have sacrificed to the gods on that roof, rolled heads down
that galvanized pyramid, Jack thought. On the right, toward Birravale
itself, there was a less-impressive square building that was half the homestead's height, with a flat roof. It looked like a shoebox but with windows.
Jack could hear the clinking of glasses and the general hum of conversation
from within. The restaurant. What made it incredible was how it sat, right
on the precipice, where the land began falling steeply away. The best seats
in the restaurant were literally hanging over the edge. In the middle of the
buildings, the driveway turned in a loop, a circle of flowers in the middle.
Farther forward, behind the homestead, the tops of the two silos glinted in
the sun. One of which Curtis had split open with his ax.

"So this is where the tourists are," he said aloud. Realizing he hadn't
seen many in the town.

"Well, the Wades are closed," Andrew said, "obviously."

"Business is good for you, then?"

"It's okay. Not many weddings. No surprises there."

"Impressive structure." Jack gestured to the restaurant.

"It's the original building." Andrew pointed to the parking lot. "Used
to be over there, but we moved it. We wanted the view."

"Sounds like a big job."

"Worth it to preserve the history. The Wades just knocked theirs down
and started again up the hill. That's why our wine has flavor." Andrew
smiled, then leaned forward conspiratorially. "Tell you what...the previous owner wasn't too happy about being asked to knock the old one
down. The Wades said they were buying the land not the buildings. Well,
the old owner, he knocked it down all right, but then he filled the underground with concrete. Ha. Now Curtis can't grow on it anyway—that bit

of land's useless. The best thing is, Curtis probably hasn't even figured it out yet." Andrew's eyes sparkled with a prank well played. But there was a spite there too.

Jack had known that the restaurant had been knocked down, the new one built up the hill, and the cellar scuttled to ruin the growth of any vines on top of it. (That last row of grapes, which Jack had always liked to imagine were dying because of Eliza, blooded into the soil, were actually wilting out of revenge.) But he *hadn't* known that knocking down the original restaurant was a condition of sale. He was about to ask something, but Andrew was distracted by a small woman hurrying past, too many bottles of wine cradled precariously in her arms.

"Hold up," Andrew called.

The woman turned. She had dyed-blond hair with silver roots, a small, tight mouth with pursed lips, as if pulling every breath through a straw. Her brown eyes reflective, she looked as if she was about to say something. Again, Jack was struck with the feeling of knowing someone he'd never met: Sarah Freeman. Her mouth relaxed; she'd changed her mind, said nothing.

"What have you got there?" Andrew said as she walked over to them.

"I thought these would be nice." She wasn't able to hand him a bottle, so proffered the spread of them. Andrew picked one up, tossed it from his left to right hand.

"Andrew, that's a thousand-dollar bottle of wine," Sarah said curtly.

"An important dinner," Andrew said to Jack. "Collectors." He turned the wine over in his hand, held it to the light. Looked at the label.

"Nope," he said, "I think we want the ones we just got in."

"I really don't think—"

"Treat them to the new ones."

"You don't have to give them those."

"What's life without a few thrills, love?" Andrew flashed a grin at Jack, who had a sudden realization that Andrew's brash business confidence was not so different from his own faux producer voice. Andrew and Sarah weren't having a discussion; Andrew was merely repeating what he wanted until she conceded. "She thinks they're too expensive. But there's nothing better than seeing a man with money *actually* pumping through his veins." Then, back to Sarah: "These are valuable men. Start them off with one of these, sure. But then let's give them what they've paid for."

Sarah nodded as Andrew slotted the bottle back in her arms.

"Jack Quick, by the way," Jack said, gesturing to her load. "I'd shake your hand, otherwise."

"I know who you are," Sarah said, and turned back to the restaurant. Jack had an image of her tripping, on her knees in a $6,000 puddle. He thought about Andrew tossing the bottle back and forth and didn't think he'd care.

"Right, that'll be fun," said Andrew. He turned. The point of his boot crunched the gravel with his pivot, as if he was grinding out a cigarette. "Come."

He led Jack through the gap between the buildings, and the silos came fully into view, towering more than ten meters high. Steel ladders ran up the sides of both. The closest had a gray metal sheet riveted to it at torso height—a repair job. Jack imagined Curtis up there, swinging from the hip. Red wine spurting back at him.

Andrew walked past the silos, fumbled a key from his pocket, and stooped over. Jack thought he was fiddling with the ground, but as he got closer, he could see that Andrew had unlocked a set of butterfly doors inlaid forty-five degrees into the sheer hillside, homestead to the left, shrubbery invading the hill behind. Andrew yanked the doors open and beckoned to Jack to follow him in.

The light thinned as Jack descended a flight of creaking stairs. The smell was musty, earthy, more like a spice rack than a cellar. There was the same tang in the air as in Andrew's car. He heard a click and a series of fluorescents stammered into life, illuminating a huge underground cellar. Stone arches divided the room, holding up the roof, which was low but not low enough to have to stoop. The walls were brick—cladded in clay or dirt,

Jack couldn't tell. The floor began as polished concrete but turned to rock and dirt farther back. It wasn't sloped; it had been built *into* the hill. The Freemans weren't afraid of a challenge, Jack realized. They wanted a cellar built into a mountainside, a restaurant literally suspended over a valley, and that was what they got. Andrew was excited by people with money pumping through their veins. And beneath them, Curtis Wade wouldn't replace his broken couch. Jack could see why they hadn't gotten along.

Jack stood at the base of the stairs, taking it all in. The arches that led to further chambers splitting off to the left and right. The series of safe-like steel doors. The oak barrels that lined each wall, stacked three high, hundreds of them. Some of the barrels on the bottom rows were two-toned in color, a redness bisecting the light-chestnut-colored oak. *Of course*, Jack remembered. *This room would have flooded too.* Curtis's couch. Mary-Anne's skirting. Andrew's cellar. Everywhere he went, Jack kept being reminded the town was tainted. Stained.

Andrew was at a rack of bottles laid out in honeycomb shelving, rifling through them. He plucked one out, tilted it to the light. He held it up to Jack as if for approval. Jack shrugged.

"Did you bring me here just to show off?" Jack said.

He felt uneasy, and he was cold. Andrew was being kind, nice, which didn't match how Jack had portrayed him in the series—as a complete arsehole. Not that he was one, but Jack had *told the nation* he was. Jack didn't know exactly why Andrew Freeman had approached him, but he didn't fancy being trapped underground with him for too much longer.

"Of course not," Andrew said, slightly taken aback—and maybe a little hurt—that Jack wasn't impressed by him. He walked back to the stairs. "I brought you here to choose a bottle. This isn't what I wanted to show you. This way."

Andrew flicked the switch on the wall and the cellar disappeared. The square of light at the top of the stairs shimmered like an invitation.

Andrew tucked the wine bottle under one arm and placed a hand on the lowest rung of the ladder. The ladder ran up the flank of the repaired silo before curling over the rim.

Andrew started to climb without asking Jack to follow. About ten rungs up, the ladder was encased in a circular cage which went all the way to the top. The chute was secured at the bottom by a padlocked grate. Andrew unlocked the padlock and worked it through the latch, the grill swinging open with a clatter. *Whump.* The sound shocked Jack. Andrew climbed into the chute.

Jack's fingers had found their way into his mouth; he was gnawing at his nails. He wasn't afraid of heights, even though he probably should have been, but he remained respectfully aware of them. He placed a hand on the ladder and felt the vibrations of Andrew's climb rumbling through his fingertips. He breathed in and shut his eyes. Besides, he reminded himself, people aren't scared of heights; they're scared of the ground.

People bounce too. Everyone thinks that when someone falls from a height, they just go *splat*. But they don't. There's a puff of dust, and then they're in the air again, rag-doll limbs akimbo, as if the earth is spitting them back out, rather than colliding into them. People bounce. Jack knew. His brother had. Only once.

Jack opened his eyes and slowly climbed. His grip was tight, knuckles strained. He took it one rung at a time.

On top of the silo, he was glad he had. The views were spectacular. Now he was level with the canopy, Jack could see the ridges of the mountains beyond, fire trails carved through the trees like veins. Turning, he had a bird's-eye view of Birravale. From up here, it looked like a child's diorama, small square blocks dotting the road. He counted the buildings—no more than thirty. Tiny cars moved like they were on rails. A toy town. Lazily built, as if the playing child had forgotten some essential parts that made it a real town. Beyond was land in square patches of yellow, green, and dark brown—a country both dead and alive, stitched together like a quilt.

And, of course, directly beneath them, the Wade property. The hexagonal restaurant took pride of place, undeniably drawing the eye. Jack's eyes followed the final vine on the Wade property, down to where Eliza had died, near where the old restaurant would have been. He wondered what the old restaurant had looked like, struck by the irony of Andrew, with his multimillion-dollar renovation, calling Curtis's single indulgence tacky. Andrew Freeman thought he was so different from Curtis Wade, but they'd both found money, though Andrew had married into it. He seemed to pride himself on technicalities. He owned a winery, after all; Curtis only owned a vineyard.

From here, Curtis's rows of grapes looked like gouges in the dirt. Some were covered in white nets, cocooned like spiderwebs.

Before the land started to really run uphill, there was the small patch of overgrowth unofficially separating the two properties, where Jack had found Eliza's shoe. And then, as soon as the elevation started, the Freeman place began. It was as if both wineries had sat flat, side by side, then someone had folded the earth and put Andrew Freeman on top.

The Freemans' trellises were different too. Because it was too steep to run them straight down the hill, their vines were along the slope, perpendicular to the Wades'. It gave the impression of a Vietnamese rice paddy rather than a winery.

"I like it up here." Andrew was sitting on the edge of the silo, knees folded out into the air, the backs of his heels drumming against the steel. Jack sat as close to the middle of the roof as possible, next to a large metal nub that looked like a submarine hatch.

"Sarah brought me up here on one of our first dates. I thought to myself, for the rest of my life, I gotta have this view. That's when I knew I was gonna marry her. You can sit on that, it's fine."

Jack sat down on the hatch. There was a picnic basket beside Andrew, but Jack didn't remember him carrying it up; he must keep it up here. Andrew swiveled around, back to the air now, which disconcerted Jack even more.

He opened the bottle and pulled two glasses from the picnic basket. The wine he poured was red, smelled fruity. Andrew handed him a glass.

"I know nothing about wine," Jack said, "if you're expecting a discussion on the *notes*." He'd been on a date once, at a tasting, and the sommelier had said his glass should have the essence of an *oak bushfire*. Jack didn't know how he was supposed to taste a bushfire, let alone the type of tree aflame, but he'd nodded anyway, said he could taste some roasted koala in there too. There was no second date.

"Me neither. My wife's the maker." Andrew took a long swig from the bottle. "I'm the drinker. This is a good one though, trust me." He filled his glass almost to the brim. Jack was reminded of an old saying: *Don't get high on your own supply*. That saying only applied to drug dealers, but Jack supposed Andrew was *technically* a drug dealer, especially if the sign in the Royal was anything to go by.

Jack took a sip. Andrew was right. It had that smoothness where it felt as if your tongue were waxed and the liquid was levitating above it. He didn't know how much this bottle was worth; he tried to imagine what a thousand-dollar bottle would taste like.

"Andrew," Jack said, "you didn't bring me up here just to show me the view."

"I thought hospitality might be in short supply. Besides, I think in order for you to come back here, you must have something pretty heavy weighing you down. Maybe you're back for the right reasons this time."

Jack took a sip of his wine. Laughed. "I thought you were bringing me up here to throw me off."

"Water. Bridge. Birravale might not have a creek, but it's under it. Not everyone here's an enemy." Andrew raised his glass. "If I can do something to help put that man away again, I will."

They sat in silence, appreciating the view. Jack could see the romance of it. But had Andrew realized how beautiful his wife was up here, in this light, or how rich? A technicality, he supposed. He remembered what

Lauren had said about being born into wine, and here was a local cop, married into it yet respected all the same. At least there was one person in town keen to help him. And, seeing as how Andrew was the sergeant, this olive branch could be useful. McCarthy hadn't replied.

"One thing I do need is medical records. The coroner's report."

"Why?"

"The detective from Sydney's too cagey. I'm only getting half the picture. Have you heard anything?"

"I wish I could help, but I wouldn't know." Andrew shrugged. "I'm not a cop anymore."

"Shit." Jack looked into the deep red of his glass. Alexis's words were echoing—*You definitely got someone fired.*

"It wasn't you," Andrew said, "if that's what you're thinking. Though you ruined a lot of reputations." He finished his glass and topped it up again, holding the bottle up to the sun, swishing it at Jack. Jack shook his head. "No? Don't act so surprised. You cost a lot of people their jobs. Not mine though. I was happy to retire. I get to spend more time up here, spend more time with Sarah. Besides, a small-town cop has only got one murder in him, I think. We're bred tough here, don't doubt that. That's not what I mean. I've peeled children off blacktop, ground fathers out of harvesters. But murder…country people are good people. We know death, more so than city folk. But the difference is that we respect death. Murder, though, there's no respect there."

"Hmm," Jack agreed.

If Andrew wasn't a cop anymore, then who was? Birravale didn't have its own police station, but at least when the sergeant lived in the town, there was some authority. Though he'd always had a lot of ground to cover. Where was the nearest station? Cessnock? Newcastle? Jack reminded himself not to get into any real trouble out here.

"Yep. One murder's enough for me." Andrew downed the rest of the glass, refilled it. He examined the empty bottle, slotted it into the picnic basket. "It didn't make sense, what you said about me. You know." He was speaking quietly; he didn't sound mad.

"I know," Jack said. "I'm starting to realize I got a lot of people wrong."

"That I *killed* a woman. Just to get back at him for emptying my tanks? Fuck that." Andrew's voice was slightly slurred. "I didn't even press charges. Some feud."

"You broke his windows, I hear."

He shook his head. "Dawson's boys did."

Jack tried not to let the surprise show on his face, mentally filed away that the blonds in the pub were Brett Dawson's sons.

"After all, they built the hideous thing. You know how expensive one of those curved windows is to replace?"

"Like a firefighter setting fires," Jack said, "to rescue the people inside." Brett Dawson smashing the windows he'd put in so Curtis would have to pay him to have them fixed. He was double-dipping.

"When I started as a cop," Andrew said, "the sarge at the time had a handshake deal with the pub. Let him know ahead of time who was headed home drunk. Sarge'd pull them over, completely randomly, of course." He tapped his nose. "Offer them a cash fine to not get hauled down to the station. Then he'd split the profits with the bartender. So yeah, I'm saying they set their own fire."

"But Curtis took it out on you. Why didn't you press charges?"

"The wine's insured. Look, it sounds bad, three million. That was the claim, anyway, but those numbers—they're all projections. They sound intimidating, but the thing is *it's not real money*. Worse than it sounded, is what I'm saying. It wasn't three million, not even close. So we didn't press charges, because we didn't want to add fuel. Look at things now." Andrew looked out over the town. "Everything's ablaze."

"You could have told me this before."

"I thought *no comment* was my best option. Sarah didn't want to get pulled into it. But you were making your show. You'd chosen your story, and I could tell you were sticking to it. What voice would you have given *me*? But now, someone you know has been killed, so I'm thinking you're on my side."

Jack was silent. Would he have listened? He'd been confronted with conflicting evidence, and he'd hidden that away. Now here he was, starting again. He thought of Lauren, begging for his help. Was he really listening this time?

"Do you know how complicated it would have been for me to even *think* about arranging a conspiracy as complex as you proposed? No. I'm sorry." Andrew waved a hand. "I shouldn't. I'm sorry. I said I forgave you and I have. I shouldn't have drunk so much. I'm trying to help you. He killed her. Killed 'em both, I'd say. So let's get him." The last few words spat from his plump, reddened lips.

"You know it doesn't make sense for a murderer to set up a body pointing straight back to him." Jack couldn't believe he was defending Curtis. "Even an idiot dumps a body better than that."

"You flipping sides again?" Andrew was exasperated, his voice high and tired. "Do you think he killed them or not?"

"Yes," Jack said, and it was true. He did believe Curtis had killed Eliza, even if he wasn't sure as to what had happened to Alexis. But he was still convinced that Eliza's murder, the truth behind it, would unlock everything else. "But I need to know why. I need to know how he got her to the middle of that field. You can see the whole town from here. Curtis's whole property. You didn't see her before she died, after she stopped working here?"

"No."

Something there. A flicker. Not a lie. Not the truth.

"You sure. Never?"

"I'm sure."

A long shadow was passing through the town now. The sun was shedding its last golden rays across the vineyards. A few lights popped on in town. Another one, closer, the windows of the Wade restaurant emitting a soft glow. Through the curved glass, it looked like a lantern, a beacon. Lauren's invite. Tomorrow.

They sat for a time without talking, the single street below hazy with a dewy mist.

"I should go," Jack said finally.

"You didn't finish your wine."

"I don't really drink. It was delicious. Thank you."

"No bother. Leave it. I'm gonna stay up here awhile longer. You right to get home yourself?"

Jack nodded. It would be a fast walk downhill. He went slowly backward down the first few rungs. Just before he dropped below the rim, Andrew called out to him.

"We're friends now, Jack," he said. "Anyone gives you trouble…" He raised his fists, tossed a few imaginary jabs, laughed. "Tell 'em they're messing with me."

Jack held his best smile until the wall of the silo rose over Andrew, blocking him out. He was careful on the descent, used a mixed grip—one hand over, one hand under. It felt a long way down and that he was going too slowly. Think of the positives, he reminded himself, it could be much faster. *Whump.*

Jack didn't know what to make of Andrew. On the one hand, Andrew had shown some true intent to bury the hatchet (provided it wasn't in his wine vats again). But there was an anger in him that leaked out too, snuck through his red lips in fits. Andrew had suffered seven weeks of a one-sided conversation, all but accused of conspiracy. Was it so strange he'd wanted to have his say, to clarify his character? But there was something disconcerting there, something not quite nice about a man who decides to marry his wife based on a view. Jack realized, somewhat uncomfortably, that he was looking forward to seeing Lauren again tomorrow. God forbid, he actually preferred the Wades. At least they spoke their minds. With Andrew, Jack couldn't tell if what he was saying and what he was thinking were the same thing. You can move a restaurant across the road, but if the food's rotten...

The sun was gone now. Dark. Jack climbed down into the abyss.

CHAPTER 16

Jack was only halfway down the drive when he heard yelling. A dog barking. The air was so still and clear that the sound flooded and filled it. Short words. *Oy. Hey. Stop.* They hung in the night.

Toward town, down the hill, he could see the Wades' field, a dampened yellow glow encasing it in some kind of ethereal bubble. Behind and above, across the tops of the trees, a harsh-white circle of torchlight scanned. Glints of possum eyes, bright as stars, sparkled then vanished as they darted off, branches rustling. The light wasn't smooth; it shuddered up and down, across the canopy. It was a feeble, shaking beam. Whoever was holding the flashlight was running.

Jack was running now too, back up the drive. Yelling from the Wade property was something to worry about. He crossed the back of the Freeman restaurant, and his line of sight cleared. In the valley below, the Wade property looked like a POW jailbreak without the air siren. Between the rows of grapes, the beams of two flashlights were scanning back and forth. At the base of the rise, a cracking sound, bushes shaking, as someone picked their way through the shrubbery line that separated the properties. One of the flashlights in the field lowered from the canopy above Jack to illuminate the bush below. A shadow lurched, on Jack's side now, hopping on one leg out of the undergrowth as if struggling with a sock, then bolted into Andrew Freeman's vines.

More yelling. *Stop. Hey. Fuck.* Barking. A car started.

The shadow heading through the Freemans' vineyard looked as if it was aiming to go up and over the hill. If Jack ran straight along a row, he'd cut them off. He knew he had to catch them. Fleeing the Wades' this late at night? That was someone dangerous.

Jack hurried past the wine silos, sparing a quick glance up. Was Andrew still there, watching? He couldn't tell. The ground opened up to the rows of grapes in front of him. The entrance to each was black, with curling vines raking backward, the entrance to a maze. A torch was flashing over the vines, that person having plucked their way through the bush as well. One of the Wades giving chase? Jack took a breath, ran into the closest entrance.

The rows were tall, immediately blocking the moon. The flashlight scanned through the gaps in the foliage in a slow pan, momentarily dipping him in and out of darkness. A zoetrope. It must have been later and colder than he'd thought, because in one flash of light, his breath was coming out in puffs and mist swirled at his ankles. The intermittent light was screwing with his night vision, the night almost impossibly dark when it moved away from him. He kept drifting downhill, shouldering the vines and fence posts on his right, ricocheting back into the center of the row. Tendrils whipped at his face. Then light. Then dark. Jack was wondering how the hell he was going to know when he was even close to the person he was chasing when he heard a yelp and tripped right over them.

He landed hard on his elbows. Rolled. Everything was dark. Something was in his hand, a sock, an ankle. Grunting. A foot kicking out. Then it was light again, the flashlight beam rotating past, and there was mist glowing around his head and a glimpse of someone in front of him, scrambling on their stomach to go under the fence. Then dark. Something wooden like a baseball bat hit him hard in the jaw, and he felt his neck snap backward and his head bounce off the ground. There was a scuffling noise. The light scanned over him again—he could tell from the glowing red across the backs of his closed eyelids.

He rolled onto his back, opened his eyes, and came face-to-face with the mouth of a hunting rifle.

CHAPTER 17

Lauren peered over the top of the rifle, lowered it, and swore.

She reached out a hand and pulled Jack up from the dirt. She didn't have time for him, spun around, and aimed her gun and flashlight up the hill. Jack turned to see the intruder burst into the tree line in a shower of broken twigs and snapped branches and vanish.

"Lauren, what happened?"

"I could have *shot* you!" She was crying, her toughness stripped away, as if the tears dissolved her back into that young girl trying to hold it all together.

"Who was that? Why do you have a gun?"

"I caught them! I heard something—it woke me up—something crashing around in the shed. So I took the gun. Just because I was scared, okay? They saw me and ran."

"Did you get a look at them?"

"Did you?" Jack shook his head. She sniffed. "Me neither. It was too dark." She was breathing heavily, shoulders ragged, shock settling in as the adrenaline wore off. Jack steadied her with an arm. "You don't understand. They took his ax. Curtis's ax. They took it."

Jack understood her panic immediately. He clicked his jaw; he thought he'd been smacked by a baseball bat, but that wasn't right. It was the wooden handle of the ax. Who could possibly want to steal Curtis's ax? Only someone who had use for it. And what possible use? Someone who could put Alexis's blood on it and then plant it somewhere later. Perhaps the same person who had slipped into the vineyard in the middle of the night, months ago, and carefully placed a pink running shoe in a place they knew Jack would have to look. A killer, covering their tracks.

And Jack had been close enough to grab them at last, but he'd let them get away. In the quiet of the night, he could still hear them crunching through the bush. They hadn't gotten away quite yet.

"Lauren, call the police." He was already running up the hill. She sat, stunned, dropped to the ground with her head in her hands, gun useless in her lap. Her flashlight beam pooling uselessly on the ground. He should have taken it, he realized halfway up. But it was too late for regrets. He crossed into the tree line.

Now that he wasn't periodically blinded by brightness, Jack's eyes were able to adjust to the gloom. Black bars, tree trunks, slotted his vision. He couldn't run in the dense bush, but he tried to hurry, arms in front, scanning for danger with his palms. Everything felt simultaneously far and close, each shadowed shrub managing to jump out at him. It was the thin branches that caught him off guard the most; the big ones he could make out, avoid, but hundreds of tiny sharp twigs jabbed at him. He felt something on his cheek, wiped it off. Hot and wet. Blood. Heard something ahead, a similar twig-crunching, skin-bruising ricochet through the bush. He was getting closer.

The ground flattened out into a small clearing, he felt a crunch of hard plastic underfoot, and then he was going downhill, steep and quickly, his heels digging in and slipping, plant litter skittering down the hill in front of him. He fell, landed in something wet, felt it soak into his jeans at the knees, bone cold. He got up, reminding himself to tell Andrew Freeman he'd found the fucking creek. Then he was rocketing downhill again. Before he had time to remember the CREST and STEEP DESCENT signs from the main road, he was going faster than he could control. The bar code of the night sky whipped past above. Then something caught him on the shins and swept them out from under him. He landed hard, skinning his palms on asphalt. Asphalt? He gingerly stood up. He was in another clearing. Night sky above. No, he was on a road. A road that bent upward to the left and snaked down in a wide turn to his right, hooking back around behind the bush. This was the long, S-shaped road that was marked on the signs, but instead of going around the curves, they were running across it. Jack looked behind him. He'd tripped on the steel safety barrier; it had knocked his shins and pitched him forward.

Someone was climbing over the barrier on the other side of the road, back into the bush. Jack followed without thinking—he was so close. *Get there. Get there, Jack.* The shadow seemed to have one leg over the barrier, and then it looked like they turned and shouted something.

It sounded like "Watch out."

Then the world exploded.

Everything turned a blinding white. Jack had about two seconds to contemplate the new brightness, enough to see his hands bleached bone white, his dirt-crusted, bloodstained fingertips. And to see the wall of light pushing toward him. Close enough now to see a huge aluminum grill. Close enough to see insects swirling inside two cylindrical beams, as if the darkness outside were solid. The ground vibrated. The squeal of brakes and hot rubber, burning brakes, thickened the air. Wind dragged around him. Close enough now to see nothing but brightness. Nothing but death.

Then light.

Then dark.

Jack was surprised that his feet lifted off the ground before he felt any pain. He was even more surprised that the pain, when it did come, was in the wrong spot. A shock through his arse that jarred his back.

He barely noticed the truck had come to a stop in front of him. Smoke was curling from the back tires, the truck bed jackknifed at a slight diagonal to the cabin. There was a hiss and the cab hopped on its suspension as someone got out. Hazards clicked behind the smoke, casting the scene in a flickering glow every few seconds, like a series of orange-hued photographs. Jack breathed in, the tang of pulverized brake pads so acrid that he could smell it with his tongue. He was sitting on the road next to the truck that should have killed him. But he was alive.

The truck driver was talking to someone. Jack heard him say "You sure?" and then a few more mumbled words. A door slammed. The rumble of an engine starting. The truck pulled away, and Jack saw a white pickup with the door open behind it.

"Fucking got away," someone said next to him, a deep familiar growl, "because of you."

Jack looked up at Curtis blankly. He remembered the noise of a car starting from back in Andrew's vineyard. While Lauren had given chase, Curtis had waited around the bend for the intruder. Then Jack had staggered out of the bushes. Curtis must have seen the truck, grabbed Jack by the collar, and flung him backward. Jack, still reeling, slowly pieced it together. Curtis had saved his life.

"Well, get up then," Curtis said, one hand raised in frustration. "You're still sitting in the middle of the fucking road."

Jack hauled himself up. Curtis was already at his truck. He got in and slammed the door. He started the car and the brake lights lit up the skid of black rubber on the blacktop. That had almost been Jack. He stood on the double white line, not sure what to do. There was a whir of a window lowering, a bang on the door.

"Fuckin' hurry up."

Jack hopped in the passenger seat. Locked in the cabin with Curtis, Jack could smell his breath, a yeasty musk. Curtis looked at him with a mixture of confusion and pity, flicked on the overhead light, put a hand on Jack's jaw, and tilted his head roughly. Jack felt his neck grind in its joints.

"Did you see who it was? When they did this to you?"

"They didn't."

"What?"

"I fell." Jack didn't want to tell Curtis he'd had the shit kicked through him.

"Here I was thinking you could take a beating. And turns out you did it to yourself." Curtis did a U-ey—there was a *thunk-thunk* as the wheels went over the reflective yellow humps that split the road—and revved it to get going on the hill. "What the fuck, man? What the fuck?" Curtis was shaking his head. "You're insane."

"They took your ax."

"And you let them get away with it too. I'll be counting on you to back me up when the damn thing turns up again, doused in someone else's blood."

He had a point. As much as Curtis liked crying wolf, this time, it seemed, he was actually victim to a conspiracy, someone picking around his property to find something incriminating. The problem for the framer, Jack supposed, was that now Curtis knew exactly what was missing, it could hardly turn up again. Jack looked out the window as they weaved around a long, sloping bend. The bush it cut through was steep, with rocky drops several meters high in places. Jack was lucky to have ended up with just a bruised coccyx, and that wasn't even considering almost getting blown apart by a semitrailer.

"I didn't save you because I wanted to," Curtis said bluntly. "The last thing I need is the attention of a journalist getting squashed flat after snooping around my property."

"I'm not a journalist," said Jack. He was cold, his jeans sticking to his legs.

"And you're not squashed flat either." They were at the top of the hill now. "You're welcome."

"I'm not complaining."

Curtis was massaging the leather on his steering wheel.

"You make everything worse, you know that?"

"I've been told."

"I mean it. Fuck, you're still not listening. People die on that road all the time. Not to mention what you've done to yourself crashing through the bush. You almost got yourself killed. Believe it or not, that's not what I want. I'd rather catch whoever's trying to frame me." Jack noticed when

Curtis was speaking that, even if it was obviously bullshit, he believed it so hard. As if he could conjure truth from sheer willpower alone.

But something was still strange. The person in shadow, as they fled from the road, had turned and yelled as the truck bore down. If it was the killer, why give Jack a warning?

"Who do you think it was?" Jack asked.

"Lauren didn't see them. But who do you think?" The accusation lay unspoken—*Andrew Freeman*. But he was on top of the tower. At least, he had been when Jack had left, and he'd only made it halfway down the drive. No way.

They were stopped out the front of the bed-and-breakfast. The engine hummed.

"Listen, Curtis." Jack struggled with the words. "Thank you."

"Go home, Jack. You don't need to be here. Someone's setting me up. You think I hated her because she sent me to jail? Someone bashed in the back of her head. With a single blow. And you think I hated her *so* much because she sent me away?" He leaned over and opened Jack's door, gave it an extra shove so it swung wide. "You're so obsessed with proving me wrong, you can't even see when you're actually right."

Curtis lowered his voice, almost reverentially, the tone that should be taken when talking about the dead—but not from this mouth, not with these words. "Because I did *hate* that bitch. But if I'd killed her, I would have done it slowly. Go home."

CHAPTER 18

Jack spent the next morning fast-forwarding through his old interviews. He could watch the interviews at speed, projecting himself back into his seat, clipboard in hand, to remember most of the conversations. He'd slow down when he needed to remember something better. The difference between the raw footage and the final cut was staggering. He'd interviewed Lauren and Vincent for four hours, and their cut had been a total of twenty-two minutes. Ian McCarthy had it worse. Jack was proud of the mise-en-scène on that one: They'd pulled over on the side of a dirt road, sun setting. Ian had sat on the trunk of his 4WD, his boots dangling above the dust. They'd talked for over an hour, but in episode 4, Ian had been trimmed to a slim six minutes.

Jack pressed Play on the raw footage. Ian was in the middle of telling him how they'd moved the body, intending to take Eliza to the hospital.

Ian: *It was when we picked her up that we realized she was actually pretty dead.*

Jack: *And then?*

Ian: *It sounds stupid, but it didn't seem real. I mean, yeah, she had her fingers in her mouth. That looked strange, but it didn't look real. So neither of us were sure what to do.*

Jack: *I'm not blaming you, Ian. It must have been hard to see whether she was alive or not. What did you do next?*

Ian: *Andrew went up to the house, while I stayed with the body and called for backup. When Andrew came back, he told me he'd arrested Curtis Wade. He said he'd cuffed him to something, and we had enough evidence.*

Jack: *How did he know for sure?*

Ian: *He said we had a witness.*

Jack: *A witness? There was no witness at the trial.*

Ian: *I know.*

Jack: *So all you had to go on was Andrew Freeman telling you he had enough evidence, and that was enough for you to know that Curtis was guilty?*

Ian: *Well, yeah. He's the sergeant. I believed him.*

Jack: *Even without any actual evidence? Just his word.*

Ian: *Even without evidence. I guess. Now that you mention it, I don't know what he actually meant. You're right, but it's a blur. I trusted what he told me, you know.*

Jack: *So tell me how you felt. Forget the trial and this show and everything. I just want to know your first impression.*

Ian: *As soon as we set foot on the property, I had a bad feeling. And by the time we left, yeah, we were certain Curtis was guilty.*

Jack rubbed his eyes. Andrew's witness had, of course, never surfaced. It was just an excuse to lay the cuffs on Curtis.

The interview was a gold mine; Jack had got his mileage out of the inferred bias here. He switched the file to episode 4, the final cut as it appeared in the show, and scrolled through to the scene with Ian. The interview started by zooming in on the beer beside Ian. Ian hadn't even drunk it, but it had been a hot day and Jack hadn't brought any water. (He had, but he didn't tell Ian that.) *Here, have this,* Jack had passed him a beer. *I don't want to look like I'm drinking on the job,* Ian had said. *We won't film it, just hold it against your neck if you want, to cool down.* Yet the shot lingered on the sweating can. Just to make Ian a little less reliable, a little more incompetent. *That's low,* thought Jack, *even for you.*

On-screen, they'd started to talk. Jack jacked up the volume.

Ian: *It was when we picked her up that we realized she was actu-*
        ally pretty dead.

Jack: *And then?*

Ian: *Andrew went up to the house, while I stayed with the body*
        and called for backup. When Andrew came back, he told me
        he'd arrested Curtis Wade. He said he'd cuffed him to some-
        thing, and we had enough evidence.

Jack: *How did he know for sure?*

Ian: *He said we had a witness.*

Jack: *A witness? There was no witness in the trial.*

Ian: *I know.*

Jack: *So all you had to go on was the fact that Andrew Freeman*
        had told you that he had enough evidence, and that was
        enough for you to know that Curtis was guilty?

Ian: *Well, yeah.*

Jack: *So tell me how you felt. Forget the trial and this show and*
        everything. I just want to know your first impression.

Ian: *As soon as we set foot on the property—even without*
        evidence—we were certain Curtis was guilty.

Jack had to close the laptop. He felt sick. He didn't remember cutting it together that badly. He'd edited out every bit of footage that may have made viewers sympathetic to Ian. He came across as dim, a bit conniving—part of the grand conspiracy against the Wades. He'd kept in that Ian hadn't known Eliza was even dead for the black comedy of it, ignoring his expla-nation that he would have been panicked, confused, and was just trying his best. But that didn't fit Jack's narrative either, so it had to go.

But worst of all was the final sentence.

Ian: *As soon as we set foot on the property—even without*
        evidence—we were certain Curtis was guilty.

Jack had even *cut away* from Ian's face to a shot of that stupid beer can, as he dubbed the words *even without evidence* (kidnapped from a different line of dialogue earlier in the interview) and spliced them into a new sentence, dropping out half the context in the process. Just like that, he'd created police bias.

He felt sick. It didn't feel like he was crafting a story anymore, as he had in the editing room, where he'd move things around only to achieve a better story. But this was so *real*. He was hurting people. Creating villains.

By the time he'd gorged himself on enough footage, the sun sat high enough to sluice through the venetians, throwing prison bars of shadow across his room. Jack got up and went to the mirror in the bathroom. His left eye was bloodshot, broken capillaries flooding the bottom of the socket in a crescent, a half-full wineglass. There was a slash on his cheek. Mixed with the only just recovering yellow of his nose, courtesy of Ted Piper, Jack had transformed into what the bigwigs call "off-camera talent." He felt a sudden surge of tiredness, sat down on the side of the bath. The toilet was just next to him, the lid up.

Andrew had lied to him about something, he was sure, but he didn't know what. He'd lied on the night of the murder as well. He didn't have anything worth putting Curtis in chains, apart from the coincidence of location and his own prejudice. There was no witness.

Alexis's funeral was tomorrow. He'd almost gotten himself killed yesterday. Why was he here? Who was he helping? He stood and spat in the toilet. Blood and mucus pirouetted in the water. He looked into the bowl. *Not today*, he thought. He sidestepped the speckling banana, still in his doorway, and went outside.

Alan Sanders served Jack a child's meal without complaint—chicken nuggets and fries. He rang it up as a rib eye, which was pricier than a chicken parma.

Jack hadn't planned on coming to the Royal exactly, but the main street lacked attractions. Besides, he knew eating on a schedule was important, and it was lunchtime. He couldn't start skipping now. His tightrope walker was wobbly enough as it was.

Pecking at his meal between sips of soda water, Jack thought about Andrew Freeman's property, his cellar, his in absentia wife. Jack's documentary had painted the conspiracy against Curtis Wade as being mostly led by the Freemans, without ever directly accusing them of murder, no matter what he'd had to deny afterward to prevent libel suits. What if his story was actually right, and Andrew *had* killed her and made Curtis the scapegoat? He shook his head. Maybe that was plausible for one murder—Eliza's—but not two. Andrew had no motive to kill Alexis. Neither did Curtis. Sitting next to him in the car last night, too exhausted and broken to be terrified by the veiled threat purring from Curtis's lips, Jack realized something else: he believed him.

Lauren thought it was the same killer. But maybe he was chasing a *new* killer, someone who just used the opportunity to murder Alexis. He thought about the threats Alexis received. He assumed the police were sifting through them. He called Ted Piper's office phone. If someone was going around threatening lawyers, that was the next best place to start. But he couldn't get through. The line must have been inundated with calls. *The office phone rings endlessly*, Alexis had told him. *We've had to switch it off.* No surprises there. It didn't bother Jack. Even if he had got through, Ted would've hung up on him, he figured.

Jack was getting used to the double take you had to do when exiting a building in Birravale, the squint, flat hand raised against the sun. Outside the Royal, a woman was crouched in front of a Forester, back door open, picking up cans and jars from the gutter. A broken plastic bag flapped in the breeze.

Jack walked over, knelt next to her.

"Need a hand?"

The woman looked up. Her light-blond hair was wisped with stress, from running her hand through it, strayed across her sweaty brow and cheeks. Sarah Freeman. She was swiping brown dust off her groceries, running a

finger down a bottle of milk where the dust was lumpy with the condensation. Jack picked up an orange, brushed it. It wasn't dust, Jack realized.
There was a broken glass jar in the bag. She'd cracked a jar of cinnamon.
They rescued the rest of the groceries: a few more escaped oranges, some
lemongrass, and another bottle of milk that had thankfully kept its lid. Sarah
shut the car door with a *thunk*. She threw the plastic bag into the bin outside
the Royal.

"Well, thanks," Sarah said without looking at him, and hopped in the car.

Jack walked back to the B and B. *Fuck this town*, he thought, lying on the
bed. He picked his nose, and the cinnamon under his fingernail made him
cough. He went to the bathroom to wash his hands. The toilet was beside
him, the lid still up. He flipped it down. Chicken nuggets were a bad choice.
Fried food. Fuck. Jack lay on the bed, feeling it inside him. He tried to doze
but couldn't. He felt heavy, a snake lazily digesting food, a lump inside him.
His head hurt. He got up, looked for Mary-Anne in the hallway, decided
it was safe enough. He went out to his car and flipped the floor covering in
the trunk, pulling out a toolbox he'd never used. He went back to his room
and sat the toolbox on the bed. He chose the right size screwdriver and set to
work on the hinges. He did the bottom first, tiny bits of wood spiraling out
from the frame like pencil shavings. When he'd finished the top hinge, the
door fell inward and he caught it, shuffled backward, and propped it against
the window. He lay back on the bed. The bathroom was open before him.

It wasn't much. A reminder not to lock himself away. A small touch
of home. The back of a bathroom door, hooks and hanging towels, and,
sometimes, a handle jiggling had been an image he'd lived with for too
long. It was pointless, he knew, taking the door off the frame. There was
always another door to shut yourself behind. All the same, he felt a little
more comfortable. The door's new position blocked out the sun from the
window, and the coolness of the bathroom tiles tempered the room. Jack
didn't remember falling asleep.

He woke after dark. Looked at his watch. *Lauren.*

CHAPTER 19

The glass door to the Wade restaurant was ajar.

Lauren was inside, behind the long rectangular service window that cordoned off the kitchen. She was cutting something. Meat. Jack caught a whiff. She had two out of eight gas burners going, blue flames in a grid, like a domino spotted with fire. She hadn't heard him come in. Her black hair was pulled into a ponytail, her shoulders rolled as she chopped, and her hair flicked and swung like a horse's tail. He noticed a string of knives across the back wall. They'd tested all of them. No matches. They hadn't expected a match anyway. Jack had learned a lot about killing: knives meant you had to saw through bone. Mangled as they were, Eliza's fingers came off quick. A meat cleaver, much more suitable, hung on the other side of the kitchen. It had also been tested. No match.

Jack thought about calling out to Lauren but decided instead to ding the silver service bell.

"Four fish for table fourteen," he said.

Lauren wiped a forearm against her brow. She smiled, cranked the gas knob nearest her off. Then she used the flat edge of her knife to scoot potatoes into her palm and flipped the potatoes onto two plates like a gambler rolling craps. She slid the first plate hard across the steel bench. Jack didn't realize he was supposed to catch it until it was almost at the edge—part of him was tempted to let it fly—but he blocked it with his hip and grabbed it. A potato made a break for freedom; Jack returned it to the plate among the others. He looked at the food: steak, a nice cut. Boiled broccoli on the side.

"Chef's out. So no fish," said Lauren. "Fuck table fourteen."

She came through the swinging kitchen doors, her plate in hand. "Feels good to say that. The entitlement of some of these Sydney tourists that come up for a weekend in"—she adopted a pompous tone, crossed her eyes, and looked down her nose—"*wine country.*" She returned to normal. "'The customer is always right,' they say. Try thinking that after running a winery for two weeks."

"Vineyard."

"Pardon?"

"Nothing."

She put her plate on the bar, went behind it, and pulled on a loop in the floor. The wooden board lifted and settled back on its hinges. Beneath, there was a compact wine cellar, the wine all bottled and stored in latticed racks, like Andrew's, but in units that looked like giant fridges, glass doors inlaid with LED lighting. It looked like the inside of a spaceship, four large, humming units glowing gently. *Tacky*, the locals would say; Jack now realized that Birravale conflated that word with *new*. Buried in the past, this town, scared of the future. He imagined the people of Birravale milling around, scratching at lesions. *Did you hear Margery's gone and got the smallpox vaccination? Pfft. Tacky. No respect for history.* Lauren emerged with a bottle, eased the cellar door shut, and retrieved her plate.

"Why not just build this over the old site?" Jack said, following her to a table—they were all set up for service, which was eerie—at the center of the parabolic windows. "Surely it's cheaper to refit the cellar and restaurant than knock it down and rebuild in a different spot?" *Not to mention*, Jack thought, *if you didn't piss off the old owner making him knock down his pride and joy, he wouldn't have ruined your land by concreting it.*

"Curtis wanted to make his own mark," Lauren said, pulling out a chair. She shot a glance up the hill and shook her head. "Such *boys.* Like dogs pissing on trees."

The night yawned before them, and at first, all Jack could see was black. His eyes slowly adjusted. From their table, he had a panoramic view of the vineyard. Andrew might prefer to look down on everyone, but the view was just as good from here.

There was a small light up the hill, in the air. Almost a star. It was Andrew's lantern, Jack guessed, on top of the silo. Was he up there? Could he see them?

"Hope steak's okay. We don't really have the full menu at the moment. We'll need a new chef when we reopen."

"You had to let them go?" His stomach rose as if on a tide, his impact on the town confronting him again, like the wine stains in all these different houses. *You ruined a lot of reputations*, Andrew had said.

"Thank God, actually. He was a shitty chef; we wanted to fire him for ages. I suppose that's one good thing that's come out of this." She laughed gently and then quieted, examining Jack, whose face must have betrayed him. "I didn't actually mean that. Just trying to... I don't know. Just trying not to think about the worst of it. Sorry."

"It's fine. I got the joke."

"Tough crowd." Lauren raised her eyebrows. "Are you always this jittery? No wonder you throw my brother off balance. Shall I open this?" She stabbed the bottle at him.

"Only if you want. I don't really drink."

She thought for a minute and then put the wine to one side.

"Well, eat," she said. "You're too skinny. I could drink wine from those collarbones."

"I'm sorry?" Jack shifted in his seat.

"I think that's in a poem I read once. If we're going to work together, Jack, you're going to have to loosen up." She started eating. Jack put half a potato in his mouth because she was watching, mushed it against the back of his teeth. Sludge.

Work together? She thought *she* was recruiting *him*. Team Curtis.

"You want me to help you prove Curtis innocent?"

"No, actually. I don't. I said I want us to work together."

"You'll help me prove him guilty? You think he did it?"

She shook her head, sawed a piece of steak, popped it in her mouth, and spoke while chewing. "No. But you do. And that's important. I figure devil's advocates are the best way to go about something like this. We've got different information. Fuck it. I'm opening this. No?" Another jab of the bottle.

Jack shook his head.

"Listen. My family lives under this shadow. *I* live under this shadow. Eliza, Alexis, they block out the sun. My surname is spit in people's mouths. You're not getting anywhere on your own, are you? I'll give you everything you need. You can come onto the property. You can talk to Curtis. Never alone." She must have seen the look on his face. "I'll be there. You can look through the house, the yard, the restaurant. Tear apart the shed if you need to. I don't care. But in return, I need your perspective and your ear. I want to know what you know. You have more details of the investigation side of things. You've got a link to that new detective. I know there's more evidence somewhere."

Jack set his face, gave nothing away, not least that his link to Winter was more that he might be arrested by him eventually.

"You can't fit everything into one miniseries. I need to know everything behind the scenes. And you know you need me too." She'd rehearsed this speech, Jack realized. She opened the bottle and poured herself a glass.

"Does Curtis know about this?"

She nodded.

"And if he's guilty?"

"If you *prove* him guilty. I'll accept that."

She was right. He needed her perspective. Her access to the property and her candor. The police had overturned the property with warrants and SWAT teams in tactical vests with assault rifles. But they'd done it four years too late, the case solved so quickly first time around. Maybe the truth was overgrown, covered in weeds. And they'd never had the Wades' cooperation. Maybe Lauren knew something and didn't even know it.

"Why are you really doing this?" he said.

"Do you have a brother?"

Jack nodded.

"You know what it's like then. You're supposed to stick up for them."

Whump.

He knew.

"Your brother," said Jack, "he's quite a bit older than you. It must be an odd family dynamic."

"Yeah, maybe," Lauren said. "I don't really think about it. You know how some people want to know the meaning of life or whatever? Why we're here?"

"We're getting philosophical now?"

"I just mean that I *do* know why I'm here. Why is any child a decade younger than their sibling?" Jack nodded in recognition. "You got it. I was born to save my parents' marriage. They hoped I'd help them reconnect. And I know what you're thinking." She must have seen the dark glimmer across Jack's face as he remembered Lauren's mother hadn't made it through her birth. "How's that for an existential crisis? My purpose was to bring my family closer together. Imagine messing up your entire existence before you've even opened your eyes."

"Family loyalty? That's why you want to help your brother?"

She wrinkled her nose. "You're overanalyzing me. I don't really know how I feel. But I think last night was evidence in my brother's favor. Alexis's killer is out here looking for something. So we need to nail this copycat fella."

He nodded again. She'd said previously she *didn't* think it was a copycat, but it seemed she was coming around.

"Listen, all I know is that women around my brother keep turning up dead." She paused. "Don't make me say it. The killer was *in my house*, Jack."

And there was the real truth. Lauren was scared. It was so simple. But it was also a subtle guilt trip, part of her polished speech: *If you don't help me, can you live with another dead woman on your hands?* Expertly done. She should make TV.

"That'll go cold, if you don't start it. Then, I know you've been itching to take a walk through here." She pointed to the window. *See what I can offer?*

She was right though; he was at a dead end without her. And if he walked away and something happened to her... He ate a few bites because he didn't want to talk and she'd noticed how little he'd put in his mouth. Two meals today. The tightrope thrummed. Jack's internal acrobat wobbled, one leg in the air, poised like a wishbone.

"We can try," he said finally. "But let's be clear. I think your brother is a monster. I still think he killed Eliza, but I can't prove it. Alexis, I'm open to suggestion. But he's a killer. You won't change my mind."

"Honesty is all I'm asking. Tell me everything you know. Do we have an agreement?"

Lauren raised her glass. Jack raised an imaginary one in return. They'd work together to work against each other. A deal.

"To innocence," she said.

"To guilt."

CHAPTER 20

Lauren and Jack circled into the vineyard. The temperature in the air had dropped, but the stones on the drive still held the heat of the day. The sky was so clear he didn't need a flashlight. The small light up the hill was gone now. Jack's cheeks felt bunched and swollen, his eyes stinging. He'd had too much sun today.

He'd done too much walking too. Far beyond his supervised allowance at the treatment center. Also, more eating than he was accustomed to, managing half his steak in prideful swallows before succumbing to the excuse of a big lunch. A fucking *kid's meal*. He could feel the food inside him, acutely aware of where it sat. It swelled, an island, the seas of his stomach sloshing against it. But the cliff faces of that island weren't eroding and falling into the sea, as they should have been. Instead, they were taking hold, scuttling ships and pulling more rocks into their tide. Clogging him up. He felt it. His acrobat, arms extended, wandered from shipwreck to shipwreck, mast to mast, above the jagged outcrop and vicious seas. Twirling his baton, jester's hat wobbling, bells ringing. The sea arced beneath the acrobat, spat up, hissed. Understanding the science inside yourself is part of accepting it, the nurses had said, so he tried to think about digestion, about food broken down. Because no matter how you prepared it, if you took away the smells and the colors and the textures, food was just sludge. The shit that went in was the same as the shit that came out, just skipping a few steps. The jester bells kept ringing. A small piece of the cliff crumbled and splashed into the acid. Lauren was talking to him.

"Where we're walking now, this is where the patrol car drove in."

"The first question is, why was she on your property at all?" Jack asked.

"It's a public winery. I mean, normally we invite only the restaurant guests to wander around. But there's nothing to stop someone else."

"Did she eat at the restaurant?"

"Well, I think we would have noticed if someone who's been away for eight months came in for a meal." She put her hands on her hips. "We did check, and no. The police checked our bank records and interviewed the staff."

"So she isn't at the restaurant, which means she comes in off the road"—Jack pointed at the junction where the asphalt hooked right and turned to pebbles—"and then walks"—he looked along the fence line, bordered by vines, down to where she died—"this way?"

Jack looked along the fence line for breaks, anything odd where someone could have come in. Lauren followed two paces behind. The grass was short and lush; it folded under his feet. Even if the police hadn't butchered the initial investigation, footprints would have still been impossible to come by unless it was wet. A few hundred meters along, the fence curved away from the road and then stopped at the patch of bushland where Jack had found Eliza's shoe. Behind them, the vines ran up toward the restaurant. Halfway between the bushland and the restaurant was where the body had been found.

"There's no way she could have gotten from there to here." Jack pointed at the northwest corner, all the way across the yard, where supposedly her footprints had been found. The truth of that was obvious. They both knew she hadn't been killed there.

"What if she was draped over someone's shoulder?" Lauren asked.

"It's possible. Hard to tell, everything was so jumbled. Curtis's footprints were all over the place."

"It's his winery."

"I know. I'm just making the point."

"Wheelbarrow?"

"Heavy, again, weighed down with a body. Those tracks would

probably be clearer. Even they wouldn't have missed that." And again, the problem was that all of these were relatively normal for a winery. Footprints, wheelbarrow tracks, a ride-on mower—not incriminating.

"So she fell from the sky." Lauren shrugged. "I think the question is less how she got here and more where she was really killed. If we can find that, we'll know how she got here."

"And if Curtis put her here. The question is why." Jack paced back and forth, the ground alternating from wet to dry. Irrigation. It was unmown. Longish grass, knotted together. And the larger question plagued him, the one Jack had built his series on: Why would Curtis place the body here, with all signs pointing back to him?

"Humor me—he planted a body that led right to him?" Lauren must have been reading his thoughts.

"That's the tricky part."

"Andrew Freeman broke our windows," she said, as if that equated to murder. "He hated the new restaurant. This is where the old one was. Do you think it's some kind of message? That there's some meaning beneath the body being right here?" She stamped her feet in a dull thud, as if to illustrate the point.

"Andrew didn't break your windows."

"He did. I told you, it's a pissing contest."

"Brett Dawson's sons broke your windows, so you'd hire them to fix it. It was a cash grab, not a feud."

She thought about that for a minute. "Fuck."

"Let's keep going," said Jack, and they walked back to the edge of the bush, turned, and continued along the property line. They soon reached the point where Eliza had smoked a cigarette. Jack had been right in his guesswork in his kitchen—the line of sight from the Freeman restaurant windows was clear. From the top of the silos, clearer still. Jack tried to picture Eliza, arms wrapped around herself, stamping her feet from the cold. On a clear night, a small ember *might* have been visible from up the hill. Even if Andrew had seen someone—and he hadn't, or so he said—there was no way he'd know *who* it was. Why did this cluster of footprints bother Jack? What was so interesting about a cigarette?

"Her footprints were here, yeah?" Lauren pointed at the ground.

"Yeah. Well. Maybe hers," Jack said, poker-faced.

"Gee," Lauren said, "your case would be a lot more solid if we knew that." She meant it as a joke, not knowing that he was the only one who could place Eliza there. Jack didn't know what to say. He swallowed. He ran his tongue along the back of his teeth. His acrobat wobbled.

"I'm thinking about all of this," Lauren continued. "And don't some killers want to get caught?" She was clearly more able to jump across to his perspective than he was to hers. "They write letters to the police. All that psycho stuff?"

"Maybe in the movies," Jack said.

"I hate that."

"Hate what?"

"Serial killers in movies. They're always supposed to be these incredible geniuses. Twisted souls but clever, deep. Deserving of their own"—she hunted for the word—"kind of mythology, I guess. They're celebrities now, for fuck's sake: Zodiac, Jack the Ripper, the Nail-Biter Killer. Whoever killed Eliza, they weren't some *genius*. Even those other words they use for criminals—*psychopath*, *sociopath*—make them sound too interesting. This is no mastermind. This is a killer of women. Nothing more."

For the first time, there was a hard edge to Lauren's tone. She hated whoever killed these women as much as he did. The world on her shoulders at the age of twenty. They kept walking, now around the house, toward the tip of the driveway.

"Eliza had a story to sell," Jack said. "She said she'd seen something. I'm wondering if it was enough to kill over. Did she ever say anything to you?"

She hesitated slightly, thinking. "No. Like I said, we knew each other, but it wasn't really a tight friendship. I'll tell you what though, I have

listened to that message, and the strange thing is—she didn't sound scared."
Jack nodded in agreement. Lauren sighed. "Another in a series of if onlys.
If only he'd called her back. Tell you what, I'm sick of these fucking
journalists. Present company excluded, of course."

"I'm not a journalist."

"Oh. Yeah."

"And what about Andrew Freeman's *witness*?"

"Andrew Freeman's full of shit," Lauren said. "I don't know why he
was so convinced it was my brother, unless he *wanted* it to be my brother."

Jack nodded again; that was what he'd said in the show.

"The cops think Alexis's murderer might be a boyfriend," Jack said,
starting to feel he was pushing Lauren too hard. "So there's no genius there.
Just blind rage, a king hit." She looked at him dully, so he added, rotating
his fingers back and forth between them, "In the interest of sharing."

"Now you're getting it," she said brightly, momentary sullenness gone.
"Look at us, a regular Robin and Watson." He was about to correct her
when she continued, "Because sidekicks do all the work."

"That's why the cops don't think it was Curtis. They're pretty confident Alexis's murder was staged."

"Did you know her boyfriend?"

Jack shook his head. "She had a second phone. The cops didn't know
about it."

"But you do?"

"They know now. But no one knows who this guy is. She took a call
on it when we met up. Before—"

"What does this have to do with Eliza?"

"I don't know. But that's why I think Curtis might be low on their list
of suspects."

"So they think the crimes are unrelated?" Lauren was thoughtful.

Jack had assumed she'd be happy about this, but she seemed more
confused. "Legally speaking, they are."

"Do you? I mean, we're talking about a copycat now, right?"

"It might have been a crime of opportunity. Which means it wasn't a deliberate copycat, rather a convenient shield. Curtis might be a mask, not a target. I think knowing what happened to Eliza will help us solve Alexis's murder. Two killers though…" He shrugged.

"Is that all the police are going on?"

No, Jack thought. "Yes," Jack said.

Jack could practically hear Lauren's Rolodex of evidence whirring in her brain. "Anything else useful you can think of?"

Plenty, Jack thought. *Your brother is a killer of women.*

He didn't answer her question. "Alexis and Curtis didn't"—he could barely get it out—"see each other outside of court, did they?"

Before Lauren could answer, a third voice cut them off.

"He wishes."

They were at the driveway, at the point where the ever-changing landscape of the pebbles precluded footprints. The point where Eliza disappeared from the earth. The front deck of the Wade house was on their right. Eliza could have easily walked straight up and knocked on the door. Gone inside the house without leaving a trace.

Curtis was leaning against the railing, drinking out of an enamel mug. "Having fun with your friend, Lauren? You're lucky she thinks you're useful, Jack."

Lauren ignored him. Turned to Jack. "Do you want to come back tomorrow?" Then she whispered, "He'll settle down."

"Alexis's funeral," Jack said.

"Oh. Shit. Doesn't make sense us both driving. Can I hop in with you?"

"You're going?"

"She stuck up for my family. Of course I'm going. Besides, her killer boyfriend might be there."

Jack wondered if that was disrespectful. Then again, he hadn't even thought of it. It was a good opportunity to have a look around.

"You're at Mary-Anne's?" she asked. "See you tomorrow, then."

Jack gave a noncommittal nod. He was aware of Curtis watching them. He couldn't be seen at the funeral with Lauren, but he'd have to talk her out of it tomorrow.

Lauren bounded up the stairs, gesturing for Curtis to come inside. He turned to put an arm around her, but she weaved out from under it, recoiling at his touch. This must be so hard for both of them. A family without a mother or a father now. Both of them untethered, their surname hated, not just by this one small town but the whole country. Lauren had some broad shoulders to take all that on. It was more than self-preservation, he thought, and more than being scared. She wanted to see justice for these dead women, the right person in prison.

She opened the door, guiding Curtis inside now. Jack heard her mutter something about it being time to go in, admonishing him for what was in his cup. A murmured protest. She gave a retort, not properly heard but Jack got enough of her tone and cadence to guess the words: *I can smell it, Curtis.*

CHAPTER 21

Lauren bobbled in the passenger seat next to Jack. He'd tried to sneak out early, stepping over the blackening banana in his doorway, but Lauren had already been there, sitting on his car hood, legs swinging in the air. She was wearing a black pantsuit with a white blouse, barefoot, her high heels perched on the roof. Jack didn't have the heart to argue; he tossed his bag in the back and they got in. Five minutes into the drive, Lauren buzzed down the window, stuck an arm out, hooked her heels with her fingertips and brought them back inside.

An hour later, they still hadn't spoken. Lauren's jiggling head matched the bumps in the road, and Jack didn't know what was pissing him off more: the elasticity of her neck or the fact that she was sitting next to him at all, which meant that he had to go back to Birravale. Though Mary-Anne hadn't asked him to check out, and he hadn't returned his key either. He was going back whether he liked it or not.

"Do you think they'll be there?" Lauren broke the silence as they purred across the Sydney Harbor Bridge.

"Who?"

"The murderer." She angled herself around in her seat, practically leaning out the window to glimpse the sails of the opera house. Jack didn't bother. Like every other Sydney commuter, he'd become numb to the majesty of the bridge and what was around it. Sure, the bridge was one of the architectural marvels of the world. But it was also just the way to work for any Sydney-sider. It still looked incredible from the aerial photos, but up close, you could barely see the opera house for the barbed-wire enclosed walkways, the train tracks, and the traffic. The opera house's supposedly pristine white sails were rust dark with water stains. Up close, seeing how things were built, the majesty was removed. Just like people themselves, the nuts and the bolts of them, the traumas and the bruises. Everyone liked the final product, but no one wanted to see it close enough to know how it was all stitched together. Just like his TV show.

Jack peeled off to the Cahill Expressway, which quickly opened up a better view of Circular Quay, the opera house, and the bridge. He feathered the brake in sympathy to let Lauren have a proper look. Then they dipped into a tunnel and into the eastern suburbs, weaving through town houses and roadworks. Another twenty minutes and they were in the beachside suburb of Maroubra. Jack slowed as they came up to Alexis's family church; he'd planned to park around the corner, so he and Lauren wouldn't arrive together. The church itself was old and regal, with rough, large-bricked walls. The front facade was peaked and triangular, though the stained-glass window and large wooden double doors were both arch shaped. The way the roof peaked, that triangular prism, the angularity of it, it looked almost like Andrew's or Curtis's country homestead. If you added a veranda, wood instead of stone, you could worship at that altar.

The churchyard was empty, the street not yet clogged with cars. They had an hour and a half until the service started.

"We're way too early," Lauren said, as if it wasn't her fault Jack had tried to sneak out early. "Coffee?"

Jack certainly didn't want to be the first one there. The last sight the grieving family needed was him sitting in a pew with Curtis Wade's sister next to him. That was next-level gate-crashing.

There'd be coffee shops by the beach, he figured. He parked on the main road. Lauren sat with her door open to put on her shoes. One of the heels was roughly glued on. Jack supposed she barely had use for heels in the country; these were funeral and court-case shoes only. Jack was in jeans and a T-shirt; he hadn't wanted to drive in his suit. He got his bag out of the back and pointed to a public toilet block down near the water.

"I have to change."

"I'll order you something," Lauren said, gesturing to a café over the road. "What do you want?"

"What you get," Jack said.

The road ran parallel to the beach. The sea hissed and rolled like it was boiling. Some tiny black dots were out far, bobbing up and down, waiting for the temperamental sea to serve them something they could use. Jack wasn't close enough for spray to fleck his cheek, but salt hung in the air, opened his nostrils. There were two men showering in the open showers just off the parking lot, a surfboard propped against the railing beside them. One was half-in, half-out of a wet suit, which was hanging off him like the black skin of a rotten banana, peeled to the waist. The other man was in his underwear, thick black hair on his chest, facing up into the stream with cupped hands around his cheeks, letting the water pepper his face. Shampoo foam bled out of his hair. Either a vain man, Jack thought, to bring his own hair products to the beach, or a backpacker.

The toilet block had a polished concrete floor and wet, crunchy sand underfoot that hung together in clumps. Glued together by salt and piss. Jack locked himself in a cubicle—there was a steel toilet without a seat— and changed by draping his clothes over the door, standing on his sneakers. He wobbled as he threaded his trousers one leg at a time. This wasn't how it used to be. He used to put his knees on such a floor if he had to. Any floor used to do. Not today.

Walking back out in his suit—which, being gray, he hoped was reverential enough—Jack saw one of the men drying himself in the parking lot and changing into proper clothes, half-shielded by the door of his car. Jack recognized the car first—a silver SUV. He caught a glimpse inside: filthy, the opposite of Andrew Freeman's vacuumed carpets. Then he properly saw the man—it was Ted Piper. Out for a surf before the funeral. Jack's first thought was that it wasn't very respectful; his second was that Ted had never struck him as a surfer. But he knew hardcore surfers didn't care for such things as grief, if the ocean's calling. They chased that pull, addicted to the drama of the sea. The swell, bro, it's irresistible. Funeral or not.

Jack hurried back toward the café. He definitely didn't need a confrontation with Ted before the funeral. And perhaps sipping a soy latte with a potential serial killer's sister wasn't very respectful either.

Because there was a pull on Jack as well, just like Ted and the ocean, that same addiction to the drama. Lauren was sitting outside; she waved. The swell, bro, it's irresistible. She'd ordered food. He really fucking wanted it.

Jack told Lauren that he'd go first, and she could follow in fifteen minutes.

"You're like a high schooler getting dropped at school by their mum," she said, but agreed.

"I thought you were homeschooled?" Jack said.

"Jesus, Jack. Creepy much?"

"If having a team of researchers look into a woman is creepy..." He got out of the car.

People were still milling on the large stone steps of the church, and Jack willed them to start heading in. He knew he couldn't get in and out completely unnoticed, but he still wanted to minimize the attention. David Winter and Ian McCarthy were talking by the door. Winter was using his hands. McCarthy, at least a foot taller, was nodding. Around them, people started to move, splitting around the policemen, as if tidal, filtering through the large, arched doors. Winter produced a manila envelope, handed it to McCarthy, patted him on the back, and joined the current of black backs into the church.

Jack watched as Ian squeezed the sides so the mouth of the envelope opened. He glanced into the church, then at the envelope in his hand. He thought for a second and then stepped quickly down the stairs, over to his Toyota. He didn't need to open the door; country cars always have their windows cracked. Ghosts of blue heelers in the back, Jack supposed. Ian slid the envelope through the window onto the passenger seat, as if posting a letter, then hurried up the steps and into the church.

The mingling on the steps had thinned. Jack didn't recognize any faces. Now was as good a time to make his entrance as any. He crossed the street, taking the long way behind the back of Ian McCarthy's car. Curious, Jack peered in through the window. There was a McDonald's coffee in the console. The yellow envelope was on the passenger seat. The window was descended generously into the sill.

Jack stood there awhile. *Last favor*, he thought, recalling his text message to Ian. He figured people might look over if he hovered too long, so he got moving, rubbing his shoulder.

As at the police station, there was a hush when he walked into the church. A few seconds of silence. Then a sound like crinkling paper, whispers trickling through the gathering.

I didn't think he'd come.

Who told him it was on?

Someone should ask him to leave.

He took a seat in the last pew, scooted to the end. People swiveled to catch a glimpse of him. Lauren would fare better—not as many people would recognize her. But if they caught on—if that whisper rippled through the church when she came in—they'd both have to leave, and quickly. It wouldn't take much to explode this powder keg of grief.

Heavy piano music ricocheted off the stone walls. Alexis's coffin was on the altar, open at the midpoint and lined with white satin. But the coffin was empty. The ever-cautious Winter must be hanging on to Alexis's body. The family would have a smaller, private ceremony later. Jack looked around. On one wall, a projector cycled through photos of Alexis. There was one of her in a mortarboard, holding a scroll, graduating from law school. Another of her hiking. One of her drinking from a comically large stein in Europe. He wondered if Eliza's family had put together a slideshow, if they had pored over the images to choose those that best captured her life. How had they felt when the memories they'd chosen to remember her by were replaced by billboards and TV ads of her bone-white skin and strangled neck?

He scanned the gathering. The church was filling up with familiar faces. Many of them from the same faux-family that had followed Eliza's ghost through Sydney, those interns and film crews and journalists who had come to know Alexis. Cameramen normally seen exclusively in cargo shorts with Bose headphones cradled around their necks, who wouldn't wear a tuxedo at their own wedding, were stuffed into black suits. He saw Lauren sidle in the back, clock him, and stand in the opposite corner. He silently thanked her for her discretion. Winter hadn't taken a pew; he was standing by the door. Was he investigating the room or here to pay his respects? Ted was there too, hair still wet, in his favorite blue suit. He'd found a seat near the middle. This was almost more a networking event than a funeral.

And, on top of it all, there might be a killer here too. The pew creaked as Ian McCarthy shuffled in beside Jack.

"I didn't know you were coming," said Jack, even though he'd seen him outside. Ian's jacket had patches of dust on the shoulders. He was another man Jack had never seen out of jeans that doubled as a dish towel. "It's odd seeing you like this."

"Whole bloody thing's odd. Poor girl," McCarthy whispered.

People were looking at them talk.

"You don't have to sit next to me," Jack said.

"She would've wanted you here."

"She would have preferred none of us were here, I think."

Ian fiddled with his tie. "Just wanted to let you know you've still got some friends. You got a program?"

Jack held his up. It was a folded booklet with an image of creeping vines on the front. *In Loving Memory*. A phone rang somewhere in the church. Someone mumbled, "Sorry, always forget that," and turned it off.

"I've been thinking," McCarthy said. "You still reckon Andrew Freeman might be a bad egg?"

Jack turned slightly, aware of the rustle of his jacket. It was a papery crinkle, too loud in the church. "It's a line of inquiry," he said.

"Three million worth of damage," Ian said. "You think it's enough to kill over?"

"Not sure." Andrew's words echoed: *It's not real money.*

"Thing is…" Ian looked at his hands. "He didn't claim it."

"What?"

"The three mill is guesswork. Andrew wouldn't have the insurers out. He didn't lodge a claim. Never a dollar in. Apparently."

"Why wouldn't you lodge a three-million-dollar insurance claim?"

Ian shrugged. "I thought that too. I'm no finance cop. Maybe it means something, maybe it doesn't. But I thought you'd like to know. Strange, hey?" Ian nodded, information passed on. He shuffled out.

Jack tried to process the information. Andrew didn't want an insurer out to his property? That made sense if Andrew was up there strangling people. But Andrew had seemed so benign, and he hadn't cared about the money, so there wasn't any motive. But then why lie about a witness? Unless putting Curtis behind bars really was just small-town bigotry. Prejudicial police work rather than a deliberate effort to hide anything more sinister. Still, Andrew wasn't in the church today, Jack noted.

Again, Jack thanked his luck that Ian McCarthy didn't watch TV, that he thought Netflix was a brand of screen doors. *You've cost a lot of people their jobs.* Thankfully, Ian seemed to be doing okay despite how Jack had smeared him. Besides, Jack thought, it was a reputation not so unearned. Not ten minutes ago, Ian had left a yellow envelope exposed, behind an alluringly cracked window that an arm—not any arm, but a particularly skinny one, perhaps—could reach, depending on the owner's willingness to risk a bruised shoulder.

Jack absentmindedly rubbed his shoulder again.

The service was starting. Jack picked up the program and opened it, could barely pay attention to the first hymn. He checked behind him. Winter wasn't looking, and Lauren was leaning against the wall with her arms crossed. He was safe, tucked away in the corner. Jack opened his jacket pocket and withdrew the envelope. It had made the worryingly loud crinkle as he'd moved to welcome Ian. Jack unfolded it, peeked inside. Photos. Splayed hair on a steel table. A bloodied and bruised face. Severed fingers. Photocopies of reports too. He looked up at the altar. The priest was beginning to talk. Photos of Alexis flashed beside him on the wall. Jack looked down in his lap, and Alexis stared back up at him there too.

After the service, everyone was welcomed to visit the community hall next door for a cup of tea and cake. The priest seemed to hang on the word *everyone*. Jack might have been imagining it, but there seemed to be a shift in the air. The people in front of him looked like they were itching to turn around. They needn't have worried; Jack was leaving right away. Unfortunately, they only opened the door beside the altar, which led straight into the wake. Jack waited until the end of the line had mostly faded down to the stragglers hanging back to talk to the priest. Someone shut the projector off with a clunk and the room dimmed, Alexis disappearing. The envelope rustled in his breast pocket as he stood. He smoothed it. It should be easy enough to walk straight through the hall and out the door.

It wasn't. The community hall was packed. Long tables of cakes and square-cut sandwiches lined each wall. A card table with a hulking steel coffee urn was at the back. Grief requires energy. People turned as he entered, though Jack avoided eye contact. He was used to the dullness in the air when he walked into a room now. He just wanted out. The fastest way to the door was by going around the end of the trestle tables, walking through the gap between the food and the door. He couldn't see Lauren. She'd already be outside. They'd agreed to meet at the car.

"Bringing a date to a funeral. That's low. Even for you," Ted Piper said when Jack was halfway to the door. Thankfully, there was a table separating them. Ted had half a sandwich in his mouth and a handful of cakes and other morsels on a paper plate. He was picking more off the platters and adding to the pile.

"Who do you—"

"I saw you at the café."

"We're not at war, are we?" Jack pointed to Ted's stockpiled plate.

"Fuck off." Ted licked his fingers. "Why is Lauren here?"

"Alexis was her family's lawyer. I imagine they knew each other."

"That's not what I'm asking. Why did you *bring* her here?"

"I have to g—"

"I know you're hanging around out there." Ted lowered his voice. "You think that will make it better? Look around."

"You think I don't know that?" Jack hissed, trying to keep the hurt in his voice to a whisper. A few people turned, aware that a table might get flipped soon. "You think I don't know that all these people are here because of me? That one person isn't?"

Jack didn't want to argue. He took a step for the door. On the other side of the room, Winter was shouldering his way through the crowd toward them. Jack was conscious of the envelope in his pocket. McCarthy, likewise, was looking curiously over now.

"I don't know whose side you're on." Ted kept pace, walking a parallel track, as if both of them were stuck on rails. "I've been digging too. Yeah, that's right, on my own. No chain of evidence, no discovery. Just what I can find and where I can stick it. I'm taking pages from your playbook now. And I'll have enough soon. You're not the only one who can build a story. Lauren wouldn't testify at the trial. You should know that."

"There are no sides anymore, Ted. I'm leaving. And I know she didn't testify." He knew all the witnesses inside out. Neither the prosecution nor the defense had needed Lauren. She hadn't seen anything. He put his hands in the air and stepped backward in what he hoped was a sign of clear surrender. Everyone around them let out a breath. Mostly relief. Some disappointment.

"That's what I'm telling you. Not *didn't*," Ted called after him, "*wouldn't.*"

That gave Jack pause. He was in the door now, sun warming his face. Lauren was standing in the courtyard, waiting, unaware of what was happening inside. Ted's parting shot came from behind.

"She's lying to you, Jack. Ask her about the night of the murder."

CHAPTER 22

"Wait here. I have to get something."

Jack stopped in his Kensington driveway and opened his door. Lauren opened her door too. Jack shot her a look. He wasn't sure he wanted her in his house. *She's lying to you.* Ted might be manipulating him, but still. Jack was waiting for the drive home to ask her about her testimony, where he'd have her cornered for two hours. In the meantime, he had a yellow envelope in his pocket that he didn't want her to see, and he needed a few of his own files from Eliza's case.

"You're coming in?" he asked.

"You want me to wait in the car?"

"I'll be quick."

"Fuck that." Lauren missed his tone and followed him. At the door, she dragged a finger under one of his wilted pot plant's ferns. She held the frond up, then slid her finger away and let it flop. She made a humming sound. Disapproval. The door swung open, and Jack led her into his home.

"It's freezing in here," she said.

"I'll just be a minute," Jack said, and headed up the stairs. He lived in a two-story town house, like Alexis's but cheaper, though he'd paid it off now. (*Who says crime doesn't pay?* his father had said when Jack told him.) He headed into the bedroom and opened his closet. Inside were half a dozen filing boxes bursting with notes, black permanent marker scribbled on each. *Interviews. Court Documents.* Jack had kept everything just in case. In these boxes was the truth of the case, before he cut it together. The box he was looking for was stacked under the *Finance* box. The Wade family assets tabulated, their wealth *significant.* The expenditure on the restaurant was no-holds-barred. And then the older accounts, the $35,000 handwritten invoice from Brett Dawson's The Concrete Company to the former owner, Whittaker, flitted past him. Jack mused at Brett's company name; country towns really suck at naming companies. He imagined the office, adorned like the bakery with blue ribbons from the local fair—*Highly Commended, Concrete Pour, Footpath Division 2004*. He sifted through more files, handwritten notes, and audiotapes: the rainbow glint of CDs, silver side up. So much written down and recorded, yet he'd turned it into so little truth. Farther back, behind his files, was the small shoebox. Jack reached in and opened it. The sneaker was surprisingly intact for four years in the bush. It *must* have been planted. But by who? *The real killer.*

"I figured out why it's freezing." Lauren's voice from the doorway made him jump. He closed the shoebox and shoved it back, grabbed the box labeled *Forensics*, and pulled it out instead. Lauren rapped his doorframe with her knuckles and said, as if he might not have noticed, "You've got no fucking doors."

"I'm redecorating."

"What if I need to take a shit?"

"Sing," Jack said.

"What?"

"If you're singing, I'll know you're in there."

Lauren assessed him. "You don't have much company, do you?"

"I don't often invite people around to take a shit, no." Jack picked the box up and placed it on the bed.

"You okay?" Lauren took a step toward him.

"Can you just—" Jack sighed. "Can you go?"

She walked over, sat on the bed, put her hand on the forensics box. Jack held the lid down.

"What about sharing?" she said.

"Ted Piper told me something at the funeral."

"Oh. Okay." Her eyes flickered downward. *She's lying to you.*

"So, you tell me. What about sharing?"

Lauren stood up; the bedsprings creaked. "What do you want to know?"

"Everything that happened the night Eliza died."

Lauren ran a hand through her bangs and sat back down again. "You want to know about Eliza. Okay. I'm Andrew Freeman's witness."

She took a breath, calmed. "We were all waiting in the lounge room for the police. The sergeant was first; he took me aside and asked me a bunch of questions. I don't remember them all, but I— He asked me if I'd seen or heard anything. I said I'd heard Curtis get up. I wasn't sure what time, around midnight."

Jack nodded, piecing it together. "But you took it back," he guessed, "so your statement never made it to trial?"

She nodded. "Dad was *so* mad. He said our family was supposed to be a team. And when I really thought about it, I couldn't actually be sure. It was, like, two in the morning when he was questioning us. I couldn't tell if what I heard was the house settling or people moving or anything really, if maybe I'd dreamed it. And Andrew was asking me *so* many questions. I was tired and I was stressed and I screwed up, okay?"

Jack put an arm on her shoulder: fatherly, protective. He could imagine Andrew Freeman beating her with questions until he pulled the answers he wanted out of her.

"It barely mattered," Lauren said, "that I didn't have to testify at the initial trial. It was finished before it started. The prosecution didn't even have to try. Until your documentary began and the conspiracy theories came into play. Then suddenly the frame-up was the center of the defense's strategy, and I guess I became important again. I begged Alexis not to make me take the stand, and, to her credit, she didn't. Andrew wasn't allowed to use what I'd said as evidence. I think the prosecution knew I'd just get up there and say I wasn't sure. Besides, I was a minor, and I didn't have an adult present at the time of the interview. But I feel like the moment I said that I'd heard him get up"—she sighed—"I made him guilty."

"Jesus."

"A family is about teamwork, my father always said. He used to punish us together. Curtis got drunk once when he was seventeen and spewed—we both had to clean the bathroom. Curtis stayed out at a friend's one night—both of us got curfews for the next month. Dad let Curtis get away with anything. Anything." She looked at the ground. "When Curtis was first arrested, it was like I'd really betrayed him. My father wouldn't talk to me. It got better, over time. But it still always felt like it was my fault. And then he got out, and the same thing starts happening again. I felt like a victim for a long time. I am not a victim anymore." She paused, considered her next thought. "We're both guilty, you know, you and I. We carry that guilt in different ways. You're doing this because you think you got him out; I'm here because I think I put him there."

"This looks bad for Curtis."

"I know."

"Why didn't you tell me?"

"Because you already think he killed her. I thought you wouldn't understand. You'd take it out of context and run with it. As soon as you put something on TV, it's automatically believed." The truth of this stung, but Jack didn't interrupt her. "It wasn't admissible evidence, and it didn't prove anything."

"Everything's important."

"Have you told me everything then?" Lauren looked at him over his box full of files. He was still leaning on it, keeping the lid closed. He held her gaze, conscious of not letting his eyes flicker to the closet.

"I know you won't want me to ask you this," said Jack, "but *did you* hear him get up?"

"I don't know." Lauren sighed. Tears had started to form. "Maybe footsteps. Maybe. I told you, I was never sure. I shouldn't have told anyone."

"I do understand, you know," Jack said. His protectiveness had really kicked in now, and he just wanted Lauren to feel better. She struck him more than ever as two different people: a woman who'd lived and a girl who never had.

"You don't." She sniffed.

"I told you I had a brother. His name is Liam. We lived in the Blue Mountains when we were teenagers. We used to love mucking around on the fire trails. We'd take our backpacks and BMXs and spend the day out in the bush. At one lookout, there's this large rock formation we used to call the Fist. It was cool; we used to love it there. But my dad, he was very clear: we weren't allowed to climb the Fist." He paused, deciding how much to tell her, but he'd already come this far. "One day my brother decided to climb it. I told him not to. I, um, I wouldn't go up with him." Now he'd got past it, the rest came quickly. "My brother went up, while I stayed at the bottom. He came down. Quickly."

Whump.

Jack could see it still—the plume of dirt as if coughed. Orange dust caked on Liam's cheek, congealed in blood and snot and fuck knows, cracked like a dried creek bed. Blood from his nose, his ears. And his chest, jumbled and broken, like a dropped bag of ice under Jack's hands. The fucking helicopter too, a hovering silhouette in front of the reddening sun, just a breath above the canopy, jumpsuit-clad men rappelling down the lines, boots thumping into the dust, the steady crump of the rotor blades above it all. All Jack could think was, fuck, how cool Liam would have found the whole damn thing. A real action hero. He'd been flown away on that stretcher, rigid in his brace, hanging above the tops of the trees. And Jack couldn't wait to tell him how badass it all was once he was recovering in the hospital.

Lauren had a hand over her mouth.

"Fuck. He died?"

"He's in a permanent vegetative state. Dad looks after him because there's still something left of him in there. We couldn't let him go. You talk about failing to protect your brother, and I understand."

"You regret not going up with him?"

"I go over all our choices that day. If we'd have gone swimming instead of climbing, if I'd been able to convince him to stay on the ground. Yeah, I regret whether I went up or not. So many forks in these roads though." He offered her a grim smile. "I get lost in the labyrinth."

"I don't know what to say. I'm sorry."

And, finally, it felt as if they'd agreed on something. Lauren thought she put her brother in a cell. So did Jack: Liam's whole body was a prison. They sat in silence. A breeze chilled them, wafting through the silent, doorless house. Jack surprised himself by taking Lauren's hand. Her skin was soft. The last woman's hand Jack had held had been Alexis's. Lauren's was warm.

"If Curtis killed anyone, that's not a betrayal," Jack said quietly.

Lauren nodded.

"So," Jack said.

"So."

"In the interest of sharing, help me look through these files." Jack took the lid off the box.

"What are they?"

"My research from the case."

"The restaurant?" Lauren recognized a blueprint on a piece of paper. "Have a look at these." She offered them to him for a closer look.

"Not those," Jack said, and passed her the stolen forensics.

"Looks official." She leafed through them. "Where'd you get them?"

"Friend of mine." Jack glanced away.

"Wow," she said, seeing through him. "Glad we're not friends."

McCarthy's files were a gold mine. The autopsy report identified the fatal wound as a severe blow to the base of the skull with a blunt object. The strangulation marks on the neck were made postmortem, pulled just tight enough and long enough to bruise and scar a still-warm body. Imagine strangling a dead person. Jack shivered. Lauren was having trouble looking at the photographs, so Jack took them back. There was Alexis, splayed on the cobblestones, on her back. Fingers in her mouth, pointing to the sky. Her limbs were twisted unevenly, as if she'd jumped from a balcony. The violence of her death bled out of the photos. There was no peace there.

There were also more clinical photographs, close-ups of the finger wounds. Hers were cleaner cut than Eliza's, Jack noticed immediately. The forensics expert had drawn small green circles where they thought there were unique markings. On Alexis's wounds, these markings formed a small tilted diamond. Jack rifled through his box and found photos of Eliza's wounds. Eliza's knuckles were chewed and ragged, they looked like raw hamburger mince. Jack compared them to Alexis's. They had been more neatly severed. A different kind of weapon.

He wondered if Winter had checked Alexis's kitchen thoroughly, if they'd found a knife missing. *No, you had to saw with knives.* There were no saw marks on the bone. *Something like a…meat cleaver?* He took out the photos of his independent silicon hand tests. They'd been comprehensive with those, more so than the police, at great expense. They'd used thick, molten silicon ladled into molds for the flesh. They'd made dozens of the hands and then systematically destroyed them all: slamming them in every door of the Wade household, severing them with every sharp object they could find. He found the meat cleaver report, the exact one from the Wade restaurant. On one side of the paper was a photo of the weapon, laid out on an evidence table next to a yellow ruler. On the other side, close-up images of the severed silicon fingers. An even cut, a fast chop. The cleaver was the perfect weapon for the job, but it wasn't the right one. No match for the tilted diamond. Jack flicked through the rest of the reports on various weapons. Nothing, nothing, nothing.

Lauren wandered across the hall. Jack could hear her singing from the bathroom: *She's having a piss, she's having a piss, don't come in, because she's having a piss.* When she ran out of lyrics to her own song, she sang to the tune of a pop song: *This piss. This piss. Unstoppable.*

Jack smiled. Lauren's ability to bounce back astounded him. She didn't take things lightly, but she seemed able to not let them pin her down.

Are you born with that resilience, he wondered, *or do you have to go through some trauma to build up to it?* He supposed all country women had thick skin. Ducks might have the market cornered on water bouncing off their backs, but Jack reckoned if Brett Dawson spat at Lauren, she'd use it to polish her boots. He was thinking about Lauren when he stopped on one photocopied page of a silicon hand. There was a constellation of markings. He grabbed Alexis's report, turned his lamp on its side so the paper turned translucent, and held the two images over each other. The markings lined up.

A match.

The typed report on the weapons test said it was a single blow with great force. A fast chop. Jack's heart danced in his chest, his cold, thin fingers shaking as he turned the paper over. Saw it. The scanned picture of the weapon. Lauren was in the doorway now. Jack held up the two matching sheets of paper. Her face turned white.

The photo of the weapon on the silicon hand report was in black and white, but they both immediately recognized the change in shading halfway up the wooden handle. Half-stained red. Unmistakable, this ax.

Jack didn't have to say anything; he could see Lauren already understood. Whoever they'd chased through the vineyard hadn't been stealing the ax at all. They'd been trying to put it back.

"We have to get back to Birravale," he said. "Now."

CHAPTER 23

Lauren was out the door and sprinting for the shed before the car had stopped. Jack had cut a half hour off the drive, only slowing for one set of well-known speed cameras on the highway, where Lauren had snapped at him: *For fuck's sake, Jack, you can afford it.* They'd blown through Birravale's lonely traffic light.

How had he missed it? An ax head had two sides. The killer had flipped the ax, hit Alexis with the blunt end of the head. That would be like getting plugged by a hammer. Then the killer had turned her over, spread her fingers. Jack had seen the white scores in the cobblestone himself. Chip marks. Not made with pliers or knives. The ax was the only solution.

"No police," Lauren said on the drive back, and when Jack was silent, added more softly: "Give him a chance."

"Don't call him."

"You can't still think—"

"Whatever else they planted, they want him to find it. If he touches anything, he's fucked."

Had she known he wouldn't call the police anyway? Surely she could see the television producer inside him wanting to see it for himself. First.

In Birravale, Jack opened his door before he flicked the car off, everything still in motion. The car, with both doors splayed into a wingspan, shuddered to a stop. The car stalled as he got out, threatened to roll back but didn't. Jack left his door open and hurried after Lauren, sprays of gravel flicking up at his calves. He could hear clanging, swearing, from the shed, then the sound of the homestead screen door rattling open behind him, but he kept running.

Sunlight spilled in a glaring rectangle on the dusty concrete floor of the shed. The pickup was on the grass outside. The off-white hatchback had its hood up, innards exposed. Jack knew nothing about cars, but it looked like something was missing. The dirt bike was unmoved. A ride-on mower sat in the back. There were black stains on the floor, which had a long crack down the middle of the slab. A workbench on the left was covered in debris and scattered tools. Lauren was over by it, picking things up and throwing them to the floor. A heavy wrench sparked off the concrete.

"Fuck," she said, hair in clumps, the tips narrowed and dark with sweat, waxed ends of cut rope. "Fucking. Just. Fuck." She saw him standing in the doorway. "Help me look."

Jack wasn't sure what he was looking for. Anything really. Lauren had interrupted them before they could properly plant the ax, but who knew what else they'd managed to hide? Lauren had chased someone out from the shed, so if anything was to be found, it was here. It wasn't an over-stuffed garage, so there weren't many hiding places. He walked around the car, bent behind the mower. Lauren was now laying into a red-metal tool cabinet, pulling out drawers in desperation. She buried her shoulder into the side of the chest, pivoted it out from the wall. Jack checked under the hatchback. While he was stooped, the light in the room changed. Someone was standing in the doorway.

"Is he here?" Curtis said.

"Curtis, I need you to tell me—"

"Is he here?"

"Jack," Lauren said loudly, clearing her throat.

Jack stood, dusting the front of his suit, registering that he hadn't changed from the funeral. At least if things went south, he was dressed for his own. Curtis was a silhouette against the cube of daylight.

"Where was the ax before Alexis died, Curtis?" Lauren asked.

"Are you kidding me? It should have been in here."

"Jack thinks that—" Jack coughed in protest as if to say *don't pin this on me*, so she restarted. "*We've discovered* the forensics match Alexis's wounds. To your ax."

"My ax?"

"We're ahead of the police."

"Why are you all so fucking dressed up? Are there cameras? There's a very good explanation, and that is that someone took it two nights ago. Come on."

"Alexis died a week ago, Curtis."

"I don't bloody know where it was a week ago, Lauren." He spoke her name through his teeth as he stepped into the room, materializing out of the dimness. "Someone took it. I don't know. I am not in possession of any weapon," he said, as if he were testifying in court.

"How'd they get in here?" Lauren said.

"You on his side now?"

"I should call the police," said Jack.

"Do it," said Curtis.

"Don't," said Lauren, holding out her palm. "Curtis, if we call the police, they might find something else in here. Even if it is planted, they won't believe you. It's better that we search first. Think about it."

Curtis breathed out through his nose. "*Even if* it's planted?" Jack saw Lauren's face fall at her badly chosen phrasing. "*Even. If?*"

"No one's saying—" Lauren started.

"Everyone's saying a lot." Curtis's voice rose. "First, if Alexis *was* killed with *my* ax, how are you ahead of the police forensics?"

"Jack's research—"

"Jack's *research*, as we're calling it, has no one checking it, no one to answer to." He shook his head. Jack wasn't sure if it was genuine frustration or his surprise that after all his insistence of framing, he actually might be right for once. Then he turned to Jack: "You say what you want, you put it on TV, and everyone believes it. I'm glad you got me out of jail, but it's bullshit that put me in and bullshit that got me out. I don't *trust* your research. Fuck that."

Curtis canvassed the two of them, decided it wasn't worth it. He turned and left. The light came back in from the doorway, scarring the concrete. Jack could hear him crunching down the driveway.

"My research isn't flimsy." Jack found his voice.

"I'm so confused," Lauren said, mostly to herself as she started rifling through the tool cabinet again. "This fucks your boyfriend theory."

True. Whoever murdered Alexis had to have planned to kill her. They'd come to the winery, broken into the shed, headed back into the city, weapon in the trunk. Premeditated.

"Is this shed locked?" Jack said.

"Sometimes."

"So the police now know the ax is the murder weapon. We can tell them what we think, but I doubt it'll help," Jack said. "Your problem is when the police come out here and *don't* find the murder weapon. It'll look like Curtis got rid of it."

Jack went to check behind sheets of plywood on the far wall. A wooden handle excited him, an irrational flicker inside him that it might be the ax returned, but it was just a stiff-brushed broom. From across the shed, Lauren said, "Oh fuck." Then a puttering of repetition, an engine kicking into gear. "Fuck-fuck-fuckity-fuck."

By the time Jack looked up, Lauren was sprinting to the door, the drawers of the tool cabinet left hanging open. "Curtis! Curtis!"

Jack followed her outside, but she was already on the veranda. Something small and black was in her hand. She banged on the door, flat-palmed, then wrestled with the knob. Curtis must have locked it from the inside.

"Open the door!" she yelled.

It swung inward so suddenly she almost fell over the threshold. Curtis looked uninterested, until Lauren showed him what was in her hand

and his mouth seemed to cave inward. He asked her a question and then guided her into the house. Jack was only a few steps behind; he followed through the still-open door. He could hear them arguing in the lounge room, Curtis protesting something. The curtains were still all closed, the walls tinged mold yellow by the setting sun.

"I haven't seen that before. I swear," Jack heard clearly, louder than the rest. Then Lauren said something about "charge." *Settle down. No one's going to charge you with murder.*

When he got to the lounge room, he propped himself against the doorframe, where Lauren had stood two days ago. Lauren was pacing back and forth in front of the window, while Curtis was standing beside the bookcase, the butt of the rifle visible on the shelf above, running his hands through his hair.

"I don't know what to tell you, Loz." Jack knew he was begging because he'd never heard Lauren's nickname before. "But I don't know where it came from."

"It's planted, is it? Everything's fucking planted with you, Curtis." She stepped up to him, paused on the balls of her feet, and Jack thought she might be about to hit him, but she changed her mind and dropped back on her heels. "The sheer absurdity of the conspiracy behind this... This is literally your *last* chance. Just own up to *something*."

"Lauren. This is what they want. Alexis's killer knows that it's not sticking to me. They're getting desperate."

Lauren crinkled her nose.

Curtis kept up his impassioned defense. "Why would I keep it? And why would I keep it in my own toolbox? I was in prison for four years. I've mopped floors with people who've jacked off to things that this... this fucking Nail-Biter killer...couldn't stomach. Jim Harrison, fuck, he'd tell you some stories. Amputated fingers, ha, that's fucking *cute*. Trust me, this is shoptalk. It's all you get inside. I spent four years listening to people talk about how they got busted. Little things. And you found this in my goddamn shed? This isn't the work of an ex-con. This is the work of someone who *wants* to get caught."

"It must be ready," Lauren said.

Jack still didn't know what they were talking about. Then he saw the coffee table. It still had the Lions football mugs on it, a skin of milk on top of both half-finished teas. But it was what was between them that caught his eye. A thin black cable squirreled its way up one of the coffee table legs from a plug into the wall. It was plugged into a touchscreen phone. Its screen cracked.

Lauren hadn't been talking about Curtis being charged with murder. They'd been talking about charging a phone.

"Is that—" Jack said from the door, and both of them looked up. Curtis looked like he wanted to pile-drive Jack through the drywall, but then there was a faint, distracting bell noise.

Alexis's second phone had turned on.

"No pass code," said Lauren, picking it up and looking at it.

"Go to messages," said Curtis.

"Go to calls," said Jack.

"Shut up."

Lauren scrolled through the phone for what felt like an eternity. Curtis peered over her shoulder. Jack couldn't see anything.

"Interesting," Curtis said.

"What is it?" Jack said.

Lauren unplugged the phone and tossed it to him. Midway through the air, he had a panic about fingerprints and tried to pull his jacket sleeve over his hand, but that led to a clumsy fumble and it landed in his bare hands. *Fuck it*, he thought. Lauren had touched it too; at least they were in it together now. Besides, now wasn't the time to take a stance on evidence tampering. He went to calls first. All the same contact—saved as HUSH with a small emoji, a yellow face with a finger to its lips. The last one the night of her murder. Just after midnight.

There was only one contact saved: HUSH. Jack checked the messages. Again, only the one contact. Some messages. Some pictures. Some sent: Alexis, undressed, the flash warping her face in a bedroom mirror but unmistakably her. Some received: a penis, close up, hotel bathroom. Boyfriend, definitely.

"This is her phone," Jack said quietly. "Why do you have it?"

"We think it's planted." Curtis spoke over her.

"Of course you do," muttered Jack.

"What's that supposed to mean?"

"It means I do believe you, Curtis, but if literally everything is planted, whoever's doing this to you must be some kind of"—Jack was about to say *mastermind*, but then remembered Lauren hated that—"very lucky."

"I'll tell you what," said Curtis to Lauren, though he tilted his head at Jack like he was sizing up a meal. "Things got a whole lot worse when you started hanging around with him."

"Stop it, Curtis," Lauren said.

"Was he in the shed with you?"

"Stop. You know he was."

"Did you bring this with you?"

"I wouldn't," said Jack.

"Wouldn't ya? What'd you say to me in prison? About words?"

"I told you words will make you famous."

"Do text messages count?"

"I guess."

"That's enough." Curtis patted the top of the bookcase, dragged something from the top. By the time Jack realized it was the rifle, it was already aimed at him. Lauren screamed.

"You want me to be a murderer. I'll be a fucking murderer."

"Curtis—"

"*Shut up, Lauren!*" Curtis had been loud before, but he'd never cut into a full, booming yell, and it shocked both of them. "The way you've been acting—you've got no respect for this family, sneaking around with him. This is my property, Jack. You know what that means?"

The gun was shaking slightly in Curtis's hand, the tip tracing a jagged circle in the air with his breathing. *He might miss*, thought Jack. He wasn't keen to take that chance.

"It means you're trespassing. I've been clear. No journalists."

"I'm not a journalist."

"Not for too much longer, anyway," Curtis said. Then he took one hand off the stock, dug around in his pocket. He pulled out his phone. Held it out.

"You can't—"

"This is my property. I can do what I want."

Jack didn't want to get into the legalities of Australian property and trespass law with a man with a gun, but he was pretty sure Curtis watched far too much American television. He figured it was hard to be smug about a technicality while trying to stop his guts from dripping on Curtis's carpet though, so he kept his mouth shut.

"Let's prove this once and for all. Call the number. Call Hush," Curtis said, shaking his phone in his hand.

"Why?"

"If my phone rings, I'm Hush. I'm guilty."

"No, Curtis," Lauren was shaking.

"*If* it rings?" said Jack.

"I'll turn myself in. But I'll shoot you first. May as well."

"Stop—" said Lauren.

"Dial it."

Lauren looked over at Jack and gave him a slight nod. His hands were shaking as he pulled up Alexis's contacts.

"You better hope I'm innocent, Jack."

Jack pressed Dial. There were a few seconds of silence where Jack was sure he was about to die, that the last thing he'd hear was a ringing from

Curtis's hand. And then a bang so loud it would expand around him, fold him into it, until there was nothing but quiet. But there was nothing. Then a small burring noise from Alexis's phone speaker. But the room stayed quiet. The house stayed quiet. No reciprocal ring. Jack put the call on speaker. The phone rang out. There was no voicemail. *Click.*

"Damn," said Curtis, "I almost convinced myself." He hadn't lowered the gun.

"Okay, Curtis, put it down," said Lauren.

"Did you plant the phone?" Curtis said.

Jack shook his head.

"Get on your knees."

Jack obeyed. He put his hands behind his head. Curtis hadn't asked him to. It just happened. A reflex. A doctor taps you on the knee, your leg kicks. A man with a gun asks you to kneel, and your elbows rise, right angled to your ears.

"Did you plant this?"

"You're scaring him." Lauren's voice was high, pleading.

"I should be."

Jack shook his head again. Lauren was frozen. Watching Curtis. She didn't seem to fully understand. Curtis had his little fictional avatars in the people around him. The world in black and white. With him or against him. Jack had shown him doubt, and that meant he was against him now. Did that mean he deserved to die? The gun was now only moving up and down with Curtis's breathing. He was calmer. More confident. He wouldn't miss from this distance.

"I think you killed her," Curtis said. "What do you think about that? You need a second series. Gotta make it juicy, huh? That's how TV goes. God. You reminded me that I *missed out* on Alexis. I'm jealous of whoever did it. I'm not a killer. But deep down, you know…seems like it might be up my alley. Imagine the press if I did just pop you one? Right here."

No one said anything. Jack could feel his heart pulsing in his throat.

His feet had gone numb. His hair felt greasy under his fingers. *Your life's supposed to flash before your eyes*, Jack thought. But for him there was no montage of the past, instead the opposite—everything reduced to this exact moment and nothing more. Nothing existed in the universe except this room. It was as if it had broken off from the earth and was floating in a vacuum. Nothing held Jack's attention except the slow, hypnotic rise and fall of the gun barrel. Jack even imagined he saw the exact moment that Curtis made up his mind. Decided to kill him.

"Words will make you famous," said Curtis, his finger feathering the trigger, "but guns will make you famous too. Faster."

A loud ding cut through the room.

Everyone stopped. It had come from Jack's left hand. He moved it slowly from behind his head. Something was glowing in his tightly squeezed fist. Alexis's phone. He'd almost forgotten he was holding it. Curtis lowered the gun. If he'd psyched himself into a murderous trance, the noise had broken it. Jack slowly brought the phone up.

A text message. From HUSH.

Who is this?

He lifted the phone so Curtis and Lauren could read it.
Two seconds later, another ding.

You're supposed to be dead.

S01E05
THE FALL

Exhibit D:

Steel-headed ax with a hickory handle. Retrieved from the Wade property garage on second search. Head is painted red, chipped to silver on the blade. Handle is two toned, maroon fading into light brown. Fingerprints: Curtis Wade, Lauren Wade, Vincent Wade, several unmatched, see Exhibits M–O. Blood: Not found.

Markings on the victim's finger wounds do not match ax head.

CHAPTER 24

PREVIOUSLY

Eliza sat on the bed and watched the wine run down the walls.

After her initial panic wore off and the fruity, fermented smell worked its way through her synapses, the scene had transformed from nightmarish to absurd. She actually wondered for a second if the place might fill up and mercifully drown her, but the flood had tapered off to a steady drip. A droplet had sizzled on the single swinging light globe.

She'd lifted her mouth skyward to catch a few drips, to prove to herself it wasn't a delusion. The first few droplets shocked her with taste and delight. He fed her, but it was plain. Once he brought a pizza, slid the cardboard box across to her, but she'd been too scared to eat it (*Why pizza now? Had he put something in it?*), and he must have taken offense because she hadn't been given anything special since. She didn't actually know if he fed her regularly or well because of the way time came to her down here. Some days, she was convinced he'd forgotten, that she'd gone weeks without food, but then he'd come with a piece of toast and a bottle of water, and she wondered if it was only a few hours after all.

The pizza had come a few days after he stopped asking her what she knew. She'd told him everything. He hadn't killed her yet, but he hadn't let her go yet either. A survivalist stalemate. A single, powerless pawn dancing a lone king around a board.

She put one of her shoes under the heaviest drip and watched as it slowly filled up. It sloshed as she brought it back to her bed. It was the only vessel she had in here. There were droplets on the floor in an odd, almost rigid, pattern.

Some days she wished he would hurry up. Others, she was thankful for the tiniest events. The rush of fresh air when he opened the door. A vivid dream, a memory, of her friends or family. A glass of wine.

She sat back on the bed, propped on her elbows so she wouldn't have to lean against the sticky wall. She took refuge in those moments. Just get through one more day. That was her philosophy. And then get through the next one. Then the next one.

She had her shoe-full of wine and was determined to enjoy it. She lifted it up to the speckled roof in cheers. It would be some time before the wine dried and the dyed-red pattern began to tell her another story.

But for now, happy hour.

CHAPTER 25

SEPTEMBER

You're supposed to be dead.

Alexis's second phone was faceup on the coffee table. Jack, Lauren, and Curtis had settled in around it. Lauren and Jack were together, scooted forward on the ravenous couch. Curtis had taken a chair opposite. The hunting rifle was propped against the chair's arm, with the stock on the floor, the barrel pointed to the roof. Someone had plugged the phone back into the charger as the sliver of battery waned, but Jack couldn't remember who. It wouldn't have been Curtis, who treated it like a hot coal, refusing to touch it.

"Hush." Lauren rolled it around her mouth like a candy.

"Asian name," Curtis muttered. "Must be."

"It's not a name, Curtis," Lauren said. "It's an adjective."

"Each letter stands for something?"

"That's an acronym," Jack said.

"Don't talk down to me." Curtis ground his jaw.

"One of my friends"—Lauren's calm, even voice tempered the room—"changed the name of her ex-boyfriend in her phone to *Do Not Call Him*. So it doesn't mean anything, Curtis, except that she didn't want to put her boyfriend's name in her phone."

"Why not?" Curtis asked, still figuring it out.

"Don't know," said Jack. "Why *wouldn't* she want to put her boyfriend's name in her secret phone?"

"Stop being a smart-arse," said Lauren.

"Devil's advocate," said Jack. He saw a flicker of a smile.

"It's weird to us because she's dead," Lauren said, scrolling through the messages again. "But to her, maybe it wasn't so suspect. There's no pass code. Then again, there must have been some reason for keeping her relationship discreet. He's the only one in there. And his messages only go back to June."

June. Just before the retrial.

"She told me it was her second phone. Just until her other one stopped blowing up."

"Okay," said Lauren, thinking. "That could be why she never bothered with a password. If it was only meant to be temporary."

"If the killer planted this," Curtis said, "they'd have deleted anything incriminating. Agreed?" Everyone nodded. "So that means they left Hush in there on purpose. Why plant a phone with your details in it? Why hasn't her boyfriend gone to the police? They're trying to guide us to him. Right? I never thought I'd say this, but we should go to the police."

"You think you're being set up as part of a setup now?" Jack said, talking Curtis down for his own benefit. Jack couldn't go to the police. They'd tear apart his house. They'd find the shoe. Potential jail time aside, that was a career ender.

"You could hand this in. But if the killer even gets a whiff that you're colluding, they *will* find a way to plant that ax on you," Lauren said. "It won't matter that he's in the phone. All he'll have to do is admit to sleeping with her. You'll still be hit with this. Point is"—she blithely dismissed Curtis's concerns—"she's used a little smiley picture. That's not real secrecy; that's cute more than anything. See?"

Curtis recoiled as if she'd thrust a snake at him.

"I'm not fucking touching that."

"It's still a secret," said Jack. "Otherwise, she would have used his name."

"Unless it's an aneurism," said Curtis.

"Acronym," said Lauren and Jack together.

"Whatever."

"He's got a point," said Lauren. "Hush-hush." She held a finger to her lips. "This was, at the very least, someone she wanted to keep under wraps."

"Someone married?" suggested Curtis.

"Someone she knew she shouldn't be seeing." Jack tapped a finger on his chin.

He must have been unconsciously sizing up Curtis, because Curtis flung both hands upward. "Seriously?"

"I didn't even—"

"Jack, lay off," said Lauren.

"Someone she shouldn't be seeing," Curtis repeated smugly. "I'd say that's everyone in this fucking town. Even you."

Jack took a moment to appreciate the absurdity of them all sitting in Curtis's lounge room throwing theories at a dartboard. Their own little crime-solving trio. Winter would have a stroke.

"You're right." Jack tried to look sincere. "Sorry."

Lauren looked over to Curtis, as if to encourage him to play nice, and he acknowledged her with a grunt. Her skyward eye roll back to Jack was clear: *That's as good as it gets.*

"That explains why he wouldn't go to the police. If it was an affair or whatever. The secrecy must be more important to him than finding her killer," said Jack.

Jack was aware both Curtis and Lauren were examining him as if they knew he'd played the truth fast and loose during his own interactions with the police. Of course they did. Curtis had guessed that whatever evidence he had, had been planted. Even Lauren had asked him numerous times: *Are you telling me everything?* And not a single time had she looked like she believed him when he'd said he had. Good radar on her.

"So what do we know?" Jack said. "Someone wanted Alexis dead. And they realized the easy way out was to frame Curtis for it. So they come here, take the ax, drive back to Sydney, and—" He clicked his tongue. Enough said.

Everyone stayed in silence considering this. The only sound was the slow synthetic clicking as Lauren scrolled back through the text messages. It was too coincidental to not involve Curtis Wade *at all*. Jack again realized he only thought this because he *wanted* the crimes to be related. Curtis couldn't have sent the text message; his hands had been steadying a rifle. Jack wondered if the irony of it escaped Curtis. That he was innocent of murder only because he was busy preparing to kill someone else.

"Nothing else in here," Lauren said, putting the phone down at last. "Though they do stop texting each other…hmm…a few weeks before she died. Their texts are all discreet; it's like business meetings. Dates and times and places. That's it. They don't talk about their days at all. There are some photos. Only close-ups though, and mostly her. He's white, by the way."

"Can I have a look?" said Jack. Lauren passed it to him. He scrolled through. There weren't a lot of messages, so it didn't take long. Lauren was right. Everything was organized and perfunctory: 7:00 p.m., Frankie's Café. If it dried up a few weeks before she died, did this indicate a breakup? Or was Curtis right, and whoever had planted this had cleared just the right amount of information to make it look that way?

"He's not Jewish," Jack said, "if that helps."

"What's the number?" asked Curtis. "We should write it down."

The shared look between them said, *In case the police take it.* The mutual understanding, that they would keep this evidence to themselves, hung in the room. They wore their motives clear on their faces. Curtis, who knew it would make him look guilty. Lauren, wanting to stick up for her brother. And Jack, here for himself.

Lauren read out the number. Jack keyed it into his phone and saved it under HUSH. Curtis jotted it down on a piece of paper and put it in his pocket. Curtis was the most animated Jack had seen him, motivated by something other than hurt or anger. Curtis wanted to solve this murder as much as Jack did. Clear his name.

"We should call it," said Curtis.

"We called it already," said Jack.

"On our own phones," said Curtis. "Of course they won't pick up when a dead woman calls."

"I don't know if I want a murderer to have my phone number," Jack said, simply because he didn't want to admit it was actually a pretty good idea.

"Man up."

"You do it, then."

"I can't. My number in a murderer's call logs? That'll play badly with the cops. And on TV." Curtis added the last two words with acidity, a raised eyebrow.

"Block the number," said Lauren to Jack. "You can hide behind that."

"I'm not *hiding*."

"Then call them," said Curtis. "We know the phone's on."

"Why don't we text them back?"

"And say what?" said Lauren.

"Dunno." Jack thought a second. "'Who is this?'"

"Of course," said Curtis, smacking his forehead. He tapped an imaginary phone with his thumbs, speaking stilted as if typing each word. "Thanks for asking. My name is Gary Murderson, and I live at 123 Confession Street."

"Well, fuck, he's not going to tell us who he is on the phone either, is he?"

"But we'll hear his voice. We might know him," Lauren said.

"Shit," Jack said. "How do I block my number?"

When Lauren had masked his phone, Jack hit Call and put it on speaker. Again, the tinny hum thrummed from the small speakers. Again, there was no reciprocal noise in the house. They all clustered forward, waiting. Each pause between rings was near interminable. Implausibly, it seemed each pause was a fraction longer, as if someone had picked up. But then the burr would return, and they'd wait again. The phone rang out with a click. No voicemail.

"Well," Jack said, pocketing his phone, "Gary Murderson lives on in secrecy."

"Maybe he's not picking up a blocked number," said Curtis.

"I'm not giving him my real number, Curtis."

"Lauren?" Curtis looked over to her.

"I'm your sister. The call logs would be just as incriminating."

And Jack finally realized why Curtis had let him on their property at all. Jack was *Curtis's alibi.* Curtis was letting him stick his fingers in places Curtis couldn't, at risk of incriminating himself. Jack's fingerprints were on the phone. He'd underestimated Curtis again.

"Fine," said Jack.

"Fine?"

"Fucking *fine*, Curtis."

Lauren showed Jack how to unmask his number. Again, he placed the phone in the center of the table, put it on speaker. Again, they hunched forward. *Ring. Ring. Click.* No voicemail.

No one had to say anything, all three of them making their own summations. Personally, Jack thought they'd called in too close proximity and Hush knew something was off.

Of course something was off; it's not every day your dead girlfriend rings you.

Perhaps it didn't even matter who Hush was, Jack thought. There was something larger than just a boyfriend hovering behind all of this. If Hush was her murderer, why give them the phone at all? Perhaps hiding in plain sight *was* the plan. Curtis such a plum suspect that he's behind bars before anyone takes a closer look. Evidence overgrown with time.

After all, the last time, a closer look had taken four years.

No one seemed to have any more ideas. Curtis went to the kitchen and came back with a beer. He didn't sit, just stood there sipping at it. Jack took the initiative and rose.

"I should keep this," he said, pointing at the phone. No one objected. He slid it into his jacket pocket, looking at Curtis for an objection that didn't come. He defended anyway: "You can trust me."

"We can't." Curtis took a sip. "But okay."

"Thank you, Jack," said Lauren. She lay on the couch, wrist on her forehead. Spent.

"Walk you out," offered Curtis.

"I'm fine."

"Walk you out," he said again. He was already following Jack into the hall.

Outside, the sun was just down. The sky was a translucent navy, rather than black, the color still siphoning from it, the chromatography between night and day. Jack had thought it would be later. He stepped off the deck without saying goodbye to Curtis. He heard crunching behind him. Curtis was following him, a few steps behind.

"Jack," Curtis said, and Jack turned. "You never told me what it was you found."

To their left, the Freemans' silos turned from glittering steel beacons to shadows stretched across the fields.

"I didn't," Jack said.

"So?"

"You said it was planted," Jack reminded him.

"Yes. Someone planted it."

"It doesn't matter, then."

"So."

"So?"

"What was it?"

Jack consistently failed to give Curtis enough credit. He'd obviously figured out that now the investigation was suggesting a copycat, Eliza's real killer remained open to scrutiny. That *he* remained open to scrutiny. Sitting in the circle, in anticipation of the ringing phone, Curtis must have been frantically spinning through the evidence in his head—how this could support his being framed not once but twice. Eliza still lay alone, stark naked, in the middle of his own vineyard. Two dead women and Curtis

Wade the only thread between them. Double jeopardy was his ally, but it was a fragile one. Especially if Jack had some unknown evidence. Another reason to keep him around: Curtis wanted to know what Jack had on him.

Jack stayed silent. If he had any advantage over Curtis, this was it. Curtis blinked twice quickly, a muscle in his cheek jumped. There was a violence lingering under his skin, something crawling.

"Does Lauren know?" Curtis said eventually.

"No."

"Is it safe?"

"Yes."

Curtis sighed, took a pull on his beer. "That'll have to do for now," he said.

Jack looked over and up the hill to the Freeman place. He imagined again that bleeding hill.

"Tell me something," Jack said. "Why'd you do it?"

"Fuck you, Jack."

"Not the murder." He pointed to the silos. "That."

"Oh."

Curtis looked up as well. Remembering. "We didn't fit in here; you know that. You're either born here or you're fucked. Like spurting out of a rich ball sack counts as skill, but try telling them that. *Grapecism*, Lauren coined it." He laughed. "They smashed our windows, yeah, there was that. But it wasn't really one single thing. It's just the general attitude here. You felt it?"

Jack thought about Brett Dawson's mockery at the pub. Mary-Anne's five-star breakfast. Alan Sanders's overpriced meals.

"The town's got a vibe, yeah."

"Well." Curtis shrugged as if that settled the matter. "That's it then."

"What's it?"

"The vibe. That's why I did it. Besides, I didn't know it would be so"—he searched for the word—"dramatic."

"That's not much of a reason to soak a town in wine."

"This ain't a town, mate," Curtis said. "It's Andrew Freeman's winery and a cluster of brownnoses at the bottom, bending over and opening their mouths for the money to run downhill. His wine's fucking awful too. I'll tell you how it went; I don't care if you believe me or not."

"I'll try."

"I was up there, you see, and I turned on one tap. Just enough to piss them off, you know?" Curtis raised his eyebrows in expectation, as if pissing off the Freemans should be an everyday activity. "I didn't plan anything else. And then I saw the view, looking down on this rubble of buildings that calls itself a town. And I looked at the dribble of wine, which was starting to run down the hill. And I thought about all the uptight pricks below. And it just came over me."

"What did?"

"I thought to myself, *Fuck it, someone needs to buy this town a drink.*"

CHAPTER 26

When buzzing woke him, Jack was convinced it was the murderer calling him back.

"Jack."

A familiar voice. Jack opened his eyes. He popped his ears by grinding his jaw. Light rimmed the border of the disconnected door over by the window. He pulled his phone away from his ear to check the time. Morning. Just.

"Ian."

"Sorry to wake you. Question for ya." McCarthy was abrupt, as curt as Jack had ever heard him. It also sounded like he was driving; there was a hum underneath everything. Jack's first thought was grim: *Ian knows about Alexis's phone.*

"Okay. Shoot." *Play it cool.*

"At the funeral."

"Yeah."

"You take something?" Not the phone. This was worse.

"From the funeral?"

"From my truck."

"Jesus, Ian."

Jack shook himself properly awake. He'd watched enough interrogations to know he needed to buy himself some time. He needed to give noncommittal answers. Let Ian lead. The fatal flaw in most criminals: no patience.

"I know," Ian continued, "and I'm sorry to ask you, mate. But listen. I lost something. I need it back. If you took it and you just give it back, no harm done, okay?"

Jack had already read the files. He could copy them, return the orig-
inals. McCarthy was his final ally. Even now, while accusing Jack of a
serious crime, he was offering an out. But what if it got back to Winter?

Jack sighed. The lie formed on his lips. Truth, edited.

"I wish I could help you, Ian." *You're a piece of shit*, Jack told himself.
"But I made a fast exit before Ted doubled the church bookings with my
own coffin."

"All right." Ian spoke on an exhale. Was Jack imagining the disappointment? "Sorry to ask. Had to, you know? I gotta go. You still out this
way? Drink soon?"

"Yeah. I'm out here. Sure."

There was silence then. Nothing but the road purring under McCarthy's
tires. Something broken between them. McCarthy hung up.

Jack's mornings were becoming ritualized. Stuck in the cycles of this town.
Dress. Shower. Step over black banana in the doorway. Out to the street.

He walked into the center of town for no reason but an abstract gravity,
stood at the single traffic light. It was too early to go back to the Wades.
Besides, he had nothing new to tell them. He'd scrolled through the phone
last night and nothing more had revealed itself. It was too early for anything really; there was a layer of mist still on the ground. It was cloudy too.
The town's buildings were shadows behind gray, slowly coming into focus
with proximity, sharp features materializing bit by bit, as if buffering into
existence. It wasn't raining; that would come later. His face was damp, the
moisture in the air pervasive.

Jack kicked at rocks as he kept walking nowhere in particular. Andrew
Freeman still bothered him. That vertiginous restaurant. That mine shaft
of a cellar. Birravale Creek had been a healthy business before he'd married into it, Alan Sanders had told him, but not a behemoth. But the
money it was making now must be staggering. Sufficient enough not only

for renovations, but also to ignore a multimillion-dollar insurance claim. Andrew had brushed it off the other night as overvalued. Out of all of his oddities, that was perhaps the worst: honesty to an insurance company.

Jack was past the pub again now. With its useless cautionary signs through the window. GAMBLING: KNOW WHEN TO STOP. ALCOHOL: AUSTRALIA'S MOST EXPENSIVE DRUG. All while inviting you in to drink and gamble. Something niggled.

His brain was addled with theories. He had to simplify the facts. He needed clarity, a calm sounding board. He pulled out his phone and dialed.

"Hey, Dad," Jack said, "can you put me on speaker?" Then, before his father could react: "Please, I want to talk to him."

There was a short pause, and then the familiar soundscape of his father's trudge up the stairs. Then more silence, a short scuffle, and Peter said, "Right," and retreated to his armchair. Jack heard the leather creak and the pencil start to scrape away at a crossword.

"Hey, Liam. What's up?" The first few words were always the hardest. His voice caught. "I've been working that case for us. Can you give me a hand sorting through some stuff?"

The soft beeps in the background audio were almost an errant Morse code. It was a comforting thought that maybe Liam was, in some way, talking back.

"Look, so I know that Curtis—he's the bad guy, remember, buddy?—didn't swing the ax that killed Alexis."

Beep. Beep.

"And I know that someone stole that ax, so they could plan the murder and a cover story to go with it, until I busted them trying to put it back."

His father's pencil rustled in the background like someone whispering. Jack ran his pointer and his thumb down his temples until they met at his nose.

"And I know that Alexis had a second phone. One that she used for a secret…" He paused. "No, you're right, Liam. I'm speculating there."

Maybe not secret, but still a discreet relationship. What kind of relationship required discretion? Someone she shouldn't be seeing. Like Curtis had said, that was almost everybody. An affair? On her end? Was she a mistress, or he a cuckold? Sex isn't murder, but the two went hand in hand more often than not. Jack clicked his teeth. Liam's machine continued its rhythmic beat. Maybe not Morse code, but an artificial heartbeat. A small sign of life that proved he was there.

"You're right," Jack said. "That is the real question. Who is the worst person she could be sleeping with?"

Jack looked up and answered his own question. The hilltop beyond the town was shrouded, as if blowing smoke rings. He could see the two silos, the windowed shoebox. Andrew Freeman had struck Jack as leading him around the circumference of the truth. Andrew knew more than he was letting on, and it was time to find out what.

"Yeah, don't rub it in. I know," Jack said. "What would I do without you?" He ended the call.

The road had thinned underfoot without Jack noticing, his walk taking him to the edge of town. He'd got the gravity of the town wrong. It didn't pull into Birravale proper. He looked up at the Freemans'. Like everything else here, the gravity ran uphill.

CHAPTER 27

Andrew's Forester wasn't in the drive. Jack lifted the bronze knocker and rapped on the front door, his shoes leaving moist prints on the stained deck. In the city, at this hour, it would be almost criminally rude; he'd be greeted by electroshocked hair, a bathrobe, *What the fuck do you want?* Out here, though, only silence. Farmers and early risers already out for the day. Jack knocked again.

Fuck it, he thought and clomped off the deck. He walked around the side of the house, past a row of overflowing recycling bins, plastic tubs with science-y names—ethyl, glycol—peeking from under lids, and across the grass to the Freemans' silos. He trailed his fingertips along the cool corrugated steel; droplets pooled and ran down his wrist. He looked down at Birravale, the sparse collection of buildings now dark spots in the gray mist. He tried to feel what Curtis had when, up here, his knuckles strained around the handle of an ax: contempt for those beneath him. It wasn't so hard to empathize.

Past the silos, Jack came to the cellar door. He stooped and yanked at the handle. Locked. That catacomb of a cellar, with its safe-like doors. Who knew how deep it went into the hillside? The perfect place for secrets.

Eliza had picked here for six months. Had she found something? What had she said on the voicemail? *Might even be, I don't know, illegal?*

Jack walked over to the trellises of grapes. There was a gouge in the dirt, lawn scuffed, from where he'd grappled with the intruder. He continued up the hill. In the light, it was an easier trek. White trunks—bones in the mist—flanked him. Sleeves of bark hung down, swinging shadows like peeled gloves from branched hands. Jack took careful steps over rotting logs and branches. Brown leaf litter swathed his ankles, slicked and dewy like dead tongues.

The density of the trees petered out. Jack stepped into the clearing. There was a blue tarp tethered to a wooden stake on the right side of the clearing. Jack recalled the crinkle of plastic when he'd run through here in the dark. The tarp was neatly pulled back over something lumpy and weighed down with a brick in the far corner. Jack looked at the irregularity of the lumps, tried to guess, worst-case scenarios playing through his head. *Lauren.* What had she said? *Women around my brother keep turning up dead.* He picked up the brick, pulled the tarp back. Under it, rather than a dead body, was a small garden. The smell was unmistakable. It wasn't quite the smell in Andrew's car. That was something earthier. This was a reason to keep investigators at bay. Especially if there was more growing in that cellar. Marijuana.

But something wasn't quite right. The garden was too small. Three or four plants. Was it just a sample of what was going on in a lab below? A handful of small plants was nothing to kill over.

"Don't tell him," a voice said from behind. Jack whipped around to Sarah. She was dressed for high tea, not for bush walking in the dew. She had black handprints on her white slacks where she'd wiped them. Her trouser legs were slicked, cladded and transparent on her calves. And she was shivering.

Jack clutched the brick.

"You were home, before?"

"I wanted to see if you knew." She nodded. "Don't worry, Andrew's out cycling."

"Why would I worry?"

"I misspoke. Sorry."

"Should I be worried?"

"No. Please." Sarah brushed some water out of her eyes, wrapped her arms around herself. "Keep this as just us."

Jack stepped toward her. She drew back. Momentarily confused, Jack thought to check behind him. He realized then, she was shrinking from him. His face was bruised and cut, hair plastered to his scalp. Still holding the brick. He must look quite threatening. He dropped the brick.

"Does Andrew—"

"It's fine. Come back this way. I'll get you a towel." She turned and guided him back through the bush.

"How long have you had this?" Jack spoke to her back.

"A few years."

"And Andrew doesn't know?"

"He's the sergeant, for heaven's sake." Her voice rose above a sullen drone for the first time. "What kind of a look would that be?"

"He's not the sergeant anymore."

"Still. A secret kept this long, it festers."

Jack rubbed the scars on the backs of his knuckles. They were back on the property now, walking past the silos. "Why?" Jack asked.

"Stress mainly. You wouldn't last one week running this place. Andrew's a genius; he's turned this business into a legacy. I think it's because he didn't start with it, you know? He respects it, but he's looking at it from an outsider's perspective. Nothing tying him to the old ways. So he sees new opportunities."

"And that's stressful?" Jack asked, dimly aware that this was the same reason Andrew said he hated the Wades. Imposters.

"He's a bit of a guru with these things. But the way we do things, it's not without its pressures."

Jack thought back to Andrew tossing the expensive bottle of wine back and forth. Telling Sarah to get a different one. That wasn't a discussion between husband and wife, between business partners; it had been an order. Andrew was intense. If Jack were married to him, he'd probably need some stress relief too.

"Those chemicals…" Jack said.

"Are for making wine," Sarah said. Jack shrugged; he didn't know what went into wine. "Alcohol is chemical," Sarah continued. "I'm not cooking meth, if that's what you're thinking."

"Do you sell it?" Jack asked. "The pot."

"To Curtis Wade, is that what you're asking?"

"Anyone," Jack said, but she'd correctly guessed his angle.

"You're trying to turn one marijuana plant into a murder investigation?"

It had started to rain. The clouds were so low that it didn't so much fall as waft onto them.

"I won't tell him," Jack said, but before she could thank him, added, "but I want you to take me into his cellar."

Sarah flicked the switch and the lights shuddered on, revealing the proscenium chamber that receded into the mountain. The honeycomb-latticed wine racks. The barrels lining the walls. Their footsteps echoed off the walls as she led him onto the clay. It was dry and musty down here. Jack could hear the rain tapping on the top step.

Jack went in farther than he had last time. He peered at the chambers that were off the main hall. Some were open, circular rooms racked with wines and kegs. Others had large steel doors, like fancy fridges. Or high-tech safes. A dragon could be sleeping on gold bricks behind these doors. He felt his wet shirt with each step, alternately sticking or peeling off. With every step, a new piece found skin, sending shocks of cold through him. The air was cold too, in the lungs.

"The thermodynamics of being under the earth," Sarah said, as if she'd heard his thoughts, or maybe she'd just seen him shiver. "It's the best temperature control there is. We take from the earth, we put it back in."

"All natural," Jack said, rapping a knuckle on one of the metal doors. He spotted a keyhole in the door. "These locked?"

"Yep."

"Can I look?"

"Nope."

"Can *I* look?" He tried to push his leverage.

"Sorry, Jack, these are private collections. It's just bottles in there."

"You sure there's no more narcotics?"

"Marijuana is hardly a narcotic." Sarah bristled, revealing too much of her politics. "I told you, these are private collections. And, well, you'll just have to trust me."

"You store other people's wine?" Jack said, thinking that it really *was* like a bank. "How does that work?"

"That's the business," said Sarah, looking at him as if he was an idiot. "Wine collecting may be niche, but it's a strong industry. Our customers want to keep their wines somewhere secure, with good conditions. There's nowhere better in the country than here."

"Why not just keep it in their own cellars?"

"Some only want short-term storage. They might be building a cellar or moving house. Whatever. Others simply don't want to. Why don't people hang a Picasso in their lounge room? Wine's the same. For collectors, it's art. We're a gallery here." She eyed him. "A *private* gallery."

"Not that private," Jack said. "Andrew took me down here before."

"What can I tell you? He likes to brag."

Jack almost snorted at that. *Give them what they've paid for*, he'd said about the collectors. Jack bet they'd paid handsomely. So that was why the leaked silo didn't bother him—the lost wine was just his supermarket product. This was the real business. And it explained him not claiming the insurance too. If Andrew's reputation depended on the trust of his customers, he couldn't have claims officers coming out and opening doors. There might be no dragon, but there were gold bars in this bank, indeed.

"This was Andrew's idea?"

"Yes, and then the restaurant followed. Originally, he just wanted to eat up some of the profits, offer employment to the town, but then the restaurant took off as well. Like I said, he transformed this place."

Jack wandered to the door at the end of the cellar, not to the left or the right but inset into the back wall. This one had a digital keypad lock.

"What's so special about this one?"

Sarah didn't answer.

"That," said Andrew Freeman, his voice booming across the cavern, "is my personal collection."

CHAPTER 28

Andrew was bare calved, in Lycra shorts and a highlighter-yellow wind-breaker, zipped to the sternum. There was a clicking sound as he walked to Jack, brushing past his wife without acknowledging her. Jack realized the clicking was from Andrew's cycling shoes, the metal cleats clacking on the floor. Jack tried to decide if the look on his face was anger or surprise.

"Moisture doesn't go in the vault," Andrew said, scanning Jack's damp shirt. He punched in a code. "But no harm in giving you a peek."

There was a hiss as Andrew pulled the door wide: so heavy it was hydraulics assisted. It didn't look like it opened from the inside. *You could sever a finger in that.* Jack filed the thought away.

Inside the room, shelving lined the walls. Bottles lay on their sides in specialty wooden cradles. The corks faced outward, lines of cannons on a tall ship. Dull tube lights emitted nothing more than a soft glow. There were hundreds of bottles, rows on rows.

"Temperature, humidity, light," said Andrew, looking with affection at his collection. "That's the holy trinity of aging wine."

"It's down here because it's cool?"

"It's down here because it's *consistent*," said Andrew, stepping inside. "That's the real key. Good wine is about consistency—you want the right temperature zone, which is coolish, sure, but it's the fluctuations that matter the most. One or two degrees across a year can put it out." He picked up a bottle and held it neck out so Jack could see. "See this? The bottle may be corked, but the wine inside is still liquid. And liquid expands and contracts in different temperatures. So if the temperature moves up and down, the volume of the wine goes up and down too. Excess air pushes out or in through the cork, meaning the wine inside, even sealed, evaporates. Minutely, of course, but when you're storing wine for a few decades, it matters. Most old wines, you'll note, have slightly lower levels in them."

"Okay. So that's temperature. What's important about light and humidity?" Jack was half-interested and half wanting to keep Andrew talking so he could keep looking around.

"Anything can speed up the process, change the bouquet—that's what they call the flavor in a wine—just by invigorating different catalysts. Sunlight's a definite no-no."

"I thought you just put wine in a closet for a hundred years—the older the better."

"No! Wine expires. It's not like spirits. Scotch you can age indefinitely—there's enough alcohol in there to stop it turning. Wine has a lower alcohol percentage, and it *is* subject to fluctuations. Sometimes, even down here, it'll go off. But we do our best." He slotted the wine back into the rack, breathed in the room, the dusty, aging smell, and looked pleased with himself.

"It's a clever business idea," said Jack. "You're making money off wine without even selling any. That's why the wine you make isn't real money."

"Very good. People say business is about risks. Good investments." Jack wondered if Andrew considered his wife an *investment*. "And, yeah, it's about those things, but it's also about guts. It's about lateral thinking. Did you know, in 1987, the CEO of American Airlines saved forty thousand dollars in a *single* year by removing one olive from each first-class salad on his flights?"

"Sounds less like business strategy and more like skimming off the top to me," said Jack. He was starting to get a hold on Andrew. Here was a country police sergeant who'd married into money, read a couple of business books, and taken it upon himself to flaunt that wisdom.

"You're missing the point." Andrew sighed. "Diversification is the key to good business. American Airlines' business is flying planes, city to city, but the real costs lay elsewhere, outside of the core business. Hell, now flying *is* entertainment. It's about the experience. It's not A to B anymore because someone had the vision to switch it up. But my point on the olives is much simpler. Lots of little changes to make one larger one. One olive, not so significant. A million olives..." Andrew nodded over Jack's shoulder, and Jack finally realized what he was saying—rows and rows of bottles, Andrew's own collection, was insignificant compared to the value of all the chambers combined. The value was in the accumulation. "You've got yourself a business."

Jack listened to the faint whistle of wind through the open doorway. Sarah had left, unbidden. He breathed in the cool air. Andrew was right: the cellar was exactly the same temperature as the last time, despite the looming mist and brewing storm outside.

"Speaking of business," Andrew said, stepping out of the vault, "have you got Curtis yet?"

"Got him? No. I, uh, the cops think the second murder is a copycat."

"The cops think?"

"Yeah." Jack shrugged.

"And you?"

"I don't know."

"Consistency applies to human nature, just as it does to wine." Andrew patted Jack on the shoulder. "It's either all truth or all lies, Jack. It can't be half of each."

Jack felt like one of Andrew's employees. Was he really being lectured? Those business books and seminars had gone to Andrew's head.

"Too bad," Andrew said.

"What is?"

"To see him walk free. Maybe he'll kill again. Next time it'll be some other poor woman."

Now Andrew was just needling, and Jack was starting to hate him again. It must have been easy to talk down to the whole town from up here.

"Eliza worked here. Yet you don't know anything useful."

"I know as much as you do," Andrew said, and Jack didn't know if that meant he didn't know anything or he knew a lot and wasn't telling. "No one even knew she was missing until she got found. The backpackers come in, they pick, they hang out together, pull beers at the Royal or the Globe, and then they just wander off when they feel like it. If I had a bottle of wine every time I was a man down at 6:00 a.m. and then found out for some reason they were in Toowoomba, well, I'd need another cellar. There's no need to come skulking around here, by the way. I've already offered you my services."

"I wasn't skulking."

"It's gotta be all lies or all truths, Jack. My wife was soaked through. There are muddy footprints here. You weren't over for a cup of tea. You must have scared the hell out of Sarah, if she came outside to find you there. Curtis definitely killed Eliza. I'm sure of it." There was a hushed serenity to his tone. "Alexis, I didn't really know—maybe it *is* a copycat. I'm not your enemy, Jack."

"How are you sure he killed her?"

"I just am. Okay? I know him. I was a cop for a long time. Let's call it my gut instinct."

"My gut's good too," Jack lied.

"Well, then, we're agreed." Andrew looked into the chamber. "Tell you what, I know it's been hard. Locals aren't exactly welcoming around here. I should have stepped in earlier, I suppose, but I'll vouch for you. They'll lay off. Then you can get on with the real job: putting Curtis back where he belongs."

"Finding the killer is the real job. Whether Curtis is involved or not," Jack said. It didn't escape him how badly Andrew wanted Curtis in jail. It seemed so personal.

"Sure, yeah." Andrew thought a second, then spread his arms toward the vault. "Tell you what. I'll give you a peace offering. Choose a bottle."

"Huh?"

"Choose one"—he swept an arm across the racks—"out of my collection."

"I thought some of these were worth thousands?"

"Some are. Others are worth much more. Go on."

"I couldn't," said Jack.

"You don't know a lot about wine, do you?"

"No."

"Then it's fair, because it's a lucky dip. You won't be able to rob me blind. We'll see what you get." He smiled, a lecherous carnie kind of smile. *Roll up, roll up. Choose a bottle. Any bottle.* "It's a game," Andrew added. "What's life without a few thrills?"

"That one," Jack said, pointing to a bottle on the middle of the middle shelf; as inauspicious a place as any, he figured, where the wine couldn't be too expensive. The last thing he needed was to feel in Andrew Freeman's debt, though perhaps he already did. He felt odd around him, the power dynamic. The way you feel meeting your boss's boss. Not shy, that wasn't it. But reserved. Andrew made him feel uneven.

Andrew clicked his tongue and picked up the bottle. He held it up to the light, tilted it at Jack.

"This one?"

"Sure."

"Not much of a drinker, you say?"

"If it's expensive, it's fine. I don't need one."

"If I play, I play fair." A grand smile erupted on his face, and then he was shoving the bottle at Jack's chest. Couldn't be rid of it quick enough. Jack clutched it with both hands. Andrew shouted like a carnie. "This one it is!"

"No, really."

"Just don't sell it, okay? It's to enjoy."

The door sighed on its hydraulic hinges as Andrew closed it. He headed across the cavern to the stairs, *clack clack clack*. The message was obvious. Jack's visit was over.

The wind had picked up outside, the rain now slanting sideways, cutting at any exposed skin. Andrew popped the collar on his jacket and zipped it up. Jack had no choice but to wear it, stinging pellets whipping his bare arms. He put a futile forearm over his brow as they waded to the house. He could hear the vines creaking on their stakes, rustling as if a thousand people were whispering together. He followed the reflective silver stripe on the back of Andrew's jacket. Then they were standing on the deck, shaking dry like dogs. Jack realized he'd been clutching the wine tightly with his spare hand. Maybe it was valuable. Or maybe he'd imbued it with false value just because Andrew Freeman had given it to him. He imagined pegging it against the wall, watching it burst in a star of bloodred, sliding down the corrugated iron in lumps, and laughing his way back down the hill.

Andrew scraped his shoes on the mat and levered them off. His socks left prints on the dark wood. Jack just stood there, shivering, unsure what to do.

"You can't walk down in this. Even with fog lights, no one'll see you," Andrew said.

Jack agreed but said, "I'm okay."

"No way. Hang on." Andrew disappeared inside with the clatter of a screen door. A minute later the door swung inward and a white hand towel was flung out. Jack managed to catch it between his chin and shoulder. He pushed it against his face, breathing into the warmth and dryness. Andrew reappeared, wearing sneakers, his jacket replaced with a polar fleece. He was holding keys.

"Right." He nodded.

They battled through the wind and sleet to the Forester. Jack hopped up and down while Andrew leaned over from the driver's seat to unlock his door. The rain slapped the car and rolled off the windshield in sheets. Andrew sat for a second, as if wondering if it would ease. Then he turned the car on and flicked the wipers. It wasn't any better. He cranked the wiper speed, tsked, and upped the speed again. Still barely a difference. Jack rubbed the back of his neck with the towel.

Andrew drove slowly down the hill, no more than ten, coasting in first, pressing the brake with a small whine whenever the roll picked up too much. He had fog lights and high beams on. It felt like sailing through a reef, slow and cautious. The visibility was so low that street signs grew out of the fog within meters, seemingly out of nowhere. Andrew guided the car on the road by the roughness under the wheels.

"The pub's fine," Jack said once they were in town. He knew they were getting close because a single red glow pierced the mist a few hundred meters away. Jack couldn't see the traffic light itself, just the red mist around it in a sphere. It flicked from red to green.

Andrew pulled into the curb. He clicked the hazards on just to be sure, which ticked like a watch and seemed to bounce backward off the mist and rain as if some laser grid encased them. The rain pounded down all around. Nothing but them in the world, no sense of time or the town in this drowning car.

"I can't take this," Jack said, offering the bottle.

Andrew shrugged. "You won it," he said, though his eyes stayed on the road. "That particular bottle, it doesn't need aging. It's all right to drink as is."

"I didn't win it, Andrew. I don't deserve it."

"You can. You will."

Jack had no more fight in him than that. He opened the door and the rain roared in, spraying the seat. The gutter was a river. Nothing for it, he sacrificed his left ankle and hopped to the curb. Two hurried steps and he was under the awning. The Forester hadn't moved. Water corralled and eddied in around the tires. Jack imagined the main street awash with red, those currant currents, bleeding from the Freemans' gouged silos. Surely it hadn't been as dramatic as that, but he was a filmmaker, after all.

Jack turned, but there was a soft clunking behind him. Andrew was knocking on the glass. He wound down the passenger window halfway. He was leaning across, one hand on the wheel, his elbow in the crook of the passenger seat.

"Open it when he goes back to jail," Andrew yelled above the rain. "Then you'll deserve it."

CHAPTER 29

The door to the pub was locked. Jack checked his phone. It was just past ten. He knocked, just in case. Nothing happened.

Jack still had the small towel Andrew had given him. He scrubbed it roughly through his hair once, then, satisfied, laid the cloth on a dryish patch of concrete. He sat. His back on the pub wall, legs scooted up, his body folded in an N. The rain hammered down in a curtain. Fingers of water pried under the awning. Jack flicked a cigarette butt that was too close to him, sending it into one of the streams, where it spun and spun and spun before wafting back past him on the tide. He propped the gifted wine next to him and leaned his hands on his knees, watching the rain. He still couldn't get a handle on Andrew Freeman. There was something about him. Something missing behind his eyes. Something fake.

How ridiculous was it that he'd gone up to the Freemans' in search of some kind of drug lab? Ironically, he'd been right. Andrew just dealt a legal drug. Jack thought of the sign inside the pub: AUSTRALIA'S MOST EXPENSIVE DRUG. That was a safety and addiction campaign, but the point stood. The value of a single vault in that cellar must have been mind-boggling. Jack wondered what the value of Andrew's "gift" was. He took out his phone and searched wine collectors. Articles about taste and culture were replaced by articles about *investment* and *valuations*. These weren't bottles of wine, Jack realized; they were retirement packages. More articles. There was a listing of two bottles of 1959 Dom Pérignon selling for $42,350 each.

"Fuck," he breathed. So much for not being in Andrew's debt if his bottle was anywhere close to that. Jack was out of his depth; he'd turned down *house* wines above $6. In his twenties, one of Jack's friends would buy boxed wine by the dollar, and squeeze the crinkled silver bag into reused bottles, before taking them to parties. He'd smile like a smarmy bastard when friends complimented him on his taste, which, inevitably, they always did. Jack just heard the stories, of course. He didn't go to dinner parties.

The Freeman winery wasn't designed for people who carried two glasses back to the table because happy hour was ending. It wasn't designed for people like him. Not for people like the Wades either. He kept scrolling through articles. Wine could be sold at auction too, he learned. Jack picked up the bottle. He chewed a nail, thinking. He picked it up and looked at the label, looking for the date. It didn't look *that* old. 1961. *Fuck.* Penfolds Grange. He'd heard of that. *Double fuck.* If you've heard of it, you can't afford it. He itched to search the value but resisted. He couldn't stomach owing Andrew something, and knowing how much the bottle was worth brought it out into the light and made it real. *Just don't sell it, okay? It's to enjoy.* It occurred to him that this might even be a bribe. He felt like Don Corleone had bought him a sports car. With a body in the trunk.

There was a rattle behind him. Alan Sanders leaned out, examined the storm, then spied Jack.

"Well," he said, "I wouldn't have pegged you as an alcoholic."

"I got caught out."

"It'll turn on you," Alan agreed, thought a second. "We're not open yet."

"I'm happy here."

"Mate, you're not happy anywhere."

"I'm content, then."

"Yeah." Alan looked out at the sheets of rain, listened to it skittering on the awning like poured rice. "This does suit you. But get inside, you idiot."

Inside, the bar was, of course, empty. Despite having not opened for the day—and, therefore, Jack assumed, being at its cleanest—a dandruff of potato chip crumbs flaked the carpet, and sticky, glossy circles varnished peeling-laminate wooden tables. The fungal, yeasty smell hung damp over everything. Jack knew the sommelier's word for it now: *the bouquet.*

Alan offered him a beer, said he had a few things to do, but could fix Jack some lunch when the kitchen opened later. Jack declined the beer, saying he was happy—or at least content—to wait out the storm in a booth by the wall. Alan insisted on at least turning on the television. "Because otherwise you're just too goddamn creepy."

In the booth, Jack scrolled through more wine articles. There were millions of dollars there, certainly enough money to kill two people over, but how was Curtis affecting Andrew's business? Why would he need him out of the picture?

The Royal was open proper now, Alan pacing behind the bar, clearly wondering if people would come in with the storm. It started with a couple of sodden tourists, their day trips ruined. Alan brightened. Then the deluge came, and the bar was as busy as Jack had ever seen it. People clogged the doorway, shaking coats and furring their hair into spikes.

Mary-Anne came in. She winked at Alan. Was there something there? It was easy to forget the people in the town were real people, not just extras in his movie. Of course Mary-Anne would have a man. It might as well be Alan.

There was an ad for Vanessa Raynor's talk show on the television, with footage of Ted Piper promising another interview. He was really milking this. *Break someone else's nose this time, buddy*, Jack thought. Just as he thought this, the advertisement replayed—in slow motion, those hacks—Ted launching into Jack.

"Credit to you," said Mary-Anne.

Was she talking to him? "I'm sorry?" he said.

"You can take a punch." She nodded up at the TV.

His hand went to his face, rubbed it. Maybe he could take a punch, but he sure wished people would stop hitting him.

"Wish I was on the telly," Mary-Anne said, mostly to herself, and then shuffled off.

A glass of beer clunked down in front of him. Jack was about to remind Alan that he hadn't wanted a beer when he looked up and saw Brett Dawson. Brett was standing awkwardly, not wanting to sit. He clinked his glass against the rim of Jack's. *Cheers.*

Brett raised his glass to his lips. Expectant. Jack picked up his own glass, raised it in reflective salute, then took a sip.

"Thanks," said Jack. He wasn't sure what else Brett wanted him to do. He looked nervous, like he had something to say. Andrew had said the locals would lay off. He knew Andrew had influence, but this quickly? Did he have a favor phone tree? Brett's unease made sense now. Jack could see it: a kid, pressured by his mother, pushed onto the playground to make friends. *You never know. You might like him.*

"Yeah. Sure." Brett fumbled for the words. "I didn't know you already had one." He nodded at the wine.

"That's for later," Jack said, turning the label away, in case Brett figured out how expensive it was.

"Right. Well…" Brett, clearly exhausting his small talk, wasn't sure what to do.

"Do you want a seat?"

Brett took the offer with relief. They sipped their beers in silence.

"I'm not here to make things worse," Jack said after a time. "Though I know it doesn't seem like it."

"Yeah. I know." Brett's voice was phlegmy with the beer.

"Did you know her?"

"Not really."

"Which one are we talking about?"

"I didn't know the lawyer. But the girl, yeah, well, she used to pick for Andrew, didn't she? I can't say I met her, personally, but the pickers, they float around town a bit. Some stay here at the pub, if they work shifts. Others at Mary-Anne's. So you see 'em round, know 'em by eye. Especially the Brits, they stand out like beacons."

"Why do they stand out?"

"They get so sunburnt they glow. Like beacons," Brett said again, as if that analogy was his only source of wit.

"You like Andrew?" Jack said, figuring if Brett was being forced to talk to him, he might as well push it.

"Yeah. Well, everyone does. Don't you?"

"He's a generous man."

"He is. That restaurant was lots of work for me and the boys."

"A big job like that though, would need better—" Jack saw the quick jerk of Brett's head. "Sorry. I mean *different* experience than what's in town. Architects and engineers, that kind of thing. No offense, but he'd have to bring some people in."

"That's the thing about Andy—he respects the town. He needed a few outsiders, but he kept us on board anyway. I was site foreman. I never had a proper job site before, let alone be foreman of it."

"And you rebuilt the Wade restaurant as well, for Curtis?"

"Yes. Well, half. The knockdown of the old site was paid for by Whittaker. The last bloke. And then Curtis hired us to build his new one."

"But you did do the entire job even if two different people hired you?"

"Yeah, okay," Brett conceded, as if suspicious of being tricked. "If you want to say it like that."

"And Whitti—what was his name?"

"Whittaker."

"Whittaker paid you to put concrete in the cellar. To ruin the ground?"

"That's not my fault. I'm just the hired hand."

"I'm not blaming you."

"Yeah. Whittaker had a chip on his shoulder about knocking down the old one. It was his family business, so it meant a lot to him. Like if you knocked down my motel."

"You still made thirty-five grand off his revenge."

"Are you saying I ripped him off?" Brett shifted at the hip. Took a drink.

Jack raised his hands in mock surrender. "I wouldn't dare. But tell me, if you're not ripping anyone off, why'd you smash the Wades' windows?"

"It wasn't just— Who told—" Brett shook his head, resigned. "Because he's a stingy fuck," he said. He looked up and saw Jack didn't believe him. "I was short, okay? I thought the build would be a bigger job than it turned out being. Nah, fuck that. Actually, he *needed* it to be a bigger job, but he let us go before we finished. It was like he just gave up."

"Looks finished to me."

"That's beside the point, and I don't want to get into it. Point is, I broke his windows because I figured he owed me a little. And I figured he could spare it. He's got the money—put in some tacky wine storage humidifier thingies, three of them, twenty grand each. Just woke up one morning and called me, said to put them in. Just like that." He snapped his fingers.

"If you were short, why not ask Andrew? He's basically the town benefactor."

"Andy helps everyone out from time to time. He put new doors on the motel after the wine stained 'em all. He repainted Mary-Anne's house for the same reason. But, just, I didn't want to ask him for too much. I thought this was something I could do on my own. Me and the boys."

Jack shook his head in disbelief. Brett saw ripping off Curtis Wade as a *family bonding exercise*. He changed the topic. "I know Andrew asked you to come here and play nice."

"Look, I bought you a drink."

"I can buy my own drinks. Be useful."

"I don't know anyone who killed anyone. If that's what you want."

"What *do* you know?"

"Man, what do you want me to tell you?" He threw his hands up. "All I know is boring country shit. Like that the yield should be higher this year than last. Like that this rain won't help Curtis's dying vines, because he's too cheap to fix the irrigation through there properly."

Jack resisted the temptation to point out that that was because of the concrete slab Brett had put there himself.

"Or that Andrew's Forester needs a new clutch soon, because I can hear it when he pulls up. That I'll be patching the roof at the bakery tomorrow because she's not ready for the hail. That Alan Sanders has gout. Yeah." He raised his voice and yelled to the bar. "Gout! Of course I know boring shit. It's *Birravale*, for fuck's sake, not Caracas." Jack must have looked surprised, because Brett added, "I watch the news. We're not all idiots… And you mope around wondering why no one here likes you? You've turned us into the murder capital of the world."

They were interrupted by Alan sliding a plate down in front of Jack. A kid's meal. Spaghetti. Jack couldn't remember ordering when he came in. He didn't think he could handle eating right now. He needed focus, even for this small war. His acrobat needed silence and calm to walk the rope.

"Thanks, Alan," Jack said, "but I haven't paid."

"You've been buying half meals at full price. I figure we can count this one sorted."

Another Freeman favor, Jack supposed. One phone call and suddenly the whole town was on his side. But the kindness was as fragile as scum on the surface of a pond, easily broken should you throw the right stone. The vibe of the place was all wrong, as delicate as Andrew's carefully stored wines. This was a kindness that required its environment to remain consistent.

Brett stood.

"Don't know why you're still here," he said. "You already know who did it. We all do. You just want to invent something bigger." He went to the door and paused a second, appreciating the gale. Decided to brave it.

Jack looked down at the pasta. He felt full to his sternum even as he twirled it around his fork. He needed Lauren, he realized. He missed her company. *Shit*, he realized. He missed her.

Brett, just like everyone else, thought the answer was easy: that the real question wasn't whether Curtis had killed Eliza but whether he'd killed

Alexis *as well*. But that just didn't sit right in Jack's gut. He'd already dis-missed the idea of Curtis sitting in his prison cell, slowly dragging a pencil across candy-wrapper thin prison paper, plotting revenge. Besides, he'd met the copycat—they'd almost taken his head off.

You get the threats too? Alexis had asked him back in Sydney, her warm hand on his. Or had she put her hand on his after she'd said that? He couldn't remember. She was a wisp in his mind now. His memory of her wouldn't stick. He thought of her cigarettes on her dresser. How he hadn't known she was a smoker either. *Best carton of cigarettes I ever bought.*

Another thing she'd said dislodged inside his brain. Those cigarettes. She'd framed an inmate about to walk on a grisly crime, her big career-making case. Alexis had a gutsy, tenacious side. One that cast aside certain morals in the pursuit of her own ends. One that could make enemies, perhaps. Jack realized they'd made basically the same decisions. Was it so different that her goals were morally superior to his own? Fuck, whoever killed her and tried to pin it on Curtis, they'd basically done the same thing too.

Was framing a guilty man as bad as framing an innocent one?

Framing a guilty man. Jack turned the thought over in his head. Curtis hated her because she'd sent him to jail. But Jack's cast was too small. Curtis wasn't the only one.

What had Curtis said to him, back in the house, when he'd been too captivated by Alexis's phone to take any real notice? *Jim Harrison, fuck, he'd tell you some stories.*

Jim Harrison. The nickname had skipped over Jack, but Curtis had been talking about James Harrison. Two of Alexis's most high-profile cases, and they'd been in the *same* prison.

Right motive. Wrong person.

Best pack of cigarettes I ever bought.

That word bubbled inside him again.

Revenge.

CHAPTER 30

James Harrison didn't look like someone who could gut a rabbit with a steady hand, let alone a teenage boy. He had a turtle's neck, sails of thick skin webbed to his thin collarbones. Adam's apple in the space between skin folds, set back into his neck: a whorl in a bushfire-hollowed gum. He was skinny too. His plain gray T-shirt fit him like a teenager's hoody. He wore cheap, gold-framed reading glasses. The type of glasses you find warped on the sides of roads, left at bus stops. Short gray stubble, chin and crown.

They shared a similarity in thin wrists, Jack noticed, though James's were chained to the stainless-steel table between them.

He had not been hard to find. Alexis's obituary had flagged the Harrison case as her big break, profiling how she put him away. His victim, Tom Rhodes, was the son of a wealthy property developer. It was kidnapping gone foul. There were gangs involved, organized crime. Jack imagined Curtis and James—in his mind, they shared a cell—throwing a ball between the top and bottom bunk. Curtis on the bottom, lobbing it up. James on top, clawing it out of the air with a flat hand before dropping it back down. Back and forth the ball—it was red and rubber in his mind—would go. And all the while, the two criminals traded battle stories of that bitch of a lawyer that screwed them. Maybe they made a deal.

After the storm had passed, Jack had walked back to the B and B. In his doorway, the black banana had been replaced with a freshly baked muffin. He picked it up and smelled it. Banana. Another omen of Andrew Freeman. He placed it on his bedside table, so it would at least look like he appreciated the gesture.

His research confirmed that Tom Rhodes had been eviscerated as

Alexis had described. That Alexis had uncovered star testimony at the final hour and convinced a deadlocked jury to convict. It all fit. And James Harrison was indeed still housed at Long Bay.

It was never hard to talk himself into the prison: the guards knew him and were, for the most part, excited to have him there—each hopeful for their own part to play in the national pantomime that true-crime podcasts and TV had turned the justice system into. It was the same with the prisoners. Jack had been worried that James wouldn't want to talk to him, but the guard had come back almost immediately with his message: *When can you come?*

He rang Lauren and filled her in. She seemed confused, not as pleased to hear from him as he'd been hoping.

"James Harrison?" She put him on speaker while she tapped at her phone, pulling up his case. "Okay, he has motive. I see it." Her voice was flat and analytical.

"You don't sound convinced."

"How'd he kill his lawyer from inside a prison cell? You've gotta find the ax, I think."

"I'm thinking that he might have paid someone, you know, with his organized crime connections."

"Uh-huh. And who's Hush then?"

"Don't know."

"Okay."

"I'm going to see him. You coming?"

"Not today."

"You're busy?" He didn't do a good job keeping the incredulity out of his tone.

"I might have a closed restaurant, but I still run a winery."

"Vineyard." It slipped out.

"What?"

"Nothing. Did I do something?"

"The cops were here. They were looking for the ax. That Winter bloke is aggressive. He almost arrested Curtis. Hell, he would have arrested me too if he could have." Jack breathed out in relief. Thank God he'd taken the phone. "They didn't, this time. But they're coming back."

"I didn't tell them anything."

"Okay."

"I didn't." He was pleading now.

"You went up to the Freemans'?"

"I couldn't sleep. Thought I'd poke around. I thought he might be Hush."

"And?"

"Nothing. Andrew gave me a bottle of wine."

"So you're friends now?"

"No. Look, I didn't even want it. I thought you'd be pleased to hear about James. It all fits. This could be it."

"It doesn't fit," Lauren snapped. "It just fits in your head. Who's Hush? Get the ax first—that's the most important."

"Alexis's death is looking more and more planned the further we go. Does he fit anymore?"

"He's the *only* one that fits. But you want something dramatic, so go chase your serial killer."

"Lauren—"

"What type of wine was it?"

He told her.

"Wow. He must like you."

She hung up on him.

The rain had sapped the morning, so it was nearing dusk when Jack finished the drive back through Sydney to Long Bay. They'd taken him straight into the interview room, switched the camera off for him. James Harrison had been set up in there already, chained to the table. Waiting calmly for Jack Quick to come for him.

As he always hoped he would.

"So glad you're here," James said. His voice was high-pitched, each word moist, as if he were chewing each thought like tobacco before spitting the words out.

"Jack Quick."

"I know who you are."

Jack was aware of the pointless introduction but unsure where to start.

"So, how do we do this?" said James.

"I'd like to ask you some questions."

"It's your show." James rocked back, which clinked his chains against the table. "Shoot."

"About Alexis White," Jack said, examining James's face for a reaction. To his surprise, the killer broke into a wide smile and leaned forward. He was excited, speaking his wet words quickly.

"Yeah? That's good. She set me up, right? Prison testimony. Bull"—he flicked a thumb up, as if counting off syllables—"shit." Then a pointer finger. He seemed to surprise himself that his finger made a gun; he pointed it at Jack. "Knew it."

"You knew Curtis Wade in here?"

"I mean, I knew he was here. Not well though. But we watched him on the TV, so I guess we all knew him."

"You watched the show?"

"Yeah."

"And you knew Curtis?"

"Yeah." He thought a second. "I see where you're going with this. The two of us. I *love* it." He smacked his hands on the table. "So good! Yeah then, if it helps, I knew him. Real well."

They seemed to be having two separate conversations at once. Jack tried to understand what James was telling him. Was he admitting that he and Curtis had planned this together?

"Tell me more about Alexis."

"She got what was coming for her."

"So you're saying she deserved it?"

"Fuck yeah I am. Curtis Wade's harder than I gave him credit for."

"I know that you and Curtis had a plan," Jack said, lowering his voice. At this, James leaned in, dropped his shoulders. "You do?"

"Yes."

"Yeah. 'Kay. Sure. We'll do it like that."

Jack wished he would stop saying *we*. James seemed to be filling in a picture that Jack didn't even know was there.

"What do you want to know?"

"I know why you did it. The two of you were burned by her. But I'm not quite sure how. Did Curtis commit the murder for you? And if he didn't, tell me who did." That didn't sound right. Why would Curtis frame himself? Another name came to him, and then it was in the air, an accusation: "Andrew Freeman?"

"Who?"

"Never mind. Who committed the murder?"

"Wait. What?" James scratched the back of his wrist—his thinness gave him a good range of movement in the cuffs—and his forearms rattled in the loops like the ball of gas in a spray can. "I did."

"Did what?" *Say it*, Jack thought, *say it*.

"Killed him." James shrugged.

Him? Jack paused a second. James was confused; he was talking about the old murder.

"You mean Tom Rhodes?" Jack asked.

"Yeah, I killed him."

"And what about Alexis?"

"Well, she stitched me up, right? That's what we'll use."

"Stopping saying *we*."

"You, then."

"I'll do what?"

"Use that."

"We're getting sidetracked. You killed her?"

"Fuck." James leaned back, and his chest hopped with his small chuckle. "I wish."

"Did you work with anyone on the kidnapping of Tom Rhodes? Were you part of an organization? If it wasn't Curtis Wade and it wasn't Andrew Freeman, is there someone you knew from back then? You know, a contract killer?"

"I think we should start again," James said after thinking for a beat. "Because I'm keen. But you gotta tell me what to say. The criminal underworld, all that business, I can't say I really know. But if that's what you need. I'll tell you something."

Jack closed his eyes. Was James such a psychopath that he was literally unable to make sense, or was he enjoying running Jack in circles? Or was Jack missing something? The oddity of sitting here unable to extract a confession from a killer who was telling him everything didn't escape him.

"We'll start again," Jack said. "Let's try simple yes and no for now, and see where that takes us."

"'Kay." James grinned and pushed his glasses up his nose. "Shoot."

"Did you kill, or arrange to kill, Alexis?"

James thought, trying to figure out something. Perhaps how the conversation had led to this. "You want honesty?"

"Please."

"No."

"Hmm." Jack tapped a scarred knuckle on the table, frustrated.

"Not the right answer?"

"Not quite."

"Well." James rubbed his chin. "Yes?"

He said it as a question, voice lilting up. As if he wanted Jack to be happy with the answer. As if he wanted to give the answers Jack *wanted* him to give. Jack sighed, shut his eyes, and squeezed the bridge of his nose. Lauren had been right; he was still chasing drama over truth.

"Was that the wrong answer too?" said James, a pleading tone to his voice.

"Why do you think I'm here?"

"You got my letter."

Perhaps it was the disappointment of it or the simple way James had said it, like it was the most obvious thing in the world, but Jack felt like he was about to throw up. He was so fucking tired and so fucking hungry and, most of all, so fucking *full*.

"Okay." Jack tried to keep the shake out of his voice as he stood. "Thanks."

"You got what you need already? But you didn't record anything."

"Sure. Yeah. I got what I needed. You didn't kill Alexis."

"'Kay, sure. Whatever you say."

And that was James Harrison, laid bare. He hadn't killed Alexis. He just thought Jack Quick, television shaman, could get him out of jail.

James Harrison thought he was the goddamn sequel.

"You're a guilty man," said Jack.

"Guilty but wrongfully convicted, yeah?"

"Tom Rhodes—"

"I killed him." James mimed sticking a knife in the table, drew it across like a child with a pencil: a curled fist, pressing hard. "I'll give you the details. Gory ones. If you want?"

"You shouldn't be telling me this."

"Huh?"

"You're supposed to tell me you're innocent."

"Does that make it easier for you?"

Those words took the wind out of him. He had to leave. He turned for the door, rapped it twice. There was a crash from behind him. James had stood, flicked the aluminum chair against the back wall, where it now lay on its side. He was standing, stooped though, still bound to the table.

He was breathing through his nose, shoulders heaving up and down, his turtled neck dipping in and out. Glasses askew.

"Why the fuck are you here then?" he yelled, the sound bouncing off the walls. He spat in Jack's direction; it fell well short. He was shaking the table. Rabid. "If you're not going to help me?"

"I won't help you," Jack said. Not *I can't*, which he almost said. *I won't.*

Jack heard the door open but didn't turn. James locked eyes with him and seemed to calm down.

"But that's what you do, isn't it, Mr. Quick?" The insult seethed through his teeth, and then a smile. "You get people like me out of jail."

CHAPTER 31

The all-night service station glowed green and white in the dark, levitating strips of neon. The light stung Jack's bleary eyes. It was ten minutes to the turn, then nothing to Birravale. He pulled in. Black bugs flecked him, spiraling up to circle the neon. Jack filled his tank and washed his windshield. Inside, it was brighter. Clinical. The hum of fridges. Jack swiped his card. It was more than a hundred bucks, so he had to sign. Walked out crinkling.

Birravale was sodden and calm in the way rain seems to pat down energy as well as dust. Puddles, mud-filled potholes—water splashed up his doors as he drove. Chalk was streaked on the bakery sign, not yet corrected. Jack waited as the single traffic light blinked, looking over at the fuzzy, warm yellow light from the Royal. He shot past the turn to the B and B and turned right into Lauren's driveway. He parked out front. The house was dark, which was no surprise. He considered honking but texted her instead. No reply. He looked in the backseat, itched.

After ten minutes, he was ready to leave when he saw her emerge, stride across the deck, and open his passenger door. Jack realized he was messy, so he brushed the front of his jacket. Lauren climbed in and wrapped her arms around herself even though it wasn't that cold. She looked pale, her eyes sunken. Like she hadn't slept.

"What do you want?" she said.

"I was wrong about James Harrison."

"Okay." Her fingers hunted the door handle. "Is that it?"

"Did I do something?"

"Fuck, Jack."

"What?"

"That for me?" She nodded to the back.

"Just stuff."

"Uh-huh."

"I don't…" He realized he was gripping the steering wheel. "I don't know what I'm doing."

"No shit."

"What happened? Here." *In this car,* he tried to say. *Between us.* But that sounded stupid. He didn't know the words. Besides, there was no *us.* Just another fake connection, intimacy through a screen.

"Of course it's not James fucking Harrison."

"I know. You told me. I should have listened to you."

"Like I give a rat's about you listening to me." Her voice rose and fell. "Goddamn it, Jack. The only thing I care about is that we're running out of time."

Jack didn't know whether he saw it in her eyes or heard it in her tone, but suddenly he understood. Winter had come out to her property and accused her brother again. He must have really scared her. And the only person in the whole country who was supposed to be on her side was off chasing stories at Long Bay.

"You're accusing people of Alexis's murder, and it shows you don't care what happened to Eliza. Or what happens to my family." She swallowed hard, and Jack saw the youth in her face. "Or what happens to *me,* Jack."

James Harrison had motive for Alexis, but not for Eliza. By treating the murders separately, he was admitting that he still thought Curtis guilty of Eliza's. *He's guilty,* she'd said, days ago in her drive. *He always will be. It doesn't matter if he actually did anything or not.* She didn't know about the shoe like Jack did. Every new copycat they looked at rammed her family's shame back at her. Once Andrew Freeman, or James Harrison, was out of the picture, Curtis Wade became a killer again.

And she was right, of course. They were running out of time. The older the case got, the likelier it remained unsolved. The more likely it hung around the Wade family like a collective noose. TV shows and podcasts aren't on recent crimes because, as the stories age, so does the truth in them, bled out like the midday color in this bleached-bright town. And you can play with that. Physical evidence decays. Conversely, and it doesn't make sense, but memory can sharpen. Not because people remember better. But because, as time wears through truth, there is less to contradict it. The real reason memory sharpens: because you can put it in high-def, beam it into people's lounge rooms, tell them what they believe.

But Lauren didn't know Jack had one extra piece of evidence against Curtis. She didn't know.

"Lauren, four months ago—" He felt tired. Light-headed. His stomach cramped. His acrobat had fallen, was drowning. He'd been eating more since he got to Birravale. Maybe it was because there was nothing to do but linger here, like the water on the road. Like festering potholes of wine. Or maybe it was because, in the "murder capital of the world," he'd started to feel safe. Lauren was a part of that. *Spit it out.* She looked at him with a tilted head, tired eyes lightly bloodshot. He ground his jaw. Realized he was gripping the wheel again, and said:

Nothing.

He couldn't tell her. Not yet.

"Four months ago?" Lauren prompted.

Jack gave her a little. "I know you're trying to see things from all sides, but I think you can't. You're blocking out the truth because it might hurt you. And it might. I understand. Four months ago, I felt the same. I was just trying to make a TV show."

"Now?"

"Now I'm just trying to find the truth."

"Truth." She laughed, had enough, got out of the car. Her back was to him, but he still heard it. "Wow." It seemed for a second she would say nothing more, but then she leaned down, just before she swung the door closed, and said: "You hold that word out in front of you like a shield. And you don't even know what it means."

It comes out in order. Reversed. Like watching a movie of people going into a club and then rewinding it. If you were really paying attention, you could pick through your day.

There, the banana muffin. That was last in, sitting on the cold rim of the bathtub. There, the bright orange of the cheesy, salt-coated Doritos, the empty bag next to bright-orange marks on the white sheets where he'd wiped his fingers. There, the brown of the chocolate he'd eaten while driving to Lauren's. He'd brushed the flecks from the front of his coat when she'd entered the car. There, the scotch finger biscuits, shoveled in crumby handfuls before turning off the highway. No one in the service station had noticed his crinkling jacket, pockets full, as he signed for the food. The food he was paying for, anyway. No one looks twice when a grown man swipes snacks. They're supposed to be better than that. Shoplifting is for women, apparently. Not a man's crime. Not a man's hands, knuckles scarred, shoving packets in his coat. The spaghetti now. Worms. Next, just spit and acid. A retching burn where the body wallows, empty, while the mind still tries to squeeze the last drop of sacrifice out of it. Eyes bloodshot, pushed against sockets. Ribs tight with pressure.

They call it a purge for a reason. With each piece of food he saw, Jack tried to vent the day, the week, the year, the life from him.

That's what you do, isn't it? You get people like me out of jail.

Thin ropes of cloudy spit hung from his lips. He wiped them away.

You hold that word out in front of you like a shield.

He flushed. Started again. Rewinding. Get it out.

Curtis's guilt, laced up in his closet. Alexis's hand. Soft and warm and alive.

The lies you can live with.

More. Harder. It's not working if there isn't pain. His fist was slicked and slimy as if freshly jellied, just birthed.

Whump.

Get it all out. Curtis. Alexis. Eliza. Dead women. Dead ends. His brother. Lauren. Andrew. His father. His brother. His brother. His brother.

Liam. In the hospital. Tubes rising out of him, bound up in a spider-web. Bubbles coasting through the transparent plastic crisscrossed against the white of the hospital wall. A nurse coming in. Pouring a nondescript brown sludge into an upright cylinder, affixed at Liam's hip, that sucked and gurgled as it slowly descended. Brown watermark stained on the plastic. Like filling oil in a car. After that, for the first time, food felt like paste in Jack's mouth. No taste or color or smell anymore. The shit that went in the same as the shit that came out, just skipping a few steps. Tar to go down a chute: a throat or a tube. So he'd started avoiding food. Overchewing. It worked. He and his brother decayed in tandem. It felt fair. Later, when people started to notice, and forced him to chew the paste into a swallow, he could always feel it inside him. Thick gunk. Remembered the brown sludge glugging down the tube. Had to get rid of it. That sludge. Unwelcome. Unwanted. His undeserved reward for still walking around. That sludge they'd literally *poured* into his brother.

That sludge that poured out of him now, small penance.

You're never really full, never really empty. There's a point where it stops coming though. Where your fingers dip the wooden bucket back into the well, but the bucket comes up empty. The bile and the spit have dried. But just because it stops coming out doesn't mean it's not in there. Jack could feel it in his blood, in his breath. Still not empty. Something inside. No matter how hard the push. How dry the well. Sleep, maybe. Pass out, maybe. Wake fifteen minutes later, cold tile pressed to cheek. The smell of vomit settling into the room. Still there, that feeling. Not empty.

He hunted for more. Those half-finished packets of food. Those new ones. He'd thought about it and bought backups, reinforcements. Worse than the preplanning was a trip back out to the all-night supermarket, if he was in Sydney. Out here it would be the gas station. He didn't think he did go back out there. But he couldn't quite remember now, because time had passed and there was more food and he was eating again. Because it was a cycle, this, and putting more in let him get more out. Like filling a glass to float a dead bug to the rim. More in. More out. Maybe then he'd be empty. Never was. Never was.

That unachievable goal. To fill himself up enough to be hollow.

He ate a second time. Purged. Brushed his teeth. Slept. *Done with it,* he promised himself as he closed his eyes. *You've slipped, but you're okay. Once is fine.* Two hours later, waking up, doing it all again. He ran out of food. Nothing left in this fucking place. He found some individually wrapped biscuits near the kettle. Fortune. He tried to remember if Mary-Anne had a fruit bowl on the table downstairs. Couldn't. Knew he was too tired to drive. Nothing useful in the room except two biscuits and a bottle of '61 Grange.

The bottle of Grange. That would fill him up. He got the corkscrew from the tea stand, near where he'd found the biscuits. Should he open it? It was too expensive. That would be wasteful. Waste. Like what they'd put into Liam—the stuff other people shit out. As if today were a day to take a stand on wastage. At his sickest, he was always poor. Every dollar on food. Either to fill himself up or just to make his fridge look normal if people came over. Fancy stuff too. The best brands. A fridge full of it, turned over every week in large green bins. Just to be normal. The bottle of wine, it had no value to him.

Jack pulled out his phone. Googled the Grange as best he could, just out of curiosity. He felt weak and pseudo-drunk. Mistyped a few times. Got it up. Easy enough to find on an auction site. Three thousand. Okay. So not ten or twenty. But still, three grand. He turned the bottle over in his hand. The label was lightly yellowed. Old-fashioned type, like a newspaper. *Penfolds* splashed in cursive red across the top, bulletin type below. He chewed a biscuit, sludge in his gums. *Fuck it*, he thought. He'd promised not to sell it anyway.

He tilted the bottle at the toilet bowl in a grim cheers; they'd share it soon enough. Stripped the red seal that topped the neck, peeling it around in one go. Cork bare in the neck.

Three thousand. Part of his conscious brain kicked back in. *Don't open it.* As if this expensive bottle were the last thinning twine that separated him from his old self. Four years sober. If that was what this represented, he was already doing shots, dancing on the bar. He plunged the corkscrew in. The cork came out easier than he'd expected for an old wine; he'd thought it would be soaked and swollen with time. Some of it sloshed down his knuckles. "Fifty bucks," he said with a laugh. Raised the bottle to his lips. Drank as much as he could in a long swallow. Filled himself up.

His first thought was that the wine had turned. The environment had perhaps not been *consistent* enough. There was grit in his teeth, not the smoothness of the red Andrew had shared up at the top of his silo. Of course, all wines were different. Maybe you weren't supposed to slug it from the bottle. Of course you weren't. That was like taking a bite of a Black Angus standing in a field. Still. Something wasn't right. Jack couldn't tell the subtleties of the flavors in a regular bottle. But this bottle had no subtlety. There was something around the rim of the bottle too. On the inside. Specks of dirt. Same as the grit in his teeth. Grit, dirt—$3,000 his arse.

Something was definitely in the bottle. He pushed a finger in the neck and ran it around. It came out pale red, as if swished in bleeding gums—specks on the fingertip. Part of his brain knew this wasn't right. Wasn't supposed to be there.

Poison. Fuck.

How had he picked a poisoned bottle out of Andrew's random selection? Did Andrew give him the bottle he pointed to? Or was there some sleight of hand? He tried to remember whether he'd actually seen Andrew get the exact bottle he'd pointed to.

Don't sell it… It's to enjoy.

Andrew was hiding something. Perhaps he did have something behind one of those doors. And he was killing anyone who got too close. Eliza had found it. Alexis, too. And now Jack.

Poison. Jack started to panic.

He didn't feel ill. Then again, he'd never been poisoned before. *Be rational.* He tried to calm himself. *Why hadn't the others been poisoned?*

And then he knew what it was. And he thought back through everything and knew the wine hadn't turned.

Why would Andrew put something like this in a valuable bottle of wine? Unless.

Unless it wasn't valuable at all.

He took another slug from the bottle, just to be sure. Dropped the half-full bottle. The curve of the bathtub caught it, so it didn't shatter, guided it into a roll up the other side, riderless in a skate park. It came to rest, sideways, in the middle of the tub. Glugged. The air rushing in countered the liquid coming out, giving the flow an unnatural pendulum-like force, vomiting the wine in slow heaves.

And Jack Quick, the man who couldn't tell tannin from an oak bush-fire when he'd arrived in Birravale, suddenly knew what had been added to the bottle: the smell in Andrew's car; the earthy spice in the cellar; Sarah Freeman in the street, gathering up her broken, dusted shopping.

Cinnamon.

CHAPTER 32

Lauren opened the door, went to close it again with one fluid motion of her arm.

Jack got a few words in. "I know why he killed them now. Andrew—"

That was all he could get out before the door clicked. He was standing on the porch, in jeans and a blue polar fleece. He knew she'd open back up. He'd gotten enough out. He was a TV producer after all—he knew how to build a cliff-hanger. He imagined her leaning, back against the door, cursing him, while her resolve faded against her curiosity. The sun was just up, slivers of light cutting through the steaming mist just beginning to dissolve. He'd had to wait until morning to come and tell her. He'd been too weak to see her. He needed the night to calm, to fish his acrobat, clinging to a rock and waiting for an errant ship, from the ocean. He'd slept little. Used the time for research. But he was filled with adrenaline now. Because he knew why he was wrong and why he hadn't been able to solve the crime. He'd thought Lauren had been emotional about her brother. But he'd been the same.

Because he had *assumed* Curtis had to be guilty of *something*. Because he needed that to justify his own regrets, to validate his own involvement, so that he could be some savior, out here, solving a murder. But because he'd already tried and convicted Curtis in the back of his mind, Jack had never really considered that maybe this didn't involve him at all. The only question Jack really needed to answer was the one Lauren had posed several days ago: Why would someone want Alexis dead?

He'd thought the motive was revenge. But put Eliza back in the picture, and that didn't work. Because the motive was the key. For both murders. If they were to be linked, it had to be the same.

Eliza had worked at Andrew's winery. Before Alexis died, she would have been prepping for the pending appeal.

They'd both found something. Something big enough to get them killed. Maybe the same thing that Eliza had tried to sell to Sam Culver in her voicemail.

Four marijuana plants weren't enough to kill over. But Andrew was peddling a different drug: Australia's most expensive, in fact. And he wasn't growing it. What both women had died for was so simple: the reason why Andrew couldn't have an insurance analyst turning over his property.

The door clicked open. Lauren stood with arms crossed, eyebrows raised as if to say *This better be good.*

"Andrew Freeman's wine"—Jack held up the near-empty bottle of 1961 Penfolds Grange—"is fake."

It was the Italian that Jack remembered first. The articles he'd read, at the start of everything, when he was reading up on wineries: the Italian who'd boosted his alcohol content with methanol, killing twenty-three and leaving dozens blinded and hospitalized. Jack had never had cause to consider that as more than a slightly interesting news piece.

But he'd learned something up at Andrew's cellar during the storm. And its meaning had sunk in as he'd accidentally slopped the Penfolds on his fingertips, immediately estimating the cash value. He'd realized the true value of Andrew's vaults, thinking of it like a bank, but he still saw the individual bottles as *drinks*. He realized now—they weren't bottles of liquid. They were gold bars. Picassos. And everything that came with those precious objects suddenly applied to wine: theft, counterfeit, forgery.

The cinnamon in the Penfolds had collided with another thought, hunkered at the back of his mind. His friend siphoning old boxed wine to impress at dinner parties. Andrew examining the label of the bottle atop the silo, assessing the value, gently placing it back in the picnic basket. It wasn't hard to do the research once he'd known what he was looking for. Cinnamon. Elderflower juice. Lemongrass. All used as additives to cheap wine to make them feel like vintages. There were a few ways Andrew could have gone about it. Collect the empty bottles of the expensive wines and refill them. Fake the labels.

The fatal Italian wine was just the tip of the iceberg in a billion-dollar industry seriously afflicted by wine fraud. In South Africa, vegetable additives were added to sauvignon blancs, which went on to pick up several awards. That was harmless enough. Some wineries, though, had started adding silver nitrate. Silver nitrate is a toxic salt—the stuff that clever vampire slayers put in bullets in movies, but instead, it was being packaged up and sent out to family barbecues. People were in jail for forging wines. They were minor celebrities, it seemed, their names unspooling in the search results page by page: Rudy Kurniawan, Hardy Rodenstock.

Again, Jack was stunned that a bottle of wine was enough to kill two people over. But like Sarah had told him, these weren't just bottles of wine—they were *art*. Rudy Kurniawan had sold an estimated *$550 million* of counterfeited wine. He'd eventually been prosecuted by the FBI and was serving ten years in prison.

Enough to kill over? Jack would drink to that.

Christ, Lauren had even told him Eliza was partial to stealing bottles.

He explained this to Lauren, standing on the deck, with her leaning against the doorframe. She held out a hand without saying anything. Jack handed her the bottle. She sipped the remnants, rolling her tongue over her gums.

"Yep," she said, examining the bottle, "that's a 2018 Penfolds *Strange* all right."

"Does that look real?"

"The bottle? Sure."

"So he's recycling them?"

"Maybe. Maybe he gave you this one because at least it was in a real bottle. The question is why he gave it to you at all."

Jack thought about his friend bringing his faux-expensive bottles to dinner. The lines he'd told Jack he loved to use: *Oh, I just picked that up in Tasmania; you know, they've just come off a strong vintage; of course, you haven't really tried merlot until you've been to the Southern Highlands.* Relishing in the approval of his friends. Andrew was the same, telling Sarah to go back and get more wine, the ones in her arms not good enough for his VIPs. They were good enough, sure, but they weren't *fun* enough. *What's life without a few thrills?* Andrew had asked Sarah then, and later, Jack himself in the cellar. He'd sauced his collectors up on real wine and then fed them the fake shit. Then he'd sat back and laughed as they guzzled Andrew's bravado in the form of cinnamon and elderflower juice. And then Andrew had washed the bottles out and sold them again. *Give them what they've paid for.*

The restaurant wasn't a restaurant. It was a turnstile.

He thought of Andrew hesitating in the cellar. It wasn't because Jack had picked a too-expensive bottle: Andrew had hesitated because he wasn't sure what was actually in it. But he'd given it to Jack anyway. Perhaps because Jack knew nothing about wine. Perhaps for the thrill. He wanted Jack to hold Andrew's guilt in his hands and, quite literally, piss it away.

Serial killers leave calling cards—those "masterminds" Lauren hated. They take pleasure in dangling clues, sitting just out of reach. The famous Zodiac Killer left letters, for example. Andrew Freeman just smiled at his collectors with red lips. Patted himself on the back for his own cleverness as his marks drank away their own evidence.

"He likes to brag." Jack shrugged.

He could see Lauren had reached the same conclusion. It was hard to disagree with Andrew's pomposity. She still had questions.

"What about the phone?" she asked. "And I think we still need to get the ax back, to build our case."

"Andrew wouldn't have had time to come down from the silo. But Sarah would have. That's why he came and got me. He knew that I'd been around here, too much probably. They must have tried before, but I was getting in the way. He wanted me up there, distracted, so that she could go and put the evidence back." Andrew had fucked up though; he hadn't kept Jack occupied long enough.

"Who's Hush?"

"Maybe him. Maybe it's irrelevant."

"I think he's still important."

"Maybe," Jack said. There was so much he didn't know about Alexis. If Andrew was Hush, there were two motives—Sarah may have wanted her husband's lover dead. She could have talked him into it, if Alexis knew about the wine. "But I think this bottle is the most important. We now know the meaning of Eliza's voicemail—why she had something big but wasn't sure if it was technically illegal. This would do well in the tabloids."

"It's convincing. I'll give you that." But Lauren still seemed unsure, the look on her face like she was trying to connect all the dots, make it work. "I'll come with you. Five percent, by the way."

"What?" Jack thought she was talking about the alcohol content of something.

She turned back inside to grab a coat off a hook. "The problem with wine fraud is that once the bottles are in circulation, you don't know if you've got a real one or a dud one. It's not like a Van Gogh, where Andrew can only paint one copy. You also can't open a twenty-thousand-dollar bottle of champagne just to check if it's real. People like Kurniawan fucked the industry good, crippled the market, and now all their wines are still out there. They reckon that five percent of any collection is fake. That's why we don't collect here."

She looked at him knowingly. Jack stared at his toes. He didn't need her to state the implication. *I know about this shit.*

She said it anyway. "If we'd worked together properly, we would have figured this out ages ago. Of course I know about this, Jack. I run a fucking *vineyard*."

She stepped on the porch and buckled her coat. Jack thought he might have cooled her down a bit. But she was still pissed. She'd even called it a vineyard.

"I'll go to the police. If that's what you want," Jack said.

"And miss out on your finale?" Lauren dropped her guard to flash a smile. "No way."

"We can't go just yet," Jack said.

"Why not?" she asked.

"Because of that." He nodded behind her.

There was a creaking and then Curtis was in the doorway. He sized up Jack, swung his gaze to his sister, who gave him the look of calm Jack had become accustomed to between them.

"So," Curtis growled, "you here to apologize?"

"Not quite." Jack looked at Lauren, then back to Curtis. "I'm here to borrow your gun."

CHAPTER 33

Jack knew Andrew would run.

The rifle hung by Jack's side as he and Lauren walked up the drive. Curtis had elected not to come. *In case someone gets shot*, he'd said. Jack couldn't tell if Curtis meant that he didn't want to get mixed up in the aftermath, so he had plausible deniability, or he didn't trust himself not to pull the trigger. The gun was light, but after walking up the hill, it was hanging heavy and pulled taut on his shoulders. He swapped hands. Sweat slicked the stock, where Jack gripped it like a club. He'd been too embarrassed to ask Lauren how to actually use it. He wasn't planning on shooting anyone—he just wanted the threat. But if events turned, the gun was about as useless as a baseball bat. So. Club grip.

It was too early for tourists, but Andrew's Forester was in the driveway. Jack jiggled the handle on the restaurant. Locked. Lauren walked around the side of the building and opened the recycling bin. Jack leaned over her shoulder as she rifled through it. There wasn't a single bottle. *Odd*, Jack thought. *A winery that doesn't put wine bottles in their recycling.* There was a regular bin next to it, filled with food scraps. Then compost. Next to that was not a bin, but a crate made out of wooden slats. Inside was a plastic tub with a sealed lid. Inside that, standing on end, were rows of bottles. Jack lifted one out and ran a finger over the rim. It came off reddened. *Andrew must clean them in the cellar*, Jack thought. Behind one of those doors.

Andrew hadn't even bothered to hide the empties very well. But maybe he didn't have to. There had never been a flicker of suspicion. Did people in town know? Probably some of them did. Andrew gave the

word, and the townsfolk fell into line. He'd given Brett Dawson a job he
was unqualified for and new doors for his hotel. He'd repainted Mary-
Anne's house. Jack didn't know what he'd done for people like Alan, but
it wouldn't surprise him if the *handshake deal with the pub* persisted, cash-
in-hand fines for drunk drivers. So maybe they knew. Maybe they also
knew that they depended on Andrew's benevolence. This town, as Curtis
had said, was not a town: it was Andrew up at the top and a rubble of
houses at the bottom. Perhaps a few bottles of fake wine were forgivable
when that wine was blood in the veins of the community.

But Curtis was an anomaly. He'd come into town an instant millionaire with no need to be bought. And then all the attention Curtis
brought with him, Andrew's wine suddenly a source of much interest,
seeing as half the town was dipped in it. If Eliza had found out the truth,
and Andrew had killed her for it, maybe he wanted to nail two birds
by sending Curtis away too. That had worked until Jack's documentary
had popped the cork again. Andrew declined to be interviewed, clearly
hoping it would come and go, watched by few, cared about by fewer.
But as the series went on, and it grew more and more popular, and then
it started to look like Curtis might get out...

Worried that the documentary might shine an extra light back on him,
it wouldn't have been hard for Andrew to slip Eliza's shoe in the bushland. Then there'd be no need for the cops to crawl over his counterfeit
operation. Probably the only thing Andrew hadn't counted on was Jack
covering it up.

Sarah made sense now too. She'd had to stand by and watch Andrew
disassemble her family business. Forced to keep his secrets while the man
that married her for the view bled her legacy dry.

The fingers in Eliza's mouth. That worked too, he supposed, if con-
strued as a message. Maybe after slamming in a very heavy hydraulic door.
Don't speak my secrets.

And then Alexis must have found out. Andrew had only one way out then, again. Someone had to die, and the suspect, again primed and perfect for him, fresh out of prison. Jack had once asked Curtis, *What's the point in framing you twice?*

"Heads up," Lauren yelled, and Jack looked up in time to see an empty plastic bottle sail toward him. He couldn't catch it without dropping the rifle, so he let it hit his hip and ricochet to the ground. Lauren walked over, picked it up, and held it out to him.

Diethylene glycol.

He looked at Lauren and shrugged. Didn't mean anything to him. *Alcohol is chemical*, Sarah had said. *I'm not cooking meth.*

"It's brake fluid," she said.

"In the wine?"

"It's used to give cheap wines a richer flavor."

"Poisonous?"

"Unlikely in these quantities." She turned the bottle over. "But you wouldn't want brake fluid in your glass if you knew it was in there, I'm guessing."

"How do you know this?"

Lauren shot him the same withering and exasperated glare as back at her house. *Five percent.* Jack had no desire to get into an argument about his lack of teamwork, so he let her have her moment.

"Someone used this in Austria back in the eighties," she said. "No one got hurt. But the entire wine industry was fucked, because you just don't know, you know? It took decades to recover."

"Andrew's serving people brake fluid?"

"Looks like."

"This is worse than cinnamon." Jack turned the container in his hands. Laymen didn't give two fucks about a counterfeit '61 Grange; they weren't the ones drinking it. Brake fluid, though, that was another level entirely. That would have mums stopping in the supermarket, seesawing over that bottle of cab sauv. Vanessa Raynor's show would be a jubilant verbal massacre. She loved the dodgy ones. *Discover!* magazine made much more sense. "At least it's not actual poison."

"Still. It might be just as deadly."

Behind them, at the house, there was the clatter of a door closing. They both turned. Andrew was standing there, cracking his neck; he hadn't noticed them yet. When he did, he paused a second. Jack felt his shoulders tense. The gun came up. An accident. A reflex.

Andrew saw the gun and ran.

Lauren and Jack bolted after him. Jack didn't know about Lauren, but he knew he'd be spent on the foot chase quickly. Especially after last night. His knees wobbled in their joints, calves trying to find the energy to push himself forward. Luckily, Andrew hadn't gone far. He was by the silo, only twenty meters away. He seemed to be levitating, which was odd. Then Jack realized he was standing on the ladder and reaching up. He was unlocking the grate to the top. It fell open with a clatter. Andrew pulled himself into the chute, then stooped and pulled the grate back into position. He pulled the padlock inside the grill and locked it.

Lauren and Jack were under him now. Only a meter below but unable to get to him.

"Andrew, come out," Lauren said.

Andrew looked down at them. He seemed tired, scared, behind the bars. An animal in a cage. He kept looking at Jack's gun. It was harmless at his side now. Harmless if raised to sight too, but Andrew didn't know that. Andrew seemed to be debating something with himself. Then he started to climb.

"Fuck," Lauren said, "should we shoot at him?"

"What? Jesus. No."

"I said *at* him. Not *in* him."

"I'll miss."

"You'll miss trying not to shoot someone?"

"He'll come down."

"Give me the gun."

"He'll come down."

"What if he jumps?"

The implication was petty, but it incensed Jack: *We might never know the truth.*

He slung the rifle strap over his shoulder and mounted the ladder. People aren't scared of heights, he reminded himself. He climbed a few rungs, until he was under the locked cylindrical cage. He leaned out, forced himself to peel a hand from the ladder, stretched out from the wall. He curled his fingers through the side of the chute. It was made of slatted bars, so there were lots of handholds. He repeated the motion with his other hand. Once he had a fair grip, he walked his feet up the silo wall. The corrugation made it easier; his feet found purchase in the grooves. Then, when his feet were high enough, he reached up to new handholds and swung backward from the wall. The soles of his shoes grappled with the metal, then lodged inside the bars. And he was there, hugging the outside of the chute, like a koala hugging a tree trunk. Andrew was above him, halfway up. Jack knew he'd already made the decision to follow him. He started to climb.

Andrew must have felt the ladder shaking, because he glanced downward. He seemed surprised that Jack was following him by climbing the *outside* of the safety chute. Jack didn't look down. People aren't scared of heights. His heart whumped in his chest. *Whump. Whump.* It was stupid. But he had to be the one to catch Andrew Freeman. He had to solve this properly. He'd started it. He'd end it. *Whump. Whump.* The ladder shook, and Jack lost a footing. He scrambled and got it back. Andrew was kicking the chute, hanging on to the ladder. It rattled and shook. Jack clung to the bars, rust biting into his fingers, vibrations shaking up his forearms. Giving up played through his mind. *You can still get down safely. Andrew will climb down. He'll have to. Or he'll jump. Either way.*

But Jack knew he wanted to be up there. This was his last chance to get the answers. The truth. That shield. His last chance.

An outstretched hand in his mind: *Last chance—you coming up or not?*

Jack gritted his teeth and kept climbing. He countered the shaking metal by making sure he had three points of contact at all times—two feet and one hand, one foot and two hands. In this way, because Andrew was busy shaking the tower, Jack started to gain on him. He grew confident. *Get there. Get there.* Andrew stopped kicking, turned back to his climb. Jack was almost close enough to reach out and grab the hem of Andrew's jeans, but he'd have to reach through the bars. Then Andrew disappeared, and Jack realized that they were at the top. The wind was roaring at his ears. He hadn't noticed the temperature drop, but it cut through him now. He shivered. The entire scaffolding was shaking in the wind. He had to go higher than Andrew, to go over the lip at the top of the cage. His sight line reached the top, and he half expected Andrew to be waiting for him, to push him off, pinwheeling into the void. But Andrew was sitting, hunched, with his back to Jack, on the hatch in the middle. The picnic basket still in the corner. The Brokenback Range behind him, jagged knuckles. Like people's spines in the clinic. Jack reached over the top. He tried to quickly scramble over the lip and lower himself to the roof but messed it up and fell the last bit with a jolt. He steadied himself, planting both feet flat, though one leg wouldn't stop jumping, up and down, up and down. He was exhausted, the climb filled with adrenaline and adrenaline only. The wind pushed him around up here, light as it was.

He stood as far away from Andrew as he could, which was difficult, seeing as he was sitting in the middle of the small roof. Jack steadied himself by the chute, raised the gun, and pointed it downward. At the back of Andrew's head.

"Olives," Jack said. He couldn't think of anything else. "You've been skimming off the top. I know about the wine."

Andrew looked up. His eyes were red. From the wind. From the tears. His face was different from James Harrison's; he looked like a tire someone had pricked, bled him partly out. Filled him back up again with brake fluid.

"You don't need that," he said.

"Don't I?"

"Are you going to call the police?" said Andrew.

"I'll have to."

"You don't. No one has to know."

Andrew must know he had the shoe. If he'd left the shoe to be found, and then the shoe had disappeared, and he'd known Jack had been rooting around... He would have known Jack had taken it. Lied. He must think Jack would do it again. For him. That was why he'd been on Jack's side since he got here. Because he thought they were in it together.

"Money," Andrew said, as if that explained it all. So rich that he didn't even need to beg. Just spat a golden promise into the air. "I can give you—"

"I'm not here for money," Jack said.

"Well, then." Andrew seemed defeated. "So we talk."

"We talk. Are you Hush?"

"Who's Hush?"

"Were you sleeping with her?"

"Who?"

Jack breathed. *Start at the beginning.* He had the gun. He had the time. He knew most of the story; he just needed Andrew to fill in the gaps.

"Eliza knew about the wine?"

A pause. Andrew gave a slow nod.

"She stole a bottle," he said. "The day she left."

Jack imagined the young backpacker, after months of picking, rewarding herself with a bottle from Andrew's collection. A parting gift for herself. Ready to start her next Australian adventure, ill-gained celebration tucked in her backpack, swaddled in a sweater. Turning. Seeing a shadow, backlit by daylight, blocking the cellar stairs.

If he'd been able to pull the trigger, he might have.

"Where was she for the next eight months?"

"I assume she never left Birravale. She was here."

Jack would bet any money she'd been underground. In the cellar. Behind so many locked doors. Just another private collection.

"And Alexis?"

"Her too." His voice full of regret. Such shame. Andrew was rubbing his cheekbones with the heels of his palms. "I can't believe that. Her too."

"Were you sleeping with her?"

"Alexis?"

"Yes."

"No."

So Hush didn't play into it at all. Just some boyfriend. Nothing worth killing over, and only interesting in the light of trying to pin it on Curtis. Sex, passion—those common motives of which Lauren had been so sure, that Andrew had tricked her into believing by clearing the phone to point toward Hush—were void. Hell, he could have even changed the name to Hush to make it seem suspicious. It only came down to Andrew Freeman's money.

"Curtis—" Andrew started. He sniffed and stood. Jack levered backward, traced him with the gun, but Andrew went the other way. He stooped over and flipped the knitted wooden lid of the picnic basket. He rummaged and brought out a bottle.

"Curtis was the perfect suspect," Jack said. Realizing now Andrew's compulsion to *get* Curtis. He needed Curtis to stay in the spotlight, in order to keep him in the dark. He needed Jack to stay focused. "Is that one real?"

"They're all real, mate." Andrew swigged it like a sailor. "The ones up here are for me, so I guess they're more real than others."

"You must have known someone would find out eventually," Jack said, "the way you flaunted it."

"Maybe. I kept thinking I'd stop. You know, at the start, it was a few quick bucks. But then I kept not getting caught. So I kept going. Every time I thought the glass was finally empty, someone would refill it."

"She's dead, Andrew. The glass is empty."

"Let's get it out of the way and then you can leave me up here to drink in peace until they come. I got her killed."

"Say it properly."

"Eliza Dacey." He yelled it at the sky. "I got Eliza killed. Happy?"

"Good. And Alexis?"

"Well, fine." He looked inside the bottle, as if it might contain an exit—Jack had a quick glimmer of Andrew smashing the bottle, lunging at him, slashing his throat—but Andrew's shoulders dropped. "Yeah. Okay. That's true. Her too, if you think about it that way."

"What way?"

"I guess they're both my fault, then."

"You stole Curtis's ax. You bashed her skull in. You cut off her fingers. You *guess* it's your fault?" He jabbed the rifle between words, as if stamping the punctuation in the air.

"Whoa, wait."

"I'm tired, Andrew. Tell the truth. You've already admitted to murdering Eliza."

Andrew blinked twice. He chugged the rest of the bottle and examined the empty. Weighing up the price, the value of this one, just like he had previously. But then he shrugged and lobbed the bottle over his head in an arc. It spun in the air, dropped out of view. Jack heard it shatter on the ground below. No point keeping the empties now, he supposed.

"I said I got Eliza killed." Andrew locked his red-rimmed eyes with Jack's. "But I didn't kill her."

CHAPTER 34

"Eliza knew that the bottle she took was a bad one," Andrew said, "and I knew as soon as I saw the gap in the shelf what she'd done. It wasn't finished; the flavors were really unbalanced. I was still learning."

"Not enough brake fluid?" Jack sniped.

"Cigarettes contain airline fuel." Andrew's rebuttal was swift; it showed he'd spent years rationalizing it. "But we still sell them."

"So Eliza figured out your scam. I'm still waiting for how this works *against* you strangling her."

"I'm trying to explain. Like I said, she would have known fairly quickly she had a rubbish bottle, especially after working here. You surprised me. I thought yours was okay."

"There was cinnamon on the rim. It got stuck in my teeth."

"It's a three-thousand-dollar wine," Andrew sighed. "You're not supposed to swig it from the bottle."

"Eliza," he said, trying to push Andrew back on topic.

"Okay." Andrew pinched his temples. "Okay. I bumped into her at the pub. She comes up to me and says she's going on a little trip up north to do some touristy things. Says she needs some money. Doesn't say she knows, but she knows. I gave her what I had in my wallet. It was a bit, you know." Andrew Freeman, thought Jack, was the only man who'd try to slide in a brag while explaining a murder. "Then she left."

"When was this?"

"I know what you're going to say. Just relax"—his eyes were pleading, looking at the gun—"okay, when I tell you?"

"The twentieth of March?"

Andrew nodded.

"What time?"

"After five."

Jack chewed his lip. Eliza had left her voicemail message to *Discover!* at 4:52 p.m. on March 20. They both knew that.

"So she tried to blackmail you." Jack watched for Andrew's reaction. "But you overheard her phone call, that she was planning to roll you to the tabloids. A few dollars from your wallet is no big deal, but this—"

"No! I swear, I didn't hear the call." Andrew wasn't looking at Jack, his eyes instead tracing the slightly wobbling barrel of the rifle. "There were others in the pub. It was pretty quiet, but Ian was with me, because we'd just knocked off patrol. Curtis was there, if you can believe I'm not trying to set him up. I swear he was. And Alan was tending bar—he's always there. Ask them."

Jack reminded himself to calm down. His mind was running from him again—he was editorializing and trying to tell Andrew's story for him, before Andrew had told it for himself. He just had to listen.

"After she took your money, what then?"

"What then? Well, I waited for her to come back. I didn't know how this blackmail stuff worked. But I assumed she'd keep coming back and asking for more. I wasn't worried about the money, but I *was* worried that she'd talk. That she'd get drunk and spill to some friend. I could spot the girl some cash—a vacation, rent, whatever. But I was constantly worried she'd tell the wrong person. Maybe someone who knew how to wield the information better, and they'd come back—all Bonnie and Clyde in my head—and they'd both turn the screws. Worse than that, I was worried she'd just go to the cops. It was very stressful."

"I feel for your plight," Jack said flatly. Eliza had been missing for eight months, but maybe she hadn't been missing? Maybe she had been traveling in luxury thanks to Andrew's cash? Then what? Maybe she ran out of money. *Maybe she came back*, Jack's brain shouted, *and Andrew Freeman killed her.* No. He didn't kill her. He got her killed. Apparently. "She came back?" Jack said.

"That's the thing. She didn't. She completely disappeared. She never came to my house, never called me, never emailed me. But all those months later, I saw her again."

"You saw her?"

"It was from a distance. I was up here. But I'm sure it was her."

"Where was she?"

Andrew simply pointed. Jack followed the line of his finger downward, across the lip of the silo and into the Wade vineyard.

"I was up here," Andrew said. "And I saw her, running for the fence between our properties. Curtis came out of the house. He followed her down. I don't think she saw him coming. I had my light on; she would have seen it. She would have known it was me. I brought her up here once. I like bringing people up here."

You like showing off, Jack thought. "I still don't—"

"I just didn't want her to tell anybody. That was all. I didn't think he'd *kill* her, though maybe I knew he would. I don't know. Sometimes I think I did know what I was doing. Sometimes I'm able to convince myself I didn't." Jack felt the truth of those words thud him in the chest. "But I knew where she'd been for eight months. He had her. And I thought that if I did nothing, that would solve my problem. I didn't do anything *wrong.*" His voice was now dripping in self-justification. "I just didn't do anything at all. He grabbed her, dragged her. I lost them when they went behind the restaurant, into the driveway. And then she shows up again, two days later. Except this time—well, you know what happened from there."

"That's why you believed Lauren immediately, even though she wasn't sure? You thought she was a credible witness?"

"She *was* a credible witness."

"You hoodwinked a minor into an unsupervised confession, Andrew. She's not even close."

"Oh. Okay. She's told you that, has she?" Andrew said. "Look, Lauren was sixteen. The youngest blokes in this town are Dawson's boys, and they would have been just shy of twenty back then. I'm not saying anything, but we searched the house. Someone had been in her room. A boy. I'm not implying it was anything nonconsensual or anything more than two young people sneaking it in. But if she had to testify, there would have been collateral. If it was Brett's boys—*if*—it would have been statutory."

"That's a flaky theory, mate. Still sounds like arse-covering to me," Jack rebutted confidently, but wondered if he'd been too distracted to look into Dawson's two sons properly as suspects.

Andrew held up his hands. "Maybe you are right. I'm just saying I always thought that was why she changed her mind. I'm not saying that makes her a bad person. I'm just saying that everyone's telling you what they need to. But now I swear I'm telling the truth. I saw Curtis grab Eliza. Eight months after she disappeared. Two days before she died."

Jack was reeling. After all this time looking for new evidence, Jack now had an actual witness. His breathing was shallow, his lips dry. The wind buffeted him. Alexis though. Andrew had said he was responsible for her death as well. How? There was still more to know. Curtis hadn't stolen the ax, kicked Jack in the face. Curtis wasn't Hush. They knew that. Was it possible that Andrew had copied the first murder he'd witnessed?

"And Alexis?" Jack said.

"Well, yeah, if you put it like that. I didn't tell anyone what I saw. But it was okay because we did our job. Myself and Ian. I don't care what you say about him—our police are good, and they're thorough. We didn't need all this extra shit to send him to jail, but you came along and made it out as some miscarriage of justice."

Andrew had been able to lead the investigation with what he'd witnessed in mind. That was why the evidence was biased. That was why the police hadn't bothered with intricacies, why some things sounded right but were clumsily proven.

"But then you got Curtis out. And he killed someone else. So I suppose, now you bring it up, that I wear her around my shoulders too."

Andrew seemed to relax now. Jack had dissected Andrew's faux-wine gift as the calling card of a psychopath, a sign of bravura. But perhaps it was a call for help. It had to be planted by someone who knew that Jack was coming back out there and where to find the evidence. It had to be someone who didn't want Curtis out of prison. Andrew *had* made his confession, just not with words.

The strangest thing was that Jack understood him. While Andrew shouldered the guilt of Eliza's death, Jack shouldered Alexis's. By both doing nothing, they'd both done a lot.

Jack looked down at the Wade property. In the town, to the right, red and blue lights blinked down the main street. Jack still had so many questions. Everything swirled. The evidence still didn't match up in his brain. He could tell from up here that Curtis's final row of vines on the roadside were drooping. Not growing as well. Death in the soil.

His gaze drifted to the fence line. Eliza had tried to run, and Curtis had come out and caught her.

She'd seen Andrew's light. Those deeper footprints.

Eliza hadn't been having a cigarette, stamping her feet from the cold. She'd been jumping up and down. Calling for help.

The lies you can live with.

Andrew Freeman had seen all of this and turned his back.

CHAPTER 35

Finally solving Eliza's murder totally sucked.

By the time Jack reached the bottom of the ladder—Andrew had given him the keys, then produced a second bottle from the basket—Jack knew he couldn't tell anyone.

Because as soon as it was out that Curtis was Eliza's real killer, the copycat killer theory for Alexis would be obliterated. Double jeopardy would implode. Ted and his team could try the new murder with precedent. A repeated MO: the ax, the phone. It would be inescapable. So Curtis would go to jail, where he no doubt belonged, but for, in part, the wrong crime. The only thing keeping him safe was that no one could tie the murders together, but as soon as he was guilty of the first, he'd be guilty of the second. He'd be a guilty man framed. Curtis's guilt was so clear it obfuscated all else. Which was exactly what the copycat killer wanted. And Jack and Lauren were the only ones that knew the copycat was still out there.

Alexis's killer couldn't be Curtis; Jack had the bruises on his face to prove it. There was someone else running around out there, trading on the case. Jack had done what they wanted. By catching one killer, he would set another free.

He reached the grill and bent down to unlock it. Lauren was waiting for him. He'd have to tell her everything. Soon. Standing next to her was Sarah Freeman, her arms folded. He heard a siren in the distance, coming up the hill.

He had until Andrew confessed to the cops. He figured that wasn't much time. Maybe he had until Winter got out here from Sydney, depending on who the officer coming up the hill was. And then Jack would have to make his own confession, hand over the ASICS sneaker, and the real killer would slink away in the ensuing chaos. And it *would* be chaos, an absolute frenzy.

Jack hopped off the ladder.

"You shoot him?" Sarah said. Emotionless.

She must have been waiting for this, Jack figured. She probably didn't know about Eliza. But she did know about the wine. Sarah looked to the ladder as if considering climbing up to see her husband. But she just stood there, stuck. It must have felt familiar for her.

Jack shook his head.

There was a crunch of gravel under tires from the driveway. A door slammed.

Lauren hadn't said anything yet. She held out a hand, and he passed her the rifle. She looked up and down the barrel, as if to check it was unfired, walked two steps toward the restaurant, placed it on the grass, and came back again.

"You should have told me you didn't know how to use it." She patted Jack on the shoulder, then put her hands in the air. "Instead of you climbing like a maniac, I could have shot the lock."

Jack allowed himself a smile. He raised his hands as well. Sarah caught on.

Ian McCarthy, gun up, rounded the building at a sprint. He saw them and slowed. His eyes darted across the scene, taking it in. Three people, elbows square, hands up. The rifle on the ground in front of them, no danger. Ian lowered his own gun slightly. He stepped forward, picked up the rifle, and, not quite sure what to do with it, slung it on his shoulder.

"Where's Andrew?"

All three of them looked skyward.

"Get him down." Ian jerked his head Sarah's way. She nodded and turned to the silo.

"Right. You two," he said to Lauren and Jack, "in the car."

Ian was driving a country police car—a four-wheel drive with bright-yellow stripes—rather than his usual Toyota. Both Lauren and Jack split off around the hood without really thinking about it, opening the doors to the back seat on each side of the vehicle like practiced criminals. The doors opened from the outside but locked on the inside, so once they were in, Jack realized, they couldn't get out. Unless McCarthy let them.

"So," Lauren said after a few moments of silence in the car, "what did he say?"

"He admitted his wine's fake."

"And they knew? And he took care of them? He admitted it?" Her voice was incredulous. Excited.

"No. Listen, it's complicated."

"When is it not?"

"If he tells the cops what he told me, it'll bury Curtis. Andrew's telling the truth. I can prove it."

"Right," she huffed.

Great place to fight, Jack thought. *In the back of a locked cop car.*

"If Curtis takes it for both murders, the copycat gets away."

"Forget the damn copycat! Look, I said when we met that if you proved Curtis guilty, I'd accept it. I've been struggling with keeping that promise."

"Me too," Jack said.

"I guess I always thought that it was the same person. I really thought that was the key. That we could tie it to the same killer. Fuck. It sounds awful, but I sometimes thought, for a flicker of a second, subconsciously... It wasn't something I wanted to think. Alexis...I thought she might be—" She almost kept going, smiled to herself, and took a breath.

Jack could see her mentally restructuring her next sentence. So as not to seem emotional. So as not to seem stupid or tricked. So as not to seem taken in by the story she was *supposed* to see. Jack sympathized. That was the problem with the whole damn thing. The case was a flimsy construct of hearsay and theorizing, but everyone's stories had their own predisposed endings. The copycat killer was banking on that too.

"Nah. It's a terrible thing to think about a dead woman." She wiped her eye with the back of her hand. Sniffed.

"What is?" Jack said.

"Useful," she sighed. "When I heard she was dead, I thought it might be *useful*." She broke the word into two syllables. A hiss and then a *thuck* like a pistol silenced. *Use-ful.*

"It's okay."

"It's not."

"No. I guess it isn't. But it is real. And that's okay."

And then Jack had his arm around her, and she was leaning into his shoulder. His neck wet. There was silence except the wind skating across the roof. They just sat, knitted together. Jack's body moving with her breath. Up and down. Up and down. Tidal sway. The swell, it's irresistible. She pulled away. "I feel like that…and I wonder if there's a sliver of him in me."

Jack didn't have anything to say to that. Lauren thought there was a seam of darkness in her. She thought that made her less. There was a sliver in everyone. Unlike hers, which was nondescript—a shadow, a vein— Jack's had a volume, a quantifiable shape and a size. You could measure his sliver: it was a size 9.

But he didn't have the words to explain that. So he waited for her to speak again.

"If my brother did this, he should rot," she said. "I'm ready to accept that now."

"And for Eliza, he will. But we both know Alexis's killer is still out there. We *saw* them. We might be the only ones who can get to them before the evidence we have against Hush gets into police hands. As soon as it does, Curtis is going to look guilty. We need to catch them first.

Otherwise, I may as well go to Winter with everything we have and hope he believes at least some of what I'm telling him."

"Don't do that," Lauren said, and took his hand. "You don't need to do that."

"I might not have a choice."

"I'll help you find Hush," she said softly.

Jack nodded. There was silence. Lauren looked out the window. Jack chewed the nails on his free hand.

"When you say you can prove it..." She let the sentence trail off. And Jack really thought he was about to tell her this time.

But then Ian McCarthy wrenched open the driver's door and settled himself into the car with a gruff sigh.

It was a short, wordless drive, punctuated only by the squeak of the brakes at the bottom of the Wades' driveway. Then the *click* in opening, *thud* in closing, of Ian's door, the crunch of gravel as he walked around the hood to Lauren's. *Click.* No words. Thrust Lauren's rifle at her. *Get out. Thud. Crunch. Crunch. Crunch. Click. Thud.* Engine.

They coasted through town. Jack focused on the rearview mirror, willing Ian to glance back at him. Ian stared straight ahead. He turned onto Mary-Anne's street and stopped. They sat in the car, neither moving. Eventually Jack pulled on the door handle. The door didn't open. Locked from the inside.

"Jesus, Jack," Ian finally said, still staring forward. "You can't go around waving guns at people. Especially not Andrew Freeman."

"I wasn't—"

"I don't care. That's it. You're done."

"Done?"

"Done. Pack up. Get out."

"I've paid until—"

"Jack."

"I have a right to be here."

At this, Ian swiveled in his seat. His forehead was splotched with red and he was sweating. Jack noticed his hands were balled into fists. Ian had a shotgun on the front passenger seat. Jack wished the car wasn't locked. His nervous fingers pried the handle regardless, levering it in false escape. No result. Ian had him trapped here.

"You have a right? *You* have a right?" Ian was getting louder. "These people *have a right* to be left alone."

"I'm not—"

"Andrew Freeman will get an order against you. Then you *won't* have the right. I'm telling you now. The judge will rush it through. He can get it tomorrow morning."

"Listen—"

Then Ian was smacking the wheel, rocking in his seat. The car heaved and shook on its springs. Jack had never seen him mad before. Locked in the car with him, it was terrifying.

"No, you listen! I am ordering you to go! I'm a fucking policeman, Jack, so for fuck's sake, just fucking treat me like one for once."

The car quieted. Steamed.

And Jack knew. And, God, he wished the door was unlocked now.

"You watched it," Jack breathed.

"I watched it," Ian said.

Jack's carefully crafted episodes, pieced together to make Ian McCarthy look like a donut-eating, ball-scratching, gun-fumbling country cop, blithely trying to figure out who *done these here murders.*

"I'm sorry."

"You're not. But tell yourself what you need to."

"Ian, I am," Jack protested. "I am sorry. For the whole series. Everything. It was supposed to just be TV. Just characters in some stupid story. I didn't realize. Why do you think I'm out here? Curtis is free.

Alexis is dead. I'm so sorry. But I'm close now. I can't fix everything, but I can set some things right. And it's real this time. And I'm *so* close."

"Leave tonight." The words scraped out of Ian's throat.

"Ian. Come on. Are these Winter's words? Hold off for a few more days. Last favor."

"Last favor?"

"Last favor."

"You took the forensics." It wasn't a question.

"Ian—"

"At the funeral. You took the forensics."

Jack nodded.

Click. Thud. Ian was out of the car. He was in his R.M. Williams boots, faded blue jeans, as usual. He was pacing back and forth. His pistol on his hip. Kicking at rocks. Arms in jagged movements. He looked like he was talking to himself. Back and forth he walked, stooping at intervals, fingers wish-boned on his temples.

Click. The back door opened, Ian against the sun. Above Jack, in shadow, he was as large and hulking as Curtis. An eclipse. Jack could smell him. His sweat. His hurt. Another man laid waste by Jack Quick. Chewed up. Spat out.

"Nope." Ian shook his head, as if talking to himself. "Nope. You're gone tonight."

"Winter doesn't have to know."

"It's not Winter, Jack. *I* volunteered to come out here on this call. *I* knew it would be you. Because you can't help yourself, can you? Your last favor *was* the forensics. I got them for you in the first place. Because you asked me to. Because we were friends. Not this time." Ian stepped aside, the sky yawned wide, and sunlight burst into the car. "I am *not* your friend. And I refuse to be your fool. Go."

"Ian—"

"These aren't Winter's words, Jack, they're mine: if you're still here tomorrow morning, I'll take great pleasure in arresting you myself."

CHAPTER 36

Jack packed. He had nothing else to do. He wiled away an hour sitting on his bed, turning things over. His betrayal of McCarthy was thick in his throat and gut. Ian had been helping him the whole time. He'd been trying to give Jack the forensic files to guide Jack to the ax wounds, but Jack had gone and screwed him over anyway. Even so, leaving them on the seat with an open window… McCarthy was a bumbling cop, sure, but that was like he almost *wanted* Jack to take them. Jack's bag was zipped by the door, reminding him that he had, finally, run out of time.

Curtis Wade was a murderer. Andrew had known and tried to guide Jack by planting the shoe. But so much was still unanswered. Why had Curtis killed Eliza? Who was Hush? Who killed Alexis? Who had stolen the Wades' ax and kicked him in the jaw? He'd only solved half of the case. *Hang on*, he corrected himself—he hadn't even solved half. He'd just *unsolved* the bit he'd fucked up. He shook his head. Making it about him again. He'd fucked it up. He'd gotten Alexis killed. And he'd helped the new killer get away.

Ian was right; he was doing more harm than good here. He'd have to figure it out from Sydney. He started loading his paper files back into their evidence boxes. He didn't care for organization, just shoved them in randomly. He filled two boxes and then neatened the bed, scrubbed the toilet bowl. He looked at the door, unscrewed and propped against the window. He thought about reattaching it, but instead put two fifty-dollar notes on the side table and scribbled a note to Mary-Anne. *If Brett charges you more than this for the door, give me a call.* He left his number below. He grabbed his bag, took it downstairs, and put it in the trunk of his car. He did a return trip with the two boxes. He was filling the last one when he saw the blueprint of the Wade winery. He remembered Lauren handing it to him, what felt like years ago, in his house. Something flapped in his mind, a door left open, banging in the wind. Lauren. He had to tell her.

He'd come into town to fix his mistakes, but before he left, he'd have to tear it apart again. Once he told the police about the shoe, tomorrow morning, he'd be in a cell. Only the truth would do now. He shoved the building plans in, grabbed a few more pieces of paper, invoices, forensics, and put them in too. The blueprint swirled in his head. He pictured the view from the top of Andrew's silo, except this time the picturesque view was superimposed with lines and schematics. The door in his mind slammed shut.

Could he be right?

His breathing quickened as he started the car. The afternoon was waning. Creeping up to five. Vanessa Raynor's current affairs show would play at half past seven. Ted Piper was clinging to the last bit of infamy with this interview. His last appearance on Raynor's show had been interrupted by the breaking news of Alexis's murder. Ted would sure be pissed off if Jack upstaged him again. Another bit of breaking news. Curtis Wade proven guilty; Jack Quick arrested and charged with obstruction. He had Vanessa's number; he could call her. He caught his tiny smile in the rearview mirror, entertaining the idea. McCarthy could even bring him in. Slight redemption for Jack ruining his career. He'd be a hero cop. He'd like that.

Jack shook it off. He was creating characters and narratives again. How to spin the story. Against Ted. In favor of Ian. Not this time. This time there was no story. Reality beckoned. He thought it finally made sense, but he had to be sure.

He parked at the bottom of the Wades' driveway and got out of the car.

He was ready to tell Lauren everything, especially if his hunch was correct, but before that, he had one more confession to make.

He dialed his father's number.

"Hi, Dad," Jack said.

"Jack," his father said, "just turned the TV off. That horrible Vanessa Raynor show is about to come on." Whether Peter believed that or was defiant in solidarity was unclear.

"Can I talk to Liam?"

"Hang on." Peter offered no resistance, no: *He can't hear you, Jack.* He must have heard the crack in Jack's voice. The sound of footsteps, stairs. Sitting down. The usual routine. Peter's voice now echoing: "Okay. You're on."

"Liam, hey buddy. It's Jack. Just wanted to say hi."

A moment's absorption, while Jack pictured his words entering Liam through one of his tubes. Volume seeping into his skin. The scratching of the pencil in the background, the crinkling paper.

"I wanted to tell you that I think we've finally figured it out." Jack was walking across the vineyard now, having eschewed the driveway. "You would have gotten it faster than I did—you were always so clever—but I caught on eventually."

The soft rasp of a pencil.

"I noticed that the schematic of the old restaurant lines up exactly with where Eliza was found." He was there now; he tucked the phone between his shoulder and ear as he worked with his hands. "And Brett Dawson was paid thirty-five grand to fill that old cellar with concrete. But then why'd he call Curtis a *stingy fuck*?"

The scrape of a pencil. The rustle of paper.

"You got it, bro," Jack said, fingers plunging deeper, digging. "Just like the windows. Smashing them so he'd be paid to repair them. Brett Dawson wanted to be paid for the same job twice. He took Whittaker's money but didn't do the job, then wanted to charge Curtis to do it again, fill it in, so the vines could grow. And the whole vine is dying, from the bottom of the field up to the new restaurant. Why? Because that's how he goes in and out. Brett only put in *three* wine storage units. Not four. So there's the answer. Couldn't have done it without you, buddy. I wanted you to know that. We did it."

Scratch. Scratch.

"And"—Jack's breath caught in his throat—"I wanted to tell you that I'm sorry."

He was crying now, his dirt-caked hands rubbing soil on his cheeks, on his knees in Curtis Wade's vineyard.

"I'm so sorry, Bro. I should have been better. That day, at the Fist—"

The pencil scratched.

"After you fell...I told everyone I wasn't up there. I told everyone that you climbed it on your own. I never told anyone that I went up with you."

Silence. No scratching.

"And I never told Dad. I never told him that I said it was too slippery, but we argued, and you insisted I come with you, and I caved. So I went up with you. And we were mucking around. And that's how you fell. I never told Dad that."

Last chance—you coming up or not?

Liam's fingers, reaching out, slipping past his. Then his body slowly leaning backward until there was nothing but air. *Whump.* So close. The graze of his brother's fingertips burned onto his hands. Just another scar for his fingers.

And Jack had been so sure he'd get in trouble that when the orange-jumpsuited rescue worker had asked him what happened, he said Liam had gone up without him. And then when the doctor had asked him, he'd said the same thing. And Peter, Peter had sat him down and asked him too.

Part of him, even then, realized that *his* story was the only truth that mattered. He controlled it. It didn't matter what was true—it only mattered what you told them. And he'd given everyone who'd asked the same consistent answer and built a fortress of half-truths. It wasn't the first time he'd told a lie. But it was the first time he'd told one he couldn't *un-tell*. And then he'd gone and made a career out of it.

Alexis had been wrong. The line isn't drawn between the lies you can live with and the lies you can't. They aren't so well defined. The lies you can live with, sometimes they turn into the ones you can't. Not this one. Not anymore.

Peter's pencil was quiet. Crossword discarded.

"I'm sorry, Liam." It kept spewing out of him. "I'm so fucking sorry. And if I had the courage to tell Dad this too, I'd tell him the same thing."

There was silence. No movement of anything in the room, even Liam's constant metronomic beeping seemed to take a deeper breath. Then Peter's voice came from a distance, the corner of the room, picked up gently on the speaker.

"Thank you," he said.

"Dad—"

"Of course you went up there," Peter said, as if it was the most obvious thing in the world. Jack heard the creaking of springs, which meant Peter had moved to the bed next to Liam. His voice was slightly louder, up close. "You were twelve years old. Liam was everything to you—you followed him everywhere. But I understand. What you saw. You wouldn't have been able to process that. Hell, grown adults lie to make themselves look better. You, just a boy, trying to digest what happened to your brother. Of course you lied. Of course. It doesn't matter."

"You knew?"

"Watching you punish yourself all this time, that was the hardest. But I thought I'd make it worse if I brought it up. I almost did. But then you got—started getting—better. I wished I could tell you it wasn't your fault. But you just never seemed ready."

Jack's nose was wet. He used his forearm, gelling the hairs on his arm to his skin.

"Tomorrow," Jack said, out of breath, "it's going to be a tough day. Some things will hit the press."

"They're all tough days," said Peter.

And Jack imagined Liam, silent on speakerphone, agreeing.

Then one of his fingers sunk into something soft. A dent. The rim of something. He told his dad he had to go, put the phone on the grass beside him. He dragged his finger down in a straight line. Across. Up. Across. He'd marked out a crude square carving in the ground, less than a meter square.

A hatch.

That was how there was barely a trace of her. *So she fell from the sky*, Lauren had mocked him. No. The opposite. She'd come from the earth.

Jack's heart galloped. The old restaurant and the old cellar. The hole in the ground that Brett Dawson was supposed to have filled with concrete but hadn't. This, the old entrance to that cellar, unnoticed by everyone, walking back and forth over the top of it, because it was supposed to be filled in. That was why the vines weren't growing here—not because of concrete—there wasn't any soil. How could they have missed it? The first time, the murder had been solved slam dunk. So quickly, there was no real need to pick holes. Besides, Ian McCarthy had parked right on top of it, pushing the already overgrown door back into the ground, sealing it with two tons of incompetence. And everyone in town *knew* it had been filled with concrete; they'd all told him. Jack could hardly blame the police, because he hadn't taken a second look either: it was like punching a rock with the expectation it was hollow. You just didn't need to check things like that: the solidity of the earth, the color of the sky. The difficulty was that the real investigation was four years later. The evidence was overgrown, Jack had often thought. How true that had been. The entrance to the cellar, unopened for four years, would have overgrown too. When the serious investigation had begun, there was nothing but dirt and grass. Eliza's tomb had sealed itself shut.

Jack wished he had a shovel. He scrabbled with his hands, pulling the surface covering of dirt and grass away. He cleared the ground around it, wriggled his fingers under a jagged edge, stood up, and pulled.

The hole in the ground yawned before him. A mouth, ready to swallow him whole.

CHAPTER 37

If Eliza Dacey had only had the common decency to wear shoes when she was murdered, Jack Quick's life would have been a lot easier.

At the very least, he wouldn't have been lowering himself into a hole in the ground.

When he'd pulled, the ground had bent upward, toward him. It was slow, heavy, but when it gave, it gave quickly. Jack stumbled. The door fell open, past its axis, coming to rest at a forty-five-degree angle. Dirt sprinkled from the vertices, rained into the black hole. The hatch was heavy, solid steel. Nestled neatly in a metal rim. It wasn't designed to be opened from the outside, and, even freshly opened and closed, the disturbance wouldn't necessarily be noticeable. Especially if you thought it was just concrete beneath. And, four years later, more invisible still. Under the earth or in the back of a closet, evidence in this case seemed to bury itself. Jack noticed rust on the sharp edges of the metal rim.

Not rust. Blood.

The hatch was heavy. Heavy enough to amputate two fingers if slammed. Jack swallowed.

Jack picked up his phone and turned the flashlight on. The floor below about two meters down. No ladder. Jack hung his legs over the dark hole and lowered himself in. The metal rim lifted the tail of his shirt, scratched up his lower back. Not much farther and he had no choice—elbows square, strength fading—he pushed outward and let go.

He landed awkwardly, hitting something soft and spring-loaded, which sent him spinning sideways to the floor. He looked up, saw the dim glint of stars, the first brush of night through the square hole above. He stood.

He'd twisted his knee. He'd dropped his phone. He winced. Limped over to pick it up.

In its light, he saw the room was about the size of a garage. Ten strides across and deep. He saw that he'd landed on an old bed. It had a flatbread of a mattress and no pillow. A cord hung from the roof in the middle of the room. He pulled it. A single light bulb flared dully, but it was enough to see better. To see the scratch marks in the floor where the bed had been dragged from one side of the room to where it stood now, under the hatch. To see the regular door at one end of the room. Riveted, strong. Clearly locked. Jack had already guessed this led to a passageway through to the modern cellar. To see the pile of clothes on the floor. A T-shirt. A pair of jeans. Worn and moldy. One running shoe.

To see the walls. Streaked with dried red. Stained. As if they'd bled.

The cord swung back and forth in front of him. Hung down to his chest. It was blue and yellow woven together. Polyester rope.

It started to come together in Jack's mind. He shone his light under the bed. It was spattered, but there was a neater pattern too. Almost as if the drips had come in a square.

Eliza, down here for eight months, believing that locked, submarine-esque door to be her only in or out. Maybe she'd tried to get out through there. And after eight months, there was nothing left to do but wait to die. And then Curtis had gone up and buried his ax in Andrew Freeman's silos. And, behold, the roof started to bleed. After it stopped, Eliza would have had a red floor with a clear square in the middle of it. She was clever; she would have figured out that the formation of droplets equaled an entrance above. The wine marked it out. So she'd dragged the bed over, those scratch marks. Stood on it. Maybe she was just tall enough, or perhaps she balanced on the edge of the frame to push up with all her strength. A little bit of light. Fresh air. She'd have been excited, shoved harder. Squeeze through it. Run. Run. Run. The Wade homestead light coming on. Andrew Freeman's light above. She'd have jumped up and down. Screamed for help. Andrew's beacon flickering off. Nothing seen. Nothing said. Curtis grabbing her. Hauling her back to the new restaurant, to that cellar, and back into this room.

What next?

Eliza wasn't a quitter. She'd have tried again. Maybe quickly. Before Curtis figured out what to do. Before he came back. He knew she could escape now, which meant she had become a liability.

In front of Jack, the floor was stained with wine, but there were darker blemishes too. Pooled under the swinging light.

Jack's mind filled in the blanks. Maybe Curtis had come back while she was halfway out. Her legs, slithering up and out into the light. He imagined Curtis yanking her ankles. Eliza grabbing at what she could as she fell backward, two fingers grabbing the lip just as the hatch slammed closed. Falling on the floor. Clutching her hand. Hatch not closed. Jammed with something. Her screaming. Sound siphoning through the thin slit of sky. Curtis roughly shoving the hatch up, dislodging the block, fingers scattered on the floor, closing the hatch properly now. Dragging Eliza up. The light bulb cord. Blue and yellow. Polyester rope. Curled around her neck. Toes skating on the floor, no purchase. The light blinking on and off as Curtis pulled on the cord. Fight going out of her. Like Andrew Freeman's light, flickering out.

The only question was why Curtis had dumped her in his field. He could have kept her down here and never been discovered. Why?

There was a metallic groan. The crunch of a bolt being slid back. Jack backed up, hobbling on his bad knee toward the bed. Sat. The tip of the rifle came first, then the man.

At least, before he died, Jack would get to ask Curtis himself.

"Who'd have thought," Curtis said, locking the door behind him, "us in a cell together?"

Jack didn't say anything. Curtis flicked the gun up. *Rise.* Jack stood.

Patted a hand in the air, in what he hoped was a calming gesture. Took a step forward.

"We could've been a team, Jack. Hell, we could've been a good one. You pretend like I'm the bad guy. You knew what this was."

"I did."

Curtis nodded at the clothes.

"I was gonna burn those. Then"—he shrugged—"well, you know."

"I don't, actually."

"I didn't have time. I took them off her. I was figuring out what to do with the body. But then she got up, I guess. Stupid of me to leave her here, but I didn't think she was getting up, to be honest."

Jack had an image of Eliza waking up. Half-dead. Undressed. Just enough life in her to crawl out of that hole a final time before collapsing. But why were her fingers in her mouth? A flash of the simplest answer. What do people do when their hands are full? Surely not. But maybe she didn't want to leave a part of herself behind. Just while she needed both hands to climb out of the hole. Courageous Eliza, dragging herself from the mouth of the earth, her own fingers in her mouth.

The most salacious part of his documentary was nothing but pure coincidence. The bareness of the truth didn't suit TV. *Of course* it was Curtis the whole time. There had never been any truly convincing argument otherwise, just a competition to see who could shout the loudest on television. As with Liam's accident, you got to be the truth teller if no one was there to contradict you. Worse still, Jack had told the story enough times that he'd wound up believing it himself.

"I listened to you while you fed me bullshit. Now I want you to tell me something real. What happened the night you killed Alexis?"

Curtis looked like he was watching a season finale loaded with fan-service moments. One hand left the barrel. Went to his mouth. *You won't believe it.* "Fuck. Wow. Jack. Wow." He wiggled the gun one-handed. "You are endlessly entertaining."

Jack didn't say anything. Curtis returned his hand to the rifle.

"I didn't *feed* you anything. I told you exactly what you wanted to hear. You should have seen your eyes when I gave you something dramatic; it was like a drug to you."

"Just tell me why."

"Because of Sam Culver," Curtis said, as if it were all so simple. "Because she left that message about Andrew's stupid wine. I overheard it. Then, when she told me what she knew, and it wasn't as much as I thought she did, well, I'd already got her down here. Roughed her up. I didn't have the heart to kill her, but I couldn't let her go either. She made me do it, in the end."

"You were partners," Jack guessed. "You thought Eliza knew you were involved, but she didn't."

"Partners." Curtis chuckled to himself. "Sure." Then he paused, looking at his hands, seemingly surprised to see the gun there. "I don't want to do this. You helped me out. But I guess I can't let you walk away?"

Jack shook his head.

"Up until now, I think you could have. But I see you've changed your mind on things. For what it's worth, I don't know why. I don't see what's different."

"I couldn't live with it anymore."

"That's easy enough." Curtis shrugged, raised the barrel. "You won't have to."

Jack lunged forward and yanked the cord, switching off the light. Everything was plunged into darkness. He took a few steps sideways in case Curtis fired. He heard Curtis's footsteps. Only two. He imagined him scanning with the rifle in the dark. Waiting for his eyesight to adjust. Waiting for Jack's shadow to cross the square prism of dull light that shot down from the hole in the roof.

"Come on, Jack," said Curtis, with his slow and heavy breathing, pauses between words. In the dark, it was like they weren't in the same room anymore, Curtis's voice crackling down a phone line as it had at the beginning. "Aren't you a little bit glad it's us, here, together. Your season finale." His voice echoed off the walls. "It won't hurt. You can even keep your fingers."

Jack had now managed to circle around Curtis in the dark. He pushed him hard in the back and, when Curtis stumbled in surprise, leaped on top of him. They scrambled in the dark. Curtis was flailing his arms, but all Jack wanted was a handle on the rifle, because if he knew where the barrel was, he could avoid it. Curtis head-butted him, and Jack felt his shoulder crumple with pain. The gun went off, and the cellar flashed white, the sound ringing in both of their ears. Jack held firm to the barrel and, with Curtis dazzled, yanked the gun away. Then he stood back up, under the square of light from the hatch, leveling the rifle at Curtis.

"We both know you don't know how to use that," said Curtis.

"You're right," said Jack, "but I don't have to."

He heaved the gun upward, throwing it through the hatch in the roof, where it clattered on the grass, out of harm's way. Curtis reacted almost immediately, pile-driving Jack into the concrete wall with a roar. Jack felt something break—a rib?—and slid down to the floor, groaning. Curtis turned and was up quickly, scrambling over the bed frame. Though he was fat, he was tall, and he'd pulled himself up through the hatch before Jack could catch his breath.

By the time Jack managed to lever himself to stand, using the wall as support, Curtis was standing in the hole, a shadow against the night. He hadn't picked up the gun yet. He looked down at Jack and spat in the cellar. Bloody mucus bubbled on the floor.

"Yeah," Curtis said. "This'll be much more entertaining."

He slammed the hatch closed.

CHAPTER 38

Plunged into darkness, Jack staggered to the middle of the room and blindly felt for the cord. He turned on the light.

The main door was locked. The hatch closed. Curtis was probably figuring out a way to seal it, and then Jack would starve to death down here. Maybe that was the way Eliza had been supposed to die. He could try to open the hatch now, but Curtis would be watching the opening with the rifle. He'd be a slow-moving target pulling himself out of a hole with a broken rib. There was nothing he could do.

There was a muffled noise from above. Two cracks.

Curtis hammering something down, sealing Jack in.

If he'd have been filming this, he would have used a split screen: Jack cross-legged on the floor, waiting for death, side by side with a reenactment of Eliza doing the same. He could almost hear the ticking clock he'd put in the background, subtly over the soundtrack.

Plink. Plink. Plink.

Hang on. That wasn't a ticking in his head. That was a real noise: a soft, wet tapping. Something was dripping. A slow, metronomic splash on the floor behind him.

Plink. Plink.

He turned around. Thick drops were steadily landing on the floor. They were coming from one of the cornices where the hatch sealed with the roof. The droplets ran together along the seam and pooled, before drawing down in tiny stalactites, stretching like chess pawns until their bulbous heads snapped off. A deep red. Dripping down through the cracks in the roof.

Thick. Like blood.

Then there was a groan of a hinge, and a beacon of light poured in. It took a moment for his eyes to adjust, but he could tell by the slim frame of the shadow above that it wasn't Curtis.

His eyes focused. There—holding the rifle and a flashlight, tears streaming down both cheeks, flashlight shaking slightly, peering down into the hole, looking both the youngest and the oldest Jack had ever seen her—was Lauren Wade.

CHAPTER 39

Regretfully, Ian had learned his lesson and this time parked on the turn, which meant Jack had to hobble back down the driveway to get to the car. His back and chest hurt. He'd been right—the main door did lead to a thin concrete corridor. There were circular stains on the floor, from long-gone kegs or barrels, and then a stepladder up to a door. The door at the top opened into the new restaurant's cellar. The fourth wine incubator was not a unit at all, just a cabinet, dressed up with a glass front and rows of bottles inside, that swung outward on hinges. Of course, Brett had only put in three. He would have chalked it up to Curtis being a cheapskate.

Ian sat them in the back of the SUV while he radioed Winter in Sydney. Their conversation was short, one sided: *Don't fucking touch anything this time.* By the time Ian had figured out what was going on and got statements from Lauren and Jack, another car had arrived from Cessnock, and the incoming officer was stationed to stay with Curtis's body, now under a white sheet.

Lauren still hadn't stopped shaking.

Ian drove back into town in silence. He pulled up out the front of the pub, of all places, and helped Lauren out.

"I'm sorry, guys," Ian said, "but I'm supposed to keep you here until Detective Winter arrives. He wants everybody in the same place, and this is the only place big enough. We've rung around, still chasing a few stragglers. I figure you can at least have a drink. Ambo's coming too." There was a lilt of optimism in his voice. As if he hoped that they wouldn't notice they were being detained under the promise of beer.

"Can I wash my hands?" said Lauren quietly.

For the first time, Jack noticed the blood and dirt. Ian shook his head.

He was playing it straight this time. Lauren grunted and headed inside. Jack followed her.

The bar was packed, but it took little effort to cross to an empty booth by the far window—everyone moved out of their way. Alan was tending bar, as usual. Cashing in on the emergency gathering. Brett and his sons were propped on stools. Even Andrew and Sarah Freeman—Andrew sawing at a steak, not speaking—were at a small table. Mary-Anne was sipping a white wine with a few people Jack didn't recognize. In an obscure remembrance, he took his room key from his pocket and handed it to her. Mary-Anne curled her fist around the key as if it were wilting and nodded. Enough said. *Good to see the back of you.*

Ian McCarthy had taken a position leaning on the bar, close to the doorway. His gun was still on his hip. Jack thought it was probably overkill, considering the real danger was under a white sheet bleeding through a trapdoor but, hey, if a gun made him more comfortable. Then it occurred to him that Ian's job wasn't to protect him; it was to keep him there.

Jack slid in next to Lauren at the booth, deliberately sitting beside her, rather than across. Alan appeared with two glasses of beer. Lauren scooted one aside to Jack, no coaster, condensation skid mark. She picked hers up and held it against her neck, shut her eyes.

"You gonna drink it or wait for it to evaporate?" she said after several minutes of Jack staring into the foam. He picked it up and took a reluctant sip. She needed normal. He could give her that. His acrobat wobbled inside. Now was not a good time. Maybe he should eat too.

Eat. He spoke it silently to himself. The way the mouth moved. Lips curled back. *Eat.* Such a teeth-baring word.

"I'm sorry," Jack said, clearing his throat. "That you had to—"

"Don't," she said. "I can't. I can barely think. It's stupid. I don't even remember it. Ian told me I shot him twice." She looked into her drink. "Twice."

"It's okay," Jack said.

"I'm glad you're still here." She gave him an unconvincing smile. "We'll never catch the copycat now though, will we?"

"There's finally proof Curtis is guilty. So now the cops have a pattern of behavior."

"It's easy to try the dead. The ax will stick to Curtis now. If it comes out?"

"Suppose so."

"I guess it's finished then." She breathed out deeply, relieved. "He probably did kill them both."

"You've been pushing me the whole time to find this copycat and now you're giving up?"

"Does this look like giving up?" She held up her bloodstained hands. "Fuck you. Maybe I'm ready to see my brother now. Really see him. And if the evidence points to him, then so be it. I should have listened to you at the beginning."

"No," Jack said, "you were right not to listen. You never should have. Winter will arrest me when he gets here, and I have to tell him what happened."

"Arrest you?" Lauren's voice dropped. "This is fucking self-defense. I'll back you up."

"It's worse than that." Jack took a deep breath. "I'm involved."

There was a blare from the roof-mounted television. Trumpets, as there always are in a news bulletin jingle, accompanying circular discs sliding over a globe. *Vanessa Raynor Tonight* was starting. That was the last thing he wanted right now. Ted Piper smiling smugly down at him. He wondered if he should call it in as breaking news, steal Ted's thunder again, but Ian had been clear: everything was under wraps until Winter arrived.

"Turn it up," yelled Brett Dawson, banging a pint down. Out of the corner of his eye, he saw Ian tense with the noise. His hand went to his hip. Surely, he didn't need that gun. *Wait. Did Ian normally even carry one?* Jack turned his attention back to Lauren.

"Involved?" Lauren said quietly.

"Four months ago." Jack took a breath—last truth. Empty now. "I found something."

Lauren hit him the way grieving women hit men. On the shoulder, fists curled but pounding flat slaps with their wrists. The quiet violence one inflicts in public. When she was done, she laid her head against him. He put an arm around her. Not quite a hug. Selfishly, more to shield her from the bar than to comfort her. It was also the reason he'd sat beside her in the booth—so she couldn't storm out and make a scene. Her back shuddered up and down. She was crying.

"You knew?" she said after peeling Jack's arm away and sitting back up. Her nose was red. "I asked you if you knew anything else. I fucking asked you."

"I know."

"That's why you were so confident Curtis was guilty when you got here. You were more than confident." Her hands were trembling.

"Yes. It was planted, but it still places her there. I knew she hadn't been dumped."

"And you knew that. All this time."

"Yes."

"None of this had to happen." She looked at him in awe, as if seeing him for the first time. "None of this had to happen," she repeated. "I just shot my own brother to save *you*. Everything I did, for nothing. And it's all your fault in the first place."

Jack didn't say anything. Because she was right. If Jack had handed in the evidence in the first place, Curtis would still be in jail. Then, whoever killed Alexis wouldn't have a cover-up. Because of Jack Quick, another killer was set to walk free.

That's what you do, isn't it? James Harrison's words raced through his mind. He felt the muscles under his jaw tense. *You get people like me out of jail.*

People like James Harrison. People like Curtis Wade.

Lauren was recovering from the shock.

"Oh, you've fucked this one," she said in one long exhale. She spun her glass side to side. "You've really fucked it."

"It's not finished. Hush still has the evidence we need."

She peered at him, trying to figure out his angle—whether he was just telling her what she wanted to hear because he needed an ally. He was just like James Harrison, guessing at the answers until he landed the right one. Lauren was quiet. Was she weighing up whether she would have done the same, had she seen the pink laces poking from the shrub? Jack couldn't tell. Had never learned to read her.

"Fuck, Jack," she said. "Move." She nudged him.

He slid out of the booth and stood.

"I need some water. Air. The bathroom. Whatever. I need something. Space." She brushed past him.

"Lauren—"

"Just give me a minute to myself, all right? I need to think about what you're telling me." She hissed, set to storm off, noticed the people around, changed her mind, and turned back, leaned into him. "You know, I was the *only* one on your side. The only one who would pat you on the back and say, 'It's not your fault.' Well, it really is, Jack. All of this, it is all you. And that's the way you wanted it. You never gave a shit about me or Alexis or Eliza. How many people have to die to fix your career?"

She stomped toward the bathroom. Ian moved a few paces down the bar, asked her where she was going.

"I'm going to wash my fucking hands!" Lauren yelled, fanning them in his face.

Ian, twice her size, almost physically crumpled, the yield rippling through him. Jack sat back down. A few people shot glances.

People had been telling him he was selfish since the beginning. Winter had. Even Curtis himself. That he had a perverse need of ownership over the crime. But, like it or not, he was tied up in this town now. He affected it in tangible ways. Andrew had told him something similar atop the silo, the first time they'd met. His words glimmered inside Jack, felt important, but he couldn't pin them down. All this time, he'd reached out of the television screen and affected real people—made Andrew Freeman look like a criminal, Ian McCarthy look incompetent, and Alexis, in her own words, *look like a bit of a superstar.*

Andrew's words came back to him. *You've cost a lot of people their jobs.*

But not Alexis. She was probably the only person he hadn't made look bad. In fact, he'd done the opposite. Getting Curtis out of jail had been a huge break for her career.

Something Lauren had said too. Something Peter had. All his memories colliding, fireworks in his synapses. Some meaning, simmering just below his consciousness. He looked around the bar. At the gathering of people here. Mary-Anne. Brett Dawson. Andrew and Sarah Freeman quiet in the corner. They'd actually tried to be on his side. Even Ian, who, if Jack hadn't have stolen the files, was trying to lead Jack to the ax; Jack could feel his hurt from across the room. The only one missing was Curtis.

It's all about you, Lauren had spat. He'd never had any problem accepting that it was his fault Alexis had died. But she'd phrased it differently. *How many people have to die to fix your career?*

No. It slowly came over him, TV blaring in the background. How Lauren had said it—did that make sense? *No. No. No.*

It was his fault. But in a different way. This wasn't some egocentric application of grief. Curtis walking free had tarred a lot of people with a brush of incompetence. Some more severely than others. Some, perhaps, enough to kill over. Maybe Alexis had merely pissed someone off—a bad breakup—and that had sealed her fate. Their real motive hidden underneath the opportunity of it all, but, hey, squeeze in a little personal revenge while you're there. But the real motive was to stage the crime scene to rekindle Curtis's guilt. The copycat was about restoring order. Trying to put Curtis away for a crime he'd already committed by framing him for a new one. *Framing a guilty man.*

His father's words clicked in as well: *Grown adults lie to make themselves look better.* The copycat was twelve-year-old Jack, standing on top of the Fist, looking down at his brother's swastika of a body. The same lie. For reputation's sake. Reputation. Jack was here to fix his career, sure. But someone else was seeking redemption too. Someone Jack had ruined.

Alexis hadn't been murdered because she'd sent Curtis Wade to jail for four years; she'd been killed because *she got him out.*

Grown adults lie to make themselves look better.

You've cost a lot of people their jobs.

How many people have to die so you can fix your career?

And, suddenly, he knew who Hush was. Why Alexis had to keep them a secret professionally. Because it would look bad for her to be dating someone so close to the case. Her funeral—things Jack had dismissed as irrelevant filled in the final blanks. He knew. In fact, sitting in the Royal, he was looking right at them. It was someone whose career Jack had damaged and who knew that a new murder was a way for them to prove themselves. To fix their career. Be a hero. His hands shook as he withdrew his phone, placed it on the table faceup, and started tapping at it. He looked around the bar. This would work. And then what? Move fast. Maybe they'd have time. Lauren was making her way back to him, a look of resolve about her. He held up a finger as she approached. She didn't ask what he was doing. She just watched.

Jack dialed the number he'd saved for Hush.

A beat of silence.

In the pub, a phone began to ring.

It was a tinny ring. Almost an echo. As Jack had known it would be.

Because the ring wasn't coming from the pub itself.

It was coming from the television speakers.

On-screen, Ted Piper fumbled with his jacket pocket, sheepishly turned to the camera, and said, "Sorry, I always forget to turn it off."

S01E06
FINALE

Exhibit E:

Interview Transcript: Andrew Freeman Preliminary Interview: 11/09/14

Andrew: Eliza picked for us for a six-month period over the previous summer. She was nice enough, but I don't remember her distinctly from the others. They're all about the same, you see: same age, same smells. Backpackers. I think she was heading up north afterward, maybe Byron— lots of them do that. They just rent a van and go. So I'm not sure if I'm confusing her with others.

Interviewer: And after her employment with you was terminated (interrupted)

Andrew: Finished. I didn't fire her. If you're writing that down.

Interviewer: After her employment with you finished up, you didn't see her alive again?

Andrew: No. I never did.

CHAPTER 40

PREVIOUSLY

Alexis breathed heavily through her nose, slowed, and held two fingers to her wrist. She had a wristband for her heart rate, but she still liked feeling it fade.

She was always pleased when she convinced herself to get up, jog, and be home before the sun rose. The regret of drawing herself out of soft sheets quickly erased by the endorphins. It also made her feel superior, that she'd achieved something before the city stirred. She slowed to a walk as she turned into the lane behind her house.

She often went this way at the end of a jog, because otherwise, she'd have to unlock two gates instead of just hauling the garage door up. She could also leave her sweaty shoes in the garage. It didn't escape her that, for someone who went running before sunrise, she reveled in these shortcuts. She'd earned them. She'd also earned a cigarette, she figured.

There was someone standing in the lane.

"Hey!" she said, thinking someone might be casing her place and hoping a short word would keep the waver out of her voice.

Half-shielded by a row of bins, they looked imposing. But Alexis recognized them as she stepped closer. "Oh. You can't come around here like this."

They nodded. Alexis fished her keys from her pocket, crouched, and unlocked the garage by twisting the anchor-shaped handle to the side.

"I know things didn't turn out the way you wanted," she said, standing. "But the case is over now. We don't have to see each other again." Still no response, so Alexis fished. "Okay. You want closure? I get it. Why don't you come in for a coffee? But let's keep things professional."

Then she bent down to lift the door, and the blunt end of an ax thundered into the back of her skull.

CHAPTER 41

SEPTEMBER

Like a race-car driver, Jack was starting to memorize the turns and the feel of the highway back to Sydney. Vanessa Raynor's show was live, a duration of sixty minutes. Accounting for makeup removal, general politeness—shaking hands with producers, making sure to get booked again—and snaking a can of Coke from the green room, they had much less time than the two and a half hours the drive usually took. Jack floored it, got the drive down to an hour forty-five. Personal Best.

Lauren had fabricated a story about getting Jack's asthma medication from his car. Ian had tried to stop them, but Lauren had stood defiantly in the doorway, firm and stoic as if carved, and said, *Shoot me, then.* And Ian had relented, because it was either that or place them both under arrest, and he didn't know which would get him in more trouble. Lauren had to run and pick up Jack's car, as he could hardly jog to her place with his broken rib. By the time Ian realized they weren't coming back, they were out of Birravale, the steady crump of a police helicopter overhead, heading the opposite direction.

Once it snapped together, it was rushing at him fully formed. People spray-painting Ted's office windows was just the start of the blowback. The vicious public response. Not getting through to Ted's office phone. Jack had thought it had just been unplugged because it was ringing off the hook, like Alexis's, but now he realized why it was disconnected. His filthy car. The ever-tattering blue suit. Ted was still on TV, but his profile had only spiked *after* Alexis had died. And he needed that profile, considering he'd just purchased a multimillion-dollar property. Jack's hindsight crystal clear, he remembered Ted getting changed for Alexis's funeral in the parking lot. The man, face covered, lathering his hair in the outdoor shower. Shampoo. It had always struck Jack as incongruous that Ted was a surfer.

He wasn't. Ted Piper was living out of his car.

His nose-diving profile, coupled with missing a few payments on his new mansion, could have been enough to put Ted out on the street. Living in his car, and hiding it, may have been better for his public image than bankruptcy. Just for a few weeks, until he could set things right.

It wasn't a surfer or a backpacker at the outdoor showers, but Ted scrubbing up because he needed to show up to the wake. The only facilities he could use. After, at the wake, loading up on food. Because he was hungry. He was doing a good job of hiding it, but Jack had cost him his career.

Jack had given a lot of people fifteen minutes of fame. Ted's just happened to be at a quarter to midnight.

It was that simple. Ted had gone rogue, running his own investigation to put Curtis back behind bars, rescue his reputation, and get his career back on track. To no longer be the dodgy prosecution lawyer Jack had made him out to be—the antagonist that Jack had *needed* to create, to drive the drama episode to episode. The problem was Ted had to create the investigation himself. In order to solve a murder, well, he needed a murder to solve.

And Alexis, she would have had to keep their relationship a secret. The head of the defense and the prosecution sleeping together? That was grounds for a mistrial, surely. Jack didn't know the ins and outs of lawyers and professional misconduct, but it sounded bad, even to him. And when she'd broken it off, maybe that was the final straw. Then it was easy. Ted had an intricate knowledge of the case. He knew the ax was the one piece of evidence that had never really played out. He stole it. Repurposed it for a new murder. All Ted had to do was play a character. Probably, eventually, come forward as a hero. But Lauren and Jack had stopped him planting enough evidence, and that must have waylaid his plans. So he had to wait for the police to prove Curtis guilty, and then he'd swan in and pick up the prosecution. He would have been biding his time until he was in the clear, and Jack, with all his bravura crime-solving, had almost done it for him. These were such carefully constructed heroics. The slow-motion replay of Ted lunging across the stage at Jack, breaking his nose. That wasn't anger and hurt spilling over. That was all for show. Ted was reclaiming his place in the narrative as the Good Guy. He was crafting his own story. Fuck. Jack wondered who he'd learned that from.

Jack told Lauren all of this on the drive. She nodded, her eyes half-hooded. She offered only one piece of commentary.

"Well, then, you made your villain after all."

The network's parking lot was multistory. It was mostly empty on a Sunday night. A few headlights reflected the sunset, glints between the concrete grid. Vanessa's crew. The Monday breakfast producers. Not many others. There was street parking too, a novelty in Sydney. Jack's pass worked on the boom gate. The rumble of the city traffic—that constant Sydney groan—dimmed as they rolled into the bottom floor.

Fitting, that it would end here. Where it started. When he hit that single key: Delete.

He told Lauren they were looking for a silver SUV. "The filthy one," he said. "One that looks lived in." They prowled the ground floor, which was designated for visitors and disabled parking. Jack half expected to find Ted's car there, arrogantly parked across two disabled spaces, but it wasn't. Maybe even murderers have standards. No silver SUV. He checked the time. Vanessa's show would have ended by now. Had Ted already gone?

"Fuck this," Lauren said, as they started up the ramp to level 2. "This place have stairs? Will they be unlocked?"

Jack nodded. The ramp leveled. Lauren held a palm up. *Stop.* She got out.

"You start at the top. I'll work my way up and meet you in the middle."

Jack had no time to argue, the door had already shut, and Lauren was jogging to the far end of the floor. Jack turned the car around and spiraled up, glancing in at each floor out of curiosity. Forests of gray pillars flickered past, like the trees on the Wades' driveway, like the bars of a prison cell. He got to the roof. Circled it. Empty. He wound down a level. Circled it. Empty. Down another level. Circled it. There it was.

Ted's silver SUV. Rubbish parking job, Jack thought. The car's nose was in, splayed across the lines in the near-empty lot. Jack reversed into the spot opposite. Did Ted know what car he drove? He couldn't be too cautious. Besides, it was too suspicious to park this close. He migrated a few spaces farther on and parked again. He got out.

This level's forest comprised green pillars. White, blocky number sevens were spray-painted on each one. He wished Lauren were here, but she'd gotten out on the second floor. How long would it take her to check five floors?

He walked over to Ted's car, approaching on the opposite side of the car to the elevator, just in case Ted popped out unexpectedly. If that happened, he would have at least a moment's protection. He looked through the back window. Fast-food containers. Paper cups. A sleeping bag, unfolded. A duffel bag, half-zipped, tongue of a sweater sleeve slithering out. A towel slung over the back seat. Folders everywhere. Papers. Handwritten notes. Lived in. Jack moved to the back-seat windows. Could feel his blood through him, down to his fingertips. His body thrumming, the familiar fear that had been, for so long, of his own body. Every sense heightened. Every heartbeat. *Whump whump.*

A shrill beep almost gave him a heart attack. All four corners of the car flared orange. The doors unlocked remotely.

Jack dropped to the ground. Knees cold on the concrete, poised as if on starting blocks. Pain shot through his side. Footsteps clunked across the parking garage. A murderer slowly walking toward him. Ted was swinging his keys. He was actually whistling.

There was no mistaking his guilt now. Because Jack had seen something through the window. Though Ted had pushed it under the seat, half-wrapped in a towel, the object had been immediately familiar. The shape of it. The two tones of the wood, maroon fading to oak.

Curtis Wade's ax.

CHAPTER 42

Jack risked a look under the car. His view was like looking through wide-screen. It was now almost nine. The sun had packed it in. Blue cuffs bisected the slit of Jack's vision. Of course, Ted had been wearing his fanciest suit. His shoes were scuffed; Jack could see one sole lifting away from the heel. That was okay, for TV, under the rim of the camera's view. Like a tuxedo with the arse cut out of it. Ted walked without urgency. He hadn't noticed anything wrong, that Jack had him.

Had him? Had who? Jack was cowering behind the car door, without a weapon. And he was on the driver's side. So, while it might have bought him a moment or two of shelter, Ted was eventually going to walk straight into him. If anything, although Ted didn't know it, Ted had *him*.

The shoes disappeared behind the back wheel. Ted was probably only twenty meters away. But he was diagonally opposite Jack now. As soon as he got around the car, he'd see Jack. Jack shuffled toward the hood. Precious extra seconds.

Ted had parked nose-in to the edge of the level, but he'd left a small gap between the hood and the hip-height barrier. Jack could squeeze through it. If he kept pace with Ted's walking, Jack could circle the car in tandem, shielded from view the entire way. He took slow, steady steps—still crouched, knees sawing under his chin—then stood. He wouldn't fit while crouched. He turned his back to the drop and tried not to think about how he was seven stories up. He needled his way into the gap. The corner of the license plate caught on his jeans. He wrestled it free and hurried through the other side, looked up, and saw Ted. *Shit.* He'd gone too fast. Luckily, Ted kept walking. He hadn't noticed. Jack waited until Ted disappeared behind the car again and then he was around it. He crouched again. Unseen, he could get back to his car now.

He figured he'd wait until Ted got in and then make a dash. Once he reached his own car, he'd lock the doors and call the police. He'd seen the proof, and that was all he needed. This was real life, not a TV show—things like car chases rarely happened. Jack sent up silent thanks that the car had made a noise when Ted unlocked it, giving him a few extra seconds of warning.

Unlocked.

The word ricocheted in his head like a basketball rattling on the rim. He paused.

The basketball flicked the net. From where he was now, there was only a single unlocked door between him and the ax. Did he really want to give Ted the chance to get rid of it?

He moved, poked his nose up, just enough of a sight line over the window. Ted, by the driver's door, was looking at his phone. Jack's missed call, maybe. Jack wondered if his name had shown up on Ted's screen—if Ted had kept the number Jack had given him at the very beginning, when they'd met in the coffee shop for the podcast. Ted hadn't reciprocated. Maybe that was why Hush hadn't picked up back in Curtis's house. He'd seen it was Jack calling.

Ted was still on his phone, tapping out a text. Jack took his chance, squeezed the handle, and gently opened the car door. A small click that sounded like a gunshot in Jack's heightened senses. Ted didn't move. Jack reached into the car and wrapped his fingers around the ax handle. *Fuck— fingerprints.* He couldn't reach the towel the head was swathed in. *Screw it.* He pulled, trying not to make a scraping sound as he levered the handle up and drew the ax head out of the towel and across the seat. There was the chipped silver head. Just as it was in the photographs. Red paint, fading to silver, rubbed off after years of work. Was there a little extra red there though? Or was he putting that there with his imagination? Jack swallowed hard. Pulled it the final inch and hefted it into both hands.

One throttled around the neck, the other at the base. He spun around, ready to run.

And crashed chest to chest with Ted Piper.

"What the fuck do you think you're doing?" said Ted, taking a step forward.

Jack rocked backward. Clutched the ax to his chest. Realized it was a weapon. So he thrust it forward, brandishing it diagonally from the groin. More like a fishing rod. Not much of a threat.

"No. What the fuck are *you* doing?" *Good plan*, Jack thought to himself. Primary school arguments with a murderer: *No, you shut up.*

"I thought you'd be impressed." Ted spread his arms, laughed, took another step toward him. "I'm doing what you do."

"Jesus," Jack breathed. Lauren's words rattled: *You made your villain after all.* He shook the guilt off. Tightened his grip on the ax. He realized Ted was pacing him backward. Another half step. Slowly backing him up, the drop yawning behind them. The barrier was hip high, but a good shove... *Whump.* "This is not what I do."

"Isn't it? Collecting your own evidence. Only the bits that *you* think are relevant. Only the bits that *you* really believe in. That's all that matters, isn't it? Not twelve unbiased adjudicators. Not experienced detectives. Not expert"—this was almost a hiss—"testimonies. If you can find fame solving a murder outside the courts, so can I."

"It's not about fame."

"Infamy, then. Trust me, when I solve this, we'll both be infamous."

"How could you—"

"How could I? How could *you*!" He was yelling now. Words glancing off the columns and fleeing into the void. Ted took another half step forward, his loose sole gently lifting from the bottom of his shoe.

Swing the ax, a thought tickled. He hoped Lauren had heard the yelling and started to hurry.

"We shouldn't be arguing over this, Jack," Ted said. "It's all good. I'm sorry about your face. That was you, right? In the vineyard?" Ted dragged a finger down from his eye, as if unzipping his cheek. "Let's put that aside. Season 2, hey? I'm sure they're asking you to sign. It'll be big for us both, Jack. You and me. Let's work together for once. The real truth, and everyone will finally get what they deserve."

"Back off." Jack found the energy to brandish the ax. Loosely. He grimaced as pain lanced his rib.

Ted laughed. "Jack, come on. What is this?" He gestured to the ax. "I'm just collecting the evidence. I'm not following the rules. That's what you do."

James Harrison, echoing in Jack's conscience. *This is what you do.*

"It's not right," he stammered.

"It's not. But we can make the best of a bad situation here."

A thought Jack had months ago, when deciding what to do with the shoe, resurfaced. The difference between doing a wrong thing and doing a bad thing. He tried to see it from Ted's perspective. Curtis was dead; bring the ax forward and he'd be found guilty of the murders. Wasn't that what they both wanted? All in a nice bow for season 2. And there'd be money—so much money—underneath it all.

Ted seemed to be waiting for an answer, as if he'd offered Jack a deal. And Jack realized what the deal was: *work with me, I'll let you live.*

Because he was right. Ted and James Harrison were both right. This. It was what Jack did.

"There are things I can tell you. This ax, it's not enough. Curtis is guilty, for a start. But the story we can tell is so much better than that." Ted was smiling. He actually *needed* Jack. He needed his storytelling to fill in the gaps. Alexis was already dead. Curtis was a murderer; it didn't matter the crime. Something good was salvageable here. Closure for the families. A comfortable truth, even if pretend. *Framing a guilty man.*

It made sense. This was what Jack did.

Did.

Not anymore.

That part of him was emptied out and left a shell in a bathroom in Birravale.

"Back. The. Fuck. Off."

Ted looked surprised. Squinted. Thinking. Calculating how hard he had to push Jack to get him over the barrier.

"Curtis is dead," Jack said, "and I got him out of jail. And I was wrong. It's not that I didn't see it. It's that I didn't *want* to see it."

Ted nodded cautiously.

"I know Curtis killed Eliza; I've known the whole time, but I was too arrogant to accept it," Jack continued.

Tension seemed to slide out of Ted's shoulders and dribble down to his fingertips—pleased that Jack had come around.

Then Jack said, "But I also know he didn't kill Alexis."

For the first time, Ted looked like he understood. "I kind of hoped you'd figure it out," he said, took a breath to say something else. Then a new voice echoed through the concrete forest.

"Hey!"

Lauren. From the stairwell. And then she was running. Things would happen quickly now. Ted saw her, then whipped back to Jack. His expression went from one of negotiation to one of contempt. His chin drawn up in a snarl. But the words, when he spoke, weren't barked. They were quiet, accepting. Defeated.

"You know."

Jack nodded.

"I know," Jack said, holding the ax out in front of him. Come on, Lauren, he willed. Run faster. Get there. "We know everything. And now we have the ax, we've got everything we need."

Jack saw something in Ted's eyes. That he knew he was trapped. That this was the end of it for him. Fear.

Then he moved, faster than Jack was expecting. He grabbed the head of the ax and twisted it. Jack felt it turn, useless in his sweaty palms. He pulled back. A tug-of-war over the ax. Ted had a grip on the metal head, fingers curled over the silver blade. Jack gripped the handle tighter. But his palms were sliding over the wood. Splinters bristled into his fingers. Ted was pulling hard. Jack was running out of handle. He jabbed it twice. Pushed Ted's palms back into his chest. Then he had an idea. He dropped to his knees and jabbed again. The height differential and the unexpected lack of tension combined to jolt Ted forward and, when his elbows folded, Jack pushed upward and the ax head clocked him under the jaw. Ted stumbled sideways, into the car.

Jack stood. Ted grappled with the flank of the car, holding himself up. *Hurry, Lauren.* Ted's scrabbling hands found what he was looking for. He yanked the handle and swung open the door. Then he leaned back and kicked it. The door cleaved the two of them apart, pushing Jack backward. In surprise, he dropped the ax. Ted was on him. Shouldering him off the weapon like he was over the top of a football. Jack reeled into the car. Took a second. Looked up just in time to see the silver head of the ax soaring toward him. Jack recoiled, forearm on his brow. Ducked. He felt air rush over his head. Heard a loud shattering. Flecks of glass tinkled on his head. He kept moving backward. He looked up. The ax was swinging again, this time lower. Jack scooted backward on his bum. Palms flat behind him. The ax wrenched into the door in front of him. Ted set to levering it free, a squeal of metal, a long gash in the panel. Ted straightened, took a step sideways.

Jack realized in horror what was going to happen next.

Ted had repositioned himself so Jack was in between him and the car, on the ground. And Ted had given up swinging sideways. He was swinging downward. Jack might get his head out of the way, but he couldn't move his whole body. He had nowhere to go. Ted raised the ax. Jack raised his arms together in a cross above his head, as if his thin wrists offered much defense.

Then Ted was thrown off balance. Lauren, barging into the side of him. She grappled, trying to pin Ted against the car. The ax clattered onto the concrete. Jack scrambled to his feet. Grabbed at parts of Ted. Whatever he could. It was a messy fight. Hands. Fists. Hair. Everything a flurry. Then he was pushed, hard, and felt the concrete break his fall. He saw Lauren struggling, also knocked down. Ted was roaring with pain, clutching at his jaw. She must have hit him. Lauren, bent over, facing away from the fight. Ted lunged at her. Then Lauren pulled herself back up, pivoted her whole body, and Jack realized why she'd been stooped over.

She was picking up the ax.

She swung it with all her strength. Like the sword of a warrior, gaining momentum from the pirouette of her swing. There was no grace or aim; she was swinging blindly and hoping.

The ax hit Ted in the stomach with a wet *thuck.*

Lauren's hand went straight over her mouth. She let go of the handle, which stayed erect in the air. Ted clutched at his gut with both hands, holding the steel head in place. As if it might help keep his guts inside. For a second, there was no blood. Then it started pulsing through his folded hands. Dripping from his knuckles. Thick, red stars on the concrete. Spilt wine. He breathed out heavily through his nose, blinking incessantly, as if trying to capture some final moments, his eyes a camera with a jacked-up shutter speed. He took two steps backward.

Then another, slightly wobbling, step backward.

Jack was up and over to him quickly, to stop what was about to happen, but Ted had backed up too far. He backed into the railing, lost his balance, and started to tip. Jack wasn't there in time. Ted let go of the ax head just long enough to reach out to Jack's extended arm, but Jack felt nothing but the feather of his fingertips.

Ted toppled backward. Into the air. Into nothing. He dropped out of sight.

Jack realized he was crying.

They may as well have been Liam's fingers, scarred as they were into him. He looked down at the inside of his wrist: a smear of blood, four streaked lines. He'd almost had him.

From below, someone screamed.

S01E07
MID-CREDITS
SEQUENCE

Exhibit A:

Size 9 women's running shoe. ASICS branding. Pink, silver trim. Confirmed to belong to Eliza Dacey, victim in the *State of New South Wales v. Curtis Wade* murder trial, 2014, and retrial 2018. The defendant is accused of harboring this evidence which resulted in the miscarriage of justice against Curtis Wade. Indirectly, this resulted in the death of Alexis White.

Handwritten Note: Don't see accessory in the White murder playing out here without intent. Obstruction to a murder investigation is sufficient for prosecution's aims. GH

EPILOGUE

FEBRUARY

The meals come on a schedule here. Can't unscrew these doors.

The prosecution had taken it fairly easy. It had been a challenge to find someone willing to represent him, given the lawyers he knew had both ended up dead, after all. The man who'd come on board, Greg Hanson, had been thorough if unremarkable. He had proposed that Jack's intent, while criminal in nature, couldn't be tied to the new murder, and the court had accepted this. Perhaps it was just too embarrassing to drag it out. Ted's death was ruled self-defense, muttered deservedly, as Lauren had taken the stand and admitted to swinging the blow that killed him. Ted's guilt in Alexis's death helped both their cases. The evidence against him mostly in the back of his car. Not only the ax, but files not unlike Jack's own, all on Alexis: building his own narrative. He'd also told Vanessa he had something big—he'd promised her an exclusive next week. He would have been planning on unveiling the ax on her show, Jack realized in retrospect. That was why he'd brought it to the station. But he'd realized at the last minute, maybe when he'd heard Curtis had been killed, as he'd said to Jack: *The ax, it's not enough.* He was waiting on the final pieces to frame Curtis, which was why he'd tried to talk Jack into helping him. So justice was served for Alexis in a way. Case closed. It's easy to try the dead.

Jack took it on the nose. Two years. Obstruction of justice. Interference with a murder investigation.

He didn't mind it. The other prisoners looked up to him. Minimum security, so not in with the James Harrisons of the world. In fact, James had to be taken to a different prison entirely; he'd been moved to Goulburn. But the inmates still looked at Jack as the ear they needed.

The food wasn't so bad inside either. It was on a schedule, so that helped, just like the hospital. And food was like a gift in here—to spurn it made you look ungrateful. It could get you offside. Besides, keeping people up at night was frowned upon. The echo of vomiting in his single silver toilet, the smell—nothing there to ingratiate himself with his fellow inmates. He wasn't better—you're never better—but the regime had unexpected positives. He'd even put on a little bit of weight, the green tracksuit hanging off him less than when he came in.

The acrobat was still inside him. He always would be. But some days— often the days Peter visited, his Skype set up to a corresponding iPad in Liam's room—the tightrope became a plank. The jester still wobbled, arms out, occasionally. But everyone wobbles.

Jack was sitting at a steel table. It was a private room. Unlike James Harrison, he didn't have cuffs threaded through an eye-ring in the center. Small privileges from the guards—nothing said, and not enough favor to piss off other inmates—but they nudged him with just enough kindness, in case he went on to make another TV show. The network had done season 2 without him. They'd gotten a lot of the facts wrong. Implied he and Lauren had slept together. That didn't matter; it had been a blockbuster smash.

These days, Jack produced a small underground podcast through the prison's media facilities. Someone had arranged for him to have a hand-held recorder. The premise was simple: he talked to the inmates. He only asked questions though. He didn't edit it either; his interference limited to hitting Play and Upload. He let them tell their own story, didn't tell it for them. The podcast was doing okay, he'd heard. But he didn't check the download charts. He refused sponsorship, advertising money, though he'd had plenty of offers. Jack enjoyed making it, just for him. If people listened, that was a bonus.

The door opened. His visitor was here.

Lauren had come to see him a few times. She'd coped with all the death and pain admirably, rarely letting the trauma show in her. The whole of her adolescence had been bundled up in murder, and with those final two deaths, she was able to start afresh. It had been a few months since her last visit though. She sat across from him, tepid coffee in front of her. Non-scalding. He might get some favors, but he was still a criminal.

"Andrew's trial is next week," she said.

Andrew's trial had taken longer than Jack's because, in the end, none of the lawyers could agree on where the criminal charges lay for maybe seeing a murderer not exactly commit a crime. And Andrew's confession to Jack was all they had, and Jack wasn't seen as the most *reliable* witness this time around. Andrew's version of events was much different, veering away from self-incrimination: the words out of his mouth were as built as his wine.

But the upcoming trial had gripped the nation more than even the murders had, it seemed. Wine fraud captured the minds of the masses and the media in a way that two dead, fingerless women couldn't even come close to. Easier to stomach, a 6:30 p.m. time slot. *Well*, said Lauren the last time she was in to visit, *people love to watch a rich bastard burn*. As Alexis had said, it was about what we were comfortable rebelling against. In this new age where social justice and social media intertwined, two dead women was horrible, sure. But fucking with a bottle of wine? That was a personal affront to every hardworking Australian! And that was great TV.

Some might think it lucky that Andrew had stayed out on bail so long until the trial, but Jack thought Andrew would probably be willing his sentence forward. He'd treasure the relative safety of a prison cell. He'd ripped off some rich, powerful people.

"And Sarah?" Jack said.

"She turned a lot over to them. She'll testify, I guess. I think a heavy fine rather than jail time awaits her, personally. As for the business..." She slid a finger across her throat. "Birravale Creek Winery isn't a creek; it's a dry riverbed now. They're bankrupt. I think she's started making soap."

"Soap?"

"Artisan stuff. Platypus Soap, she's calling it, or something."

He chuckled to himself. "Landmark, plant, or animal."

"Huh?"

"Nothing. Soap maker's joke."

"Okay."

"Lauren." Jack leaned forward, the steel of the table cool against his wrists. "I've got a lot of time in here, and I still can't get one thing clear. Andrew wouldn't admit what he told me, up on top of his wine silo, to anyone else."

Lauren shrugged.

"And here I sit now. Because I grabbed that shoe. All because Andrew Freeman fetched it and set a trail of bread crumbs for me to follow, to clear his conscience. But now he won't talk about it."

"What's your point?"

"It's incongruous."

"You're starting to sound like my brother. What are you implying?"

"Andrew knew that Curtis killed Eliza, but he never knew where she was. Just like everyone else, he thought that the cellar was filled with concrete. So how did he even get the shoe? There's only one answer: he didn't. You put it there, didn't you? Her shoe?"

She shifted.

"You knew I had it. That's why you kept asking me if I'd told you everything. You were the one pointing me toward everything that suggested Curtis's guilt. Devil's advocate, you said. But we were on the same team, and you were trying to guide me without alienating your family? Is that right? Because when you told Andrew Freeman that you heard footsteps the night Eliza was found, you had to take it back. Even though you did actually believe it. But I understand—you were sixteen, and maybe your father convinced you that you'd done something bad, made you doubt yourself. And then the show. It would have started to make you nervous. You're older, a woman now, and you saw a chance to correct your mistake. You wanted to make sure he didn't—that he couldn't—get out. And you gave me that option. The shoe wasn't Andrew's confession; it was yours. And I fucked it up for you. I'm sorry."

There was a long pause. The sound of the prison's everyday filtered through the air, through the door. Prisons are like ships; they groan and they rattle.

"Yes," she said, "I heard him get up. In the middle of the night."

"I'm sorry."

"After all this, you still don't know how to listen. I *know* that he got up that night."

The way she said it again—*I know*—with such sincerity. Jack remembered her standing in her driveway, neck tilted upward at a passing cloud. *We both want the same thing, you know?* she'd said. *I want the world to see what really happened to Eliza too.*

She knew.

"That night, I think I finally understood that what Curtis was doing to me was wrong," she said. "And I just knew that when he got up, that when he went down to the restaurant...I knew what he'd do. And I finally summoned the courage to tell Andrew the truth. Enough to get rid of him."

Partners, Curtis had chuckled, *sure.*

And Jack suddenly knew why Curtis had killed Eliza. He had overheard her leaving the voicemail to Sam Culver, but he'd misinterpreted it. He'd heard her trying to sell a story to a tabloid. Something *weird* was going on in town. And she thought it might make some trashy news. And Curtis had thought she was talking about something else. Not wine.

Her recoiling at Curtis's touch on the porch, the night they'd traced Eliza's steps. Something she said in Sydney, leafing through files: *Dad let Curtis get away with anything.*

"Oh, Lauren—"

Andrew, confessing on top of the silo: *Someone had been in her room.*

A boy. She knew Curtis got up in the night, because he was in the bed with her.

Lauren averted her eyes. Talked at the ground.

"I thought I was ready. I wasn't. I realized I would have to be the central witness in a major murder trial. I'd be questioned on the stand, and I'd have to tell the truth. There might be TV cameras. And I was ashamed. I was young, and it had been so long, and you feel like it's your fault. And I didn't want the world to see me like that. So I retracted my testimony."

"She didn't get out of the hatch twice, did she?"

Lauren shook her head.

"Who do you think opened the door?" she said. "I swear, I tried to help her. Then he got her, and after that is when she found the hatch in the roof. If she'd just made it to the road... Why do you think he had a bed down there in the first place, Jack? Why? Fuck. You're only the second person I've ever told this to." She wiped her nose.

The second person. Eliza? He didn't have the heart to kill her, but he couldn't let her go either. Until he had to. This was about keeping his abuse a secret.

In a distant echo in Jack's mind, he was sitting on the floor of the cellar. Two muffled gunshots. One in panic, but why the second? She'd finally stood up to her abuser. Blood dripping through the ceiling.

Lauren must have been terrified, watching the show, that public opinion was changing. She couldn't go to the police or confess that she knew about the cellar, or any of it, without revealing her shame. She'd tried to do it all without confessing. She'd tried to help Eliza escape on her own. She'd left Jack the shoe to find. Sitting on Jack's own bed, she'd handed him the blueprints that showed where the old cellar was, begged him to look closely. With Curtis in jail, she was, at least, safe.

"You let him out," Lauren breathed. Tears tracked her cheeks. "None of this had to happen." Such regret there. Then she stood. "I have to go."

"Lauren, wait."

"Why? I've told you enough."

Something distant. In the parking lot, Ted's hand slipping from his. Falling. Liam. Air. Dust. *Whump.* Something there. Distant. Memory locked up too.

It was guilt rising in him, he was sure, this unease. Lauren had given Jack the keys to help her, and he'd shoved them right back in her face. She'd been helping him the whole time, trying to point him in the right direction. Trying to help him catch Curtis, but so she'd never have to admit her part in it. It never occurred to him that she had an agenda of her own. Jack was her shield too. She'd never really believed in the copycat; that was why she got so upset whenever Jack had turned his thinking away from Curtis. Only when he was finally dead did she seem, at last, relieved. Jack should have known.

That was the memory. Ted's last words. To Jack. *You know.*

Something wrong there. That unease in his gut. Because he hadn't said it when Jack had shown up with the ax. No. He'd said it when he had turned. When he had seen...her.

I've been digging too. You're not the only one who can build a case.

What if Ted wasn't out there planting evidence? What if he was out there stealing it for himself? Because he was building a case, not against Curtis but against...

Ask her about the night of the murder.

Ted had told him that at the funeral. The night of the murder. The murder. Jack had assumed Ted had meant the night of Eliza's death. What if he hadn't?

Watch out, the ax thief had yelled as the truck bore down. Why had Ted warned him?

You know. His voice. Sadness. *You know.*

"Ted knew," Jack said.

Lauren turned. Cocked an eyebrow.

"What?"

"He figured it out. I shouldn't have been thinking who would gain the most by Curtis being in jail. It was who *needed* him there the most."

Because Lauren was okay while her brother was in prison. But then Vincent started getting sick, and Curtis was set for release, and she must have known he'd come for her again. So she'd left the shoe and hoped it would be enough to keep him inside. She wasn't counting on Jack fucking it all up. "You pushed me for the police details," Jack said slowly. "You asked me for the police side of the investigation. Questions about the copycat, if the police knew who they were yet." Lauren, in the restaurant, *I need to know everything behind the scenes.* "Because you knew they hadn't bought Curtis doing it, that they knew the second murder was a setup. Because you were worried they'd catch up with…you."

"What are you talking about?"

"But Ted knew first. And he wanted to play the hero, we got that right. That's what got him killed. His refusal to tell anyone, so he could have all the glory, saving up his big exposé. He took the ax that night. And you saw him do it. That's why you were chasing him with the gun; you could have defended that with self-defense. It's so easy to try the dead; you said it yourself. And you would have got him red-handed in the middle of 'planting evidence.' But he ruined your plan, because he took the ax, the one that you had ready in the shed for the police to find, except they hadn't come yet. Because Winter didn't want to cause a scene." Lauren, sweeping tools off the bench in frustration. Because she knew what Ted had taken. "And then you knew you were fucked. Because Ted Piper had the evidence that you'd planted against Curtis. And you started to realize he was going to use it against you. The police were looking for a copycat instead of Curtis—you learned that from me—and you could see it falling apart. But you saw a second chance. Your initial plan to frame Curtis had fallen through, but now you knew who Hush was, didn't you? You figured it out at the funeral. That's why you insisted on coming. You didn't know it was Ted yet, but you knew Hush would be there. You stood in the back. You had Alexis's phone already, so you called him, and when his phone rang, you marked him in the crowd. Because, of course, Ted never turns his phone off."

Jack recalled a phone ringing at the funeral. The words were coming out of him faster than he could make the connections in his brain, but they were coming, and they kept coming.

"How convenient that her sad ex-boyfriend was the person who was stockpiling evidence against you. Then it was a race against time—could you frame him before he had enough to pin it back on you? So you had your scapegoat. And you then started to try and bait me into that line of thinking too. Looking back, it was only *after* Ted took the ax that you decided the copycat was a plausible theory worth pursuing." He remembered finding the phone—Curtis had wanted to call the police. So had he. Lauren was the only one who objected, talked them around. She'd even had Jack call the number: *I'm your sister. The call logs would be just as incriminating.* "Because at first, you were guiding me to all of the answers I needed about Curtis. But you needed *me* to be the one that pieced it together. Because if you accused Ted directly—well, he had the ax, didn't he?"

Memories of her, trying to get him to do what she wanted. *Tear apart the shed if you need to.* She wanted him to find the ax first. Sitting on his bed, handing him the old restaurant blueprints for a closer look. *Do you think it's some kind of message?* she'd said when they were standing in the field, stamping her feet in a dull thud on the actual trapdoor. *That there's some meaning beneath the body being right here?* Some meaning beneath, indeed. She wanted him to find the cellar. Curtis's words: *This is the work of someone who wants to get caught.*

"No wonder it sounded so ridiculous that Curtis thought *everything* was planted. Only the person right next to him could do that. You wanted another quick case. You hoped the cops would haul Curtis away and not ask too many questions. And in me you had a biased party, so desperate to find Curtis's guilt. I was the perfect foil."

Same killer, she'd said when they first met. Because she needed someone to go down for her crime as well. But then Ted had interfered. He remembered Lauren begging her brother: *This is literally your* last *chance. Just own up to something.* His response: *Alexis's killer knows that it's not sticking to me. They're getting desperate.* He'd been right.

"But after the ax went missing, you knew that Curtis's arrest wouldn't be enough anymore, because as soon as Ted came forward, it would stick to you. You needed to cover your tracks first and get Curtis second. You changed your mind and I didn't even notice. You planted the phone. You deleted everything in it except for the one path you wanted me to take. Steering me back on your course. Suddenly you believed in the copycat. Andrew Freeman—you hoped that might work because at least it tied the murders together. But he talks too much, and I..." A slow dawning. *Should we shoot at him?* "You asked me for the gun. I didn't give it to you." He wondered if Andrew might have *accidentally* met his end if he had. Lauren had known that Andrew wasn't a perfect solution. She'd gone along with it, but what had she said? *I think we still need to get the ax back...* "Then I figured out the cellar. And you took your opportunity. In the pub, you insisted your brother was guilty for both murders. You hoped the drama of his death would again cover up that he wasn't the second killer. And you were right; most of what Ted had would have stuck to a dead man. Most people would have believed it too. But then I figured it out. Too slowly, and in the wrong order, but I saw what you'd wanted me to see the whole time—your scapegoat, Ted. And suddenly you had the added advantage of silencing him properly."

"Ted attacked *you* in the parking lot." A nervous smile.

"He attacked me, yes. But only after he saw *you*. He must have thought I was your accomplice. He didn't attack me before you showed up. Before that, he was actually asking for my *help*. He really was fighting for his life. And you swung that final blow. There's no one to say otherwise now."

None of this had to happen.

"Ted murdered Alexis," Lauren said, "because he knew that sometimes there's a bigger evil at play." *Framing a guilty man. The lies you can live with.*

"Maybe he thought that sometimes you have to stoop to their level to do the right thing."

"The right thing? Murder?"

"Careful. I'm just guessing at Ted's mindset, Jack." Lauren spoke slowly, large breaths between every few words, tiptoeing through a minefield. Careful not to slip. "Alexis got a murderer out of jail, remember. He must have struggled to let her live with that."

"So she deserved to die?"

"No, she didn't, Jack. But maybe other people made that decision for him."

None of this had to happen. So that was how she computed it. As Jack's fault. Her justification was that he'd forced her hand. Something else she'd said: *When I heard she was dead, I thought it might be useful.*

"You can rationalize it by blaming me, but I didn't make any choices for you."

"For me?"

"Admit it, Lauren. This was exactly what I thought it was about. Revenge. Revenge on Curtis. Revenge on Alexis. There's more than a sliver of him in you. There's a fucking beating heart."

That seemed to hit her hard. Lauren breathed through her nose. Slow.

"Tell me something," Jack said. "Why kill her? You did it to right a wrong, but you've gone and done the same thing?"

"Please stop accusing me, Jack. Ted killed her. You said it yourself—because she got Curtis out. Just like you, she knew everything but didn't act."

There was the slip, under her words. *She knew everything.* Another statement: *You're only the second person I've ever told this to.* Not Eliza, as Jack had assumed. Eliza hadn't known anything—Curtis had said so himself in the cellar, Jack recalled now. Lauren had told *Alexis* everything—the real reason why she couldn't testify—in order to keep herself off the stand. Jack imagined Lauren telling Alexis that she knew the truth, that she was the witness the prosecution needed, and the reasons she couldn't come forward. Alexis knew that. But this was a huge case. Too good to pass up. So she'd gone and let Curtis out anyway.

Jack tried to picture Lauren in the laneway. He saw her startling Alexis. *Why did you let him out? I told you not to let him out. I told you what he did to me.* Alexis telling her to calm down. Come in for a drink. We'll talk. Bent over, starting to lift the garage door. Lauren, the ax heavy in her hand. Filled with hurt, hate, and revenge. It was revenge on both of them, Alexis and Curtis. *I am not a victim anymore.* She'd shot her brother twice. Twice. The second one in the head. Anger, there.

"Put your recorder on the table," she said.

"Huh?"

"Your podcast recorder. Put it on the table."

Jack took it from his pocket and placed it on the table. Busted. It was recording, the orange display glowing. He went to turn it off, but she shook her head. *Leave it on.* She hadn't said anything incriminating yet. He'd done all the talking. She knew it. He knew it. The recording was useless.

"Good theory," she said, consciously raising her voice so the recorder would pick it up. "It'd make a good TV show."

But as she said it, she put two fingers to her lips. Two fingers. *Shh.*

Then she slowly pushed both fingers between her lips. Bared her teeth around them.

Animal.

Nail-Biter.

Reading Group Guide

1. Why do you think people are fascinated by true crime? Is there a true-crime case, book, TV show, or documentary that has particularly piqued your interest? What about it pulled you in?

2. Do you believe Jack, as a TV producer, has a responsibility to tell his audience the truth, or is he simply obligated to tell the best story? How does this question haunt Jack?

3. How does *Trust Me When I Lie* relate to our relationship with media outlets today? Do you think they are toeing the same line as Jack?

4. Do you think Jack's docuseries is to blame for Alexis's death? Why or why not?

5. What are some of Jack's vulnerabilities? What are his strengths? How do they influence his actions as he attempts to solve the Eliza and Alexis cases?

6. Describe Birravale. What was the Wades' relationship like with the town? Why do you think Curtis was the perfect scapegoat for Eliza's murder? Do you think the town's reaction to the Wades was fair? Explain.

7. What do you think Lauren and Jack's relationship is like? Why does Lauren help Jack during his investigation? Do you think she is ultimately remorseful for the part she plays?

8. Describe Andrew Freeman. Do you think he should hold blame for his role in Eliza's murder? Do you think he is ultimately a good guy?

9. Many times throughout the story, Jack asks himself what lies he can live with. Describe what that means. Do you think there are actually lies you can live with, or is the truth always the best option?

10. What do you think happens to Jack after the story ends? Do you think he pursues his career again, or is he forever burdened by Eliza Dacey's murder?

A Conversation with the Author

What inspired you to write *Trust Me When I Lie*?

Like millions of others around the world, I found myself engrossed in the plethora of true-crime television shows and podcasts. My friends and I would have lively debates on who we thought was innocent or guilty. But when you go down the rabbit hole, looking further online or for published books, to see the other side of the story—you never see two aligned halves. The story is told in parts, by the people who have an ulterior motive in choosing what they show you. That got under my skin, and then I started to think how these TV shows are now making their way into our justice system and affecting it real time (with appeals and arrests). So, I asked myself what all good storytellers do: What's the worst that could happen? And that led to the question: What if one of these shows got a killer out of jail, and they knew about it... And that's how Jack Quick was born.

Did you have to do any research to bring Birravale and Jack Quick to life?

Absolutely. I had to immerse myself in stories and the environment in order to make sure it felt genuine. I've traveled the breadth of Australia many times and have a good eye for a country town, or a small winery, so I had that fairly ready to go in my mind. A country pub with one bartender, bad food, and cold beer—I'm an expert. I also have a background as a stand-up comedian, so I have been on set for many television shows, which I brought into the novel. Where I did have to do extra research was on the background of wine-making, to make sure I got the essence of it correctly. Wine drinkers are keen-eyed and know their stuff, so I had to make sure it was truthful. And Jack's illness took a lot of sensitive research and observation; it's a delicate issue and one I wanted to do justice.

Which character did you connect with the most? Which was the most difficult for you to write?

I like Jack a lot, and I think there's a lot I connected—he's grumpy but with a sharp wit—so I have a soft spot for him. *Spoiler:* Lauren was probably the trickiest as she slinks through the novel in various forms. How to make her a casual teenager but also a calculated "mastermind" (she'd hate that word) was a tough balancing act!

Why do you think Jack's audience was fascinated by his Eliza Dacey docuseries? Are you a true-crime fan as well?

I think we love looking into the dark side of humanity, and we're all a bit scared that it could happen to us. But also, these shows are constructed, like any good narrative, out of unanswered questions. I think that's why we're all obsessed with these shows—because they promise a journey of discovery, they make us feel like we're a part of these discoveries, and we get hooked on that. I'm absolutely a true-crime junkie—while writing this book, *The Jinx* and *Making a Murderer* were large influences on how I wanted Jack's show to be, stylistically and the way it was received.

Jack is an incredibly fascinating and layered character. How did you distinguish him from other detective protagonists we might already be familiar with?

I didn't deliberately distinguish him in any conscious way, but I knew I wasn't writing a police procedural, so my main character couldn't be a cop. I wanted a regular guy who gets pulled into things. And I didn't want him to be afflicted by something we'd seen before. (How many books are there about alcoholic detectives?) But I wanted the novel to be a suspenseful mystery, but also a character study for Jack. He's a real guy who's fighting a complex illness and laden with PTSD. So it wasn't deliberate to distinguish him from other heroes, but I wanted him to be more real. He's not an action man—in fact, he gets beat up a hell of a lot—so I suppose that was my conscious effort.

What are some of your favorite authors and books?

Peter Temple's *The Broken Shore* is one of my favorite books of all time. Anything by Stephen King, *On Writing* in particular. Jane Harper's *The Dry* is impeccable and let the world know that we Aussie writers aren't half bad, so we all owe her big time! A few I enjoyed recently: Stuart Turton, Sally Rooney. I'll cheat a bit and say anything by screenwriters Noah Hawley or Shane Black.

When you're not writing, what are you up to?

I'm a stand-up comedian by night, so I travel the world doing shows. It's surprisingly helpful when writing crime, as it's all setup + punchline. I also like playing the piano (I'm not terribly good), films, camping, and guessing twist endings.

Acknowledgments

A novel is a product of many hands. It's a lot like the jigsaw puzzle my mum pulls out over Christmas, where visitors flit past and insert pieces over the holiday season. I have many contributors to thank for the finished product.

Thank you to my first Australian publisher, Kimberley Atkins, who saw the pile of pieces for the picture they would make from the very start. My editor, Amanda Martin, the dedicated puzzle solver who strikes up camp at the table, thank you for sorting every piece into matching piles and making it easier for the rest of us. I appreciate your compassion and patience in the face of authorial stubbornness and an army of errant tabs. Ali Arnold, a fiercely observant and talented copy editor, for matching up the sky blues with slightly different sky blues. Sarah Fletcher, who proofread the novel, thank you for testing each piece in all four directions to make sure it fit properly. I'm very fortunate to have a second brilliant publisher work on this book, so my thanks also to Beverley Cousins for her assistance in slotting in those final pieces. Once the jigsaw was finished, then came the challenge of showing it off around the world. To that end, I would like to thank Nerrilee Weir for her international efforts.

My editors will surely say this jigsaw metaphor has worn thin, so I'd like to thank the brilliant team at Sourcebooks for championing the book's new home (like every Aussie has to do, I see this as my book backpacking!). MJ Johnston has been my biggest supporter. Thank you for believing in the novel and for publishing it perfectly. Dominique Raccah, for getting behind the book and welcoming me to the Sourcebooks family. It's a pleasure to be published by such an innovative and independent publisher. Kaitlyn Kennedy, thank you for passionately getting this book into readers' hands. Gretchen Stelter and Heather Hall, thank you for your work with the book's production and editing. This book looks amazing, and that's thanks to Adrienne Krogh and Heather Morris for the cover and Ashley Holstrom for the internals. To all at Sourcebooks Landmark, thank you.

Of the many people who visited the house and filled in a piece, I would also like to thank Mary Rennie for her support and energy in the building blocks of this story. I am grateful I landed at your desk on my first day as a nervous publishing intern; you were invaluable in kick-starting my career.

An unquantifiable thanks to my kick-arse agent, Grace Heifetz. Grace, your enthusiasm is impervious to damage. Thank you for all you've done. You have really gone above and beyond on this novel. To all staff at Curtis Brown Australia, thank you for welcoming me into the Curtis Brown fold.

I can't look past the support and positivity from my family—Peter, Judy, Emily, and James. A thank-you to my early readers: my brother, James Stevenson, and fellow writers Helen Scheuerer and Tom Gibson. My particular gratitude to Aleesha Paz, a fantastic editor. Her opinions have made this a better book and me a better person. And all pro bono, lucky me.

About the Author

Benjamin Stevenson is an award-winning stand-up comedian and author. He has sold-out shows from the Melbourne International Comedy Festival all the way to the Edinburgh Fringe Festival and has appeared on ABCTV, Channel 10, and the Comedy Channel. Offstage, Benjamin has worked for publishing houses and literary agencies in Australia and the United States. He currently works with some of Australia's best-loved authors at Curtis Brown Australia. *Trust Me When I Lie* is his first novel.